SELWOOD
OF SLEEPY CAT

SELWOOD
OF SLEEPY CAT

BY

FRANK H. SPEARMAN

AUTHOR OF

NAN OF MUSIC MOUNTAIN,
WHISPERING SMITH, Etc.

NEW YORK
GROSSET & DUNLAP
PUBLISHERS

TO
EDWIN R. COLLINS

CONTENTS

SELWOOD
OF SLEEPY CAT

SELWOOD OF SLEEPY CAT

CHAPTER I

DOCTOR CARPY'S STORY

"Just when did this happen?" asked Wentworth, leaning forward in his chair, and dragging the chair forward with him—like a man quite ready to listen.

"The Fourth of July," repeated Carpy, surprised at the interruption. "You sure heard about it?"

"Forty kinds of stories!" exclaimed Wentworth, somewhat irritably. "Every mule driver between here and Medicine Bend has a different one. You say you saw it?"

"Saw it?" The Doctor in his turn echoed the words with a touch of scornful gusto. "Saw it?" he repeated, with an emphatic twang of vanity. "Man! I was in it."

Doctor Carpy was sitting with Benjamin Wentworth in the morning sunshine on the narrow porch of the Doctor's new hotel in Sleepy Cat.

"There was a suicide that night," he continued reminiscently, "—a girl down in the River Quarter. They sent for me. I couldn't do anything. She was lying on the bed on her back with her arms stretched out over her head. She'd caught two of the old-fashioned wood spindles at the head of the bedstead with her hands and lay there with her eyes shut, moaning. While I was trying to find out what she'd taken, she went into a tetanic convulsion. I tried what antidotes I had, but it wasn't a bit of use; I saw right away I had been called too late.

"Of course, everybody sneaked out. I didn't like it, myself; and I'm pretty thick-skinned. About all I could do was to wipe off her forehead and wipe the froth off her lips; and every time a spasm was coming on, she'd draw herself up with her lips quivering and cry out: 'God have mercy on my soul!'

"'God!' I says to myself sitting there listening to her, and like as if I was talking to myself, 'You sure picked a hard death!'

"She heard me. She looked up, with the water dripping through the paint on her face. 'I picked a hard life! Oh, Doc,' she says, moaning-like, 'could you get me a priest?'

"'Hell, girl,' I says, 'there ain't a priest this side Gunlock Reservation. But *no matter*,' I says, 'don't you worry too much. They ain't a-goin' to be too hard on you up there. Mary Magdalen's there—talk to her; you'll be a blamed sight better off there than you ever been in this country.'

"Well, I wished you'd seen that girl's eyes when she began to go. They'd got pretty hard in Sleepy Cat: they turned all soft—kind of pleading—kind of like a youngster's looking to take a hard licking. Everybody'd slunk clean out o' sight, so I stayed—that's all a doctor's good for, anyway. After a while I managed to get her hands loose from the spindles—and there I set like a dum fool, holding 'em myself—seemed like when she was going, she wanted to keep hold of something. But I'll swear you'd never known her when I got her straightened out and laid her hands across her breast, and smoothed the spread up over her face—you wouldn't, I'll declare.

"Well, I walked down the blamed stairs doing some thinking. You remember that joint of Bunty Bartoe's? It's down close to the lower river bridge. The saloon is pretty big. Next to it is his barber shop, with a big arch opening into the barroom. I stopped in the saloon to tell Bartoe his wife was dead—hoping that some fine day I'd have a chance to hang him and hang that partner of his, Atkins. Then I took a drink—he's got the meanest stuff 'tween Council Bluffs and Salt Lake—but I was fair desperate.

"Being Fourth of July night, the place was pretty well filled up. About the first bunch I noticed was Frank Sanger's gang of horse-thieves from Calabasas—they were makin' most o' the noise. I knew they were in town that day and Bartoe's place was their hang-out. Frank Sanger and Buck Boyd were the brains of the outfit; they bossed the stealing, and George Osage and a couple of cowboys from the Panhandle got rid of the horses. They were all handy with their guns, and they'd got so bold they'd try to sell a man's own horses back to him—everybody was afraid of 'em. For a couple of years they'd been running the Spanish Sinks to suit themselves.

"You remember old Dave Tracy from Thief River? Dave's been running a kind of one-horse freighting outfit between Thief River and Sleepy Cat. About six months ago Frank stole a team of mules from him, not thinking Dave would be much trouble. Dave is an old soldier. He's a gambler, too—his young mining partner at Thief River set him up in a big place here in Sleepy Cat—everything swell—up street, this side the hill—but Dave's a square gambler and he ain't afraid of nobody on earth.

"So next day Dave rides down to Sanger's dugout at Calabasas, seen his two mules in the corral, and starts for Thief River with 'em. About half way home Frank meets him and Frank said they'd talk afterward—and pulled on him. He wasn't quick enough. Dave knocked him off his horse with a bullet through his shoulder; but, unluckily for Dave, he rode away from Sanger without making a job of it. Sanger come to me. I told him I'd have to take his arm off—he said if I did he'd blow my head off: so away he went—and got well with his arm on; that's the way a doctor gets treated out here.

"Well, that was Tracy's start with the Calabasas bunch. After that they were laying for Dave. He know'd it. He'd been up to see me in the spring about a young fellow—this mining partner of his—that he said was in the last stages of consumption. I gave him some medicine and told him to tell the fellow to drink plenty of good whiskey. Dave said that was the trouble, he wouldn't drink any kind of whiskey. I told Dave, Boyd and Sanger was in town with their gang, and warned him to keep away from Bartoe's—that's all the good it did.

"So Fourth of July night, when I came down the stairs, I walked from the bar out through the archway into the barber shop to get shaved—would you believe it, the only barber shop we've got in town is down there in Bartoe's den !—and there was Tracy at the cigar stand paying for a haircut. And there in the first chair was a slim young fellow getting lathered up—there was only one barber on duty. I spoke to Tracy again, friendly-like, and told him to lay low. But he wouldn't pay no attention to me. He just stepped out like a fellow twenty-five years old into the saloon.

"I wasn't in at the start. But they said Tracy didn't see Frank Sanger. He walked up to one of the Panhandle men and asked where Sanger was. Sanger was right behind Tracy and he drew. He meant to shoot Tracy through the head, but Tracy saw the move in the eyes of the man he was talking to. He swung 'round quick and the bullet caught him in the neck and partly paralyzed him.

"I was standing talking to the barber. When the first shot was fired he was lathering the man in the chair. That man was out of the chair—well, you might say before the barber actually heard the shot, or before I heard it. The chair faced the saloon, and the man must've jumped six feet the first clip; he was through that opening into the barroom 'fore you could say 'Bingo!'

"Tracy pulled when he was falling or had pulled when he swung 'round; anyway, he pinched the trigger on Sanger from the floor and the blamed cartridge missed fire! Tracy was up on his elbow full of fight, but he was going, and Sanger covered him again to finish him—and that shot was never fired. I ran into the doorway myself and there, three feet to one side of me, the man with the lather on his face was cutting in. He had his gun down on Sanger before Sanger could pull the trigger the second time, and he just naturally threw a bullet right across the room into Sanger's middle. More than that: before Sanger struck the floor, the slim man in the lather put another bullet through Sanger's head—if I hadn't seen it I couldn't 've believed it. No man could ever told me two shots could be fired so close together from one gun.

"By this time the whole Calabasas bunch was shooting at Slim and there I was like a dummy, not three feet away from him: one bullet glanced off the jamb and nicked me right here in the ribs." Doctor Carpy put the forefinger of his right hand dramatically into his right side to indicate the exact spot.

"Hang it, Wentworth," he resumed, "I'm sorry you didn't see it. There I was, and there was the man in the lather dancing around like a happyjack, shooting faster'n you could think and actually for a minute taking the fire of five men; and every time his gun went off, the cuss knocked one of 'em down. It was too fast to watch—I just kind of saw 'em reeling around like tenpins and I watched the slim fellow, paralyzed. He was shooting with his right side turned to the bunch and his left arm straight out behind him, crooked up in the air —and dancing on his toes!"

Carpy laughed at the recollection. "I heard him shout something, but of course I couldn't get it; Dave Tracy got it, though. The slim fellow capered all the time nearer to Tracy, and Tracy, all the time, had been dragging himself toward the slim fellow. What he shouted was—so he told me afterward—'Your gun, Dave, your gun.' And, by hokey, when he'd emptied his own gun, he dropped it like a hot potato and grabbed Tracy's out of his hand. But there wasn't any need of another gun—four men were down—three of 'em never did get up. Sanger—well, he was sentenced twice—once through the heart and once through the head; it was against the law, for no man's life ought to be put in jeopardy twice for the same offense. Two of the bunch were on their feet—one man's gun was empty and his hands were up so high he broke his fingers trying to poke 'em through the ceiling; the other fellow was legging it for the door, and a shot from Tracy's gun fired by his partner nicked the yellow man in the leg—down he went.

"Wentworth, the room was so full of smoke I couldn't see the middle at all. And there was the slim fellow on one side—gun in hand and watching the room with eyes as green as a cat's—stooping and helping Dave with his left hand to crawl behind a table that was knocked over.

"I stepped forward to the end of the bar and put up my hand. 'Boys,' I says, 'I call this fight fit! Whoever you are, partner,' I calls out to the slim fellow, 'put up your gun. You've done the job and done it right.' Then the spectators that hadn't spectated crawled out from under the chairs and tables and began to peek in at the doors and windows. 'This has been a pretty fast celebration,' I said, loud as I could. 'But I want to tell you all something. This place is closed for the night; finish up somewheres else. There's a young woman— well known in this town for the good was in her and more particular for the bad was in her—lying dead by her own hand, up-stairs—let us have peace!'"

Doctor Carpy had finished. He sat silent. Wentworth spoke. "It's a kind of curious thing," said he reflectively, "but I came up here to Sleepy Cat this time, Doc, to buy that freighting outfit of Tracy's—and I suppose now it can be bought right. However, after all that hard luck, I'm going to give the old man what his stuff is worth.

"But I never did expect," continued Wentworth, "to hear of Frank Sanger, George Osage, and Boyd going down in a one-man fight. Was the slim fellow hit bad?"

"Wentworth, I was the only man hit on that side the house. The slim fellow wasn't so much as scratched——"

"Poor shooting."

"Well, yes—and no, Wentworth. Mind you, they were standing right in the centre of the room—in the full light of a big lamp hanging from the middle of the ceiling. Slim was over to one side, and I noticed afterward, when he jumped from the doorway he jumped away from the bar side and toward the dim corner. You see, there's another ceiling lamp in the barber shop that shines right through the arch, and outside that shine there's more or less shadow. The bar, of course, has its own light, so Slim just picked the shadow side of the

archway and worked from that corner. I set the leg of
the thief that was hit running out. He told me he
thought it was a ghost shooting from the corner. You
see they'd got all ready for a good time with Tracy. It
must have been a surprise party for 'em.

"Then, they were bunched, too. They tried to scatter, but they had to shoot at the same time, and, by
gum, as fast as they scattered, down they went. I
looked that room over since, Wentworth, to figure it
out—and if one man *had* to make a fight with a gang he
couldn't pick things better than the boy picked 'em.

"But I want to tell you, Mr. Slim was about petered
when it was over. He helped Jim McAlpin and me get
Dave up to the hotel after Jim brought a wagon from
the barn; and he watched Dave like a hawk till we got
him in bed and fixed up—acted as if he thought I was
going to poison Dave myself; however, I made him sit
down in a rocking-chair and stick to a quart of champagne—wouldn't drink nothing else—till he pretty well
finished it. That steadied his nerves and he was all
right again."

"What did you say the slim fellow's name was?"
asked Wentworth. "Who is he?"

"Why, it's the sick fellow Tracy came to me to get
the medicine for—he's a gambler—a mining partner of
Tracy's. Tracy staked him in a claim at Thief River,
so when he struck it, he staked Tracy here—and staked
him right. I don't rightly know just who the young
fellow is. He's got some good blood in him—somewhere. How do I know? Look at his nose and his ears
—just like you would at a horse—or at his hand—long
and slim—I can come pretty close to spotting them fellows. There's some story behind him, maybe. He goes
out here by the name of Selwood—John Selwood—and
trains with old Dave."

Little wreaths of smoke from Wentworth's cigar curled up from his fingers; he was looking into the sunshine from under the broad brim of his hat, out across the Spanish Sinks. "I wonder," he said, after a pause, "whether he knows anything about freighting?"

"Freighting?" echoed Carpy. "Why, Tracy claimed that man's in the last stages of consumption!"

"We shouldn't need him very long," responded Wentworth, undisturbed; "the railroad will be in Sleepy Cat inside a year——"

"Glory to God!"

"General Roper's got three survey parties working between here and Point of Rocks."

"Do you mean old General Roper, used to command at Fort Pierce?"

"Same man. His son, Lieutenant Roper, was killed in the Crawling Stone massacre. Maybe," continued Wentworth, reflecting, "I can get this young fellow you're talking about to run our freighting business between Medicine Bend and Sleepy Cat. Why, Doc, they steal our mules, here on the West End, faster'n we can ship 'em in from St. Louis. It's something scandalous."

CHAPTER II

WHEN the town of Sleepy Cat was throwing its excited head over its no less excited heels in a rapid growth, there were few quiet stretches along the Overland Trail. It had lost its earliest leisurely air, imparted by the vagrant adventurer and the philosophic trader—men that penetrated the West without any very definite idea of just where or how they should bring up.

Now, the sunshine trail of the earlier day lay rutted wide and deep by the remorseless tread of sweating teams and heavy wagons; it resounded with the picturesque abuse of hardened teamsters; its hollows echoed the sharp blows of complaining hubs at helpless axles and the rhythmical creaking of harness, straining on the backs of plodding mules: and sent up its whole story of begrimed effort in far-reaching clouds of alkaline dust, that tortured the rebellious eyes and nose and lungs of man and beast, and floated away in gossamer clouds so light and filmlike as to tint the lazy air for miles.

It was on one of the long, winding stretches of this trail, between Point of Rocks and Sleepy Cat, one May morning nearly a year after the tragic affair at Bartoe's place, that a mountain man, seated in a light but serviceable buckboard supplied with a comfortable lazy-back seat, and driving a team of rangy bay horses, was headed westward quite alone on the trail. The horses trotted smartly along, and a heavy shower during the night had laid the dust and polished the folds of the wrinkled trail till they sparkled in the dazzling sun.

Wearing the long-gauntlet, soft buckskin gloves, the

stout, broad-brimmed hat, and the knotted bandana neckerchief of the seasoned denizen of the trail, he was comfortably clad; in fact, his aspect at all points marked him as one likely to be at home in the inevitable emergencies of frontier life.

The horses slackening presently their lively pace aroused their driver from a reverie. Glancing up, he saw that he had reached the bluff of an important crossing; the horses were starting down-hill toward the bottoms of the Crawling Stone Wash.

The trail thus lay exposed to his view for some miles, since it made its slow way up the western hill by following the bench of the creek south. The traveler's eyes swept the scene before him: the tortuous course of the creek itself marked by a narrow fringe of trees and shrubs, the rock-outcroppings of the valley, and the sentinel-like boulders that rose at infrequent intervals from the level face of the bottom lands—these were all familiar sights. Interest in the landscape—one like a hundred east and west of it—would lie for the lone traveler only in the chance sight of another traveler within the broad field of vision. And in the west he did see two freighting wagons toiling up the long grade— but only these two, and he realized that the larger outfit he himself was driving to overtake must have made a good start after camping beyond the Wash and got well on their way during the morning toward the next divide. He slipped once more into his reverie, only looking up now and again as the horses needed checking where the shower of the night had cut fresh gullies across the way.

Driving faster for a few minutes as he gained the creek bottom, John Selwood turned his horses off the trail toward a growth of small trees on the border of the creek. Along this creek wild plums grew, and Selwood

knew where to find them. In his frequent trips back
and forth on the freighting trail under his supervision he
had watched the spring suns ripening these plums and
knew the thickets. Guiding the team close to an inviting tree, he was able without leaving his seat to break
off a branch loaded with fruit and eat of it at his leisure
as he guided the horses again toward the road.

He was sitting quite at his ease with the lines buckled
about his left arm while he picked and ate the plums,
when, as the horses turned into the beaten path, his
eye fell on a horseshoe. He paused to see whether it
belonged to one of his mules—that is, to one of the
Company mules. He saw it did not; for these were of a
particular style and make, easily identified by the practised eye. He hesitated, still picking and eating plums,
and debating whether it was worth while to add any in-
surance to luck by picking the horseshoe up, when his
eye fell on an object lying on the road a few feet farther
ahead.

It was a woman's shoe. Selwood's eyes fixed on this
at once with curiosity. It was a high shoe, narrow and
apparently of good quality. He drove closer. Reading
the wagon tracks within range, he saw that emigrants
had camped for the night near at hand; the trail, swept
by the shower, showed where their wagons had turned
that morning into the road again. This shoe had evidently been jolted from one of the wagons, of which
there had been two. All of this information was easily
absorbed and the inspection of the shoe resumed. To
Selwood it looked small and quite new. It was not
unusual to see along the way articles of every description discarded or lost from travellers' outfits. Worn
boots and old shoes were a common sight, but this was
something very different—to Selwood, at least. With
his horses switching and stamping at the flies, he tried

to decide whether to pick up the horseshoe or the woman's shoe.

"I've been picking up horseshoe luck ever since I came to this country," he said to himself at length—"and it's been rotten luck. I'll take a chance on beating it." So saying, he laid aside the plum branch, stepped down from the buckboard, and picked up the woman's shoe. It bore inspection well—and Selwood inspected it critically. It was built to come well above the ankle. It was fashioned for a high and slender instep, and as Selwood held it up, the more he looked at it the better he liked it, and he ended by lifting the box seat of his little wagon and throwing the shoe into it. Realizing that it would ruin all his chances of luck thereafter to touch the horseshoe, he spoke to the horses and started on.

Driving faster as he gained the bottom land, he reached the approach to the ford, a quarter of a mile ahead, where he saw two canvased wagons halted. One had made the ford crossing. Just the top of the other wagon showed through the trees that lined the creek itself. Voices raised high in mule adjuration reached his ears. It was an ordinary sound and told him all of the story he needed to know—the second wagon was mired.

Selwood, easing the lines, let his team down to a walk. His way passed now close to the trees and the air, filled with the fragrance of the rain, cooled the nostrils of the restive horses as their driver, reaching a vantage point, stopped them where he could see the ford and the mired wagon in the shallow waters of the creek.

On the other side of the creek stood the wagon that had made the crossing safely. The team had been unhitched and two men, doubling this team with that of the mired wagon, were working in the water.

Selwood, watching from the buckboard, had no need to speculate as to what the probable outcome of these efforts would be. The men were obviously novices at their job and in all likelihood unacquainted with the particular danger of the ford they had attempted. The few inches of clear water rippling over the sandy bottom looked inviting to the unwary, but after a shower the place was avoided by better informed travellers. Selwood spoke to his horses and, moving closer to the scene, halted them on the creek bank. The men in the creek were too busy to notice him until he called out.

At the sound of a voice both looked up surprised. Laconic greetings exchanged, the older of the two men waded across the sandy bottom at Selwood's suggestion to speak to him. While he discussed with Selwood the awkward predicament in which he was caught, Selwood looked him closely over. He was a man of forty-five to fifty years, and Selwood saw that his longish thin hair was streaked with gray, as was his still thinner beard—trimmed, apparently, for sidewhiskers, but neglected during the exigencies of travel. His face was very thin, and this accentuated his features. His eyes were large, dark, and hollow; naturally bright, they were unnaturally so now in his excitement. His mouth was rather large, and his teeth, seeming thin also and spread rather wide apart, showed prominently when he smiled, as he was doing now—talking rapidly and apologetically to Selwood, who had already got down from the buckboard and was looking not very hopefully, as he listened, toward the wagon in the treacherous ford.

"You'd have saved time by going half a mile higher up," commented Selwood after he had heard the story. "All the freighting outfits go there for the rock bottom. This is all right when it's dry enough. It's a mean place after a shower. And if you don't get that lead team out of that sand pretty quick, you're liable not to get them out at all."

"What should you do, stranger?" asked the settler, apparently realizing that the buckboard man knew more than he knew about the situation.

For answer, Selwood spoke sharply to the teamster, an overgrown boy, who was geeing and hawing the pole team with the sole effect of settling the fore wheels of the wagon deeper into the sand. "Drop your lines where you are," cried Selwood, "and get that lead team ashore. Don't you see the near horse is going down?"

Perceiving the awkwardness and stupidity of the young fellow, Selwood, not waiting to see his order executed, walked into the creek and, followed by the settler, splashed across to where, struggling to free their feet, the head horses were floundering. Hastening to their heels, Selwood unhooked the singletrees, threw them over the backs of the frightened horses, and, slapping them by turns smartly on the haunches, got them, splashing and struggling, ashore. Then bidding the teamster follow, he recrossed the creek, turned up the seat of his buckboard, took out, hand over hand, a length of heavy chain, passed it to the teamster to carry over, and, unhooking his own team, walked behind them, doubletree in one hand and reins in the other, across the creek. It was the work of but few minutes to fasten one end of the chain to the tongue of the stalled wagon and give directions to the two men as to where to stand and what to do. The settler was put with the team still hitched to the wagon. From the end of the wagon tongue the chain drawn taut reached ashore, where, on the sandy approach to the ford, Selwood had hooked his own team into the chain and, passing it between them, had hooked the rescued team to the chain's end.

With everything ready, Selwood gave final instructions. "Now if your king-bolt holds," he said, "we'll yank that wagon out; if it gives, you'll have to wait till you can rig another—there's a freighting outfit coming along about two hours behind—now everybody—all together!!"

Selwood loosed a stentorian yell; the six horses, galvanized by the shock, bent to the job. The boy lashed with his lines and the settler shouted. The mired wagon creaked violently, groaned, and with the wheels ploughing through the gripping sand moved uncertainly. A fresh roar from Selwood signalized the success and spurred the horses to renewed efforts; and the partly released wagon, plunging ahead, was jerked and rattled ungraciously through the sullen quicksand and up the ford approach to dry land.

The emigrant turned to his rescuer with a joyful breath of relief. "Stranger," he exclaimed, "that's a big lift! My name's Fyler—what's yours?" he asked, holding out his hand.

His benefactor was taciturn. He took the extended hand, but without enthusiasm. "That's not the first time I've helped pull a wagon out of that hole," he said good-naturedly; "it probably won't be the last. I had to be pulled out of there once, myself; nobody uses this ford that knows it."

"We camped here last night—" said Fyler, beginning to explain.

"Where?" asked Selwood, interrupting him mildly.

Fyler pointed to a spot near by. "In that little grove."

Selwood looked at the place designated and looked at Fyler. "Well," he observed candidly but without particular harshness, "they say the Lord looks after fools and drunkards. I don't know how much you drink, but he certainly looked after you last night. He may not do it again. Never camp in this country in a creek bottom.

This is Crawling Stone Wash and the creek empties into Crawling Stone River. If there'd been a cloud-burst last night, instead of a shower, you and your driver and horses and wagons would be in Kingdom Come by now. The water sweeps down here twenty feet high. Where you headed for?"

"Sleepy Cat. Where you bound?"

"Looks as if the whole United States is heading for Sleepy Cat. Give me a hand with that buckboard, boy, and I'll be moving." The three men pulled the buckboard across the creek without difficulty, helped Selwood to hitch his team and put back his chain. In the box seat under which he carried it were various spare pieces of harness. Selwood explained in answer to pointed questions that he was in the freighting business and looked after the Russell & Wentworth outfits through the mountains. Fyler, in turn, said he was taking some merchandise out to open a store in Sleepy Cat and expected to ship by Russell & Wentworth wagons and more out by rail; he was surprised to learn that the railroad had not reached Sleepy Cat.

Selwood, answering laconically a rapid flow of questions, was glad to be ready to drive on. He gathered his reins to step into the buckboard. As he lifted his foot, with one hand on the dash and the other on the seat, to do so, his eyes fell on Fyler's first wagon, standing twenty yards away. The canvas opening at the hind end was parted and to his great surprise he saw that at the moment it framed the face of a girl of eighteen or twenty years. Her face was turned toward where her father was helping the teamster swing the tongue of the rescued wagon round to take the team. She did not see Selwood, and he stood motionless, staring at the unexpected sight.

She was bareheaded, with her hair parted in the middle and drawn plainly over her temples. On her neck a simple kerchief rested loosely above a simple dress. Women-folk were not uncommon in emigrant trains; indeed, they were the rule. Yet Selwood paused as if petrified at the ordinary sight. Unluckily for him, his horses, less interested in the situation, champed at their bits and tried to start. The girl turned her gaze toward the buckboard. More even than the clear profile had promised was revealed in the full face; it was mere girlhood—simplicity and frank innocence—but it made Selwood catch his breath.

When her eyes fell on Selwood she looked rather quickly away and the parted canvas flap softly closed. Selwood stepped gingerly up into the buckboard and settled himself in his seat. The impatient horses leaped ahead. He did not attempt to look back.

CHAPTER III

SELWOOD, after various delays during the day and time lost in straightening out transportation tangles among his freighting outfits on the trail, reached Sleepy Cat late that night. His tired team headed without guiding for the Russell & Wentworth horse barn. Their plant at Sleepy Cat comprised a horse barn, a stage barn, a freight warehouse, a bunk-house for their teamsters, and a blacksmith and wagon repair shop.

Selwood threw his reins to a waiting hostler. He got stiffly down after his long ride, tipped up the lazy-back seat, took out and stuffed into a side pocket of his coat the good-luck girl's shoe, and walked forward. As he passed the open door of the office he saw the barn boss, McAlpin, in confab with a little woman sitting in the chair at the desk. Near them, listening, stood an over-grown boy of twenty. The woman was talking earnestly and rapidly. Selwood was hungry, dust-covered, and tired, and without speaking to McAlpin he passed out through the gangway doors and started for his room at Doctor Carpy's hotel.

McAlpin in the barn office stood profoundly attentive to the story of the little woman sitting at the desk, with a handkerchief, much knotted, in her hands and with great trouble expressed in her tear-stained eyes.

The barn boss was usually a busy man. He walked the barn gangway at a pace very close to a run; and in his habitual haste rolled on his heels like a boat in a choppy sea; so much so that when he brought to, standing, it sometimes took him an instant to balance himself.

Yet this evening he was plainly interested in the tale
the strange woman was pouring into his ear. Of the men
that profess they have no time to listen to other people's
troubles, James McAlpin never was one. He had almost
a morbid flair for other people's troubles; and the worse
they were the more he—I ought not to say enjoyed them
—but the more closely they held him. He had come
from far across the sea and crossed forbidding deserts to
reach the Great American West, penniless but thrifty,
and fortified with the resolve to weep with the weepers
and rejoice with the glad. As a Scotchman, nature had
fitted him for the difficult rôle of being all things to all
men, and as he listened in the stuffy, strong-smelling,
cluttered-up little office of the big Division barn of the
Russell & Wentworth Freighting Company—the first
barn, by the way, ever built in Sleepy Cat—as he looked
from the little wisp of a woman, weeping and pouring
out her woes before him, to the husky, overgrown
twenty-year-old son at her side—sheepish now and
hang-dog in looks—McAlpin felt that in coolness and
confidence in himself he was pretty nearly master of
the situation; and he looked his part.

"What's that, Mrs. McCracken?" he demanded, suddenly eyeing the woman, and throwing more emphasis
into the words as he repeated the sharp question purely
for effect. "What's that you say? Moses was gambling? Why, no! I couldn't say the boy was *gambling*
when he lost *that* money. If it's gambling, two men
have got to have a chance—don't you know that, Mrs.
McCracken?" McAlpin spoke fast, because Mrs. Mc-
Cracken herself had hardly checked her own sorrowful
tale in the interval; she was, in fact, though weighing
under ninety pounds, the first woman he had ever met
that could talk faster than he could. "That boy didn't
have a chance," insisted McAlpin, "he was just plain

robbed—that's what I call it, robbed. Why didn't you
come in here to buy your team?" he demanded of Moses
indignantly. "I'd have sold you a team of mules. Was
the six hundred all the money you had, Mrs. Mc-
Cracken?"

"Every cent in the world," wept the woman, "and
Moses knew better than to go near a gambling-house."

It was nearing the close of the greatest day, up to
that time, in the history of Sleepy Cat—this haphazard,
helter-skelter, frame, dug-out and tent high-country
town, flung by a chance tidal wave of civilization far
beyond its own border, up into a gap of the Rocky
Mountains; for that day the railroad surveyors had
reached Sleepy Cat—destined to be, in the imagination
of its sponsors, the mountain metropolis of the country.

As a distributing point for a widespread mountain
territory, Sleepy Cat even at this time boasted trading
and supply houses out of all proportion in size and importance to its population, and these stores, with frontier disregard of fire hazard, were housed mostly in one
long block. Perhaps the early day tradition of traders
keeping close together, stockade fashion, through fear of
Indians, exercised a subconscious influence in this regard.
Whatever the reason, the substantial Sleepy Cat merchants sat cheek by jowl in their long row. In that
block could be found the widely known establishment of
John Cole—the tall, spare brother of the town blacksmith; the long, rambling store of Alexis Roubidoux, the
French trader, with nearly all the business of the Gunlock and the Falling Wall reservations—Roubidoux with
the squaw wife, the brown toupee, the gray glass eye,
and the dyed mustache and goatee.

In this row, too, were the Kickbusch brothers, Chris
and Otto—big men with bristling mustaches and perspiring foreheads, always hustling, always sweating—

who controlled most of the supply business from the mining camps at Horse Head and Thief River, north and south. Last of all in that block was the man whom nobody knew, not even his own clerks, Van Tambel, the silent Dutch trader, tall as a Pomeranian, ungainly as a Hollander, the man that never answered a question or rose to greet a customer, but sat with his feet on a flat-top desk, behind his long, boxlike stove, his feet, winter and summer, encased in arctic overshoes, his head, winter and summer, in a home-made fur cap, the long visor pushed well back from his forehead and above his dark, cavernous eyes—sitting always with his large mouth and long jaws fortified against conversation by an unfailing supply of chewing-tobacco—the man who heard all and said nothing. He had the Mormon trade.

A riot of celebration had been loosed on the great day to greet the advance guard of the coming railroad. The pioneers and adventurers within a radius of two hundred miles had congregated in their picturesqueness to do the occasion honor. And as the celebration was now drawing to a close, the bruised and injured in the frays of the day, with groggy heads and despondent looks, were taking store of their hurts.

Sleepy Cat lay on the chief transcontinental trail of its day—an overland trail—and the railroad was only nosing slowly along westward, behind and parallel to another well-established travel stream—the wagon stream of the settlers seeking new homes and facing new adventure in the farthest West.

Patiently, McAlpin waited again for Moses's story of how that morning his mother had given him six hundred dollars to pay for and bring back the team of mules. Moses, on his way, had met an entertaining man who had come from the same town in Iowa as the McCrackens

—at this point McAlpin ground his teeth. The man had volunteered to go with him to help bring back the team. He had offered, incidentally, to show Moses where the new round-house was to be built. They had stopped in at an interesting place where different games were being played, and Moses, in earnest and repeated endeavor to pick the right one of three cards, had gradually wagered and finally lost the six hundred.

McAlpin had already heard the story once; but it was his custom, if he could manage it, to hear a particularly harrowing tale twice. He listened to the second recital with the same sharp ejaculations, the same screwing and twisting of his features and his heels, and the same angry jerking of his head, with which he had absorbed Moses's story the first time. Sympathy for the unfortunate was only one of McAlpin's grievances in the circumstances; Sleepy Cat sharpers had picked up in ten minutes as much money as McAlpin had to work ten weeks for—and it didn't seem right.

"Now I'll tell you," he said domineeringly and to cut off further discussion, "I'll go with you to where they took your money and see what can be done."

Calling a hostler front, McAlpin, with Moses, walked rapidly down the ragged highway that was to serve as Sleepy Cat's principal street, in the direction of what was already known as the River Quarter.

Originally a stockade fort and Indian trading-post, Sleepy Cat, when it assumed town airs, straggled up and down the flats on the north side of the Rat River. The transcontinental trail of the emigrants crossed these flats somewhat diagonally, seeking easy grades down from and up again into the hills, and the first Sleepy Cat buildings were strung along both sides of this trail. At the eastern end, where the trail ran nearest the river, one bridge had already been flung across and the emigrant and freighting outfits made this a halting place, close to water and, once upon a time, to grass.

Near this camping-ground the earliest Sleepy Cat adventurers had opened their eating-houses, saloons, blacksmith and wagon shops, sales stables and traders' stores. These places were housed in hastily thrown-together log and rough-hewn structures, but often they were no more than condemned army tents or half frame and half canvas affairs that might do as a place to work in, or to dispense drinks from, and to serve as a partial protection against the winds—sand, gravel-laden, and at times ferocious—that swept at certain seasons down the defiles through which the Rat and its tributaries made their escape from Sleepy Cat Mountain. Thus the lower part of the town, as it grew, took the name of the River Quarter and gradually gained an evil precedence in mountain story as the resort of hard men and scenes of violence.

McAlpin had a very definite idea of the general direction in which Moses had parted with his money, and took him directly down toward the river, talking and gesticulating as fast as he walked. Reaching the suspected district, McAlpin slowed and pointed from a conservative distance to one disreputable joint after another, asking his companion whether this or that place looked like the one he had been taken into.

Moses, confident at first, found himself hazy when it came to identifying the precise scene of his disaster. He remembered then that he had been taken into several places, and these now looked very much alike. With his guide he walked clear to the camping-grounds without success, and McAlpin, on the way back to the stable, was growing very impatient when Moses, of a sudden, stopped his companion and pointed to a man just going into a large and quite pretentious frame saloon.

"That's the fellow," he exclaimed eagerly.

"What fellow?"

"Just going in there—he dealt the cards. And that's the place!" whispered Moses with excitement.

McAlpin stopped in his tracks, somewhat flabbergasted. "In that place there with the blinds?"

"Yes," insisted Moses. "I know it now by that broken window," he added, pointing.

McAlpin looked at the place pointed out and turned a hard stare on his companion. "Man alive!" he cried. "Were you in this town only twelve hours and picked out that joint to lose your money in?" Moses looked mystified. "What kind of a fool are you?" demanded McAlpin angrily, "to pick out the worst place 'tween St. Joe and Sacramento to leave your money in? Come along to the barn!"

"Ain't you going to talk to 'im, as you said you would?" asked Moses timidly, but dreading to face his mother again.

"Talk in *there?*" echoed McAlpin scornfully. "Do I want to get knifed? Not yet. Come along. You're lucky you didn't get knocked on the head and thrown into the river. That's Bunty Bartoe's place."

McAlpin returned to the barn out of humor. He wasted little time, when he got back to the office, in explaining things but, leaving Moses to take the brunt of the storm, became very busy with some mules just being brought into the barn by teamsters putting them up for the night. It was nearly supper-time, too, and McAlpin, to avoid further discussion in the office, dodged out the back way for something to eat. A hearty meal restored pretty well his naturally placid outlook on life, but when he got back to the barn this was upset again by the spectacle of Mrs. McCracken sitting alone in the twilight of the rough office, silent and woebegone. Another long talk resulted in an opening of his heart again, and ended in his telling her to go get her supper and come back. He would see, meantime, whether something more might be done.

"If only my poor brother William—William Pardaloe —was here, Mr. McAlpin—he'd make these thieves hunt their holes," sobbed Mrs. McCracken. "I'd not have to ask nobody for help if I had William."

"Well, if William, whoever he is, was here, Mrs. McCracken," retorted McAlpin tartly, "he could have the job for all of me!"

CHAPTER IV

THE HALL ON THE HILL

Mrs. McCracken could eat no supper, but she spent thirty minutes back in camp weeping, and then rose to a resolution of her own. With Moses as a guide she resolved to seek the men that had robbed Moses—and did so.

Naturally, she got scant recognition, and was hardly given time to introduce herself at the place with the blinds and tell her story, before Moses was thrown bodily into the street and Mrs. McCracken was strongly urged, under threat of arrest, out after him. Neither storms nor tears availed; the two arguments that had always subdued her dead husband had no weight in the River Quarter.

Baffled and disheartened, she returned with her son to pester McAlpin and, having cornered him, told of the fresh indignities she had suffered in her efforts to reclaim her own.

To her surprise, the barn boss was angry at her. He told her flatly she had disobeyed his orders, ruined everything; and on this the two joined issue.

It was in the very midst of their animated discussion that a well-set, leisurely man, under a broad hat, whitened from its round crown and the wrinkled sleeves and shoulders of his loose-fitting coat to the toes of his high-topped boots with the dust of the trail, walked unobtrusively into the office. This was John Lefever, head wagon boss for Russell & Wentworth, just in with a long string of wagons, west-bound. With feet of small size and notwithstanding the largeness of his frame, Lefever

27

walked gingerly and with hardly any noise. He carried
in his hand a long whip; this he placed in the rack
quietly in order that he might lose nothing of the talk
going on behind him; and, to emphasize his ostensible
indifference to the subject-matter, he whistled softly to
himself as he fingered the other whips in the rack and,
having selected one to try out, turned slowly around,
the prey of curiosity, to see what manner of person was
matching Jim McAlpin for once in fast talking. Having
satisfied himself on this point by a brief glance, Lefever
started for the door leading into the stable.

McAlpin, pressed for help and still indignant at Mrs.
McCracken's new story, was not minded to let him
escape. He put up his hand and spoke. "Excuse *me*,
Jim," protested Lefever, not halting on his way, "I'm
for supper."

McAlpin darted between the big fellow and the door.
"No—stop, John, look here a minute. I want you to
hear this!"

"I don't want to hear it. Look you, Jim: I brought
Selwood's new saddle pony up to-night—see that he's
curried till you can part your hair on his flanks."

"Yes, but, John Lefever, listen!"

Lefever saw there was no escape, and he was forced
to hear the whole story. "Well," he asked, at the conclusion, "what are you going to do about it?"

"What can I do? It's Bunty Bartoe's place, John.
Can I afford to get dumped into the river?"

Lefever, as if disclaiming personal responsibility,
moved out into the barn. But McAlpin hung on to
him. Then Lefever said something, whatever it was, in
a low tone that caused McAlpin to lower *his* tone. A
whispered conference followed. "Do you think it would
be all right to ask him, John?" urged McAlpin, as Lefever turned to get away.

"If he doesn't want to do it, he won't do it, will he?" snapped Lefever.

"Would he get angry with me asking him, d'y' think?" called McAlpin after his retreating friend.

"If he does I'll get your job, won't I? No! He won't get angry."

Lefever was half way down to the stalls. McAlpin stopped long enough at the office door to tell the "Mrs." and Moses to bide—speaking sternly to Moses. Then grabbing his cap he hustled into the street.

Head down, and only glancing, without lifting it, from under the short visor of his cap at the men in twos and threes and scattered groups—teamsters, emigrants, frontiersmen, adventurers—that loitered in the open spaces or moved aimlessly along the middle of the street, McAlpin made straight up the hill above the River Quarter toward a large frame structure set some fifty feet back from the street below the brow of the hill and isolated. This position raised it above all other structures and made it a conspicuous object among the crude buildings, up street and down. And its situation on a corner of the cross street that opened on the trail leading from Sleepy Cat north into the Falling Wall country marked the dividing line between the River Quarter and that part of the town to the west that held all the slender hopes of Sleepy Cat for a fairly respectable future.

At a considerable expense, young and fast-growing trees had been set in generous numbers about the grounds of the place—box elders, soft maples, and poplars—indicating an effort to civilize one of the bare slopes of the barren hills above the town. And a broad sign, high above the large double doors of the building —thrown wide open now—reading "John Selwood, Gambler," left no doubt as to the nature of the owner's busi-

ness. Though but of a single story, the framed ceiling
formed below by the shingled roof was so high as to
give the interior an air of spaciousness and an appearance
very different from the places along the river. This difference was further signalized by the more elaborate
character of the equipment and furnishings, which were
complete beyond any elsewhere in the mountain country.

David Tracy—the old "partner," afterward so seriously wounded—whom Selwood had originally set up in
the establishment, had been given carte blanche—and
used it—in spending money to make his gambling hall
a Western place to be talked about.

With Tracy disabled, young Selwood had assumed
entire responsibility for the place. And as a further defiance to any aggrieved enemies of the Sanger-Boyd
following, Selwood's name, at Tracy's behest, though
against Selwood's wishes, had been conspicuously placed
above the doors. It was known that when not engaged
with his Russell & Wentworth duties, he could be found,
by any one interested, on the hill.

Being quite as reckless in the spending of money as
Tracy, Selwood had not let their common reputation for
extravagance suffer. New York had supplied the rich
velours draperies and the soft silk shades; though in
colors calculated rather to startle the frontier eye than
to win the approval of the refined. And tapestried and
brocaded overstuffed chairs, and the large mahogany
tables had been brought far, and likewise from cities of
renown.

Whatever of expensive devices marked the frontier
gambling of the day were mostly to be found at Selwood's, though some of these, set about the room—which
opened nearly in the form of a hollow square, with tables,
wheels, and dealers facing the players on three sides—
were given so little attention as to be hardly more than

curiosities; the frontiersmen, who lived chiefly for the
adventure and excitement of the hour, found more to
attract them in the faro tables than in any of the more
fashionable imported devices supplied by the open-
handed management.

These various characteristics, taken together, gave
Selwood's place unusual advertising, of the only kind—
oral—then known in the West. But the strength of
that advertising and its wide extent could hardly be
equalled nowadays by the most active printing-press.
Selwood's was known from the Missouri River almost to
the Sierras as an exceptional place and one of repute—
where there was no saloon and no disreputable adjunct,
and none near it; where no one was asked to play, and
where no limit was placed on the player.

CHAPTER V

GENTLEMAN JOHN

FEATURES such as these counted strongly in the gossip of the camp-fire on the overland trails, and few were the adventurers who could not describe the marvels of the interior, or who failed to lay claim—whether truthfully or not—to the distinction of having at some time played in Selwood's at Sleepy Cat, or to tell the story, though now nearly a year old, of the fight at Bartoe's.

The evening was young when McAlpin stepped briskly into the gambling room. It was well lighted by handsomely bracketed kerosene lamps on the side walls and by elaborate hanging lamps. The centre hanging lamp was a particularly brilliant affair, the pride of the janitor, Bull Page, a broken cowboy, who always saw that this particular lamp was in the pink of good order.

Owing to the crowds in the town that evening the place already presented an active scene. Various signs were hung on the panelled walls. One, sponsored by Tracy, read: "My money is here. It's yours if you can win it." Another, and perhaps the most singular sign and most widely quoted on the trail, was one at the head of the room, reading in bold print: "If you can't afford to lose your roll, keep it in your pocket; nobody here will rob you." This was usually ascribed to Selwood.

Like one familiar with his surroundings, McAlpin walked directly up the middle of the long room, nodding here and there to an acquaintance, and directed his steps to the upper right-hand corner, in which, apart somewhat from the tables, a flat-topped desk faced McAlpin diagonally. Behind the desk stood a swivel armchair; on a wall shelf behind the chair there reposed a card photograph, crudely framed, of a man in the uniform of a Union soldier. Beside this, but more conspicuous because much larger, stood a glass dome of the kind used to cover French mantel clocks. Under this dome there reposed already, in place of the expensive clock, which had been removed to make place for it, a single slender high shoe, evidently the shoe of a girl of eighteen or twenty years. It showed but little wear and, during the evening, attracted much attention and elicited many questions. But beyond the vague statement that it was there for good luck, no explanation to any one was then or afterward forthcoming from Selwood. His employees knew nothing whatever about it—nor was it their custom to put too many questions to the taciturn head of the house.

The chair behind the desk was empty as McAlpin walked toward it. The door of Selwood's small private room opening into the gambling-hall was closed, and McAlpin, trying it, found it locked. He turned to the man dealing faro at the nearest table—a pale little man, swearing just then in a violent undertone at a dissipated fly that droned persistently about his nose and eyes. "Where's Selwood?"

The pale little man had no information. McAlpin watched the play a few minutes with the air of one that had graduated from that form of entertainment, and sauntered back toward the front door. There his active eye fell on a man of medium stature standing with his hands in his pockets, leaning against the door jamb and looking out into the street. He was inconspicuously dressed in frontier garb and showed in his copper-colored face the hue of an Indian. Bob Scott, partly of Chippewa blood, and carried—a Sioux captive—far from the hunting grounds of his fathers, was now a retainer of

John Selwood's. McAlpin ambled up to him like an old acquaintance, which, in fact, he was.

"I'm looking for the boss, Bob," he said with some importance in his tone.

The Indian only drew his hands from his pockets to place them behind his back on the jamb he was leaning against, and smiled in friendly fashion.

"Where is he?" persisted McAlpin, who assumed to lord it a little when it seemed prudent to do so.

"He never tells me where he's going. But," added the Indian, after a pause during which McAlpin looked restively about, "I'm thinking he went up the river. If he did, he ought to be back by now."

"What would he be going up the river for?" asked McAlpin with native suspicion.

"To see a man."

"What man would John Selwood want to see up river?"

Scott smiled enigmatically. "Maybe the old padre— the one that travels that way sometimes with the Black-feet."

"I hear he let Big Haynes go this morning, Bob," said McAlpin cavalierly.

"Last night."

McAlpin was both animated and inquisitive. "What for?" he demanded. "He was the fastest dealer in the house."

Bob Scott, smiling, only held up his right forefinger and crooked it.

"What does he want to see the old padre about?" demanded McAlpin with an air of impatience.

Scott, looking over McAlpin's shoulder down the street, made a definite announcement. "There comes Selwood, Jim; suppose," he added, smiling evenly, "you ask him."

Few men could equal McAlpin in a lightning change of attitude. And without being meanly obsequious, the barn boss understood, to the mildest petition of a drooping eyelid, to the slightest cadence of a falling syllable, how to show a boss that he realized his presence and knew exactly what was due to it.

Moreover, McAlpin cherished a genuine regard for the young boss, as he sometimes called Selwood, and with all his turns and quirks, loyalty was in the fibre of McAlpin's make-up. He gave value received to whomever he sold his service, and in return had things in his official servitude mostly his own way. He understood perfectly well how to wheedle a boss and how to bully him, when to say things and when to keep silence.

" I can't be put off much longer, John," he declared, low but emphatically, keeping just half a deferential step behind Selwood as the two walked up the gambling-hall toward Selwood's desk. McAlpin was quite aware of the curious eyes that followed his companion, and he made the most of his opportunity to show how close in confidence he was to him. "We've got to have more room down there or push some of the mules into the river. The harness room is that crowded you couldn't skin a cat in it without nicking a breech strap—there's more harness right now in the office than there is in the harness room; and in the stage barn, half the wagons are in the street."

Selwood walked at a leisurely pace past the well-filled tables, listening to McAlpin but with his eyes, keen and grayish blue, taking in the scene before him. He was slender, evenly built, and carried himself very lightly— walking with much the springy step of a West Pointer. Two spots of color in his cheeks revealed the constitutional weakness that had brought him to the mountain country—a weakness now so well checked that at twenty-seven he looked fresh and boyish among men who, though hardly older in years, seemed to have felt more heavily the hardships of frontier life. Small and regular features gave him no particular distinction in looks, but his quick movements heightened the impression of nervous activity.

He was smooth-faced among men for the most part bearded; and in his personal rig different from those frontiersmen that filled the room. He wore a soft gray hat, so high-crowned and large it might have topped a Spaniard; a close-buttoned, grayish, double-breasted chinchilla peajacket of the fashion of the day. It cut him off across the middle, but his legs, in snug-fitting trousers, were long enough to modify the effect and to carry a pair of black top-boots with the high heels and short vamps favored by the cowboy. There was nothing aggressive about his appearance; but his gray eyes chilled his manner when his face was in repose, and he was known to waste but few words in reaching a conclusion, and none in pursuing a vain dispute.

He heard patiently McAlpin's complaints as to the crowded condition of the barn, and only reminded him that the coming of the railroad would mean the cutting off of much freight and that there would soon be more room at the barn than business. "And," he added, "don't lose a chance to let go any mules you can sell to advantage."

So saying, Selwood tossed his hat on the desk and sat down. McAlpin, leaning on his right elbow, cap in hand, threw himself well down on the end of the desk to reach an ingratiating attitude for what he now had to ask. He hurried through the preliminaries of his story with every indication of nervousness, twirling his cap at intervals over his fingers and hesitating at times for a word or phrase to estimate the effect on his hearer, who was looking, as he listened, over a batch of reports Lefever, the wagon boss, had left on his desk.

But try as he would, McAlpin could gain no clue to the impression he was making. It was only after Selwood looked up at the close of the recital that McAlpin could even guess what he might expect; then Selwood shook his head as if annoyed and his first words dashed McAlpin's hopes.

"Why bring that kind of a story to me?" he asked. He spoke without feeling, but as if his time were being imposed on. "They rob people down there all the time. That's their business," he continued, fixing his eyes again on the papers before him. "Our men are warning the emigrants all the time. And these crooks don't like it. They come right back after us. They steal from our wagons in spite of the dogs. And when they get a chance they poison a dog or cripple a mule or beat up a teamster. Go back to your den and forget yourself."

"John," pleaded McAlpin, low and softly but persistingly, "I want to tell you: this is a hard case, a blamed hard case. It's Bunty Bartoe's work—he's the biggest all-round thief in Sleepy Cat. Starbuck's got an interest in that place. Half the money—I'm saying half, John—goes straight into Starbuck's pocket. It's a crime," exclaimed McAlpin in half-whispered desperation, "the way that man Starbuck is picking up money."

It would have needed a full knowledge of the local situation to realize McAlpin's craft in his last appeal. Selwood, he knew, liked Starbuck less than he did any man in Sleepy Cat. With but a slight acquaintance between the two, there was, on either side, no regard lost. And McAlpin knew that if it worried Selwood as much as it did him to see such men picking up money easily, he could be stirred by the reminder of it.

Yet all he could urge on this score left Selwood cold.
And perceiving that no impression was made, but rather
that Selwood's eyes were wandering over the room,
McAlpin added that Lefever had come in with the new
saddle pony that afternoon, and perhaps Selwood would
like to step down to the barn a minute to look it over.

This news had quite a different effect on the hard-
headed gambler. The pony, a present from Ben Wentworth, the active owner of the wealthy freighting-com-
pany of which Selwood was a division superintendent,
had been eagerly awaited a week—for Selwood loved a
horse and the record of his early years in the saddle
entitled him to judge one.

It was easy for McAlpin to coax Selwood down to look
over the long-expected pony, but he knew better than
to try to induce him to join in a drink en route. Mc-
Alpin, however, having prudently stopped for one on
the way up, felt less disappointed at the conventional
refusal of his boss. The sight of the pony, groomed to
an actual polish, did gratify Selwood. "If her action is
up to her brag, she's all right," he said, as McAlpin
swung the lantern away from the box stall. "I'll try
her out later this evening."

Sounding her praises craftily, McAlpin steered his
boss into the office, where Mrs. McCracken and Moses
sat in solemn silence. Selwood, paying no attention to
them, drew a roll of bills and handed one to McAlpin.
At that moment McAlpin, thanking him earnestly,
jerked his head toward Mrs. McCracken to bid her rise.
He hurriedly introduced her to Selwood and pointed to
Moses dramatically as Bunty Bartoe's victim.

Moses stood miserably up, but, despite McAlpin's in-
sistent nodding, the woman appeared unable to rise.
She tried to, but could not. Selwood cast a cold eye on
her. McAlpin bade her tell her story. Fortunately for

the unlucky woman, she could not even do that: telling
it so many times in so few hours had left her too exhausted even to speak. But she looked the story out of
her mournful eyes. They stirred something in Selwood
that words would perhaps not have reached. "*This is
the man, ma'am*, that can get you back your money,"
said McAlpin, pointing emphatically to Selwood, "*if he
wants to*. Tell him," he bawled, starting for the gangway door, "you want him to!"

Hobbling quickly from the room, McAlpin left Selwood at the mercy of the dumb appeal. The woman,
galvanized into a sort of life by McAlpin's words, started,
rose, sank back into McAlpin's chair, choked, and managed to ask one unfortunate question: "Are you the
sheriff, sir?"

A faint grin overspread Selwood's features—it was his
only answer.

"Or the marshal, sir?" she ventured.

McAlpin, listening outside, decided she had killed
every chance of help. He could not see Selwood's face
but felt a heavy silence.

"Is this your mother?" McAlpin, after a pause,
heard Selwood ask the question of the boy and heard
the boy's affirmative answer.

"What kind of specimen are you——"

McAlpin hurried down the barn to get away from the
tongue-lashing that he knew was to follow—for Selwood
was credited with a frontier vocabulary not alone
uniquely forcible but also extremely biting.

The barn boss was brought back to the scene by a
sharp call from Selwood, who bade him look after the
woman. In the excitement—and much to Selwood's
annoyance—she had fainted and fallen into Selwood's
arms. When McAlpin had taken her in hand—and as a
widower he knew how to hold a baby or a woman—Sel-

wood spoke sharply to Moses and told him to come
with him.

He had said no word as to his intentions, but McAlpin
knew exactly what they were. "Just a minute, John!"
he called warningly, as Selwood jerked open the street
door in no very amiable mood. Selwood paused, knob
in hand. "Are you heeled?" demanded McAlpin in a
vigorous undertone. Selwood looked at him as a man
looks at a child. "Are you crazy?" was all he said.

"Stop!" exclaimed McAlpin, never more in his element than in giving advice. He caught Selwood's arm
and in an earnest whisper urged care on him. But the
gambler was stubborn, and, pushing the boy impatiently
ahead, stepped into the street and slammed the door
behind him.

CHAPTER VI

BARTOE'S place, in the River Quarter, was not only larger than others of its kind, but it was commonly regarded as being the worst of its kind. It has already been in part described. A crude bar extended along one side of the room, next to the opening from the barber shop. But back of the barroom was a second, shacklike room with wings opening on either side. These wings, provided with rude bunks, served, when needed, as quarters for the ruffians that made headquarters at Bartoe's. This back room was used to rig up such games as were introduced, or improvised, on the spur of the moment, to take a man's money from him—it was said that many strangers had entered that room with money but that none ever left it with any.

Yet Bartoe's, besides those periodically victimized within it, had a regular following of the characters that haunt the border-line between honest men and rogues— always a considerable one on the frontier—and a sympathetic following of the parasites moving in and out of Sleepy Cat; men who, like the habitués of Bartoe's, lived wholly by their wits.

It was ten o'clock at night when Selwood walked into this place with Moses McCracken in tow. The room was not crowded. Two men were serving behind the bar. The one nearest the front door, whose eyes, by a sort of instinct, usually covered the unusual, paused in surprise when he saw Selwood.

Selwood, Moses dutifully following, walked straight through to the rear. The bartender's keen eyes followed

him, but found no explanation in Selwood's decisive
step. He then tried to read the riddle in Moses's presence, but made no progress in that direction. Selwood
reached the entrance to the second room; there he encountered Bartoe coming out and there on the threshold
he halted the proprietor.

Bartoe, soft-spoken and with all the words needed for
a colloquy but few to waste on compliments, met Selwood with the doubtful grin of a man that can't figure
out exactly what is coming. His neck was short and
his shoulders were sloping; his face was rather small,
his eyes mildly congested, and his voice cut to a subdued mellowness by drink. With his eyes roving apologetically from Selwood's words to Moses's solemn face,
Bartoe listened attentively to all that was said. Moses,
meantime, following earlier explicit directions, was looking carefully at the few men standing in the room. As
Selwood finished, Bartoe, resting his eyes on Moses, spoke
mildly: "I never saw this fellow before, that I know of.
We ain't seen six hundred dollars at once here in a
month. This fellow's picked the wrong place, that's all."

Selwood gave no credence whatever to the expected
denial, but Moses saved him the trouble of saying so by
pointing suddenly to a man sitting alone at a card table
across the room, poring over an old and well-thumbed
illustrated newspaper. The paper was dog-eared, torn,
and much soiled—in the condition suffered by newspapers that have been read and re-read on frontiers that
few newspapers reach. This printed sheet, however,
held its reader fixed in a stony trance. "There's the
man that brought me in here—and this"—he looked
Bartoe in the eye—"is the man that was dealing the
three cards." Bartoe only laughed. Moses, he insisted,
quite unruffled, was mistaken—a thing that might happen to any man. "I make mistakes, myself," he said

pleasantly to Moses, whose stubbornness in repeating
his accusation gave Bartoe no offense.

But Selwood showed immediate interest in the man
with the newspaper. He was a liveryman who traded
in stolen horses when he safely could, and in stolen
goods—using his barn for a fence. Selwood had already
suffered at his hands—or his employers, Russell & Wentworth had—and this seemed a time to "round him up
proper," as Jim McAlpin would have expressed it.

Selwood raised his voice. "Atkins!" he said. "Look
here a minute."

Atkins did not look up. He was, as Selwood perceived,
quite awake to the situation. A second call in sharper
tones, Bartoe and Moses looking on, caused Atkins to
raise his head. He glanced stupidly over at the three,
who stood with their eyes on him. "Come over here,
Atkins," said Selwood again.

The expression of Atkins's face promised a poor response to the curt request. A sandy beard of several
days' growth covered his cheeks—he had not even taken
the trouble to shave after robbing his victim. His face,
red, freckled, his almost shapeless mouth with a loose
underlip, yellow teeth, and eyes half-hidden under ragged brows—all gave him a most unlikely appearance.
"I guess it's about as far from me over to you as it is
from you over to me," suggested Atkins, making no
move to rise. Selwood wasted no time. He walked
straight toward Atkins, who started up in alarm as Selwood briskly approached. "It may not be any farther
one way than the other," retorted Selwood, "but you've
picked the expensive way. I was willing to let you keep
part of your stealings—now—you and Bartoe hand out
the six hundred dollars you robbed this lad of at monte."

Men crowded up. Selwood knew every one of them.
He knew about what each represented in the way of

danger. But he abated nothing whatever of his aggressive insistence. Atkins, sullen and evasive, denying and threatening by turns, was for standing pat, as he had often done before. Bartoe, with better judgment, realized the man they had to deal with. Selwood was known as a man fixed in purpose and certainly capable of backing a demand. He gave little heed to the war of words kindled by his arbitrary attitude—the only sort of an effective one with the ruffians he was facing. When Atkins had wearied himself with brave words, Bartoe, encouraged by Selwood's silence, intervened more boldly himself. Selwood put up his hand to check both.

"Atkins," he said, without raising his voice, "this isn't the only score I've got to settle with you, but I'll settle this now. No man outside a lunatic asylum would believe a word you had to say on any subject. You robbed this fellow; you're going to pay him back every dollar you took. Now I'm done with you for the present—shut up. Bartoe"—he turned on the accomplice— "if the six hundred isn't up on my table by eleven o'clock to-night, I'll close this joint in the morning and run you out of town—or, what's just as good, I'll give you a chance to run me out. Just get together your friends— no, don't talk back. You've said it all. Starbuck? Why, yes, call in Starbuck, by all means." Selwood hardly took the trouble to laugh at the threats flung at him. "Yes, I know that, too. Just as much a gambler as you are? Well!!" Selwood caught his breath in pleasant acknowledgment. "I hope," he said "—for the honor of a dishonorable profession—that I am more of one. Anyway, if you want a real game in the morning, with Starbuck for an opener, you know now just exactly how to get it."

CHAPTER VII

STARBUCK INTERVENES

A WRANGLE between Bartoe and Atkins followed Selwood's departure—forced and acrimonious on Atkins's part, not cheerful on Bartoe's. The two had returned to a corner for a confab. Atkins counselled defiance. But Bartoe reminded him sullenly that he had nothing whatever at stake. Atkins had nothing more to do than strike the trail for fresh pastures—he was reputed to carry his roll all in his pocket—and come back to his barn when things blew over; whereas Bartoe faced the immediate loss of his whole establishment. And in the heat of their quarrel Starbuck, the man whose name had been thrown menacingly at Selwood, walked bluffly in on the angry men.

"Biting the nail again, eh?" he said in contemptuous cavalier fashion. "Why don't you two get out in the street to make a noise? What's disturbing you, Bunty? Shut up, Atkins."

"Yes, Harry told me Selwood had been here." Starbuck named as "Harry" the fat, busy Harry Barbanet, by turns barber and bartender, who had first spotted Selwood and who by dint of some crafty bustling about, some skilful eavesdropping, and the exercise of some extraordinary instinct, had possessed himself of the whole story and "scooped" the house by getting first with it to Starbuck's ear. "I know all about what he wanted," continued Starbuck. "What're you going to do?"

His appearance had a quieting effect on the disputants to the degree that they left off abusing each other and turned together to abuse Starbuck. Still in his early thirties, Starbuck, well built, frank in manner, more than equal in suave speech to the worthies in Sleepy Cat, and game in such local encounters as had befallen him, enjoyed an accredited reputation in the River Quarter. Not unpleasing of feature—rather light of complexion and alert in bearing, he was looked to as a local arbiter of River Quarter difficulties and was, moreover, *de facto* mayor of Sleepy Cat. I say *de facto* because the franchise was only a nominal part of Sleepy Cat politics and Starbuck held the title principally by acclamation, so to speak: and held it successfully against other possible claimants. His eyes were gray, but not over-large among other good-sized features; his voice, the least bit husky, was agreeable, and helped him to make friends among men much his inferiors in natural gifts. Drink he cared little for beyond its convenience for social purposes among hardy-conditioned frontiersmen; yet his face carried a trace of something in it that suggested caution to careful men and had brought rude awakenings to confiding women.

"What are *we* going to do?" echoed Bartoe. "We can't do anything without a fight—and nobody can tell how a fight's going to come out. Go talk to Selwood yourself, Starbuck. Is he running this town or are you?"

"What are we paying a mayor for?" demanded Atkins, unpleasantly significant.

Starbuck silenced his nervous baiters by confining a few brief remarks strictly to one-syllable words. Then, tarrying only long enough to absorb all pertinent details of the row, he strode up street to interview Selwood.

Starbuck realized the delicate position in which Selwood's action left him. Two bosses could not exist at the same time in Sleepy Cat any more than they could in Rome; and there was in the situation this further element of uncertainty that Starbuck wanted to solve. He

knew Selwood but slightly and knew him chiefly as a
man who minded strictly his own business. Did he mean
now to aspire for local leadership? Starbuck hoped not
but wanted to know. Thus, in Selwood, a new factor
had apparently been projected into local affairs and his
attitude toward Starbuck remained to be ascertained—
all of this Starbuck had in mind as he passed Bob Scott
talking with Lefever near the door and walked into Selwood's place.

The big room was still filled with a crowd three times
as large as any gathered anywhere down street. Starbuck entered with a confident gait. He threw his feet
forward somewhat apart, with the toes turned out, land-
ing with each step squarely on his heels; his chest was
set well forward, and his general air was at one with
these characteristics.

He bent his steps straight toward Selwood, who stood
smoking while he watched with mild interest the play
at a table where a new dealer sat installed. He noticed
Starbuck's approach and looked expectant as his caller
came up.

"Selwood?" said Starbuck, inquiringly, putting out
his hand. "Yes. You're Starbuck," answered Selwood
laconically as he gave him his own hand.

"Can I have a word with you?" asked Starbuck. For
answer Selwood, proffering a cigar from his waistcoat
pocket, led the way to his table in the corner and
pointed to a chair. Both men sat down. Starbuck
spoke.

"I don't like to see a quarrel get going in the street,
Selwood," he began, with an air of good-fellowship.
"Dave Tracy and I didn't always agree. Tracy was
getting pretty well along in years and he was a little
cranky once in a while—I guess maybe I was, too——"
Starbuck smiled faintly with the candid admission.

Selwood's face was receptively non-committal. "But Tracy," continued Starbuck, "had enemies where he might have had friends, which is a foolish policy, in my opinion, for any man." There was no covert hinting in Starbuck's manner—just frank disinterestedness. "Now Bartoe," he went on quietly, "has turned up a little grievance against you. I told him I didn't think there was anything serious to it—nothing but what could be ironed out between man and man—so I said I'd just come and have a little talk with you."

Starbuck paused—not as a man that has said all, but as if inviting the other fellow to say something. Selwood only took his cigar from his mouth, waiting courteously for his interviewer to continue.

"I suppose," resumed Starbuck, not discomposed, "I'm less acquainted with you than I am with most men around town. But I've always heard you spoken of as a reasonable man, a man who didn't want anything more than what's right. Bartoe feels you came down on him pretty strong—I suppose you had some good reason for what you did."

Starbuck, feeling, naturally, that he had put his own cards fairly on the table, and in nowise upset by his peculiar reception, now sat silent, in turn, and waited for the other man to play.

Selwood knocked the ashes from his cigar and broke the pause with a question—not precisely an expected one. "What difference did you ever have with Dave Tracy?" he asked, without changing the expression of his eyes, and speaking in friendly tones and in a merely casual manner.

"Why, none at all that I recall this minute," declared Starbuck, covering the retreat of his surprise with a little celerity of answer. "I said we didn't maybe always agree. But I'm no man to remember little differ-

ences—they don't mean anything to me. And nobody
was sorrier than I was to hear about it when Dave was
shot, down at Bartoe's. You sure dosed the bunch that
did it. Dave can thank you he's alive."

"It *was* poor shooting," murmured Selwood, inoffen-
sively meditating. "And, as you say, Dave is getting
on in years. And it was pretty near enough to finish
him. Dave says," he rambled on, quietly, "that you
and he split because he wouldn't pay you money for
protection."

Starbuck showed his first impatience. "If Tracy said
that—" he began.

"What's that?" demanded Selwood, with a shade
more of life and carefulness in his tone—"*if* Tracy said
that——"

"Not doubting your word at all, Selwood—not at all.
But somebody in a town like this always has to act as
peacemaker—you know that. The boys seemed to pick
on me for the job. It ain't much of a job, nor one I was
looking for. But I was foot-loose and took it to oblige.
I found I was getting all the kicks and the boys getting
all the money, so I asked them to chip in down along
the line. Most of 'em did. Tracy and a few others
didn't——"

"Wasn't Tracy the only one that didn't?" asked Selwood impassively.

"That may be—I don't remember. But I never had
any hard feeling against Tracy on that account. I want
you to know that, Selwood. You seem," continued
Starbuck with some irritation, "to want to stick to that
subject. I didn't come here to-night to rake over old
scores; I came here to try to patch up new ones, Selwood."

"Before we get out the sticking plaster," Selwood
went on evenly, "let's get Dave's position clear—and

mine. Dave felt that a place run like this place, where
a straight game is dealt, didn't need any protection—
neither the place nor the proprietors. It may be he
made a mistake, but that's the way Dave felt—that's
the way I feel. Now about this Bartoe business. He
robbed to-day, among others, a boy here with his
widowed mother, of six hundred dollars. I told Bartoe
to give the boy back his money. He refused. I told
him I'd clean him out in the morning or he could clean
me out. There's no use of more words about it—that's
all there is to it."

"Well, I wouldn't say that's all, Selwood," observed
Starbuck, asserting himself. "I'm here to keep law and
order and I can't have any places burned in the business
quarter of Sleepy Cat. He's in the gambling business
same as you are——"

Selwood jumped as if stung, and used a strong word.
"Same as *I* am?" he echoed angrily. "Do I send out
jailbirds like Atkins to drag men in here to rob them?
What do you mean?"

It needed all of Starbuck's diplomacy to quiet things
down. He rehearsed Bartoe's defense. He urged good
feeling—all to no purpose. He found he could make no
impression whatever on Selwood's firmness. He rose at
length, indignant. "I see I can't reason with you. If
anything unpleasant happens—don't hold me responsible!"

"Not if you keep out of it," observed Selwood, unper-
turbed.

"I'm here to keep the peace, not to 'keep out,'" retorted Starbuck, rising to his full height before his
troublesome customer. Selwood rose in turn. "I believe you left Thief River just before I went there," he
said calmly. "You had some trouble regarding claim
signs."

Starbuck blazed. "What do you mean?" he demanded.

"Miners will travel all night to round up a claim jumper. But I feel exactly as you do, Starbuck. Why rake up old scores?"

"As far as I'm concerned," exclaimed Starbuck, advancing hotly, as Selwood purposely retreated, "if you mean the bunch that tried to jump my claims down there—bring on your miners!"

"I'm not much on old scores, Starbuck," said Selwood soberly. "I don't think we're going to have any trouble here—not you and I, anyway. Our teamsters can take care of Bunty's outfit to-morrow. I'm riding down to Thief River myself to-night on business and I've told McAlpin to keep a horse saddled for me. But I shan't start till eleven o'clock. I expect before that Bartoe will have that six hundred here. Come over here and look at this roulette wheel—yes, it's a new one—they say you can beat it with a system. But, anyway, you've got to keep the boys interested—or stand 'em on their heads and shake the money out of their pockets the way Bartoe, Atkins and Company do. Drop in any time. Starbuck. Always glad to see you."

With this judicious and even-handed mixture of threats, hints, "anyways," and small talk, Selwood let Starbuck go, with feathers once more unruffled. But neither had fooled the other in the slightest degree. Both understood it was only a possible preliminary to situations that might carry far into the future. But Starbuck left at least enlightened—in some directions— and Selwood walked back to his desk, with a fresh cigar between his fingers—one that Starbuck had asked him to try.

At one minute past eleven o'clock Selwood, giving a few directions to George Skillman—the pale little man

that dealt faro and was always bothered by flies—left
the gambling-hall for the barn. His pony was waiting.
Climbing into the saddle he headed south for the Thief
River road, trying out the new pony's steps. There was
a moon and a glory of stars overhead, but these gave
Selwood little food for thought: the gaits of the spirited
pony were of more moment. He had crossed the river
bridge and was swinging out on the Spanish Sinks when
he heard the clatter of hoofs behind him. A horseman
riding fast overhauled him and he looked around to
greet Bob Scott. Scott reined in beside the gambler,
with his pony on its haunches. "The money's up," he
grinned. "Skillman's got it in his pocket. So I guess,"
grinned Scott again, "you won't need to bother the
miners."

They rode back at a leisurely pace, put up their horses,
and walked together up the hill. Selwood took the
money from Skillman, counted it, handed it to Scott,
told him where to find the owner and deliver it. "Tell
her to get her boy out of town before somebody else
gets it away from him," was his only injunction.

CHAPTER VIII

THE MOCK-AUCTION STORE

"IF there's any human scum in the whole blamed United States that ain't landed in Sleepy Cat," grumbled Carpy, "it must be because they ain't heard of it yet."

Doctor Carpy was an educated man, who knew quite well how to speak good English. But, like many another frontiersman of his kind, he had caught the slovenly English of the men with whom he was thrown in contact. At times he spoke well, but usually not well. There was, too, perhaps a tinge of bravado in his murdering of the King's English when he knew better.

"Now look at that coat," he continued, calmly aggrieved. "I bought it new at an auction yesterday! Last night I rode down to see a sick teamster at the bunkhouse—one o' your men, Selwood. While I was fixing him up it began to rain. When I started for home I put on the coat. By that time it was raining all-fired hard. I lifted my whip to touch up the horses, and the whole sleeve parted at the shoulder joint! When I reached around to see what the matter was, the other sleeve fell clean off. When I stepped out of the buggy, the coat come in two right across the back! Look at it!"

With some violent punctuation of his complaint, the Doctor, who in Sleepy Cat never by any chance received more than the first syllable of his professional title and rarely his surname, was telling John Selwood of how he had been cheated.

"Where did you buy the coat?" asked Selwood,

though less moved as a listener than the Doctor was as an orator.

"Down at that new place—opposite the warehouse—in the old blockhouse. A man name' Fyler is running a dry-goods store there. And Big Haynes is running a mock auction, on one side of the store. Come on down. You lick Haynes and I'll lick Fyler!"

The two men were talking in the one-story building adjoining and communicating with the hotel, that bore the small wood sign—known as the "shingle"—of the sole doctor in Sleepy Cat or within a hundred miles of Sleepy Cat—an open-handed, profane, and not always cool-headed surgeon, but one whose failings were in rough measure redeemed by a generous heart and the benefits of a skill free, without question, to all comers. The room in which they were sitting—not over ten by twelve feet—served as the doctor's office, as his bedroom when the hostel was crowded, and as his drug-store; at the moment the Doctor himself was sitting in his one chair, before a battered pine table, and Selwood was sitting on the camp cot where the Doctor sometimes slept and on which lay the remains of the offending garment.

Selwood, travel-stained and dressed in the rough gear of the trail, had evidently just come in from a trip over the division and sat listening to his friend with the air of a man who has more serious matters on his mind.

"How is Dave coming on?" he asked, without responding to Carpy's flippant invitation to help "clean up" the new trader.

The Doctor, one elbow on the table, scratched his head. "Hang Dave," he said, perplexed, "he ain't coming on. I can't get any life into him. It's close to a year now since he got hurt. But you've got to remember, John, he's an old man, and put in three years in the Army of the Potomac. Now look at you. The first time Dave came to see me, a year ago, to get some medicine for you he said you were in the last stages of consumption. It wasn't so; but you were headed that way all right. Look at you now—spry as an antelope. You'll be able pretty soon to whip your weight in wildcats. You'd never make a mule-skinner nor a blacksmith; but you never was built for ary one; you're built light."

"You took good care of me."

Carpy disclaimed. "Good care nothing: It was this dry mountain air—not too high and thin, neither—that took care of you; and you're young. Now, Dave is just teeterin' along—wound all healed up, but just kind of slow paralysis. Nothing I can put in him seems to pull him up. It sure was hard to get what he got here in Sleepy Cat, after three years in the army. This town is certainly tough—and getting tougher."

"It was tough before you and I saw it, Doctor; and it will be tough after we're laid up on the hill," replied Selwood indifferently. "If you can pull Dave through you'll save one good man for it—if he is a gambler."

"Where you going?"

"Down to the tent." Carpy understood what he meant—that he was going to see his wounded partner. Tracy had been moved from the gambling-hall to quieter quarters on the edge of the tent colony of the town.

As the two men parted and Selwood walked down the hotel steps, a tall, odd-looking man accosted him. "Stranger," he said with a suspicious air, "I'm lookin' for John Seltzer."

Selwood answered promptly if not definitely. "What do you want with John Seltzer?"

"I'm a Russell & Wentworth mule boss, stranger, from Medicine Bend. This man Seltzer is our superintendent here."

"You're William Pardaloe——"

"Just plain Bill, stranger—Bill Pardaloe—what do they call you?"

"It depends somewhat, Bill, on who does the calling; my friends call me John Selwood."

"Then that's what I want to call you, stranger—I don't give a hang who you are or what your name is— we're friends."

Selwood looked Bill over with some curiosity.

He was an unusual man even among unusual men. In his left hand, with the stock resting on the ground, he held, as he talked, a double-barrelled shotgun, of a size and calibre unique in the mountain country. It was, in fact, an old eight-gauge English gun with barrels thirty-six inches long. Its normal charge, as Selwood afterward learned, was ten drams of powder and "a handful of buckshot" in each barrel. This extraordinary weapon was carried ostensibly as a protection against "hostyle" Indians—though Indians had for years ceased to molest freight wagons on that trail.

In size, Pardaloe matched up with his gun. He stood well above six feet in his moccasins—which he wore when he became confused as to where he had left his boots—and he carried his arms and legs pretty much akimbo. He was long-limbed and gaunt of figure, with a browned skin drawn like parchment over a face as lean as a hound's. A sharp nose shot out like an interrogation point upside down, between beetling cheekbones, and his upper lip and lower face were covered with a scraggly growth of beard—a growth that in a beauty contest would have damned Adonis himself.

But it was, after all, amid these prominent features, a pair of deep, close-set, beady brown eyes that dominated his face and fixed themselves on the object of his inquiry with a suspicion that was meant to pierce the last reserves of duplicity.

"Ben Wentworth spoke to me about you, Bill," returned Selwood; "said he was going to send you up here——"

"That wasn't what I looked you up for now—Jim McAlpin told me I'd find you at the hotel. I want to say, stranger——"

"Selwood," suggested the superintendent encouragingly.

"I'm a brother of Mrs. McCracken—Mose is my nephew. She wrote me how you got her money back from them river rats——"

"That was nothing."

"Well, I want to say—I'm with you, stranger! And I'll get your name set after a while."

"Wentworth told me he was transferring you to this division. What were they paying you on the plains job?"

"Thirty-five."

"Forty up here, Bill."

Pardaloe gradually caught the import of the words. "Much obliged, John," he said gravely. "Everything costs a quarter here."

"I see," said Selwood significantly, "you've found that out. Wait for me over at the barn—I'll be there in a few minutes."

Pardaloe, picking up his gun in his left hand and resting his right hand on the haft of a huge bowie knife, fashioned from a blacksmith's file and slung at his hip, wandered on his way. Selwood directed his steps toward Tracy's tent.

To this tent quarter had also come Christie Fyler and her father for temporary lodgings. Selwood paid little attention to the flotsam of the tent colony. He had only been careful to pitch and equip a tent for his friend, a hundred yards from any other tent. But Dave had

lingered—refusing to die and not quite equal to getting
well; in consequence, the newcomers encroached on his
privacy until the Fyler tent was pitched almost back to
back with his own; and all that Christie had ever heard
of her neighbor's tent—a larger and better tent than
the others—was that it sheltered a sick gambler. Christie
saw at times an Indian-looking man coming and going
from the gambler's tent, and at times a woman—who
came daily from somewhere—to bring broth and to tidy
up the quarters of the wounded man.

Once Christie, at her own work, had caught a glimpse
of this woman's face. She was not old in years, but her
complexion, ruined by the sun and the winds of the
mountains, made her look old. Her features showed
traces of an earlier beauty, and her elastic step proved
her health and strength; it was care and unhappiness
that aged her expression. Her eyes fixed themselves in
Christie's memory; they were dark, rather deep eyes,
with a hard look, as if of hope, like her youth, faded.
Meeting her again in the street, as the two passed on
their ways, Christie had paused to ask a question. The
response had been cold—not calculated to invite acquaintance.

Margaret Hyde, indeed, courted no acquaintance.
Many women passed through Sleepy Cat, but among
the few that called Sleepy Cat their abiding place she
walked alone. She was housekeeper at Doctor Carpy's
hotel, which was elastic in this, that Doctor Carpy added
a room or a wing to it whenever he could get together
money enough to buy a load of lumber. She was a
hard-working housekeeper under the hardest possible
conditions; but she stuck to her job and walked her way
—alone. And cold and hard though she was, she was
never too tired to bring delicacies to the ailing or to sit
up at night to care for a sick teamster.

On this morning that Selwood parted from the irascible surgeon, Christie Fyler, leaving her own tent to go up street, caught sight for the first time of a new visitor at the sick man's tent. This was Selwood. No day passed, indeed, without Selwood's seeing Tracy; he made his visits usually in the early evening, before going to the hall. On this particular morning his anxiety had got him up early—for him—that is, before noon, to see Carpy and discuss his friend's chances.

Selwood spent some time in the tent. Bob Scott, under the adjoining fly, was cooking the noon meal, and Selwood, sitting with a cigar beside Tracy's cot, gossiped with him—prolonging his stay to observe as narrowly as he could the sick man's condition. From the tent Selwood walked back to the hotel for his own breakfast and dinner—usually one meal. On the way he had to pass the old building made over into a store by the trader, Fyler—the man of whom Carpy had so feelingly complained—and, passing, Selwood, moved by an impulse of curiosity, looked in.

A midday auction was in progress. Fyler's stock, chiefly shoddy clothing, rough staple dry-goods, heavy boots, shoes, hats, and cheap furnishings for men, was piled loosely on rough shelving hastily put together and stood in boxes and barrels in front of a rude counter that extended down one side of the store. Before this counter, where Selwood entered, was gathered a small crowd of men—emigrants, settlers, teamsters, and loafers; while on the counter, red-faced and in his shirt-sleeves, stood Big Haynes, running an eloquent auction. Paying little attention to those moving in and out of the front door, Haynes, perspiringly intent on his selling, did not even nod in recognition of Selwood as the gambler moved unostentatiously along behind the outer fringe of the onlookers and reached a quiet spot in the rear where he could see and listen unobserved. But he had been seen and inspected by one man, the man behind the counter at Haynes's side—the man that passed the merchandise up to Haynes to be auctioned off; this man was Atkins.

Atkins always made his moves from cover, and by no look or word did he indicate he had seen anybody. The bidding was good, stuff was moving briskly. At the rear end of the counter Fyler, behind a dry-goods box, was wrapping up purchases and taking in the money. It looked like a queer combination to Selwood, the new trader and the two Sleepy Cat worthies, but Selwood had no comments to record on that point, either to himself or to any one else. However, he scrutinized the trader with some interest. Fyler's thin, scattered hair, his bony face and large eyes were as he had seen them on the trail; and Selwood remarked again his nervous smile and somewhat separated teeth, showing prominently when he smiled or laughed—which was much of the time.

Selwood, listening to Big Haynes's thundering praises of his wares and complaints of the astonishing coldness of his buyers, used his eyes about him. Not a merchant himself, Selwood had profited enough by his brief experience as a freighter to know something about merchandise. He saw that the stock was of a sort not infrequently shipped to the frontier because out-of-date elsewhere. It contained good goods that nobody wanted and poor goods that nobody should buy. It was desperately ill-assorted for the needs of Western men, though it might have suited Western women, had there been any number in Sleepy Cat to suit. Selwood edged gradually over to where Fyler was at work wrapping goods near the money till. He remembered then that he had some business with Fyler.

"You seem to have the best part of the job," he

said presently, and solely because he wished to talk to him.

Fyler looked up without recognizing his benefactor of Crawling Stone Wash.

"How's that?"

"Next the money drawer."

Fyler laughed. "Mighty little in it!"

."My name's Selwood," said the gambler, without raising his voice. "I look after the Russell & Wentworth freight here. My wagon boss tells me we're short some goods for you in the last shipment."

The trader looked at him with a new interest. "You were; twelve cases of boots—all I had coming; just about put me out of business. Where were they lost?"

"They weren't lost. They were stolen. I came in to get a description—when you're through with the sale."

As he spoke, a man that would invite attention entered the front door. He was short, almost squat in stature, and square-built—practically everything about the man could have been measured by a right angle. He was smooth-faced, his head was square, his forehead square, his shoulders square, his feet broad and square, and his jaw was square. He walked slowly and planted his hob-nailed boots squarely before him. His legs were short, his arms long, and he would have disputed build with a gorilla and strength with a grisly. This was Abe Cole, the Sleepy Cat blacksmith. Other blacksmiths there were in Sleepy Cat; but Cole was known as and designated as the Sleepy Cat blacksmith.

Fortunately he was as peaceable as powerful when not aroused, but his disposition was naturally positive, and he was known as a fighter. His utterance was abrupt and heavy with decision. He was bareheaded now, with only heavy brown hair for protection from the sun. He wore a short-sleeved thick red wool shirt,

cowhide boots, and blue woollen trousers tucked inside
the boot-tops.

Abe shouldered himself through the crowd without
hesitation or difficulty—whenever his shoulders encountered an obstacle, the obstacle gave way. He walked
straight to Fyler, holding out a handful of soggy scraps
of black felt. A bedraggled hatband hung from his
wrist. "There's your hat!" he exclaimed, throwing the
remains down on Fyler's box and closing his jaw with a
snap. While Fyler gazed in consternation at the exhibit, Abe raised his eyes to the portly auctioneer.
"Look here, Haynes!" he thundered. The auction
stopped. "Here's the hat you sold me yesterday!"
Cole added, in no uncertain tones. Haynes gave him
prompt attention. "That's what the rain did to it!"
bellowed Abe.

Haynes, leaning down, picked up the shoddy wreck,
the hatband last and very carefully, for fear it should
fall to pieces, and examined the remains with solicitude.
He took the pieces one by one in his fingers, holding the
sodden black mass up from time to time for his crowd
to see, and closely examined the hatband.

Abe Cole started in again to say a hard thing, but
Haynes put up his hand as a doctor might in the presence of approaching death demand restraint from a very
angry man. While his abundant, glossy black hair fell
with a serious expression across one side of his forehead,
almost down to his eyebrow, Big Haynes rose from his
stooping position, held up the rotten felt that all might
see, and spoke so loud all might hear.

"Gentlemen," he said, speaking as a troubled man
might speak on a painful occasion, "you can see here,
all of you, what difficulty an honest purveyor of merchandise has in selecting his goods for a new country.
This hat, gentlemen—hold on, Abe!" he interjected in

stentorian tones, for Cole's safety-valve of anger gave strong indications of popping, "hold on till you hear me; I sold you this hat, didn't I? I did! Very well. I want to say to you, gentlemen, one and all, that when a mistake like this happens, we make it good! This hat"—the definition cost him a laugh from the crowd, but Big Haynes was an artist and ignored it—"this hat got into my sale yesterday by mistake. It was never intended for this country. I bought this lot of hats for the Indian trade—down on the Gunlock Reservation. This hat," he exclaimed, holding the offender out for personal reproach, "never should have been sold in the mountains; it's a desert hat, made light and porous for a dry country. The Indians along the famous Spanish Sinks buy these hats freely for their squaws; they're porous, gentlemen—but they won't stand rain."

"Porous monkey!" stuttered Cole. "They're rotten."

Haynes courteously protested. "Don't crowd me, Abe! Don't crowd a peaceable man trying to die honest——"

"Whatever you do, you'll never live honest," blurted out Cole indignantly.

"I wouldn't had it happen, Abe, for one hundred dollars. I replace it cheerfully. Mr. Fyler," he shouted, pointing a commanding finger, "be kind enough to hand me that box of hats." From the box passed up Haynes, carefully picking over several hats, selected a brown one—never for a moment losing the thread of his easy and plausible flow of words. Abe Cole continued to growl, but he was in effect silenced, and stood under his new hat, a sturdy onlooker, while Big Haynes pulled out his watch. "Gentlemen," he exclaimed, as solemnly as if about to lead in prayer, "it is twelve o'clock—time to eat. My heart is weak and I eat three times a day. I never keep men beyond their dinner hour, anyway—

their wives pick on me, and a hungry man ain't a good customer. And if you think I've got an easy job here, try it, some of you! Next sale at two o'clock sharp, and the biggest bargains ever offered in Sleepy Cat—don't miss it!"

The crowd began to file out. Big Haynes climbed down. "What kind of a hat did you give him?" whispered Fyler.

"Same kind I give him yesterday," growled Haynes. "Doc Carpy come in here a while ago with his overcoat —wanted to cut me up for bear bait. I hope to God I get out of this town before it rains again."

The auctioneer followed the crowd as they straggled out. At the door a young girl waited. She had a lunch basket in her hand. When the store was emptied, she walked up the two steps and in. She wore a tan cape that fell below her shoulders and a little poke bonnet that gave her a quaint expression, but made her look older than she really was. Selwood stood near Fyler, and he watched the newcomer with an unrestrained interest until her eyes fell on his, as she came up. Selwood looked then at Fyler. Christie—and Selwood recognized her as the girl in the wagon at Crawling Stone Wash— set down her basket on the dry-goods box in front of Fyler. "Here's your dinner, father," she said. "Eat it now while it's hot."

Selwood moved back out of the way, watching Christie for a moment while he could do so unobserved. Fyler busied himself setting his dinner out of the basket.

Selwood tried to think of something to say, but could not. And though he felt he was an interloper, he could not get started to go. Christie, her back to him, talked and laughed with her father. Her voice was completely new music to Selwood's ears; it transfixed him. But the moment could not last. She turned partly and looked at Selwood. Whatever she may have had in her mind, he could think of but one thing, for her glance seemed to him to say: What are you doing here? And Selwood, barely returning her look, just caught sight of her eyes, pulled himself together, and walked out of the store.

CHAPTER IX

PARDALOE INVESTIGATES

SELWOOD found it possible to happen in occasionally at Fyler's, and, although it meant getting up a little earlier, about at the time Fyler's dinner was due.

But he could never get a chance to speak to Christie, who rarely loitered. She was accustomed to walk in just at the close of the auction, and Selwood, who usually took his place close to Fyler's dry-goods box, made into a sort of a desk, was forced to content himself with hearing a few words, or a little laugh, as she spoke to her father and walked out again.

But such a moment Selwood thought worth waiting for. He looked forward to that moment. At night, under the glare of hot lamps that cost a fortune in coal-oil brought two thousand miles to burn; in an air reeking with the fumes of tobacco smoke and breaking at times into boisterous ribaldry, Selwood seemed yet sometimes to hear, between the monotonous clicking of chips, the calls of the dealers, and the whir of roulette wheels, the echo of a laugh that took him from his surroundings. On the trail, as he rode it alone, in the burning sunshine of a summer morning with only granite peaks for company and chattering prairie dogs to beat with abuse at his ears, he could hear—with the dogtown passed and the horses falling back into a walk up a hill —from somewhere out of the shrill air the cadence of a girl's voice—a cadence to start into life a man's first dream—one that may find place even in the heart of a man already case-hardened.

Selwood's indolent inclination, when not in bad humor, to oblige people, made him now and again an innocent capper at the vagabond auction sales. When Haynes couldn't get a starting bid on a slow article he would appeal to Selwood, who to afford some excuse for his presence would at times start and even bid in things for which he had no possible use. Money in Sleepy Cat came easily and went easily; few set store by it beyond the fanciful impulse of the moment—fewer still hoarded it. McAlpin was a man who saved his money; Atkins was one greedy for it; Selwood made and spent money carelessly; but most men in Sleepy Cat parted with it recklessly.

Chance, which always favors the persistent, came one day to Selwood's aid. Fyler lay in the tent ill, and that day Christie had to act as cashier. Selwood put in an appearance just before noon and saw Christie in the receipt of custom. The advance guard of a big emigrant wagon train had reached Sleepy Cat the night before and the selling was brisk. Big Haynes, perspiring, was knocking down the merchandise glibly and Selwood wormed his way among the buyers back to Fyler's box. Christie, her cape carefully folded and lying on a shelf behind her and her bonnet held loosely by the strings, hanging back on her neck, stood newly revealed to Selwood. It was not so much that she looked prettier, but that she presented new charms—her brown hair was only like many another woman's brown hair, but to Selwood it was something never before suspected in the world; her cheeks suffused and her eyes bright with the excitement of her unaccustomed work, were just a repetition of nature's eternal challenge to mankind.

Not for an instant did the gambler hesitate—he who so often staked a frontier fortune on the turn of a card knew too well how long it may be before the same card turns again to fill a hungry hand. He took off his hat as he walked to her—that alone set him apart from the other men—and caught her eye in spite of her resolve not to see a man, but only men, in her enforced servitude.

"Father away?" asked Selwood, meeting her look with the necessary decision in his own eyes. Christie was wrapping up a package. She had seen the man of silence more than once near her father's desk and was the less afraid of him. "He's not very well; I made him stay in the tent this morning."

Selwood seemed to understand and accept the entire situation without need of further words. Haynes was redoubling his shouting, and his success kept Christie busy at the settling counter. A miner, although it was summer in Sleepy Cat, bid in a pair of fur gloves. To pay he threw down a twenty-dollar bill. Christie looked desperately in her cigar-box cash drawer for change. It was not to be found. Selwood drew from his pocket, without speaking, a roll of bills, a bigger roll than Christie had ever seen, and tossed it toward her. The roll stopped almost under her hand. She looked up, and in doing so met Selwood's eyes. "Make the change out of that," he said dryly. And, as there still seemed a question in her eyes he added: "Help yourself."

She attempted to laugh. "Oh, would you give me a little change? They've swept the drawer just about clean," she confessed with another nervous little laugh, and held the twenty-dollar bill appealingly toward him.

He pointed to the roll. "Plenty of small bills there," he suggested, with only a trace of interest. "Help yourself." And with this invitation he walked away, while the man in front of her waited.

Christie called in consternation. He could not, or would not, hear. The men about her laughed; one offered to take the roll if she didn't want it; the miner asked for his change; Selwood had disappeared.

Next morning he was back—and at eleven o'clock.

The main body of the big wagon train had pulled in the evening before and the town was alive with sightseers and buyers. The auction-room crowd was gathering when Selwood arrived and the buying had begun to be spirited. Christie stood again condemned to the cashier's desk. She looked up in a moment and saw the silent man in the big hat standing almost beside her. Pressed by her work and intimidated by the presence of so many strange men, a face somewhat familiar seemed a welcome sight.

"Father laid up yet?" Selwood put the question as soon as he caught her eye.

Christie, heightened in color by her confusion, told him she feared her father was quite ill. Then, stopping her work, she delved into a corner of the big cigar box, and from under the loose money drew a roll of bills carefully tied with a number of strings and held it toward him. "You ran away yesterday and left all this money!"

She waited for his comment; he made none—only regarded her gravely. "Please take it, quick," she added hurriedly; "I've been frightened to death for fear I should lose it!"

"You may need it again this morning," objected Selwood. But Christie would listen to no blandishments, and Selwood, knowing when to quit, took his roll— leaving her to wonder, when she could find time to, what manner of men these mountain men were who trusted strangers with their money. Selwood, with an unlighted cigar in his hand and entertained by Big Haynes's jumble of bluff and eloquence, watched Christie. One of her weightiest cares was that of making in a blank book a record of each article sold. This took time and required more knowledge of goods than she could muster; Haynes kept a duplicate book under his own hand, but he jotted things down fast, never stopping his talk. Selwood be-

fore long had taken charge of Christie's book, though
this seemed not precisely to Haynes's liking.

The room became crowded. As Haynes continued to
knock down the goods, Christie's work grew heavy. Selwood edged closer to Haynes and began to take care of
articles as Haynes threw them on the counter toward her.
These he entered and held under his hand until she was
ready for them in turn, telling her the sale price of each
and passing the items to the buyers as they were paid
for. It was not long before he was wrapping parcels
himself, and by noon he had his hands in the cash-box,
making change, with Christie keeping the check of the
goods as they came from the auctioneer.

During the time that Fyler lay ill, Selwood was a frequent visitor at the store, and though her father had
forgotten the incident, Christie remembered him at the
Crawling Stone Wash. She had heard him tell her father
he was a freighting man, and had heard him talk with
her father about his missing goods. Christie, without
thinking much about him, began to look for Selwood as
an incident of the day, which was exacting enough even
when she had help—and he could always be counted on
to keep her cash straight. She had, during the time he
was around, almost unending questions to ask; Selwood
was equal to answering most of them, whether of the
nondescript population, the mountains, the desert, the
Indians, the mines, or the wild beasts. He knew something of all of these things, and all of some of them. He
was better mannered than the other men, always reserved,
always freshly shaven, and always neatly dressed. He,
too, asked questions, but without seeming inquisitive,
and by easy degrees and without serious effort picked
up more information than Christie would have realized
about her father and his affairs and herself.

He learned, too, about the arrangement under which
Haynes had introduced the auction into the store.

Haynes, so the story ran, had a partner—a man of mystery, as far as Christie's information went—who had a small stock of merchandise. Haynes had suggested the two stocks be combined and sold by auction. Selwood heard all, never by any chance interposing comment, and at the end of each day helped Christie settle with Haynes, who held rigidly to prompt settlements, refusing to wait for her father's return. Selwood had not actual knowledge enough of the two stocks to know just what the equities were, but he knew enough of Haynes and of Haynes's "silent" partner to reach without difficulty the conclusion that Christie was to be cheated whenever feasible.

There were some discrepancies in the two sales books. Some of these, apparently in her favor, Haynes conceded to Christie on the days she made settlement; others he held out for. When Selwood took hold of the settlement —coming back in the afternoon for that purpose—there was sharp colloquy between the voluble auctioneer and the stubborn gambler. But the settlement followed Christie's and Selwood's record.

In the meantime Bob Scott and Bill Pardaloe had been detailed by Lefever to investigate the disappearance of the Fyler shipment of boots. And as their reports began to come in, it was not hard for Selwood, who always used his eyes and ears, to reach the conclusion that Haynes's merchandise consisted chiefly, if not wholly, of stolen goods—and that these were of a much better quality than Fyler's stock. By kicking a packing case here and there under the counters, Selwood likewise found reason to believe that some, at least, of his boots had found their way to the auction—and although he had never seen a pair of boots put up by Big Haynes while he was present, he had seen men in the street carrying boots away from the store.

When Fyler, recovered, came back to his place, Selwood had told Pardaloe his suspicions and directed him what to do. Pardaloe, who loved nothing so much as a row, dropped in at times at the auction. To Big Haynes he was not a welcome visitor. Pardaloe would talk as long and as loud as Haynes himself, and at times would carry on with bystanders wrangling arguments that distracted the crowd's attention.

One day Haynes, exasperated beyond endurance, stopped his sale to remonstrate sharply with the noisy wagoner. This nearly precipitated a personal encounter, or, rather, it seemed nearly to do so—for neither warrior had any intention of closing in. Pardaloe, with much foot movement, insisted that Haynes come down to make good his threats; while Haynes, with equal violence, invited Pardaloe to come up and fight out a man's fight on the counter—a suggestion that every one but Pardaloe applauded. Pardaloe, however, objected—the ceiling being low—that if he attempted this he would have to fight sitting down. He was then invited to wait outside till the close of the sale—which Pardaloe professed himself willing and ready to do. At this juncture Fyler interfered—and the belligerents permitted themselves for a moment to be calmed down. In fact, Pardaloe's orders were not to fight but to seem to fight—otherwise he would have eaten Big Haynes alive.

Haynes, with the air of a man who has restrained his might in deference to the situation, resumed his selling with fresh vigor, and Pardaloe's patience was at length rewarded by seeing Fyler pass up to the auctioneer a pair of boots, on which Pardaloe fixed his beady eyes; and, to show that he harbored no resentment, he promptly bid for them. Despite spirited opposition he secured the boots, and in the purchase he had the opportunity he wanted. Sitting on the floor, surrounded by the crowd, he tried the boots on. He complained to Fyler they did not fit, and called for more boots to try on. In this way he got his long nose in behind and under the counters, and before he quit, by rowing and quarrelling over his purchase, secured a pretty fair description of the boot stock.

Bob Scott also made progress in his research. He made friends with a hostler of Atkins, and, prowling about in Atkins's barn, down by the river, at opportune times, he found hidden in a binful of oats one whole case of boots and six barrels filled with boots. From one of these barrels he filched a sample pair of boots and took them to headquarters for investigation. They matched those Pardaloe had bought at Big Haynes's auction.

The next evening Pardaloe and Scott were sent to the barn to levy on the stolen property. And on the principle of least said soonest mended, Scott, keeping a good fire going in the office stove, held the attention of the night barn-man with Indian scare stories while Pardaloe, aided by a Selwood teamster, dug the boots out of the oats, loaded the case and the barrels on a wagon, hauled them to McAlpin's barn, and locked them up in the harness-room.

Selwood repaired early next morning to the store. Haynes had not come down. Fyler was alone. Selwood waited until Fyler should ask about the boots. He himself never introduced an unpleasant subject when he could count on the other fellow's doing it, particularly when he held the better hand. When Fyler's impatient question came, Selwood was ready, made his report, and offered to restore such of the missing goods as had not been sold over the counter.

Fyler seemed not altogether pleased. He was skeptical concerning the reputation that Selwood unhesitatingly gave his auction partners.

And Selwood was cruelly blunt. "You may not know

it, Fyler," he said composedly, "but you've got a pair of crooks in here with you. Haynes's partner is this man Atkins. When the Angel Gabriel blows, he will have a separate and distinct horn for Atkins; and if he doesn't watch out, Atkins will steal the horn on him. All of the stuff that Atkins supplies for this auction is stolen—if you don't know it, you ought to. Your twelve cases of boots were stolen from our warehouse in Medicine Bend by some one of Atkins's cronies and turned over to him to get rid of—this is the way he is doing it. I've got hold of about two-thirds of the boots—my men found his cache. They're cleaning the boots up. The cases have disappeared, except one; they couldn't steal enough empty barrels to get all the boots into."

Fyler was unpleasantly skeptical. "This is all good talk. Where's your proof the boots are coming in here?" he demanded.

Selwood, standing outside the counter up front, leaned over and pointed under it. "Haynes has been selling all the boots he could while you were sick. Pull that box out under here and I'll show you some of your boots." Fyler refused to touch any of Haynes's property. Selwood had no such scruple; he swung over the counter, stooped, ripped the cover off a packing-box, and drew out a pair of boots. "There," said he, "is a pair of your boots, Fyler."

The trader looked at the exhibit suspiciously; the fact that he did not fail to smile irritated Selwood, but he kept his temper.

"How do I know they're my boots?" asked Fyler.

"You know what you bought."

"These fellows may have bought the same style of boots I did."

"Yes," echoed Selwood, "but these fellows never bought a case of boots in their lives, Fyler; they couldn't show an invoice for one pair. These boots are of a style we never see out here—too fine, Fyler, too fancy for this trade; they are called opera boots—that's what they're marked on the original case we dug out of the oat bin; nobody but a greenhorn would ship such boots into this country. They're for Mexican trade."

Fyler bridled. "If you know so much more about my business than I do, you'd better run it for me."

"I don't know as much about a good many things in your business as you do, Fyler, but I know a whole lot about a few things in it that you don't seem to know at all. And if you can show me another pair of boots like these in any store in Sleepy Cat or Medicine Bend, I'll pay your claim in full and throw these nine or ten dozen boots in for good measure."

No man is to be convinced against his will. Fyler raised objections as stubbornly as Selwood insisted on his evidence. When the acrimonious dispute was at its height in walked Big Haynes, lifting his eyebrows in amazement at Fyler's story of the boots. Haynes did not, however, take any radical stand until he felt he had to. Selwood left the talking to Fyler, with occasional astonished interjections on the auctioneer's part. When all had been said, Selwood addressed Haynes. "Of course, I can't make this man"—indicating Fyler—"think I have his boots if he doesn't want to think so —that's his privilege. But, Haynes, don't waste any breath talking to me. These boots are stolen property— every pair—don't you sell one more pair of them. This stuff was stolen by Atkins. He stole it and you can tell him for me that I know he stole it; and we'll jail the men that steal our freight if we have to—so you keep clear of it."

CHAPTER X

THE trouble about the boots came to Christie's ears, of course. It came piecemeal—just as she happened to catch fragments of talk at the store, or asked an occasional question of her father. But the reports all left her obliging friend, Selwood, whose name she knew chiefly through hearing it from the others, in a most unfavorable light. When she spoke of Selwood's kindness, Atkins told her Selwood had helped her in order to spy around the store. When Christie looked to her father for denial or confirmation, Fyler, not honest enough to admit what he felt must be the truth, only smiled and beat about the bush, and Christie was left to her own surmises.

Atkins himself rarely appeared at the store; like the mole, he worked underground, only appearing after hours with auction supplies. His anger, when he was told of Selwood's raid on his oat-bin cache, was violent. As the recital progressed, he eyed Haynes malevolently. Always suspicious, Atkins would suspect anybody or everybody of treachery, and was never backward in expressing his suspicions; nor was he better pleased when Haynes, who was not of a humor to take unlimited abuse from his partner for not having sold the boots faster, told him that when he stole goods he ought to steal better sellers, and expressed his own belief that the disputed goods were actually Fyler's—though apparently Fyler had not sense enough to know it. This hint concerning the trader's stupidity suggested new possibilities to Atkins, but of these he made only a mental note for himself.

Fyler did, however, after a few days, show some un-

easiness over the situation laid out so bluntly by Selwood, and Atkins suggested to Haynes that Starbuck be
brought in to reassure Fyler. He came one day at noon
and encountered Christie. She had never seen just such
a man as Starbuck—big, well-dressed, with so engaging
a manner and inspiring such confidence. And Starbuck,
his eyes once on Christie, was at his best. He strode up
to the counter and away from it; to the rear of the store
and to the front of it, all eyes following. He talked to
Haynes, to Fyler, talked at Christie, that is, for her bene-
fit, and with an air looked everything over.

"Pay no attention to what any irresponsible person
tells you about the men that are in here with you," he
said to Fyler. "They're all right. Selwood works for a
big freighting outfit here—Atkins runs a little freighting
outfit. The big fellows are always trying to down the
little ones—and they're getting lawless at it. Selwood
is liable for grand larceny, sending his men to take goods
from Atkins's barn. We can't run things in this city as
you would in a Wild West camp. Men can go too far in
Sleepy Cat. Just keep still and 'tend to your business.
I'll see you're not bothered again. This your daughter,
Fyler?"

Such was Christie's first meeting with Starbuck. He
proved attentive. Christie thought she had never seen
a finer-looking man—he carried himself so straight, and
spoke with such decision. When she left the store, he
insisted on walking down to the tent camp with her.
Christie objected, but her reluctance made no impression
on Starbuck. If she would go, he would go; if she would
stay, he would stay. So at length he had his way, though
his persistence in the face of her hesitancy went the
least bit against her. Christie had a vein of stubbornness in her own make-up, and did not quite like being
overborne.

On the way to the tent Starbuck led the talk, in the
vein of a kind adviser and a candid friend. "This sort
of life must look pretty rough to you—I know that.
How? Why a fine-grained girl from a nice home in the
East couldn't look at a frontier town like Sleepy Cat in
any other way. But you'll like it. Never? Oh, yes.
Things will settle down, and you'll see a great city rising
right here where your little feet are pressing the earth
this very minute."

Christie swallowed her surprise. She had never regarded her feet as particularly "little," and was not in
any case prepared to have them, big or little, brought
into play as "pressing the earth" the first time the man
had ever spoken to her. She had lost one of her only
pair of nice shoes on the wretched trip out, and was
slightly sensitive about the coarser shoes she had been
reduced to. "There must be one great city," continued
Starbuck, quite impersonally, "between Denver and
San Francisco—that city will be Sleepy Cat—wonderful
air. Be patient and you'll see it all."

Christie, with some little calculation on her own part,
sighed: "I'm afraid I can't live to be a hundred, even
in this wonderful air."

She stopped in front of her tent. Starbuck stopped
with her. "Your father is new to the West, too. I can
see that. He'll need a little advice, maybe, but he'll do
well here. Tell him not to believe everything he hears,
or trust everybody that talks to him—that's all."

"Thank you, Mr. Starbuck." Christie caught the
tent flap in one hand, as if delicately to dismiss her kind
friend.

"This where you live? Well! You've got a nice big
tent——"

"We brought it with us," said Christie distantly, and
hoping he would go. But Starbuck was in no haste. He

kept up his talk, telling her how he knew a woman could make even a tent homelike. He looked at the flap intently—as if he would like to see inside—his eyes fairly hinted as much. But Christie was resolved he should not, if he stood an hour. When he saw it was useless, he changed the subject. "I've got to take a little drive this afternoon—down river. Come along, and I'll show you the prettiest team and buggy this side Denver—will you go?"

"I'm sorry——"

"Have you back here before supper——"

"I *am* sorry; but I've got a dress to make this afternoon."

"Bring it along—you can sew while I'm talking to the man I want to see at the tie camp."

"Oh, it's not cut out yet. Some other time, perhaps; to-day I couldn't possibly. Good-by!"

By the time she had rid herself of him her cheeks were flushed with the effort and her heart was beating a little faster. There was something surprising, at moments exhilarating, in his challenge. But Christie could not be at all sure that she liked him—she felt, after quieting down, that he must be slightly infected by the wonderful Sleepy Cat air.

Whatever his difficulty, Starbuck made a point of seeing Christie frequently. He was so kind in every way that she more than once revised her early distrust; and he was so well bred and knew so much about everything.

He was well liked by her father, and generally popular; yet he more than once confessed in confidence to Christie that he was a lonely man; that he longed for something different from the crude life of the rough men he was thrown among; and this mark of confidence touched Christie deeply, for he added that she was the only one in whom he could confide—the only one, in-

deed, in the whole big, half-wild town that understood
him. This, too, touched Christie very much—he was
so big and strong and so lonesome. She could well
imagine what it must be to be misunderstood by hardened men and women; so she kept his confidence quite
sacredly—little Christie was nothing if not conscien-
tious; but also she liked it.

Of course, any good impression that Selwood might
have made must fade before all of this. Moreover, Selwood was much in disfavor with those about her. She
was out of humor with him herself because he stubbornly
insisted that her father was denying his own goods, and
Selwood had refused to settle his claim unless her father
would first accept the Atkins boots.

So Selwood's face when he appeared at the store was
rather set. He still came, but not so often, nor did he
stay so long. Christie was distant with him. He had
never, even when he had a chance, offered any grave
confidences, had never complained of loneliness or confessed a need of sympathy. Christie could not say he
was ill-mannered, or that he suffered in any way in com-
parison even with Starbuck, who had become her stand-
ard; nor was he less well dressed, but more quietly.

And Selwood—not slow of apprehension, whatever his
faults—could see that he had quite lost out with Christie.
He suffered; reflected; resolved; and made a desperate
bid for reinstatement.

He called one afternoon at the store before the auc-
tion hour. Selwood walked up to the cashier's desk.
Fyler stood behind it, opening accounts for the day with
Big Haynes.

Selwood drew from one pocket Fyler's bill for the lost
shipment and threw it on the counter. From another
pocket he drew a roll of hundred-dollar bills. He counted
off fifteen and threw them on the invoice. "There's your

claim, Fyler," he said briefly. "Fourteen hundred and forty dollars; there are fifteen hundred dollars in currency. Give me sixty dollars and receipt your bill."

Fyler's eyes bulged. His face lighted with a great smile. "Well, Selwood! What does all this mean?"

"It means you're paid."

"Well, but——"

"It doesn't mean the company is settling this claim in this way," he added, as Fyler counted the money. "All it means is, I'm tired of hearing about those boots —receipt your bill, paid in full, Fyler."

Fyler, pocketing the money, tried flattering words to soften Selwood's cold manner; admitted he might have been wrong in his stand, but urged he had tried to be fair.

Selwood was not particularly moved. "You're paid, aren't you?" he said bluntly. "All right. I know who stole the goods—they'll pay me for 'em sometime."

The bell had been ringing up and down the street, the crowd had gathered in the store for the auction. It chanced on this afternoon that Pardaloe was among them—perhaps on the distant chance of stirring up another row without being compelled to stifle it; at all events, he was talking in full voice, disputing with any one that would dispute, and keeping Big Haynes nervous for fear he should "start something" and injure the sale.

Selwood, taking his change and putting the receipted bill in his pocket, was about to leave the store when Christie came in to help her father. Selwood lingered, only to find that he was greeted with a distant air instead of with one of the earlier nods that had cautiously ripened into more cordial smiles. Provoked at the situation in which he found himself in her eyes, and obstinate enough to be mean himself, Selwood stayed on. He edged over to his old place near Christie's desk, not offering a word—that, obviously, would have been unwelcome—but defiantly present. When, after some selling had been done, Starbuck loomed up at the front door and, pushing briskly through the crowd, walked toward the back of the store, Selwood's humor was not improved. But when Starbuck strode confidently and straight to Christie's desk, took a sprig of wild flower from his coat lapel, gave it to Christie and was greeted with a smile, Selwood's teeth set.

Starbuck paid no attention to the gambler except to glance at him coldly. Selwood paid none whatever to him. Big Haynes was casting about for something to put up. Fyler handed up two pairs of women's black stockings.

"Latest thing in our Eastern marts of fashion, gentlemen, the very latest—double toes and heels, every pair —made for the Queen of Sheba—she was dark-skinned —and imported especially by Mr. Fyler for fine Mormon trade," sang Big Haynes. "But Mr. Fyler couldn't pass by Sleepy Cat. He camped right here among us, leaving hundreds of Mormon women to run around barefoot while the Queen of Sheba stockings are offered to you and yours at an absolutely fearful sacrifice; and his big stock of them must be sold for spot cash, here and now. What am I bid for the first pair? Take as many as you please at the price of these! Buy 'em, wear 'em, give 'em to your wives and your sweethearts—what am I bid?"

But all Big Haynes's eloquence couldn't start a bidding on women's stockings in Sleepy Cat. He had more than once told Fyler, nobody but a lunatic would bring such merchandise to the Rocky Mountains. However, Haynes was feeling good that day and resorted to strategy to get a bid. He began "kidding" the bachelors in the crowd and fastened on Selwood. Selwood, absent-minded, almost inadvertently responded to Haynes's agonizing plea, and when he begged for an opening bid of a dollar for the first pair of Queen of Sheba stockings, Selwood nodded.

That inadvertent nod started an auction row, long remembered in Sleepy Cat; toothless pioneers tell stories about it yet. Starbuck immediately raised Selwood's bid to two dollars. A train of powder lighted on the counter could not have started things faster; before the crowd had heard the words, Selwood had bid three; four came from Starbuck, ten from Selwood, twenty-five from Starbuck, one hundred from Selwood.

The astonishing bids came like pistol cracks. The crowd stood breathless, almost speechless. But with the Sleepy Cat instinct for a fight of any sort, a dog fight, a man fight, or a gun fight, men from no one could say where began pushing from the street into the little room. Fyler's eyes bulged. Christie stood amazed. Big Haynes, his forehead beading with a sudden perspiration, his dark eyes flashing, and his heavy black hair flopping on his brow, quickened his patter to a pace never before achieved by him, if ever by any auctioneer. He bellowed with an unction unchallenged and flung at his listeners, with prodigal eloquence, burning periods on the Queen of Sheba and her stockings.

At Selwood's rather staggering bid of one hundred dollars there was a momentary pause. Starbuck looked serious—perhaps whitened the least bit around the nose and eyes. But he saw what he was in for and knew what he had to do. His position before the crowd he could have perhaps held without further sacrifice—turned a coarse joke on the contest and made his escape from the situation. But there was more than a rough crowd and much more than a pair of Queen of Sheba stockings between the adventurer and the gambler. There was that which since the days of the Queen of Sheba, and long before, has started devastating fires for mankind— there was behind the cashier's desk a shrinking bit of femininity—Christie Fyler—all, or certainly almost, unconscious that she was in the least contributing to the excitement into which the crowded room found itself plunged. Selwood stood near her, his eyes fixed chiefly on a match he was whittling, in a desultory manner, with a pearl-handled pocket-knife. He apparently saw no one and heard no one except the fast-talking auctioneer. But he knew the prestige that Starbuck wanted to carry off in the heart of a listening woman, and he stood there to block the move or—go broke.

"Let's see those stockings, Haynes," demanded Starbuck, beckoning with his extended hand. Haynes, all the time eloquent, stepping along the counter toward Starbuck, passed down the stockings for inspection. Starbuck made a show of examining the texture of the hose made for Solomon's distinguished guest, but it was only a show. He turned to Christie. "Are those pretty good stockings?"

Christie blushed scarlet; the crowd guffawed; Selwood whittled. "Why, yes," stammered Christie in confusion, "I suppose so—yes, I guess so."

"If I get 'em I'll present 'em to you." He handed the stockings up. "Two hundred dollars, Haynes."

"Three hundred."

There was a roar from the crowd. Starbuck shot an angry glance at Selwood. "Four hundred!" he shouted.

Selwood, apparently oblivious to everything except the remnant of the match under his knife blade, only lifted his eyes to Haynes. "Five hundred dollars, Haynes."

The crowd was growing hysterical. A dispute had already arisen in it. Pardaloe, lest he lose a syllable of the fight, pushed his way to the front. "Look here, Haynes," he thundered, "there's misunderstandings here right now. How many stockings are these fellows bidding for —one pair or how many? Clear this thing up, Haynes, *now*."

"Gentlemen," roared Haynes, "there's no misunderstanding here. The terms of this sale are absolutely bona fide spot cash. The gentlemen can bid five hundred for one pair or bid at that price for as many as they want—is that clear? Mr. Starbuck, how many pairs of these are you bidding for at your bid?"

"One pair."

"Mr. Selwood," continued Haynes, raising his voice impressively one notch above the now furious din, "how many pairs of these stockings are you bidding for at five hundred dollars a pair?"

"All you've got."

Like the onlookers at every fight, the crowd had already taken sides in as deadly earnest as the principals. Men crowded up to Selwood and to Starbuck as retainers, and when Selwood's terrific bid for all went up, a roar followed it that could be heard a block. Haynes levelled a deadly finger at Starbuck. "Mr. Starbuck," he shouted, "do you bid for the lot?"

"I'm not buying a pig in a poke," retorted Starbuck. "How many stockings you got?"

There was a hurried movement on the part of Fyler, whose long thin hair tumbled about his ears as he dug into a drawer for his unexpectedly valuable asset. He knew that he had, or should have, somewhere, two dozen of those stockings, but, fatefully, he could turn up but a dozen; these, with an excited smile, he handed to Haynes.

"A dozen," shouted Big Haynes, "twelve pair—one dozen! Mr. Starbuck, do you bid for the lot?"

Pardaloe, standing under Big Haynes's nose, struck in

loudly: "For spot cash, Mr. Auctioneer—this sale's for spot cash——"

"Shut up, Pardaloe," cried Big Haynes; "I'm talking to you, Mr. Starbuck," he continued, shaking his stubborn finger. "Are you bidding for the lot?"

Starbuck faced the music. "I bid five-fifty a pair for the lot," he snapped.

"Spot cash," cried Pardaloe, feeling for the enemy's weak point, "spot cash!"

A dozen men put in, some abusing Pardaloe, some backing him.

"Yes!" echoed Starbuck angrily, above the din, "spot cash!"

His sympathizers cheered. Haynes, his batteries loaded with Starbuck's bid, had alreaded turned on Selwood. Selwood had produced from somewhere another match and was gradually dismembering it. He took his time under Haynes's browbeating, not, apparently, disturbed by its urgency.

"Is that all the Queen of Sheba stockings you can find —twelve pair?" he asked of Fyler, while the crowd surged back and forth. Fyler grinned from ear to ear— a dozen pairs, he declared, were all he could find.

"I'm sorry about that. I was kind of hoping you had more," remarked Selwood, while everybody kept silence to hear—for he raised his voice very little. "I never owned any black stockings. But I always thought I'd like to. I guess a dozen pair ought to be worth a thousand dollars a pair to me, Haynes."

Starbuck put up his hand. "I want them stockings, Haynes. I'll put up the cash. Hold up this sale a few minutes till I get back."

Pardaloe, sitting on the counter, turned on Starbuck. In doing so, he swung one leg around in a half-circle—it threw back half a dozen men. "Not on your life," he shouted. "This sale ain't a-goin' to be held up one minute, nor half o' one minute, for no man. It's f'r spot cash here and now——"

"Get out of my way, you blunderbuss," exclaimed Starbuck, enraged. Pardaloe leaped like a hound from the counter. Swift as thought the two men confronted each other. Selwood whittled. "Get out of what?" shouted Pardaloe, eyes aflame, and drawing back viciously. Haynes jumped down. He landed between the two men like a ton of brick, and held them apart while he roared pacification. The place was a Babel. Fyler stood white as a sheet. Christie, frightened to death, shrank back—she would have run, but there was nowhere any chance to escape. "No man can leave this sale nor hold it up, not for one minute," thundered Pardaloe. "Spot cash means cash on the spot—not all over the Rocky Mountains, by a blamed sight!" he bellowed. "Bar the door, Abe!" he yelled to the gorilla blacksmith near the front; "I'll brain the first man that tries to leave this room before them stockings are sold!"

The wrangle deepened. Selwood, match in one hand, pocket-knife in the other, pushed through the ring to where Pardaloe and Starbuck glared across Big Haynes's shoulders at each other. "I think this is a mistake, boys," he suggested. "I think every man should have a chance to play his whole roll in any game. And there's a better young woman than the Queen of Sheba ever dared be in this room with all us men right now—we don't want to scare her to death. Let everybody keep quiet. And let Mr. Starbuck bring his friends——"

"Not by a blamed sight," roared Pardaloe, quite beside himself. If the tall man could have spit fire the place would have been in flames.

"His friends," repeated Selwood, impressively, "and his roll. And Bill"—he addressed Pardaloe calmly—

"take Abe Cole—pick up a sledge at the shop, Abe—
bust in the safe in my room at the hotel. Get Bob
Scott to help you, and bring down the currency and the
gold dust. Haynes will hold this sale open till you get
back."

His eyes bulging with the importance of his position,
Haynes glanced at his big silver hunting-case watch. He
looked from one to the other of the two contestants and
delivered his decision with solemnity. "In fairness,
gentlemen, to this audience," he said loudly and impressively, "I can't hold this sale open—not over ten
minutes by the watch, gentlemen, not *over* ten minutes.
It's now two o'clock—at two-ten this hammer falls, gentlemen, and the sale goes on."

"That suits me," said Selwood, drawing his own
watch. "Two-ten; and my bid stands."

Starbuck whirled on Haynes. "Look here," he exclaimed, "this is snap judgment. You know blamed
well I can't get anywhere and back in ten minutes by
the watch. I'm not here to be made a fool of by your
outfit. Go on with your sale—you needn't wait for me.
I thought you fellows wanted a real showdown—you
only want an imitation."

"But——" protested the astonished auctioneer.

Starbuck cut him off. "Go on with your fake, you
monkey," he said to Haynes loudly. "I'm done." And
so saying, he strode with great indignation, and with
everybody looking on, out of the front door. Haynes,
crestfallen and perspiring, walked around behind the
counter and climbed up on his box. He got his eloquence
under way again slowly, with many desultory side remarks about men not knowing their own minds: and
whether a few minutes meant ten minutes or some other
minutes. Starbuck's friends stood abashed. Selwood's
following grew uproarious. "Don't talk about that fel-

low not knowing his own mind. He know'd it blamed well," exclaimed Pardaloe—to anybody. "He seen he was beat," he grinned, turning for an aside to Christie, "ary way he fixed it."

CHAPTER XI

BOOTS WITHOUT SADDLES

CHRISTIE looked like a frightened fawn at the giant mule-boss as he spoke to her. Pleased at having made an impression, although it was in the nature of frightening her to death, Pardaloe followed his advantage. "You needn't 'a' been scared, not for one minute, no matter *what* happened. Think I'd see *any* man scare you? Not f'r a second! I'd break a man in two like a match that ever give you a word or a look! I ain't nothing on fine clo'es—but I know what's a-comin' to a woman!"

Christie could only stare and gulp down her fears; but she tried to smile, and both turned to listen to Big Haynes.

There really remained only the formality of knocking down the Queen of Shebas to Selwood. Would he take them? He would.

At his bid?

At his bid. The gambler threw away the third match he was working on, snapped shut his knife, put it in his pocket, and stepped to the cashier's desk, where Fyler, his eyes dancing in nervous expectancy and his facial muscles twitching into appealing smiles, was counting and re-counting the twelve fateful pairs of stockings and wrapping them up.

The crowd, with craning necks, closed in to witness the last act in the turbulent drama—they wanted to see the actual money paid. Haynes thought it more dignified to keep his post, but he was high enough above the onlookers to see everything. Selwood, from a roll of bills that he drew from a trousers pocket, counted off twenty-two five-hundred-dollar bills; to these he added, from another roll, one-hundred-dollar bills to make up his bid and silently watched Fyler with trembling fingers count the payment over.

When the trader had done this and thanked his extraordinary customer, Selwood, taking the package of stockings under his arm, turned to go. Christie had managed to disappear, and, somehow, Selwood was glad of it. When he stepped with his purchase out of the front door, Haynes was trying to regain the attention of his audience. It was useless. Pardaloe and Abe Cole, sputtering talk, and close behind Selwood, led the way, and on their heels half the crowd pressed to be first to tell the story up street and down.

Next morning a Russell & Wentworth Conestoga wagon stood in front of Selwood's place. The wagon was filled with boots. The mules had been sent back to the barn and Bill Pardaloe, in charge of the wagon, had painted a rude muslin sign and fastened it to the side of the Conestoga.

The sign read simply:

FREE BOOTS TOMORROW

All that day Pardaloe was the busiest man in town explaining the odd announcement. He managed to make it clear to everybody except to a stupid Gunlock Indian, loafing for the day in Sleepy Cat, that the sign meant exactly what it said and that precisely at noon on the following day every man applying to Pardaloe would be given a pair of boots absolutely free; the only stipulation being that they must be tried on on the spot and worn away. When asked why not to-day for a free pair, Pardaloe explained that Selwood was giving away the boots and meant that his friends at Thief River should have an equal chance with his friends at Sleepy Cat.

Early next morning men began to drift along Fort street. They brought up, for the most part, near Selwood's gambling-hall. By ten o'clock a crowd out of all proportion to the importance of the event filled the street about Selwood's place. On the Thief River horizon there was a show of dust at daylight. By sun-up, as they expressed it in Sleepy Cat, it looked as if a sandstorm were brewing on the Spanish Sinks. When Sleepy Cat men turned out of doors after breakfast, the town was alive with strangers, and an hour later the mob surrounding Pardaloe clamored for the boots. It was decided to avert a riot by advancing the opening of the distribution to eleven o'clock, and at that hour Pardaloe, bursting with the responsibility of his job as almoner, and moderately fortified with mountain high-wines, mounted an up-ended beer keg, and announced for the last time the conditions, namely, that each man must wear his boots away. Pardaloe stood backed by Bob Scott and McAlpin and held in his hand a hickory singletree with which to moderate objection, adjust disputes, and prevent crowding.

For two hours the pressure on the open end of the wagon was severe. The united efforts of the three worthies in charge were needed to curb the ambition of three hundred applicants for one hundred and fifty pairs of boots. Within the space rigidly roped off and in charge of McAlpin, for the trying on, a dozen men at a time sat in the sun and dust, each struggling with his pair of opera boots. Feet reflecting all conditions of frontier hardship and foot-covering—not to say stockings— ranging from nothing whatever to muskrat skins, buck-skin shirting, and army blankets, were common run.

Scott, passing out the boots, was loudly and continually petitioned for large sizes and larger sizes, but with his characteristic shrewdness he emptied only one barrel at a time, making each comer take his chance. In this way alone, he insisted to Pardaloe, staggering, so to speak, under the outbursts of profane protest with which he was assailed, could fair play be accorded to all comers. A heap of discarded boots, shoes, moccasins, and fragments of buffalo robes began to pile up under the wagon. Men strutting away in brand-new opera boots aroused the sleepiest of the natives as to what was going on at Selwood's.

But not a few men, unable to find their fit and determined not to be left out, stalked off in boots too tight, and, with feet gradually swelling a protest in the sunshine at their violent cribbing, sought solace along the bars of the River Quarter. Some of these victims, inflamed with a growing sense of their discomfort, rejoined the crowd and assailed Pardaloe with abuse. Nothing could be more to Pardaloe's taste, for he only ached for opportunities to meet objectors with the singletree—and did it. Others, discomfited and dissatisfied with the result of complaints to Pardaloe, wrangled with one another in the crowd itself, and at times a vigorous fist fight ended a profitless dispute.

When the Thief River contingent reached the square the confusion deepened. Fifty men had come thirty miles for boots, and as the supply dwindled the uproar grew. McAlpin sent pressing messages to Selwood for help. The bearers only succeeded in getting Selwood out of bed. He professed he had no relief to offer, and sent word to give away what boots they had and close up shop.

This was easier said than done, and McAlpin, relieved by Pardaloe, went at length to Selwood in person to plead for some kind of help. He managed to get the gambler down to the scene—now almost one of despair, for the small sizes and narrow widths remaining were a mere source of hopeless rows and bitter recriminations.

Selwood's appearance was greeted with loud cheers. Everybody yelled—some were in no condition to do anything more. Selwood despatched Pardaloe down to John Cole's general store to buy a fresh supply of boots. The Kickbusches were raided, Roubidoux was cleaned out, even Van Tambel was coaxed and threatened out of stock. More than another hundred extra pairs were picked up and dumped as quietly as possible in with the original stock—and they were cowhide boots, much more useful and of bigger sizes than Fyler's French-calf opera goods.

With this relief it looked as if the crisis had been met, but in the midst of the second distribution an alarm was raised. Again the Spanish Sinks were enveloped in a storm of dust. Seasoned scouts soon cried "Indians!" and a scare was on. But as minute-men rushed to the river to burn the upper and lower bridges, it was further declared that the oncoming horde were friendlies, that is, Gunlocks, and had their squaws with them. This allayed fear of hostilities, and the excitement both ebbed and rose again, when the first bucks to reach Fort Street announced they were about to take the warpath against the Crows, but had halted at Sleepy Cat for boots.

Selwood stood nonplussed. He was in no position to offend the Gunlocks; they had, in fact, come to his rescue on at least one occasion, when the hostiles had attempted to hold up a wagon-train crossing the Spanish Sinks, and were in the habit of appearing in Sleepy Cat at reasonable intervals to visit P'Chink-nazee, or Big Nose, as they called Selwood, and receive such further reward of virtue as might suggest itself to their esteemed friend.

Ben Wentworth had forcibly declared that the mild-mannered red men of the desert had already collected more reward than the value of the train they had saved, but Selwood did not feel in that way, and after the company refused to authorize further allowances in their behalf, Selwood jollied them along as pensioners of his own.

Such boots as were still to be found in Sleepy Cat Selwood bought—some pairs of the opera boots were secured from dissatisfied, or, rather, already satisfied, wearers, and such were distributed to the waiting bucks; and the more provident of these, without waiting for new boots, investigated the discard and supplied themselves with better footwear than the white man had carried away.

But with every resource to supply their needs exhausted, the Gunlocks still hung in silence around the wagon. They exhausted Pardaloe by refusing to understand his harangues, and the louder he talked the less they seemed to comprehend. The shadows of the Superstition Peaks were creeping over Sleepy Cat, but the now gloomy bucks did not disperse, and it looked as if they meant to demand supper and camp on Selwood for the night. It was Selwood himself who in the end solved the problem of getting rid of them. He sent out trusty henchmen who bought up all the plug tobacco in town, and Selwood in person explained to the ancients of the invaders that, being resolved no red friend of his should go home without a testimonial of his affection, and since no more boots were to be begged, bought, or stolen in Sleepy Cat, he had resolved that every waiting brave should be presented with a sixteen-ounce bar of rough-and-ready Battle-Ax plug tobacco. This offer, conveyed by Bob Scott in good Gunlock to the assembled braves, was received with guttural acclaim.

The butts were split open. Bucks that had already

been supplied with boots were, of course, excluded, by announcement, from this further gratuity. But as increasing numbers of warriors in single files approached the wagon, Pardaloe and McAlpin were instructed to cease their disputes with such barefooted worthies as they accused of having already taken boots, and told to give a sixteen-ounce plug of chewing tobacco to every man in line. Dusk saw the swarthy caravan, their war spirit apparently satisfied, again disappearing into the brooding dust of the Spanish Sinks.

CHAPTER XII

PARDALOE IS MILDLY DISAPPOINTED

SUNDAY in Sleepy Cat was not the best day of the week; usually it was the worst; but Sunday morning early was fairly quiet, and on the Sunday following Selwood's sensational performances, Christie, in trouble, was abroad early. The sun was scarce an hour high when she hastened up-street from the tent camp toward Doctor Carpy's hotel. Slender in figure, light of foot, alert, almost swift in action, Christie looked neither to the right nor the left, and the few men stirring at that hour caught none of her glances.

The front door of the hotel was open. She entered the narrow hall with the caution of the inexperienced, and looked through another open door into the office, which was empty. The morning sun, prodigal of values, shone gloriously through the dusty east windows, and a dog, old and overfed, lay peacefully dozing before the battered office stove. He paid no attention to Christie when she walked in and halted in perplexity at the desk —which consisted only of a shabby piece of old counter and a half-empty cigar-case containing with a few cigars an abundance of old bills rendered the proprietor for merchandise had and delivered.

But on the counter stood the dinner-bell, and Christie, after some looking about and some hesitation, seized and rang it.

Startled at the noise it made, Christie set it down in trepidation and waited for results. For a moment there were none; then men, some in coats and some coatless, some bearded and some unshaven, but all very much face-washed and with hair very wet and plastered, began

97

appearing from nowhere, or, rather, from everywhere—
at the doors and through the windows Christie saw them
coming, some slowly, some eagerly, but all with great
accord, toward the entrance to the dining-room across
the hall. The doors were closed, but one adventurer,
more bold than his fellows, pushed open the door, walked
in, and the rest trooped heavily in after him.

Christie, watching this eruption of men, stood with
eyes for the most part cast down. Yet there was one
man she sought, and her glances swept at least the backs
of all the men as they passed in. Then she heard a
woman's voice and one not pitched in an amiable key.

"Ready? No! It's not ready and won't be ready
for half an hour yet. Who rang that bell?" were the
words that floated across the hall to Christie, and on an
ascending scale of emphasis and volume. Some one was
clearly annoyed, and the apologetic murmur of various
bass voices did not assuage the woman's impatience.

Christie felt like dropping through the floor. Very
positive steps were coming rapidly her way. The next
moment she was faced by a stern-looking woman.

"Did you ring that bell?"

Christie felt it would be useless to deny. "I didn't
know it was the dinner-bell," she explained. "I just
wanted to speak to somebody——"

"What about?"

There was rude resentment in both questions; the
second, coming so sharply after the first, started Christie's own quick-triggered temper. "I want Doctor
Carpy."

"What for?"

"For my father."

"Well, he's not here. There was a fight this morning
down in the River Quarter. A man got shot. He's down
there. What's the matter with your father?"

Each question was chopped off with a mental axe, and the question flung with about as much consideration as a bullet.

"My father," retorted Christie resentfully, imitating and beginning to feel the harshness of her questioner, "needs a doctor. He was robbed last night and beaten!" She spoke her words with due feeling; but if she expected to make any impression with the news, or to arouse sympathy for her anxiety, she was disappointed—stories of Christie's sort meant little to Margaret Hyde; she had become too inured to the violence of a frontier town.

Christie studied her strange face with unconscious interest. The once fine features had grown hard with the years that should have softened them; the years that ought to have crowned her womanhood had withered it. The eyes that once had hoped and danced and smiled on young life shone now coldly on all alive; Margaret was not coarse, not common, but it seemed as if with hope dead all human interest and all human sympathy had died.

"If you want the Doctor you'd better wait here till he comes back," she snapped. As she spoke the two women heard a heavy step on the porch, and the next moment Doctor Carpy walked in.

He threw down his bag and threw off his hat with the air of a tired man. Then sitting down as his housekeeper left the room, he heard Christie's story. Whether Christie herself appealed directly to the Doctor's blunted sympathies, or whether his professional sense of duty impelled him, who shall say? At all events, Christie told him her father had been called out of the tent late the night before, set on by two men, robbed of all his money, brutally beaten about the head—and that she had not dared leave the tent to hunt up the doctor till after daylight.

Without discussion, Carpy told her to wait one minute till he could get a cup of coffee and he would go with her. "A teamster got hurt last night. I stayed up with him till twelve o'clock. Then about two o'clock a man got shot down-street—he didn't take long; but the fellow he cut up took two hours and most of my—thread." The Doctor, with instinctive restraint, modified the last word and, excusing himself, bade Christie wait.

But the cook had overslept, the coffee was not ready. Carpy muttered somewhat and sputtered, rummaged about for some bandages, and was ready to go with Christie.

Selwood kept a room at "Carpy's Hotel," as it was locally known, and usually slept there, but his hours were irregular and he did not often appear in the dining-room before noon. This Sunday morning he was up early because he had a two-day drive to Medicine Bend ahead of him, with only a night stop-over at Point of Rocks. Moreover, his first morning trip, whenever in Sleepy Cat, was to the tent of his wounded partner. On this particular morning, before he went to the barn for his team, Selwood, leaving the hotel, walked down to the River Quarter on his way to Tracy's tent. Near the bridge he saw Christie coming up from the tents with Doctor Carpy. He would have passed them, and preferred to do so, without comment, for he was in no mood, being jealous and resentful, to make any appeal for Christie's favor; accordingly, he tried to pass on.

Carpy, however, held him. "John," he began, without preface or apology, and catching the lapel of Selwood's coat to make sure of his victim, "I said to you only the other day, 'If there's any human scum in the whole blamed United States that hain't landed in Sleepy Cat, it must be b'cause they ain't never heard of it yet.'"

Beyond touching his hat, and that almost without

looking at her, Selwood did not acknowledge Christie's presence. He held his eyes strictly on Carpy, and received the Doctor's outburst without visible emotion. In fact, he made no comment of any sort—only stood waiting for, and as if entitled to, some further explanation, before troubling himself to speak. "Why don't you say something, you big galoot?" demanded the Doctor, fussed, to tell the truth, by the presence of the slip of a young woman at his side—so young, indeed, that she should be called a girl rather than a woman.

"What do you want me to say?" asked Selwood, without a smile. "You always ask me that when you get mad—and you're mad most of the time. What's bothering you?"

"John, it's nothing that ever bothers *me* that bothers me; it's what bothers other folks that makes my bother. Now here's this nice little girl"—he looked toward her and knit his brows in perplexity—"dash it!" he continued apologetically, "I never can remember your name——"

The Doctor had taken off his hat and was scratching his ear when he appealed to his companion for help.

"Christie Fyler," interposed Christie. Just the sound of her voice pulled Selwood's eyes to her eyes. And he saw she had been crying.

"You know this big hulk, don't you, Christie?" asked the Doctor with genial informality. "If you don't," he continued, "meet Gentleman John."

Selwood was impatient. "Don't be a fool, Doctor," he protested, pleased neither at the mention of his Sleepy Cat nickname nor at the situation before him.

"Well, it *is* 'Gentleman John!' You can't get rid of it," persisted the Doctor. "You just tipped up your hat to her, didn't you? Nobody else within a hundred and fifty miles of Sleepy Cat would do that, would they?"

Selwood, perceiving the source of the Doctor's loquacity, ignored the rest of it. He turned his eyes on Christie, whose face showed her distress.

"Is your father sick?" he asked, without much feeling.

"He was robbed and beaten last night," she replied, looking at him and speaking quickly. "Two men came to the tent, called him out, knocked him senseless, and took all his money——"

"A pocketful, too!" interjected the Doctor.

"And yesterday morning Mr. Atkins took possession of the store and put Father out of it entirely."

Selwood could no longer pretend indifference

"Why?" he asked mildly.

Christie wrung one hand nervously in the other. "Oh, I don't know—I can't understand it, neither can Father. He says Father owes him money—he doesn't—not a penny. But he's taken all our goods, and *everything!* and put us out in the street!"

Selwood listened without batting an eye. Christie's restrained grief was plainly acute.

Carpy thought it should have called forth some expression of sympathy from the gambler. "Why don't you say something?" remonstrated the Doctor. "That man"—in disgust he addressed Christie—"got out of the wrong side of the bed this morning."

Selwood asked a question of the Doctor. "How bad is Fyler hurt?"

"Well, aside from his head being cut wide open and bein' pounded up generally with a wagon spoke, he ain't really hurt at all," replied Carpy ironically.

"Doctor," murmured Christie, naturally indignant, and anxious to get away from an unsympathetic atmosphere, "ought we not to be hurrying to get the medicine back to Father?"

Selwood turned to Christie. "I wonder whether I could see—your father—a minute." He didn't want to say "your father," being just that resentful; Selwood *wanted* to say, not "your father," but "Fyler"—so little was he in love with him; and being just mean enough to feel the trader had "something coming to him."

"Why not?" interposed Carpy. "He's down there in that tent right back of Dave's."

"I'd better wait till you come back," suggested Selwood, appealing to Christie.

"Come along to the office then; I'll give her the medicine and you two can go back together."

Until the two left the office, medicine in hand, Carpy kept the talk going. But when Selwood found himself on the way to the tent in company with Christie only, the situation grew embarrassing. It was all very well to be glum when the Doctor filled in the gaps, but now it was different. Moreover, Selwood's hardness of heart was fast giving way before the innocence of Christie, who, properly, chilled as she perceived Selwood's attempts to warm. Altogether, by the time the tent fly was reached, Selwood's fine poise had about failed him —he was feeling uncomfortable.

The tent was a good one—of ample size, with a side for Christie neatly curtained off. But the curtain happened to be drawn back, and Selwood's eyes, though decently restrained, missed few of the feminine touches that revealed a woman's presence and a woman's hand in little decorations and conveniences where ingenuity counted for much and conditions contributed few. "Doctor Carpy has been promising us rooms at the hotel ever so long," faltered Christie, holding back the fly when Selwood, stooping a little, passed inside. "But we never can get two empty near each other at the same time!" And Selwood's knowledge of how Margaret hated women about the hotel made this easy to understand.

Carpy's presence was not needed to enable him to pass on Fyler's condition. Selwood had come in contact with many injured men, and saw at once from Fyler's eyes that he was more scared than hurt. He had been beaten, but he had evidently escaped pretty well at the hands of men that meant to kill him. He looked up from his cot at Selwood all eyes—his eyes were big as saucers, and in the circumstances Selwood could hardly suppress an instinctive desire to laugh at the sight of the mass of bandages in which Carpy had swathed his face and head.

"I'm sorry I haven't a chair to offer," explained Christie, embarrassed; "they seem to break as fast as Father brings them down. Please sit down on my cot."

Selwood, however, would not sit down while she stood, so Christie was forced to sit down on the cot first. She chose the head. Selwood disposed himself at a respectful distance toward the middle. But as he settled himself, down went the cot with both of them.

Christie repressed a little scream. Selwood scrambled to his feet, helped her up, adjusted the underpinning, and insisted it would hold Christie; but neither tried it again.

Sitting on the edge of a box, Selwood listened without comment to the story—told partly by Fyler and partly through excited interruption by Christie. Violence was all so new to Christie, her view of it as something too horrible for men to resort to was so naïve in the surroundings to which she was now condemned, that Selwood regarded her as the most innocent person he had ever met, and felt sorry for what might be ahead of her on the frontier.

Despite his dislike for her father, moderating now at his unlucky experience and ludicrous appearance, Selwood offered what perfunctory consolation he could, but not being skilled in that sort of thing, did only reasonably well at it. He asked Fyler at length whether anything had been done to find the men that had robbed him—nothing had been done. He asked whether he thought he could recognize his assailants. Christie intervened. "How could he? It was pitch dark—but Mr. Starbuck warned Father just the other day to be careful"—Selwood pricked up his ears—"he said the town is bothered every night with men that come in in the evening," continued Christie excitedly. "They rob people and leave again before morning."

Selwood nodded regretfully. "That makes it hard on the local talent, doesn't it? Well, you got off with your life," he said to Fyler. "That's better than some men do. I'll see whether I can find out anything. And I'll drop in again to see how you are coming on; hope you'll be feeling better soon."

Christie followed him outside the tent and, pausing a few steps away, appealed to him with troubled eyes. "Do you think my father will get well?"

Selwood, struck by her anxiety, answered with less than his ordinary hesitation, "I do."

"If he died, I don't know what could become of me."

"I'm not a doctor, Christie"—her name came in a kind of gulp, the first time he had ever spoken it to her—"but I've seen a good many men pounded on the head," he said, flushing a little with self-consciousness at the admission. "If your father were hurt badly he'd be unconscious—and he would breathe like—well, like a man snoring pretty hard."

"He says he doesn't want to get well, now he's lost everything."

"If all the men in Sleepy Cat that have lost everything were to die, there wouldn't be Indians enough on the reservation to bury them. He'll get over that. Sleepy

Cat money comes easy and goes easy. Besides, I would-n't say your father's lost everything; he'll get his store back, somehow."

"And he's begun gambling, too, in this horrible place," murmured Christie, fingering the fringe of her shawl and holding her eyes down on it as she yielded to the impulse to unburden her over-anxious heart, "and that's like death to me—I hate gamblers!"

Selwood turned red as a turkey gobbler—where was his poise now? But Christie's eyes, fortunately, were bent on the fringe in her nervous fingers.

"Where's your father gambling?" asked Selwood, swallowing, but resolved to bluff it out.

"Oh, down in that horrible River Quarter."

"If he's taking his money down there," observed Sel-wood calmly, "he's not gambling—he's just getting robbed. If he's bound to gamble he'd better pick a place where he has a chance. But your father ought to know," he continued, in fair-minded appraisement, "that wher-ever he plays the chances are always in favor of the house—that's what gambling-places are run for—to make money for the owners."

Christie looked at him. It was as if she were placing a wholly new confidence in him, one that was reflected in her immediate appeal. "I wish *you* would talk to him, Mr. Selwood—tell *him* that."

Again Selwood began to burn—inwardly and out-wardly. "It might not do any good," he said, to hide his retreat, "but I could at least speak from experience."

With these words he skated as rapidly as possible from that part of the pond.

Fortunately, too, Christie was diverted by the sight of an unexpected visitor. Bill Pardaloe, rolling on his lean legs like a ship in a long swell, hove in sight, coming toward them with a napkin-covered tray. "Look at that man!" exclaimed Christie. "How he reels! What can he be balancing in his hands? It must be somebody's breakfast—I'm glad it's not mine—oh! I thought it was gone!" she cried as Bill stumbled, reeled, and by a herculean effort regained his balance. "He'll surely drop it!"

"He won't drop it," Selwood assured her in tones of velvet calm, though inwardly he was thinking violence.

Why, unless out of meanness, Meg had given Pardaloe the tray, after he had been down town all night, Selwood could not surmise. Whatever the situation, Bill was heading, with more or less certainty, for Selwood and Christie.

"I'll make a guess," suggested Selwood, thinking it best to advance the spark a trifle; "Doctor Carpy is maybe sending your breakfast down, and something for your father. What's the matter with you, Bill?" he demanded tartly, as Pardaloe approached. "Hold the tray quiet—can't you see you're spilling everything? Is this the stuff Carpy sent down for Mr. Fyler?"

"No," growled Pardaloe, not pleased by the reception, "this is not the stuff Carpy sent down; this is the stuff *you* sent down for Miss Fyler. Where d'y' want it?"

"I sent nothing down," said Selwood, vexed and denying untruthfully. "No matter," he added, cutting Pardaloe's insistence brusquely off. "Whoever sent it, it's to eat—where will you have it?" He asked the question of Christie.

With a protest at somebody's kindness—and she thought she knew whose—Christie very gratefully took the tray and Selwood held back the fly for her to pass inside with it. On the threshold she turned her eyes to his. "Father mustn't eat anything to-day, Doctor said. And there's a great deal more coffee here than I can drink—won't you come in and help?"

While Pardaloe listened and stared, Selwood coughed
decently. He thought on reflection he *might* go in, for
just about a minute—and followed Christie. But before
doing so, he told Pardaloe to go to the barn and get his
team ready. Pardaloe, left alone, stood a moment, his
mental perplexity revealed in the almost permanent
scowl that furrowed his brow; then he lifted up the fly
and, stooping, pushed slowly into the tent. In the ex-
cess of his politeness, Bill removed his battered hat as
he entered, and, to adjust his sight to the interior, knit
his brows still closer over his beady eyes. Selwood and
Christie were too much engaged with the tray—which
had been set on the box at the head of the cot—to notice
Pardaloe's entrance. "Where's the man t'w'z hurt?"

Pardaloe, without minding his tone, asked the blunt
question rather to announce his presence than to seek
information, for Fyler lay immediately before him. The
injured man started. Christie, turning, saw the tall intruder and, apologizing lamely, welcomed him perfunc-
torily.

Selwood was not pleased, but knowing Bill's peculiarities, made the best of it. Pardaloe, listening, bareheaded and silent—his shiny eyes close on her—to what
little Christie had to say, and vouchsafing no acknowledgment, felt his way gingerly forward, sat down un-
invited on Christie's cot, which she expected every moment to give way under him, and looked hard at Fyler.
Pardaloe's neck was long, and when he shot his head
forward it supplied an angle of about forty-five degrees.
This gave his gaze an intensity somewhat felt by the
person he looked at. Fyler regarded him as if expecting
another assault. Pardaloe, however, had only peaceful
intentions. Leaning forward, he studied Fyler's eyes,
which were all he could see of his face among the bandages, and just turned his head toward Selwood. "Who

is he?" asked Pardaloe, instinctively awed by the bandages, and speaking in that hushed voice that even the irreverent use in the presence of the dying.

"Who is he?" echoed Selwood tartly. "Why, he's this young lady's father—Mr. Fyler."

Pardaloe bent his head a little farther down. His eyes bored through the bandages till he penetrated the disguise and recognized Fyler. He twisted his neck around to Selwood again, and screwed his face into an expression in which surprise and disgust struggled for precedence. The corners of his mouth fell till they were lost in the depths of his beard; two heavy lines springing from the sides of his nostrils drew down after them. In this wise he regarded Selwood, who with good reason feared some sort of a "break" but could not avert one. Pardaloe, turning, looked just once more at Fyler and put his hat on his head. Rising, he drew himself up under the ridge pole as nearly as he could to his full height. "Hell!" he exclaimed in tomblike tones, fixing his eyes on Selwood. "I thought 'twas a friend o' yours!"

CHAPTER XIII

SELWOOD ISSUES INVITATIONS

SELWOOD made the best of an awkward moment. "Pay no attention to Bill," he said, as the tent fly closed behind Pardaloe's disgust and the mule boss strode wrathfully away; "nobody does. He probably didn't understand me and didn't recognize your father. I'm driving to Point of Rocks and Medicine Bend to-day," continued Selwood. "I'll be gone two or three days, it may be. You say Starbuck promised to clear those fellows out of the store for you?"

"He's coming back this morning," replied Christie, with great confidence, "to talk with Father about it. So I'm sure that will be all right."

"Your father is going to get well," predicted Selwood, without comment. "You needn't worry about that, anyway."

But he was not gone two or three days. That night at dusk, with the moon rising, Christie heard a man's voice outside her tent. "Is Doctor Carpy there?" She was alone with her father and made no answer. The question was repeated. Christie peeped through the fly. Selwood stood at the tent door. She opened the fly farther and answered him.

"I thought he might—or might not—be here," he said in the same slow, even tone, "but I wanted to ask a question, anyway. Yes, I expected to be gone until Wednesday. I found a teamster hurt at Point of Rocks, so I drove him back this afternoon and I'm looking for Carpy." He did not add much that he might have added, namely, that no real emergency had made this return necessary, and that he was inquiring for Carpy where he was quite certain he should not find him. "Have you any idea," he added, "where I could get hold of the Doctor?"

Christie stepped silently just outside the tent. "Father is asleep," she said guardedly. "The Doctor hasn't been here this evening."

"Sorry I troubled you—Father any better?"

"Oh, I hope so. He slept a lot to-day."

"He'll be pretty sore to-morrow morning. But that won't mean anything. Did Starbuck get those fellows out of the store for you?"

Little escaped Selwood. She turned her face quickly to one side. "No," she said, looking down, "he did not."

"But he's going to?"

"No."

"What's the matter?"

"I—he——"

"Well?"

"I'm afraid I can't explain."

Selwood was coldly silent. Christie's eyes were still on the ground. But he saw she was keeping something back and began to rage with suspicion. "Are you so close to him," he demanded at length, "that you can't talk to another man about a couple of thieves?"

Christie, stung, looked sharply up. He saw her eyes were swollen as if with weeping. "If you knew my situation you wouldn't say that. I only wish"—she spoke from the heart—"I might never see him again!"

"Well," exclaimed Selwood, cooling with relief, "if that's the situation I won't ask any more questions. So he wouldn't do anything?"

"No," blurted out Christie, now angry at the recollection, "not unless——"

"Unless what?"

She clasped her hands. "Unless I'd do something I refused to do——"

An expletive, like a pistol-shot, escaped the listener. The two faced each other in silence. Christie, unable to support the interval, was looking down again. "I promised to ask no more questions," said Selwood, after a pause, "but I've got to ask just one. Is he fit to live—or isn't he?"

Frightened, she looked up. "I'm making it worse and worse—I didn't mean to—please don't be so terribly angry. I see I must say what I hoped I might escape—he said he would help Father—if I would marry him!"

Selwood did not laugh. His distress was too evident. "And you refused?" was all he said. "What did your father say?"

That cut deep. Christie could only hold the gambler to his word. "You said you wouldn't ask any more questions," she replied simply; but she had a turn of simplicity that was silencing.

Selwood drew a breath. "I'm glad I happened back to-night, anyway. Perhaps something can be done. Can your father hear us here?"

"He's asleep."

"But he has ears. There's nothing he might not hear, only I don't like listeners. I don't believe you're afraid of me. Step over this way a minute."

She hesitated to let go the tent fly. "I'm not going to ask you to marry me—I wouldn't ask any woman to marry me, Christie. But that needn't prevent my helping you get back what belongs to you. If you're really afraid," he continued, for she was not looking at him, and was plainly reluctant to follow, "I'll talk here, no matter who hears—and even though it might mix things up."

"I'm not afraid," protested Christie—but he knew

she was afraid—"if you'll just tell me whatever it is quickly."

Selwood spoke when they stood together, away from possible eavesdroppers. "Your father isn't hurt so much," he said quietly, that he might not startle her. "But he can't very well do this, so you must. The minute day breaks to-morrow morning be dressed, leave this tent, and walk straight to the store. You needn't be afraid. You won't see anybody, but you will be watched, and safe, from the minute you leave the tent till you're back in it. When you get to the store, if you see an Indian sitting on the front steps, walk right up to him and ask for the key to the store. He'll give it to you. Ask him to watch the store till you come back after breakfast. He will. Then get Carpy, early, at the hotel, and have your father carried up to the store on his cot. He'd better stay there day and night—and you, too—till he's up!"

As Christie listened, a wave of contrition swept over her. She felt rebuked. To have slighted such a man as these words and this darkness revealed Selwood to her, in favor of a man such as she now realized Starbuck must be, was quite enough to humble her.

"What shall I do if there's no Indian there?" she asked, promptly connoting that she meant to do exactly as he directed.

"Then straight back to the tent, for"—he laughed slightly—"if it means anything, it'll mean I'm dead. But you'll be protected in any case. Just don't be afraid to do as I tell you. Will you?"

She looked at him without answering. Where he stood the big moon lighted his face, for he had surrendered the shadow to her own. "What," she asked, "are you going to do?"

He smiled, a leisurely, sickly kind of smile, a reassuring but non-committal sort of smile—for smiling was not

Selwood's regular occupation. "It's pretty hard," he said, "in this town for a man to say just exactly what he's going to do till after he does it. It depends sometimes on what the other fellow does—and, generally speaking, on who does it first."

She regarded him gravely. "I hope you won't go into any danger on my father's account."

He suppressed a laugh. "Not as much as I'm in now." It was a foolish thing to say. He tried to hedge, but, alarmed, she cut him off. "What do you mean?"

"In Sleepy Cat," he replied, getting back to his senses, "a man doesn't have to *go into* any danger; he's in it the minute he hits town. The only way to keep out of it would be to pick a dark night, when it's raining hard, and quit the blamed place."

"You've been far too kind to us to get into any trouble for our sakes," she repeated, almost mechanically. "I only wish we were away from here."

"I'm willing to get into trouble if you'll stay. I'd rather hunt for a little than see you leave."

Christie tossed off a sense of embarrassment. "My leaving couldn't possibly mean anything to—any one in Sleepy Cat."

"If I could tell you what it would mean to me you might change your mind on that point." She regarded him in the moonlight rather bravely till he had said that much. After he spoke she was silent—almost receptive; but he added desperately, "There's just one miserable blamed reason why I can't."

Christie changed the subject instantly. "Wherever we go we couldn't find a kinder friend—Father said this morning. It's when trouble comes that real friends count. And your influence would be good on Father." Selwood started a little. "I'm so afraid now of his running with these awful gamblers, down in River Street."

Selwood looked away. Christie spoke on very seriously:
"Of all men in the world I think gamblers are meanest
—don't you?"

Selwood coughed. He had taken off his hat and was
twisting it a bit confusedly in his fingers. He studied
the hat a moment and presently looked at Christie. His
face, open to the moonlight, showed his eyes clearly.
"To tell the truth," he said simply, "I never thought
much about it. But," he added, pausing, "I guess
maybe you're right. I'll be going. You'll remember to
do just as I've told you? And please don't say anything whatever to your father about the matter till it's
all over."

They walked together to the tent, then he turned his
steps, reflectively, up-street toward the gambling-hall.
At the entrance he paused. The lights were on; men
were moving in and out of the place, and the peculiar
silence, at times, of a gambling-room was broken by the
clash of chips or the infrequent call of a dealer.

Selwood did not go in. Instead, he retraced his steps
in the direction of Fyler's store building; this he sauntered circumspectly about, inspecting each side with
deliberate care and walking away from it thoughtfully.
It looked like a hard nut to crack. He walked thence
to the hotel, went upstairs, followed the narrow, low
corridor to his room, unlocked the door, and went in.
He lighted a lamp, adjusted the wick and the shade,
and sat down on the side of his shabby bed. On the wall
opposite him hung a framed woodcut of a missionary
padre. In the silence Selwood looked long and thoughtfully at the old print. A cloud had long hung over the
story of his own life, a cloud that Selwood had always
felt might possibly be lifted by this old man—if he were
yet alive. The uncertainty of this was one reason that
helped to paralyze Selwood's resolve to find him.

To-night the gambler acted with his natural determination. He rose, took the picture from the wall, turned down the wick of the lamp, blew it out, and with the woodcut under his arm, returned to the hall.

Carrying the picture to his room, he wrote and painted on a sheet of paper a sign and, returning to the hall, hung the picture on the wall beside his desk—about the most conspicuous place in the room. Underneath the picture he tacked the written sign:

FOR RELIABLE INFORMATION AS TO THE WHEREABOUTS OF THIS OLD PADRE I WILL PAY ONE HUNDRED OUNCES OF GOLD DUST.
JOHN SELWOOD.

Bill Pardaloe watched him put the portrait up. He read the sign and turned to Selwood, who had sat down at his desk and lighted a cigar. Pardaloe read the sign haltingly at least twice before he turned to ask questions.

When he spoke, Selwood answered inquiries laconically. "I want to talk to that padre," he said. "To anybody that can bring him to me—or me to him—I pay a hundred ounces of gold dust."

Pardaloe's sharp nose pushed well forward. "Where is he?"

"If he's alive," answered Selwood, "he's wandering somewhere around the mountain country among the Indians."

Pardaloe studied again the features of the long-haired old man in the print. "Won't any other padre do?" he snorted, picturing to his imagination the good times latent in one hundred ounces of gold dust.

"No other padre," said Selwood unfeelingly, "will do."

"What do you want with him?" demanded Pardaloe.

The answer was prompt and decisive. "That's my business. Get hold of Bob Scott, Bill, and bring him in here."

For ten years John Selwood had wanted to meet— yet lived in a certain dread of meeting—this padre; he had finally resolved to face him and, if it must come, to know the worst.

Other frontiersmen, drawn by Pardaloe's talk, crowded up to look at the picture. The usual discussions ensued, in which optimists declared they had seen the padre and were sure of the reward; while others tried to belittle such pretensions and were contemptuously skeptical of the statements.

Selwood rid himself of the first rush of questioners and retired to his room, with Pardaloe, who had reappeared, bringing Scott. "There's been a mean deal put over this trader, Fyler," Selwood began, addressing both men. He told them the facts in the case, about which they had already heard the town talk. "And after robbing him of his stock of goods," continued Selwood, "they called him out of his tent, knocked him on the head, and took all his money, to make things easy for themselves."

"Will he die?" asked Pardaloe.

"No."

Pardaloe's interest diminished. "Poor work," he mumbled.

Nor did Selwood extract from him any sympathy for the trader's plight. He was, in fact, cold and crusty on the whole situation. "The blamed fool went down to Bartoe's place," he grumbled, "and paraded around with a big roll of money—that's what the boys say. What they didn't get while he was there they went after at the tent. What else could you expect?" he demanded, with his long face, his hang-dog stubble, and twinkling eyes.

Selwood cut him off—for one of Bill Pardaloe's peculiarities was to pursue a subject to the limit. "I know, Bill," he admitted, "but that doesn't change matters any. Fyler's girl is an innocent sufferer for his foolishness. Her father may be a blackguard, but she didn't pick him out. Now this is what I called you both in for. I'm going to clean those fellows out of Fyler's store to-night. I'll need some help. Do you two want to join me? There'll be a fight. Take it or leave it, just as you like—no harm done either way."

Bob Scott never responded, to Selwood at least, with anything more than an affirmative grin; he wasted no words.

Pardaloe, however, had to have his talk, and from the number of objections he habitually raised to any proposal, he might have been thought desperately opposed to everything suggested by anybody, anywhere, at any time.

"Look here, John," he growled, "I know who's in that store."

"So do I," assented Selwood, unsympathetically.

"It's Atkins and Bartoe and Big Haynes."

"What then?"

"Yes, that's all right—'What then?'—but those fellows are loaded. They'll shoot. How' you going to do it? Here's the moon pretty near full. Why don't you wait a few nights till you can work under some kind of cover?"

"One reason, Bill, is that if we wait a few nights, those fellows will steal the whole stock and move it out of the store before Fyler gets on his feet."

"Goin' to coax 'em out with candy?"

"I'm going to smash in one of the doors. There are

two, a front door and a back door. All I'll ask you to do," explained Selwood, addressing Pardaloe, "is to watch one door, where you'll be in the dark, while I take the other door myself."

"What's Bob going to do?" demanded Pardaloe, acrimonious with suspicion.

"Bob's going to hold up a lantern for Atkins to shoot at."

Pardaloe did not join in Scott's laugh at his own expense, but he was silenced. And as Selwood warming to his subject revealed the high points of this purposed attack, the pupils of Pardaloe's eyes could be seen to dilate with interest. Selwood, speaking low and quietly, continued to lay out his plan. It promised the warmest kind of a time. Pardaloe's backward, skeptical expression changed into an anticipative glow. He offered neither further comment nor criticism, but rose on his bony shanks. "Let's go, John."

Scott ventured an amiable inquiry—he was, after all, the more prudent of the two adventurers that Selwood had called to his aid. "What kind of firearms have them fellows got in there?"

"Atkins is a little dangerous," said Selwood, for he felt he must be reasonably honest. "It's no use denying, Atkins is handy with a Colt's. Bartoe carries a bottle. He may not wake up until it's half over. He and Big Haynes use shotguns. They're as likely to hit each other as to hit us. What do you say?"

Pardaloe was ready. "I'll take the old gun along," he mused in cheerful anticipation.

Selwood was firm. "No artillery on this job."

Pardaloe protested with some violence. Selwood overbore him, threatening that if he persisted he should be left wholly out of the venture.

"I'll meet you at the barn at twelve," said Selwood

finally. "See Abe Cole, Bill, and get a sledge-hammer. I'll bring a couple of axes from the barn. By the way," he added, "here's something I want you two to do before you go."

The three men passed unnoticed through the hall, and Selwood stopped them outside. He pointed to the big sign over the wide doorway:

JOHN SELWOOD, GAMBLER

"Get a ladder," he said to the two men, "and take that sign down."

"What for?" blurted out Pardaloe, all his suspicions rising together. "What are you doing that for?" he asked.

Selwood, with his cigar, was reasonable and calm. "It never should have gone up there. Dave coaxed me into putting it up, after he got wounded that night down at Bartoe's—said it was too good advertising to lose. Well," he continued with an acid touch, "I'm advertised! Everybody along the Mountain Divide knows I'm a gambler. Why advertise it any longer?"

"Yes," growled Pardaloe, "they know you're a gambler. But if you haul down your sign how's everybody going to know where to find you?" he demanded triumphantly.

"Better for some of 'em if they didn't find me," retorted Selwood indifferently. "Stop your talk, dash it. Bring out the ladder and pull down the sign."

CHAPTER XIV

AN EARLY MORNING PARTY

FILLING in for one of his men, Selwood sat dealing at the large faro table near his desk. It was two hours since he had left Christie. In that interval she had had another visitor at the tent. Her father had already wakened, when Christie was called to the tent door by a voice and, looking cautiously out, saw Starbuck standing in the moonlight.

"I didn't want you to think I went away with any hard feelings," he said, explaining himself calmly to Christie and throwing into his words that touch of sympathy and interest he was always able to summon. Christie listened with reluctance. But as her caller was at no loss for words, he was soon heard by her father, who, raising his voice, called him, over Christie's protest, into the tent.

From this unpleasant situation she could not escape, but in some way, remembering another voice and another's words, she felt immensely strengthened in her resistance to its possibilities. These were not long in unfolding. And when an unpleasant subject was opened again under cover of sympathetic interest in her father's affairs, she was very positive in what she had to say.

Her father unfortunately intervened in the most trying way. "Here's the man," he said, "that can give us the help we need, Christie, if you'll treat him in the way you'd ought to."

Christie burst into tears. The obligation of secrecy was on her—she thought she knew why, now; but she would not resist the satisfaction of a covert threat. "If Mr. Starbuck won't help us," she exclaimed, "we may find *somebody* in Sleepy Cat that will."

Her eyes flashed the words at him like a challenge. She was sorry the instant she had spoken, but it was too late to recall her words.

"Anybody that goes near the store without me," Starbuck said calmly, "will get riddled with buckshot—so," he added, looking first at Christie and then at her father, "don't make any mistake like that."

He marched with dignity out of the tent. Fyler kept up a weak fire of reproach. Christie was used to such things on more subjects than one, and only continued to listen silently. When her father quieted down she sat in the dim light of the lantern, hung between the beds, gazing thoughtfully into the dull yellow flame. What thoughts were in her mind, her father, least of all, could have surmised. She gave him some refreshment presently, and he fell into an uneasy sleep. That moment seemed to rouse her from her apathy and signalize her resolve.

She rose cautiously but hurriedly, caught up a shawl that lay across her cot, opened her little trunk, and stealthily drew out a scarf.

Pausing, and looking at her father only long enough to be sure he slept, she carefully lowered the wick of the lantern, blew out the light, and stepped with as little noise as possible to the tent door. Wrapping herself in her shawl, and winding her scarf about her head and neck, she pushed open the fly and stood alone out in the moonlight.

She had set herself a difficult task. Women, it is true, might sometimes be seen in the streets of Sleepy Cat late at night. With the constant presence of emigrant trains, emergencies might and did arise that took women up-town; but these were rare. Once started, Christie did not hesitate. She walked swiftly along the street, hardly knowing which way to look in her quest, but determined to follow it. At one time she hurried directly past the gambling-hall up the hill; but she shrank from exposure to the glaring lights, though had she looked within she might have seen Selwood where he sat. The only place where she hoped she might make a successful inquiry was at the big barn; and toward this, after repassing the gambling-house, she directed her steps.

She was being trailed, though she did not realize it. Believing herself unobserved and unseen, she pursued her course, and it was only when Bob Scott stepped out of a shadow in front of her that she was frightened.

"Were you looking for somebody, lady?" he asked.

Christie jumped, but Scott's inoffensive manner reassured her. She had seen him in company with Selwood at the store, and some instinct told her he meant no harm.

"I *am* looking for some one."

"Who is it?"

"He's the superintendent of the freighting line."

"I guess I know who you mean. He was down to see your father to-night."

"Oh," she cried in confusion, "I don't mean Mr. Starbuck."

Scott was confident. "I don't either. You mean John Selwood. If you do want to see him, I think I can find him. But I'll have to be gone a few minutes. Now here's the barn"—he pointed to the big structure close at hand. "If you'd walk down with me and wait a few minutes in the office, I'll have him here."

"Who's in there?" asked Christie, looking at the barn with proper suspicion.

"There are two men on duty there all the time, but I'll give you a better guard than that."

Still in fear and trembling, Christie accompanied her

guide to the barn office. Two formidable-looking dogs rushed to the door as Scott opened it. Admonishing them, he turned with a quiet grin. A lighted lantern on the desk revealed the interior to Christie. "If you can sit here for five minutes," said Scott, "these dogs will guard you better than anybody in Sleepy Cat could do it. Just pet them a little." Christie made friends cautiously with the two dogs. "We call one Chloe," explained Scott, "and this is Sweetheart. They're Mr. Selwood's favorite wagon dogs—half bull and half mastiff—and if anybody tries to come into this office while I'm gone, they'll eat 'em up. Are you willing to wait with them?"

Christie smiled rather mournfully. "I suppose I can't help it," she said uneasily. "Will you be long?"

"Three minutes—maybe five."

"Please hurry!"

Scott lost no time in getting to Selwood, whom he found at his desk. The Indian whispered to him. Selwood seized his hat, followed Scott out the back door, and the two, singly, and walking in different directions, joined Christie.

Chloe and Sweetheart, barking furiously, sprang up to be fondled when Selwood opened the door. Scott took the dogs outside, and Selwood turned to Christie. "I've been looking everywhere for you—and if I hadn't seen Mr. Scott, I never should have found you."

"You can get me any time by leaving word at the barn," suggested Selwood.

"Are you in business here, Mr. Selwood?"

"Why—yes."

"What is it, may I ask?"

He answered haltingly—glad it was dark. "Well, I'm mixed up in different kinds of business here—that's what got me into trouble with your father." He spoke with a laugh—or tried to. "I run this Russell & Wentworth freighting outfit," he continued. "I suppose if I called myself anything, it might be a mining man. What has happened?"

She was so confused and overcome now that she could hardly summon the words she wanted. "Nothing *has* happened. I feared what might happen—to-night. You didn't tell me," she ventured, "just what you were going to do about the store." Then she added, disconnectedly, "Mr. Starbuck came over again."

Selwood looked keenly at her. "What did he want?"

"First he said," she began brokenly, "he wanted to turn the store back to Father."

"Was that all?"

"No."

"What else?"

"If——"

"If—what?"

"The same condition he named before."

"If you'd marry him, eh?"

"Yes."

"Well, what did you say?"

"I said—what I said before."

"Tell him," suggested Selwood, "if he must marry somebody, to apply to me."

Christie could summon no lightness. "Then he made a threat," she went on. "He said that anybody who went near the store without him would get killed."

"And you wanted to let me know?"

She fingered the fringe of her scarf, but looked steadily at him. "To be careful," she said.

He took her back to the tent and parted with her, hard as it seemed to do, at the fly. "Why did you want to warn me?" he asked.

"To repay your kindness." They spoke in low tones.

"Nothing more?"

"What more could there be?"

"Well," he said lightly, "if I get hurt, you'll know it was while I was trying to follow your advice."

He was still laughing as she slipped hurriedly into the tent.

The old store building in which Fyler had housed his earthly possessions stood, detached, on a corner of Fort Street. Originally a log structure, it had been enlarged and added to, but it was, all of it, well put together and capable of standing a pretty stiff siege if defended by resolute men—and none knew better than Selwood that it would be well defended by men of the character of those now inside. If he had minimized to Pardaloe the hazards of a fight for the store it was only to meet his objections. For while Pardaloe would rather fight than eat, he needed to be petted till plunged into the mood for action—after that, it was only necessary to hold him back.

Shortly after three o'clock that morning the moon, still bright, was drawing close to the western peaks that guarded the town. It was the hour in which the dissipations of a frontier night are ordinarily over and hardy men are deepest in sleep. At that time, two men with the barest of shifts for disguise, and followed by two dogs, whining and leaping at their heels, left the stage barn. One man carried three common axes, of the heavy type used in the tie camps along the river; the other carried a sledge of a size and weight that would have rendered it useless in the hands of an ordinary man. But Pardaloe, Scott, and their companion in the adventure were not ordinary men; the first was a giant in physique, the second dangerous in encounter, and the third fertile in resource.

As the two men neared Fort Street, Selwood, stepping

out of the shadow of a building, joined them. He wore, like the others, a bandanna tied with little ceremony across his nose; a flat wagoner's hat shaded his eyes. "You brought the right dogs?" asked Selwood, looking at them.

"I did," muttered Pardaloe, as Chloe and her mate tangled themselves up between his legs, "'n' if ary one of 'em gets killed, somebody's goin' to get dumped right down on the rock pile along with 'em."

Fort Street was quiet as a graveyard—not a soul was stirring and the party reached the store unobserved. They halted in the shadow thrown on the north side of the low building. Pardaloe dropped his sledge with unnecessary noise, and Scott, true to instinct, laid his axes noiselessly on the ground. Selwood tiptoed to the corner and inspected the front doors—they looked substantial. The whole front was exposed to the blaze of the moonlight, and it appeared like suicide to attempt a forcible entry. Every aperture, he well knew, was barred or nailed and would give way only before a determined assault. Pardaloe, who could not keep quiet long at a time, stamped to the front to join Selwood. "What y' going to do?" he demanded in a hoarse whisper. With these words he sneezed. It was a suppressed sneeze, but it shook the solid earth.

"I'm going to wake everybody up inside first and tell 'em to shoot," murmured Selwood. "Put your handkerchief up over your nose, you lubber——"

Pardaloe, with the bandanna loose on his neck, was obstinate. "Can't do it, John. It's full o' dust—can't breathe. Let's get at 'em."

Selwood led his retainer back to Scott, and, approaching the high shuttered window on the north side of the building, felt carefully all around it. The two dogs, cowed, crouched at Scott's feet. Selwood studied the building a moment. Then he turned to his companions.

"They'll look for us first at the back door—that's the natural way to open this oyster. I'll smash this shutter. Bill, you go around to the south side and slam away at the other window. Bu'st it if you can, but, whatever you do, make plenty of noise. When I get through this shutter with an axe, Bob drops the dogs in here, one after the other—they won't get both of 'em. When you hear me yell, Bill, it will mean the dogs are in. Then run to the back door with your axe, Bob, and chop at it. I'll take the sledge and an axe around to the front door, Bill. When you hear the dogs inside, join me at the front door and give it the sledge for all that's in you. Now get to your place, Bill—when I hear your axe, I start here—keep out of range, best you can; there's at least one hard shooter in there."

A moment later the thud of Pardaloe's axe against the hollow shutter on the opposite side of the building would have waked the dead, had there been any in Sleepy Cat proper. Timed at the expected signal, came the crash of Selwood's axe into the north shutter. Clad loosely in shirts, belted trousers, and boots, the two men sent a shower of rapid blows into the stout barriers opposing them. Selwood, working in semi-darkness, chopped and smashed at the jamb of the stubborn shutter without an instant's let-up. A loud shout from within, followed by a shot, greeted the attack; Chloe and Sweetheart, savage with excitement, yelped and whined. Selwood's axe sank to the head into the splintered jamb. A second shot rang out. A shotgun discharged from close inside the north shutter warned the besiegers what to expect, and a buckshot glancing from the blade of the axe caught Selwood above the ear. Scott, crouching with the dogs, jumped as a second bullet stung his wrist, and a third brought an angry yelp from the dog Chloe. Atkins, if it were he, was firing a shotgun from the counter, standing on it so as to range his fire down.

There was no sign or thought of a retreat. Working his axe loose, Selwood redoubled his blows—one or at most two more charges of buckshot, he believed, were all that were to be feared for a moment, and the sooner they came, the better it would suit him. He sank the axe head again and again into the thick lock-rail of the shutter, intent on reaching the hook-fastening. Again a charge of buckshot hurtled through the damaged casement and sprinkled the axeman, the Indian, and the dogs, but there was no cessation in the ferocious shower of blows. The splintering crash that followed each one told how fast the shutter was giving way, and the sound of a fourth report from a shotgun also told Selwood that Pardaloe was under fire. Throwing all his energy into one last swing, Selwood drove the axe completely through the jamb to pry out the staple. The axe helve, weakened by the blow, broke. With an oath, Selwood called for the sledge and the next minute what remained of the shutter hung loose.

Within, Selwood and Scott heard the shouting of the defenders.

"The doors, boys!" roared Selwood. Pardaloe, yelling like an Indian, was plying his axe. Selwood tore the shutter from its hinges, stopped, caught Chloe in his arms, unsnapped her leash, and threw her like a shot into the store. From Scott's arms, Sweetheart flew in after her.

In an instant pandemonium raged inside. Wild shooting, the snapping of the infuriated dogs mingled with the cursing of the bewildered defenders, the crash of Scott's axe at the back door, and Selwood's axe with

Pardaloe's sledge at the front. Wood and iron could not withstand such assault. Bullets from two revolvers were thrown desperately from within, but the positions of the two parties were now reversed; the trouble was all on the inside. Darkness, the danger of shooting one another in shooting at the dogs—and with it all the three men in the store were having all they could do to keep from being torn to pieces. The hickory cross-bar that held the front doors splintered before the first blows of Pardaloe's sledge, and the stout front doors gave way. Throwing himself against the weaker one, Selwood smashed and shouldered through it and fell into the store. He was greeted by a charge of buckshot which, because he had slipped and fallen, went over his head. To dodge to shelter behind the front end of the counter was the work of an instant. Pardaloe, unopposed, dashed in from the front end, and Selwood, springing from his momentary shelter, grappled the form of a man in the darkness. The two clenched on the floor.

"Call off your dogs!" came in a stentorian voice from somewhere; it sounded like Big Haynes. Selwood, rolling his man in a fierce scuffle toward the front, dragged him to the doorway, threw him into the street, and ran back to help.

Scott, from outside had set a lighted lantern up in the battered window opening, and hastening to the door with a second lantern, ran in to secure the dogs just as Selwood reached Pardaloe. He sat astride a prostrate defender, his bony fingers fastened on the man's windpipe. Selwood understood too well what that meant. Catching a lantern from Scott's hand, he held it on the man's distorted features under Pardaloe's hand. Grasping Pardaloe, Selwood broke his grip and jerked back his arm. "Let loose, Bill! Let loose, I tell you! You're killing him."

"Dash it, John," protested Pardaloe, struggling to get away from the gambler's hands, "that's what I'm trying to do—le' me alone—he tried to plug me! Who is he?" demanded Pardaloe, with a wealth of surly epithets. "Atkins!" he exclaimed, as Selwood held the lantern closer to the man's swollen face.

"Get your knee out of his chest, Bill," remonstrated Selwood. "Can't you see he's slipping? He can't breathe."

"Time to finish a bear's when you got him," mumbled Pardaloe, stubborn and unconverted.

With many reproaches aimed at Selwood for unwarranted interference, Pardaloe, shaking himself loose, baffled and eyeing his prey, stood by till Selwood, bending over the gasping man, saw he was coming to, and started to drag him forward to throw him out.

Pardaloe bared his arms. "Stand away!" he exclaimed in a hoarse growl. "Stand away, John! You throw'd your'n out. I throw mine."

He picked up and carried Atkins forward bodily. Selwood turned to help Scott with the dogs. These had Big Haynes, greatly embarrassed, behind two big boxes in a corner—and, held back by Scott, they were tearing to shreds with fiendish delight the blanket Haynes had slept in. Haynes called loudly for quarter, and as Selwood went forward again, Scott, while he held the dogs, advised Haynes to hustle out the back door.

When Selwood reached the front door, he saw Pardaloe toiling back up the steps, carrying Atkins, kicking wildly, into the store. "What are you doing, Bill?" demanded Selwood, amazed.

"Didn't throw the blamed critter fur enough, first time," Pardaloe panted. "Stand back, John! Dod blast you," he muttered to his struggling victim, "stop your bitin'! Out y' go!"

CHAPTER XV

THREATS AND CONFIDENCES

It was the work of only a few minutes for Selwood to regain his room back of the gambling-hall. He slipped out of his rig and began to wash up. His face was disfigured by blood that had trickled under his hatband from the wound above his ear, where the buckshot had torn his scalp. The furrow was not deep—little more than a scratch—and he checked the flow with the rude styptics of teamsters and frontiersmen.

Within fifteen minutes he was back at the post he had left an hour earlier, with the few sitters around him who had gathered at the last table where faro was being dealt that Sunday night.

Hardly ten minutes later three men appeared at the open doors of Selwood's place. Starbuck, accompanied by Atkins and Bartoe, walked into the hall and stood for a moment looking about. Selwood, his eyes shaded for the table, saw them without difficulty and, while not losing sight of the play, kept them in his field of vision. He knew what they were there for—to see whether he was missing from his ordinary post. Selwood impassively pressed the case spring and kept an untroubled eye on the layout. His visitors lingered only a moment, but it was past the closing hour, and while the last of the players straggled out, Starbuck came in again.

With his hair brushed back, his features unruffled, and his dress in order, Selwood stood at his desk, preparing to lock it. Starbuck strode across the empty room, with his usual energy, and Selwood, turning the key in the lock, looked around at him.

"What have your barn bullies been up to to-night, Selwood?" he demanded, without preliminary.

Selwood asked what he meant. Starbuck told of the attack on the store. "Atkins and Bartoe hold a bill of sale for that stock," he declared, indignantly. "Things have come to a pretty pass in Sleepy Cat when legitimate owners are to be chewed up by dogs and thrown out into the street. This thing has got to stop, or you'll have to move your headquarters out of this town." Selwood parried with civil answers the questions roughly asked, and met untroubled the threats roughly made, and asked only an occasional question himself.

"Have you heard any talk of Vigilantes organizing in Sleepy Cat?" he asked. "I don't know much about it." Selwood, as he spoke, dropped the bunch of keys dangling from his fingers into his pocket. "But the little talk I heard here a few minutes ago about some kind of a fight at Fyler's store was that the Vigilantes had got after the men who had robbed Fyler and tried to kill him. There's no use your talking to me about my men; they do as they please—you know that. Talk to them," he suggested, while Starbuck, very angry, continued to blow off. "If Atkins and Bartoe can show title to the goods, why don't they get their friends together and go back and claim them?"

"Bartoe says there were half a dozen or more men in it—and they're in the store yet, he says." Selwood thought Pardaloe and one Indian in possession must be making a good deal of noise, but he said nothing. "There's going to be a clean-up in this town before long," added Starbuck significantly. "Folks that are making trouble ought to get ready for it."

"Meaning just whom, Starbuck?" asked Selwood, pacifically.

"Meaning whoever's behind all this rowing that's going on here lately."

"Well, Starbuck," returned Selwood, with some slight

appearance of fatigue, "you know, or ought to know, that I'm the man that threw Atkins and Bartoe into the street to-night; they ought to know it; if they don't, tell them so. Of course, I wouldn't have done it, if I'd known there were friends of yours in the store. If it hadn't been for me, they would have been hanging to telegraph poles by this time—that's the fact. And tell them the next thing like that Fyler job they try to pull off, they *will* be hanging to the poles—that's the plain, straight, every-day English of it."

Starbuck had never been faced quite so bluntly. Selwood never had shown his hand quite so carelessly— parted with his caution quite so completely. But a woman stood between them, and she meant the more to Selwood because, though he cherished slight hope of holding her himself, the thought of her going to Starbuck was bitter enough to make him ready for any manner of fray.

Starbuck eyed the gambler intently. Then he spoke with composure. "Selwood, you're cutting quite a figure here in affairs that you've got no business in. You've tried some steps that don't fit the music you dance to in this establishment. You're playing too many games to win all of them—do you know that?" Selwood was too absorbed in watching Starbuck's eyes to make the slightest response in words. If there was anywhere in his demeanor an answer it lay in the inscrutable expression of his own eyes; he seemed poised for an issue. "Whether you do or not," Starbuck went on evenly, "you'll find your 'du-al' rôle will wind you up if you play it long enough. It won't work in Sleepy Cat."

Starbuck paid his enemy one compliment. Without any attempt to back out of the room, he turned and walked straight to the door. There he paused and looked around.

"Good-night, Mr. Selwood," he called out calmly.

"It's pretty late for that, Mr. Starbuck," retorted Selwood. "Good morning."

Daylight was really breaking. "Hold on a minute," he added, walking forward to where Starbuck stood at the door. "You're giving me some advice. I'll give you a little. There's Vigilante talk brewing in Sleepy Cat, Mr. Starbuck. And Vigilante talk in Sleepy Cat means—sometime—Vigilantes." The word carried a sting—as Selwood well knew.

"When the Vigilantes get me," cried Starbuck, "they'll get you, Mr. Selwood."

"In that case the cross-arm of one pole will do for both of us. But why wait for the Vigilantes? We can fix up our differences any time."

"Sometime—not any time, Mr. Selwood."

"Sometime for you, Mr. Starbuck," smiled Selwood, as Starbuck stalked heavily down the steps; "any time for me."

It was late that Monday before Selwood appeared. At noon in his room at the hotel he was pulling himself together for a shave. After lunch he walked down the street in the sunshine, with a careful eye for enemies, but passed Fyler's to see what the place looked like, after the change of owners.

Scott had patched up the scars. The front doors showed fewer traces of the rude assault than Selwood had expected. But there was a deathly quiet about the place. Selwood missed the noise of the auction crowd and the shouting. The town knew that there had been a fight at the store during the night, but for various reasons the principals concerned had kept their own counsel. When Selwood approached Fyler's, two men stood on the corner talking—Big Haynes and Harry Barbanet. Selwood understood perfectly well that Harry, chief gossip of the River Quarter, was up-town to bore

into Haynes for all the information he could get as to
who the pseudo-Vigilantes had been—that his sore and
aching friends might be posted accordingly. Big Haynes,
however, had been uncommunicative and, when Selwood hove in sight, left Barbanet unceremoniously and
drew Selwood aside.

"I want to explain things a little, John," said the big
fellow. "This sneak"—he nodded toward Barbanet,
who, left alone, was walking up the steps into the store
—"is up here trying to pump me about who was in the
party; he didn't get anything. I know Pardaloe was—
but I didn't tell *him* that. I could make a guess at
another friend of mine——"

"A friend of *yours!*" exclaimed Selwood.

"Easy, John—just easy for one minute, will you? I
want to call a white man like you a friend as long as I
live—and that ain't goin' to be a great while, if I don't
get out of this town, I see that. But who I guessed, or
didn't guess, is my business—not the business of these
bums! What I want to say to you is this: I wa'n't in
no way mixed up in this scheme to rob Fyler. I had
some goods of my own in there and stayed with them
fellows so as not to get robbed, myself. I've got no
money, John—you know that. It's come easy, go easy.
Last night I fired no gun and hit no man. I was asleep
under the counter, and if I hadn't got my head and
shoulders into a drygoods box them blamed dogs would
have eat me up. As it was, they chewed my legs something shameful! Carpy's been cauterizing me all day.
That's all, John. Right is right, ain't it, John? 'N'
you know the facts. I helped the girl 'n' the Indian and
McAlpin get Fyler up here early this morning—they'll
tell you that, too—they understand the situation. And
I want to tell you, 'tween you 'n' me—that man Fyler
ain't hurt much, neither."

Selwood had no reason to doubt Haynes's story. "I hold nothing against you, Haynes, as far as I'm concerned. And I don't know rightly what you're talking about. Somebody at the hotel said there'd been a fight. If any of my men were mixed in it and have injured anybody, they'll have to make it right."

Barbanet came down the steps with a satisfied smile on his face—a wise smile meant to ingratiate him with the two men talking on the corner. Nothing lacking in assurance, he addressed Selwood. "That's a nice girl in there." He nodded back toward the store. Selwood only looked at him in silence. It was really an ominous silence; but Barbanet had confidence and sometimes faced such silences down. Big Haynes, on his part, had one characteristic that had saved his skin where better men got into trouble; he had learned to stare at a man and keep his mouth shut at the same time. In this manner he listened to Barbanet, but he was in nowise surprised to see Selwood turn his back abruptly on the impudent loafer and walk away.

Haynes thought it well to interpose a philanthropic warning.

He nodded toward the store. "Go slow on what you say about anybody in there to Selwood, Harry."

"How so?"

"They're friends of his."

Barbanet smiled anew. "She thinks Selwood is a mining man."

"Well, he is, isn't he? Made his money down at Thief River, didn't he? And got his mine down there yet, hasn't he?" Haynes blurted the words out staccato fashion.

"She and her old man were talking about him just now," continued Barbanet with fatal persistency. "I asked whether she meant Selwood the gambler. She said no, she meant the mining man—the man that runs the Russell & Wentworth wagons. She don't know he runs the place up the hill," grinned Barbanet.

Big Haynes took the information all in, but took it stonily. "I don't know it, either, when I'm around that store, Harry," he said significantly. "And speaking of bartenders—and barbers: did you ever hear of the one that died of old age by not knowing too much?"

"Maybe Selwood thinks I'm afraid of him," suggested Barbanet, head down and eyes up, facing Haynes.

"Why not cut your own throat, Harry—you've got the tools—why wait to get your head knocked off? That's what I'm askin' you?"

"I guess from the way Mr. Gentleman John walked off just now, he wouldn't like her to know he's a gambler," retorted Barbanet.

"I've got a better guess than that: when he wants her to know it he'll tell her himself."

"Wonder how he'd like me to tell her?"

"He wouldn't like it."

"Wonder how much it would be worth to him for me not to tell her?"

Big Haynes was prompt in his reply, and disinterested. "Not a cent to him—not if I guess him right. But before you cross his trail, Harry, send for the buzzards; they're quick workers and they'll make a clean job of you."

Selwood walked down street quite unconscious of the corner talk behind him. But he felt cheated out of his visit and, feeling that he had a perfectly good excuse, made occasion to walk around by Fyler's an hour later. This time he found Christie alone and behind the counter in the front of the store.

Her face lighted when she saw him coming up the steps. She lifted both hands instinctively to her hair to smooth it as he walked toward her. She had evidently been at work among the goods and was still busy. Her face, already flushed, seemed to deepen in color under his gaze, and the slight disorder of her dress matched the pretty disarray of her hair. She stood a picture of youth in the freshness of health and endeavor. "Things were in such *awful* shape this morning," she said, with her fingers running around like mice among the hairpins and with her eyes fixed in dire apology on Selwood's eyes. "I know *I'm* a sight!" she exclaimed. "But you'll never know what this poor store looked like!"

"If it looked anything like you," he ventured, "I shouldn't have touched it."

Could Christie have blushed more deeply she probably would; but, unable to do so, she did something worse, as far as Selwood's composure was concerned. She laughed. And it was the happiest care-free laugh in the world—no fret, no worry, neither regret nor apprehension—just the young, happy laugh of a young, happy moment. Selwood felt himself rudely shaken with every vibration of her throat, but he clung to the lifeline. "You got your father over all right?" he asked, swallowing mildly.

"Oh, yes, Mr. Haynes helped—he felt awfully ashamed, he said, of the way things had gone—and Mr. Pardaloe and Mr. Scott——"

"How's your father?"

"Oh"—Christie heaved a big sigh of relief—"ever so much better. Oh, I keep saying 'Oh' all the time. Please stop me. I think I'm excited. I know I shall never be able to say all I want to to thank you—how am I *ever* going to do it?"

She looked at him with eyes so wide open and so appealingly perplexed that Selwood momentarily wilted.

His eyes fell. The man who could look at any sort of a hand at poker calmly, or into the muzzle of a gun without visible hysteria, faltered before Christie's eyes. He kept his wits just enough to answer her appeal. "You've done it," he managed to say—and continued: "I hope you'll have no more trouble. Bob Scott will be sneaking around here for a while at night; Bob doesn't sleep much."

"He just saved my life, helping this morning. And"— she hesitated and twisted her fingers a little as she stood behind the counter. Then she summoned courage and went on—in truth she had much the more courage of the two. "And—he, when I spoke of you, he told me you were not here at all last night! And I just knew *that* wasn't so. And *you* told me you were not here at all last night! And I just knew *that* wasn't so. You told me you'd prefer I shouldn't mention your name; but I just couldn't help it once—I—I—felt so happy over our getting our store back. And Mr. Scott just didn't seem to know anything about *anything*. And he said that Mr. Pardaloe had gone out of town early this morning——"

"He took a wagon train out," explained Selwood. He did not add that, knowing there was but one way to keep the mule boss quiet, he had sent him out.

"Where *were* you last night?" demanded Christie, growing in pretty boldness—pretty because it was nothing but gratitude and fast-kindling confidence—with just the merest dash of receptive feminine curiosity. "Oh, you needn't tell me if you don't want to," she added hastily, "I know I ought not to ask."

Her head hung down—about far enough down to reproach herself for hardihood—and her eyes looked up just far enough to reach his; and just innocently enough to shatter his good resolutions of every sort.

"You've full permission to ask me any kind of a question in the world," he said. "Just remember that. I *was* here a little while last night. But Pardaloe and Scott did the hard work."

"Somebody certainly did it. How *can* men be so mean as those men were to really steal everything we had?" Christie sighed at the thought. But it was not the sigh that shook Selwood; it was the appealing confidence of her question to the one man she felt sure she could trust; and it was so satisfying to him to be even for a few moments in that position.

He stumbled at some effort to answer or explain her difficulty, but Christie rode right on. "I suppose," she said impulsively, "I might as well ask: How *can* men be as good as you and your friends were to risk their lives to get back what was taken away from us—when they couldn't have the *slightest* personal interest in helping Father and me?"

Selwood demurred. "I wouldn't say just exactly *that*. I know Scott feels very friendly to your father and you—and Pardaloe, too."

"Oh, Mr. Pardaloe doesn't like Father *at all!* I think if he had followed his inclination he'd have dropped poor Father in the middle of the street on the way up here!"

Selwood retreated and advanced together. "He may not like your father. But he does you. I'll tell you how it is, Miss Fyler"—Selwood gulped a little on the solution. "Men like Pardaloe and Scott and myself don't see a nice young lady like you often——"

"Nonsense!" exclaimed Christie, flushing anew at her success as a nice young lady.

Selwood, once started, warmed to the subject. "It isn't nonsense. You're the first one I ever saw in my life——"

"I wish you please *wouldn't* make *fun* of me!" protested Christie meekly; but, in matter of fact, not un-happy in her embarrassment.

"All my life, since I ran away from home——"

She opened her eyes. "Did you run away from home?"

"I never had a home, rightly speaking, but I ran away from an uncle I lived with. And ever since I've lived on the frontier and seen nothing but these poor, half-starved emigrant women—or worse. When I see any-body like you—I—why shouldn't I help, if I can?"

"But the other men, Mr. Pardaloe and Mr. Scott, are not a *bit* like you." She did not trust herself to look up when she said it; and her tone was so soft!

"They may be a little rough, but they're a whole lot better men than I am."

She glanced at him saucily. "Don't fish for compli-ments—I'm just in a silly complimentary mood. You make yourself as little as you can, but you don't deceive me. I just know you planned things and risked your life to do this for—us."

"Christie, I'd do anything for you—I mean it, every word. Just give me a chance to do things for you. If my own affairs were as straightened out as most men's are"—he stammered—"I never would ask anything more than the chance"—he leaned toward her in his in-tensity. Christie, frightened at what she had aroused, stood with her eyes down on her hands, clasped nervously before her on the counter.

—"to do everything for you," he exclaimed.

Her heart beat a tattoo. She breathed fast in spite of herself. This was a new tone in a man's voice for Christie, and she was afraid.

—"and kill any man that stepped between us—do you hear, Christie?"

It was not hard to hear words such as these words,

but difficult to know what to say. However, the simplest answer was the best. "Yes," she answered faintly.

"Look at me, Christie," he said almost sternly. Christie summoned up her courage. She raised her eyes. Selwood's face was red to the temples. His eyes glowed. Her heart almost stopped at their expression. "Sometime," he said in deadly earnest, "I'm going to tell you everything; then—you'll be the judge, Christie."

He walked down street with his head thrown well back, and kept on to the tent quarter for his daily visit to Tracy.

Selwood found him much disturbed. He had just received a visit from an unusual caller—Harry Barbanet, one of his old-time enemies. Harry had told him a long story about Selwood's uncalled-for meanness in cleaning Atkins and Bartoe out of Fyler's store, threatened reprisals, and left the sick man worried. Selwood made light of the complaint, but Tracy took it seriously. "What did you do it for?" he asked with invalid peevishness. "Do it for?" echoed Selwood, surprised. "Should you stand around and let a couple of thieves take a whole store away from an old man like Fyler?"

"He ain't so very old. It wasn't our funeral, anyway."

Selwood flared. "So you don't like it?"

"I don't like to get that bunch stirred up. What's the use?"

Selwood tried in vain to bring Tracy around to his way of thinking. Tracy was much upset that Selwood should dip into a quarrel not his own. "I dunno, John," he said at last; "I don't guess you're fitted just exactly for keeping out of other folks' rows. You ain't that kind, John. You're too much of a gentleman—the fellows that nicknamed you hit it about right. Oh, I know you don't like it. I didn't used to like to be called 'Smooth' Dave Tracy, but they had me right. You're too much of a gentleman—so you're fightin' all the time with these river rats——"

"'All the time'?" echoed Selwood indignantly.

"Well, a good deal of the time, Carpy tells me. You're a cool bird, John, and you play a good game of poker—but that don't make a gambler—not by a jugful——"

"Why, Dave," protested Selwood, willing to humor the sick man, "you've always said I could swear worse than you could."

"You didn't learn that gambling—you learned it knocking down mule-skinners."

"Another 'gentleman's job,'" said Selwood, releasing his accumulated bitterness. "No matter, Dave," he added, in the same vein, "I never made a success of anything I undertook——"

"Well, everybody knows that ain't so. But why stir up Atkins and Bartoe and Starbuck for this man Fyler? What's he to you?"

Selwood squirmed but held his peace.

"I know, he's got a girl——"

"Don't drag her name into it," exclaimed Selwood savagely.

"Suppose they are robbing people," Tracy went on, shifting ground instantly, "or shooting people—they ain't robbed you——"

"They've robbed my company," interrupted Selwood sharply; "that's robbing me; they shot you, didn't they? That's shooting me! What are you talking about?" he blurted out in a rage. "I——"

Tracy feebly put him off. "That's the trouble; you get mad—if you was just a gambler and wasn't a gentleman, you wouldn't get mad."

Selwood, in a heat, flung out of the tent.

CHAPTER XVI

BAD NEWS FOR CHRISTIE

No further attempt was made on the store, and while her father was getting well, Christie acted as manager. Haynes, having partly acquitted himself of evil intent, started his auction sales again, and business went on. But one day Haynes called on Selwood to say his own stock of goods would not last over a week longer, and begged Selwood to reinstate him at the hall. And, on promise of good behavior, Selwood told him when his goods were sold he would give him another chance.

Christie, meantime, walked on air. To herself she scarcely concealed her interest in Selwood. Indeed, she found herself sensitive after a few days because Selwood did not call oftener. He had kept track through Carpy of Fyler's improvement, but Christie rarely saw him even passing. Yet some remembrance of their last talk was pleasant in her heart—some thought of a confidence in her worth expressed by the only man in her new and strange surroundings whom she felt sure she might trust.

Starbuck was not so backward in expressing sympathy. He came in one day especially to tell her that he had learned all the circumstances of the row between her father and his partners, and thought if her father would figure out his damages, when he was well enough to do so, he, Starbuck, would see that Atkins paid. "And, Christie," he added, in earnest of his intentions, "tell your father not to be modest about fixing the amount. Atkins is a bad egg—that's the truth of it. I get along with him. I have to keep the peace here and I get along with everybody. But your father ought never to have had anything to do with a man like that."

He made no reference whatever to the unpleasant alternative he had offered before and seemed to wish it lost sight of; for he showed now only an interest in seeing what appeared clearly a wrong properly righted.

Fyler accepted the olive branch. He would accept, so Big Haynes said, a red-hot poker from the devil himself if it were offered him. Christie received Starbuck's overtures coldly. A man may be fooled more than once; but a woman, provided her affections are not involved, is not easily deceived the second time by a man she has once distrusted. Starbuck's new approaches to her favor were deftly made, but the doors of the heart that beat in Christie's brown eyes were no longer open to them. She liked Starbuck's bluff, taking way, but she no longer warmed to Starbuck himself. The result was a certain critical attitude on her part. She was just enough afraid of the man to treat him civilly; but she threw into her talk with him little carping bits that kept Starbuck irritated though they did not cool his ardor. Indeed, they rather inflamed it with a resentful resolve to bring the girl, in some wise, to time.

"There's a hussy that's got 'em all beat," declared Doctor Carpy to Selwood. "Shy as an antelope and as trim on her feet. We never had no women like that down in my country. What? New Mexico. They're fat—not up and coming like this pert youngster. But she's got a mind of her own, boy—don't you ever forget that. Fyler? Oh, he's all right—I go in there just to rattle a few words with Christie. She asked me this morning what had become of you."

Less than that much of a firebrand would have sent Selwood's good resolutions to keep away from Christie Fyler up in smoke. What he ought to do, and what he wanted to do, were as far apart as the north pole and the south—and in the clash of opinions the south pole won.

Leaving Carpy, Selwood walked up to the hall on the Hill. The only sign of life about the place was Bull Page, who was filling and shining up the lamps. Selwood spoke kindly to him—Bull was a devotee. Walking to the back of the hall, Selwood went behind his desk. He lifted the glass clock dome, doubled the shoe up, and put it into one of his capacious pockets. Giving Bull a cigar as he passed out, with the caution not to light it till he had put away the big can of kerosene, the gambler retraced his steps to the hotel and his room. He had resolved mentally to ask Christie to-day whether this was her shoe; if she claimed it, he meant to make her prove her claim by trying it on for him.

It was useless to pretend he could visit her without careful preparation. The least vain man would have tried to look his best for a call on the only pretty girl in Sleepy Cat—Bill Pardaloe "claimed" she was the only pretty girl on the Mountain Divide.

And Selwood was vain. He probably did not think so, but his careful dress among careless men condemned him. This afternoon that he went to call on Christie he was in that dangerous state of preparedness that had given him his unwelcome nickname. He was not a mere fop nor a dandy of any sort; the serious expression of his face was quite enough to dispel any unpleasant impression of that kind. No dandy looks at times—indeed, much of the time—as if his friends were all dead; but when Selwood walked into Fyler's store his sober air might have misled a careless observer into thinking they were.

Fyler sat in a chair near the door, sunning himself. At the whip rack Big Haynes was helping a man pick out a wagon whip. In the darker rear end of the store Selwood, pausing at the door to shake hands with Fyler and ask after his health, caught a glimpse of Christie talking to some man whose back was so turned that Selwood could not see who it was. The quiet gambler, with his left hand resting easily on the toe of the shoe in his side coat pocket, chatted for a moment with the father of the girl who claimed so much of his thoughts —talked with him about the news from the East, the increase in travel, the growing disorders in the town, and at length, getting away from him, walked into the store.

Big Haynes stopped him to help sell the whip. "Here," he said to his reluctant customer, "here's a man knows all about whips. I call that a good whip," he added, cracking his choice vigorously. "There's a lash that'll wear forever. What do you say, John?"

Haynes, with a flow of commending words, handed the whip to Selwood, who, cracking the whip—which was a poor one—managed in turn to give a qualified approval. "It will wear forever," he said calmly to the buyer, "if you don't use it too often."

"Why, of course," assented Big Haynes with a wealth of apparent honesty, "a man can't use that lash for snaking ties out of the woods—nor pull a wagon out of a creek with it. But rightly used that lash'll put cheerfulness into the heart of a mule when he's a thousand miles from home—that's all *I* claim. John," he continued, "I understand Wentworth will be here to-morrow."

"Yes."

"Bringing old General Roper with him——"

"So I'm told."

Selwood heard Christie's voice just then in the back of the store. And it was raised in indignant protest. "I don't believe any such thing," she was saying hotly.

Selwood heard a man's laugh. He recognized it as Starbuck's. He heard also Starbuck's subdued but satisfied retort: "Ask him sometime."

"I will," exclaimed Christie vehemently. "I'll ask him the very next time I see him."

The talk between the two had evidently gone on in ignorance of Selwood's presence. To know that Starbuck was in the store—and talking with Christie—was quite enough to stir Selwood into an ugly mood—and some intuition suggested that they might be talking about him. Resisting an impulse to walk back where he could be seen, Selwood, his left arm resting on a bale of blankets piled on a dry-goods box between the two counters, and holding in the fingers of his left hand an unlighted cigar, stood perfectly still, eyes and ears open, watching Haynes's tactics in selling the whip.

He had not long to wait. He soon heard Christie's footsteps, light and quick—she came down on her heels with such decision! He had listened for and listened to those footsteps so many times that he could have picked them out among all the footsteps in Sleepy Cat. And they were coming toward him.

She stopped as she saw Selwood. He looked around. She was standing within arm's length. Her flushed face, her challenging expression and questioning eyes betokened her excitement. She looked fixedly at him. Returning her gaze, he lifted his hat with his left hand and laid it carelessly on the blankets. Then he waited for her to speak, and, as she did not at once, he broke the pause himself. "Good morning," he said, "—if it's not too late."

Starbuck, who had followed Christie, halted a few feet away. The passageway was narrow and he could not have passed forward if he would. Selwood gave no intimation that he was aware of his presence.

Christie, struggling apparently with some sort of suppressed feeling, hesitated. She forgot to return Selwood's greeting. Then, looking at him as if she would look clear through him, the question pressing for answer burst from her lips. "Are you a gambler?" she asked bluntly. The words were loud and clear. Even Haynes heard them. He stopped his sale to look surprised across the counter and saw Christie confronting Selwood with appealing eyes.

There was a moment of straining silence—with Selwood returning Christie's gaze. That question had been expected, but it was none the less dreaded when it came.

He spoke deliberately—and only to ask another question; but his voice lacked its accustomed pitch and resonance. "Who told you I was a gambler?" he asked.

Christie whirled. "This man"—Christie pointed to Starbuck—"told me so just now—is it true?" The words came like bullets.

Selwood looked at Starbuck coldly and long; then he turned his gaze back to Christie. The truth had to come. "I am a gambler," he said.

He saw her horrified amazement as the realization of what his words meant sank in; it made it the harder to face her with what now seemed even to him a shameful fact. "You told me," she responded with a tremor and with anger fast rising in her eyes, "you were a mining man."

It was no time for evasion; in the parlance of Selwood's kind, Christie was calling. Nor would he if he could have tried to deceive her further. There was only one person in the world that Selwood felt ought to have the truth and nothing but the truth at his hands—and she should have it.

"I am a mining man," he said. "I didn't tell you I was a gambler—because I didn't want to be classed with the cutthroats and jailbirds that infest this town and call themselves gamblers." He spoke slowly and pointed with his left hand, his arm resting on the blankets, to

Starbuck—"the kind of thieves," he continued evenly, "that call themselves gamblers and divide their stealings with this man—" Starbuck started, furious. "The kind," Selwood went on, without raising his voice, "that this man blackmails for a living."

"Stand away, Christie!" Starbuck shouted the words. With a violent oath he sprang forward. Haynes jumped and, grabbing him, threw his arms around him. Selwood, motionless beside the blankets, waited with only his eye fixed on his enemy, while Haynes remonstrated with the enraged man and reminded him of Christie's presence. Christie in a panic found herself caught between the two men. She tried to signal Selwood to let her pass, for words stuck in her throat. But he would not budge, and he compelled her to stand and listen. "I'm just a common gambler," he went on remorselessly, "but nobody can say I'm not a square gambler. I back my game against the game of other men—no man can say worse than that of me. Turn him loose, Haynes," added Selwood, contemptuously; "you're not doing me any favor by standing there."

Christie, thoroughly frightened, called desperately to her father, who had heard the commotion and came hobbling back. Fyler intervened and, remonstrating in turn with the two angry men, asked Selwood to step to one side that Starbuck might pass out.

"I'll settle with you and your establishment both together. You've bothered this town long enough. Watch out!" exclaimed Starbuck viciously as he passed Selwood.

Selwood, much to Haynes's surprise, did not even attempt a retort. He was compelled, with his life at stake, to watch Starbuck's eyes. But apart from that instinctive caution, it seemed as if he did not hear Starbuck's threats or gave them no heed. There was much more

weighing on his mind than Starbuck's words. Haynes
and Fyler walked with Starbuck to the door in wordy
talk. It was a chance for three talking men to express
themselves, and for one man who disliked talk to main-
tain a moody silence. Christie, hurrying to the back of
the store, left Selwood to his pillar of blankets. He
gazed, rather discouraged, after her retreating form;
lifted and inspected his unlighted cigar as if looking for
company. Then, summoning resolution, he took his hat
in his hand and followed Christie to the rear of the store.
She was busying herself with the shelves. He stood a
moment beside the counter; she gave him no attention.

After a moment of being ignored, he broke the silence.
"You haven't heard the whole story——"

"I've heard enough." She did not look around; her
voice told the story of her suffering.

"I didn't mean to tell any more now," he said steadily.
"But some day I'd like you—to hear everything."

She whirled toward him with her old impetuosity
but without her light heart. Her eyes flashed. "And
I thought," she burst out resentfully, "I *thought*, that
among all the vile men of this vile town there was at
least one who was clean-handed!" Selwood made no
effort to break the silence. "Well!" she exclaimed, turning back to her shelves, "it's no matter!"

"I suppose this means—you're through with me!"

"I am."

"You haven't heard the whole story," he repeated
quietly. "But if you're through with me—it wouldn't
interest you—anyway."

CHAPTER XVII

FATE TAKES A HAND

McAlpin had been working furiously all the day before, and had every hostler and barn boy working his finger-ends off to make the big barn ready for the expected visit of the head of the firm, Ben Wentworth. Lefever had sent word from Medicine Bend that Wentworth was bringing with him General Roper, chief engineer in charge of the railroad construction, and reminded McAlpin that Wentworth would be looking for a clean barn and that both distinguished visitors would be looking for a pony race or a game of poker. The summer tide of travel was in full swing, exceeding anything ever before known on the Overland Trail. A new gold field was being staked out at Thief River, and Sleepy Cat was overrun with a population that changed faces every twenty-four hours. Night was turned into day in the lower town, and the River Rats, as the sharpers were usually designated, did with their victims pretty much as they pleased.

Selwood had been down at Thief River looking after his mining operations; he had some time before sold a half interest in his mine to Wentworth.

On his return he despatched a driver with his own team and a light wagon to relay the distinguished visitors through from Point of Rocks, and Wentworth, with his guest, reached the foothills overlooking Sleepy Cat by noon.

One of the busy places in Sleepy Cat, particularly at stage time, was the open square in front of the company barns, blacksmith shops, and paint and wagon shops. The Medicine Bend stage had pulled in and pulled out again for the West, and the Thief River wagon, with mail and express, was making ready to start south, when the light rig with Wentworth and General Roper drew up before the barn.

As the company representative Selwood received the two men. Wentworth, almost as tall as Pardaloe, with large features, sweeping mustachios, aggressive eyes, wearing a broad plainsman's hat, a dusty velveteen suit, and huge solitaire diamond in the bosom of his gray woollen shirt, was a familiar figure to Selwood, who knew his peculiarities well.

General Roper was an object of much greater interest to Selwood. He was shorter and stouter with the advance of years than his companion—wore a black slouch military hat and a soldier's mustache, gray and close-cropped. His features were small, his eyelashes burnt out with sun and alkali, and years in the saddle had emphasized his slender bow legs. Selwood, when he could decently do so unobserved, looked at this man very closely and inspected him very coldly—he felt that he had particular reason to do so.

The usual programme of Wentworth's inspection trip was observed. The visitors were taken to Selwood's private office at the barn, where the best of refreshment was set forth. Selwood took, especially at the General's hands, the usual rallying and chaffing suffered by a man who sets forth good whiskey but does not drink it. However, McAlpin, serving as attendant and waiter, being urged, atoned for any abstemiousness on Selwood's part. Wentworth and Roper, with interiors well pickled, were pretty good trenchermen, but McAlpin was such a wonder with the black bottle that he was nominated as one of the inspecting party.

After the horses, wagons, equipment, and shops had been gone over, Selwood took his guests to the hotel for dinner, stopping on the way at Tracy's tent that Wentworth might go in to speak to him.

The old man looked frail. "I'm going to miss my game of poker with you, Dave," remarked Wentworth, in the rough sympathy of men of his kind. "Brought up a man to trim you this time—General Roper."

"You won't miss me," retorted Tracy huskily, and the old gambler, in turn, named Selwood. "He'll give him a game."

After dinner the construction engineers took Roper away, and Selwood drove Wentworth to Thief River for the mine inspection. They got back late to the hotel, where Carpy and Roper joined them. After a good bit of talk and more or less action in the barroom, the four went to the dining-room for a late supper. The meal was prolonged after the manner of those men of the mountain West who meet after long intervals of separation. When they do meet there is so much ground to be covered in reminiscence; there are so many stories to be told—and there is no other country in the world to supply such stories—why should not the hours be mellowed and golden? There was no pretense of saving the country, of uplifting their fellow-men, no taint whatever of hypocrisy latent in the make-up of the four men at Carpy's table; their virtues and their faults were writ large on their foreheads, and to know them for twenty-four hours was to know them for life.

Roper, old army officer and steeped in the traditions of autocracy and action, was first to manifest impatience as the early night wore on and no game was in sight. He walked with Carpy to the hotel office, sent a telegram, and was ready for new venture.

"When does this poker player of yours show up?" he asked of Carpy. "What did you call him—'Gentleman John'?"

Carpy touched the old gentleman's breast with his finger. "He was with us at supper to-night—John Selwood."

"That young fellow? Wentworth's superintendent?"

"That's 'Gentleman John'—but don't call him that," explained Carpy with his broad smile, "unless you want a row."

Roper shrugged his shoulders. "We're going to miss Dave Tracy to-night."

"You may; you may," assented Carpy enigmatically. "But the young fellow will do the best he can."

The four men sat down in Carpy's room. Carpy supplied the chips and opened a big box of cigars while Selwood placed a new deck of cards on the table, the seal of the packet unbroken. He acted as banker.

A game of poker is a monotonous affair to all except the players themselves. Its constant hazard of hopes, blasted with every hand that fails and taking new life with every hand that wins, supplies to the gambler that sting of uncertainty and the hope of loss or gain that prick anew his hardened sensibilities. But these afford to the onlooker only an academic excitement. As the hours pass, fewer irrelevant words are wasted—even the night grows more silent. The religious, spending on his knees the midnight hours in meditation, is not more absorbed in his devotions than the seasoned poker player in his deal, his hand, and his draw.

Midnight found the four men fresh at the work, the gains and losses seesawing from one pile of chips to another. At two o'clock in the morning Carpy, a moderate winner, dropped out on the plea of necessity. Wentworth and Selwood were behind; Roper was winning and in excellent humor. He found that Wentworth, whose game he knew, was easier than Selwood to win from, and directed his batteries chiefly against him.

Selwood, willing to see Wentworth eliminated from the game, encouraged this; and with the day breaking in the east and the air of the room, vitiated by the kerosene lamps, heavy and enervating, Wentworth, a considerable loser, quit.

"I hope you're not done, young man," exclaimed Roper, whose palate was whetted for further victories.

"I don't usually sit in a game longer than this," responded Selwood, whose composure seemed proof against adverse fortune. "But if you want to make it noon, I'm agreeable."

Wentworth threw himself on the bed beside Carpy, whose snoring was of a peaceful nature. Selwood pushed aside the calico curtains, threw open the windows for air, put out one of the hot lamps, dashed some cold water over his face, and sat down to finish with the man best known among the poker players of the Mountain Divide.

The young gambler meant to trim him; and all that had gone before was only preliminary to what was now in hand. From the moment Selwood had sat into the play the night before, he had done little more than to study Roper's game. It was a so-called gentlemen's game, equally without bad manners and without mercy —bold on winning streaks, guarded on losing streaks; a game difficult to beat because it was a game well in hand. Selwood set out to beat it. Roper liked the two-handed game—Selwood meant that he should—meant that his confidence should be firmly established. The General continued to win until within half an hour of breakfast, when a bad streak cost him heavily. Over-confidence—enemy of cautious men—led him for just a little while too far afield; that mysterious agency of chance, poker luck, momentarily deserted him. In a fit of pique, the General tried to discipline it—to drag it rudely back to his aid—with the mortifying result that in half a dozen hands he lost every dollar he had made in the early morning hours. Selwood was showing his teeth.

Nor was the strategy he made use of altogether in the monotonous turn of the cards and the nerve-wearing bet against the unseen. He reasoned that before General Roper would lose his winnings he must first lose his temper; this the six disastrous hands had cost him. But now the General, like a prudent soldier, retreated. He drew into his shell, silent and crabbed, and Selwood saw that something was necessary to encourage him. He ordered breakfast, and while it was being prepared the General won some consolation pots.

The meal was brought to the door by the housekeeper, Margaret Hyde, pale, silent, emotionless. Selwood thanked her, tried to slip a bill into her hand, but could not, and took the tray from her hands. The better part of the pot of strong coffee was conceded by Selwood, who took only a cupful, to Roper. The General lighted a fresh cigar from the big box, tilted back in his flimsy chair, and looked his opponent carefully over. What he thought, what conclusions he reached, were his own. Selwood, calm under the inspection, only toyed, thoughtfully—while General Roper smoked—with the cards on the table before him. When Roper was ready to resume he, himself, drew a sealed pack of new cards from his pocket. "Let's have a fresh deck, young man," he said indifferently—or with an air of indifference—as he produced them. "It seems as if I can't remember your name."

"It ought not to be hard for you to remember," was all that Selwood retorted. But the remark was unnoticed, as Selwood meant it to be. When Roper brought out his own cards, Selwood without comment took the cards they had been playing with all night, tore the pack through the middle, threw it into a corner, and opened Roper's pack. The play went on.

Within an hour, by nursing the play along as a practised hand at a cue nurses three balls within the balk line around the table, Selwood had his game where he thought he could manage it. It was not merely poker; it was the mental attitude of the exasperated man facing him. When Roper played for safety, Selwood was patient; when the General dashed at him headlong, Selwood stopped the charge and exacted his pound of flesh. By ten o'clock that morning Roper realized he had found a man his superior in nerve and his equal in strategy, and his anger was the anger of that master of fence who realizes that his skill has been matched and his rapier outpointed.

But the General lacked the caution to profit by his discernment. As a frontier gamester, he had a reputation to sustain—and to be beaten by a mere sitter-in at a friendly game—to be held up, in reminiscence, to the ridicule of his acquaintances in recalling a circumstance such as this—was too much. And egged on by that arch enemy of us all, vanity, General Roper pressed his enemy.

Selwood recognized the symptoms as the beginning of the end. Roper's recklessness was stimulated designedly by minor successes, and his hopes were repeatedly dashed by staggering losses. He was gently decoyed into boldness and brutally punished for his temerity. His discomfiture was studied and his feelings trodden underfoot. In no other possible way could his pride have been so humiliated and his pretentious autocracy abashed. He rose from the table at noon—although Selwood offered to play longer if he wished—exhausted physically, his eyes on fire, his voice shrunken to a rasping treble, a beaten man. It was not the money lost—

though he had been completely cleaned out—but he had been mastered at his own game and knew it.

"Get my I O U's together, and see what I owe you," he said brusquely as he pushed his chair back. "Look here," he added insolently—Selwood in leisurely fashion was casting up his accounts—"where did you learn to play poker?"

Selwood did not take the trouble to look up. "Among the thieves and cutthroats at Thief River," he answered with no lack of curtness and a complete indifference to the result of his words. "Why?" he asked in turn and with no less of insolence. "Don't you like my game?"

"What's your business?" demanded Roper. The General had cast aside the mask of suavity worn for so many hours; Selwood met his rudeness with rudeness. "Playing poker," he retorted, indifferent to results.

"What!" exclaimed Roper, kindling. "Do you mean to say you're a professional gambler?"

"That sounds like it, doesn't it?"

"You insult me, sir!" exclaimed Roper with an oath.

"You insulted me when you refused to play with my cards. You called for your own, didn't you? And I cleaned you out with your own."

Roper flew into a passion. "Do you play with marked cards?" he thundered.

Selwood was impassive. "Nobody would need marked cards to play with you, General," he returned. "I play with marked cards when I play with thieves—they furnish them."

"Wentworth! Carpy!" roared Roper. "Come in here!" The two men, smoking, and with their feet on the table, were in the Doctor's office. They appeared at the door together. "What do you mean?" he demanded with a string of expletives, "by running in a professional gambler on me for a gentlemen's game of poker?"

Carpy looked blank—but the look was mostly assumed. "Has he cleaned you, General?" he asked, with medical innocence.

"Wentworth," blurted out Roper, "you told me he was your superintendent here."

"Dash it, he is," returned Wentworth testily. "Last time you were up here you cleaned out Dave Tracy. You weren't so blamed particular then whom you played poker with."

Roper stamped about in a tantrum. "I've been played on—taken in by a common card sharp—I've been robbed."

Selwood, who had been sitting as an unconcerned listener, slapped the cards with which they had been playing sharply down on the table. He rose instantly and confronted Roper.

"I wouldn't call a man of your years a liar, General. But you can't crawl away after a game with me with any such word as 'robbed'——"

"Why, you blamed old martinet—" shouted Carpy angrily.

"Hold on, Doc! Hold your horses!" interposed Wentworth hastily. "The General is my guest—we're gentlemen here."

Carpy could not be suppressed. "Every man on the Mountain Divide," he thundered at Roper, "would call you a liar if you called John Selwood a crook——"

Selwood put up his hand. He was white with anger. "I'll do the talking, Doctor," he said. The men watching him made no further attempt to interfere. Roper, sullen, glared at him. "This man"—Selwood pointed to Roper—"calls me a card sharp—he has good reason to—a better reason than he knows!" He was looking as he spoke at Wentworth and Carpy and directed his words to them. "I want to tell you, gentlemen, who that man is"—his finger pointed remorselessly at Roper. "And I want to tell you who I am. That man sent my father to his death at the hands of Indians! That man tried to send my mother and me to the same death. That man put a stain on my mother's name. He sent me out into the world without a name. If that man's word is good"—he shot the words out like bullets—"my father never married my mother!"

"Damnation!" shouted Carpy, enraged. "Why don't you kill him?"

Selwood went steadily on. "I'll tell you that, too. I came out on the Divide ten years ago. I was fifteen years old. I went to this man up at the Fort—told him who I was—he cursed me. The only man on the whole trail that showed me honest kindness was the old man who lies down there in the tent—Dave Tracy. Dave Tracy was a gambler; he could teach me no trade but his own. He never tried to make a gambler of me—I made one of myself—I liked it, I drifted into it, I expect to die in it. I don't excuse it. I don't whine about it. I know the cards—they know me. They're false friends, like all friends—with you when you win, against you when you lose. But I don't forget what that man has done to me and mine. You ask me, Carpy, why I don't kill him—it's because his son, Lieutenant Henry Roper, was my father!"

An instant of silence, terrible to sustain, followed the astonishing words. Roper, apoplectic with emotion, started and clutched at his shirt collar.

Before any one could reach him he fell heavily to the floor.

CHAPTER XVIII

SELWOOD'S STORY

WENTWORTH and Carpy, with much lifting and tugging, carried Roper to the bed in Carpy's room, and while the Doctor administered restoratives, Selwood, assured that no fatal issue threatened, went down-stairs. Wentworth joined him presently with the news that Roper had recovered consciousness and had been given a sedative.

Carpy came down within half an hour and, accompanied by Wentworth, went at Selwood's request to his room. There Selwood sat down before a supply of champagne.

"I told you the bare fact of this man's relation to me," he began, addressing the two men. "But you are entitled to more. My father was Lieutenant Henry Roper; my mother was Annie Selwood; she was the daughter of a post trader at old Fort Pierce. Young Roper fell in love with my mother. His father, then Colonel Roper, commanding officer there, was violently angry—he wouldn't listen to their getting married—he thought a post trader's daughter wasn't good enough for the Roper blood; but that didn't chill the young couple. Their one object in life was to get married.

"It would be a poor kind of a man, gentlemen, that wouldn't speak well of his own mother—who wouldn't deal gently with her weaknesses and draw a veil, if need were, over her mistakes. But, gentlemen, I want to say, I'm not called on to apologize in any way for my little dead mother. She was a whip of a girl, eighteen years old. He was twenty-one. She weighed ninety pounds when Henry Roper married her—only ninety pounds, but every ounce of that ninety pounds was true womanhood, as you will say when you hear me; and she knew what was due to herself. And I can say no word against my dead father—he knew what was due to the woman he loved, and respected it. She was the better educated, he was the older—and I know nothing of either of them but what is to their honor and mine.

"There were few chances at the old fort, in those days, to get married, and if there is one thing for which my father should be blamed it was that he was afraid of his own father and let him bully him. But in spite of the bullying he wouldn't give up the girl; and to break up the attachment, this old man up-stairs arranged to have his son transferred to Fort Calhoun.

"Before the transfer order came, and while the young couple were growing desperate over their situation, a party of Crows started on the warpath. They attacked a party of emigrants in the Peace River country, burned their outfit, and killed two of them. Colonel Roper ordered a troop of cavalry out after the Crows.

"It happened just when there was an outbreak of smallpox at the fort. It was light, but many of the men were down; the captain who would have ordinarily commanded the expedition was down. My father was assigned to the job of punishing the Crows.

"But he had to wait for men. Colonel Roper, like an old blunderbuss, sputtered around trying to hurry things up, but a week slipped away before they could get a handful of men ready. Father, of course, was likewise impatient to be off and greatly elated—and before he got away something else happened.

"Father had an orderly—a half-breed Chippewa Indian who was to act as guide. He had been brought up among the Sioux, and his name was John Frying Pan.

Frying Pan learned from friendly Indians that a black-robe missioner was travelling with an escort of Blackfeet into the mountains, and that the party was camped at what was called Old Mission, twenty miles down the river. My father went to my mother with the news.

"He was in high spirits, of course. He told her his father had given him the great chance to make his name; that he was going to make the best of the chance, and would come back with a record that would make his father relent. He asked her to go with him to the black-robe and be married. When he came back he would tell his father, have it out with him, and all would be well; they would be married, anyway, and there would be no more trouble.

"It all sounded good to my mother; the little Crow expedition was to be a holiday affair—soon over, military honors, brave young husband—and all that.

"She consented. Frying Pan, the orderly, arranged things. An old sergeant, devoted to Father, rode out with him one afternoon after antelope. Mother rode out later alone. Frying Pan met her, and they rode down the river together and met Father. Frying Pan and the old sergeant were taken along for witnesses.

"A thunderstorm overtook them before they reached the Indian camp. They had to halt and even got lost in the storm, but they made the camp and found the black-robe. My mother belonged to his faith. He made necessary inquiries, told them he would marry them, and asked them to come back the following day for the ceremony. They begged to be married at once.

"Night had fallen. It was raining to beat hell. But that wild night, in that little Indian camp and in that downpour, before the gray-haired padre, with Frying Pan, the sergeant, and the Blackfeet lighting the scene with pitch-pine torches, my father married my mother.

"They got back to the fort. Came next day the orders to start. There were only half as many men fit as should have been sent against the meanest Indians ever bred in the Rockies. My father was no greenhorn —he protested. The sick captain begged the old man not to send the boy out with so few men—the old man was iron—he listened to nothing. He waited a few days and sent him out with fewer men than he would have had a week earlier.

"Any old scout in the mountains can tell you the story of that fight. Henry Roper followed the Crows a week, and surprised them at daylight, up past the lava beds, in Crawling Stone Wash. My father attacked. Colonel Roper's scouts, who were no good, had reported that the war party numbered fifty—but a bigger party had joined them, and there proved to be three hundred warriors in the Wash; Roper's men were surrounded in thirty minutes.

"He saw what he was up against. He knew there was only one thing to do—to cut through the ring and make a dash back for the lava beds.

"A few men—about a dozen—got through. The old sergeant—I never got his name—was shot through the head. Frying Pan was left for dead on the field. My father did not reach the lava beds. He fell at the head of his men, in Crawling Stone Wash; his body never was recovered."

Selwood paused. "Gentlemen," he said, wiping his forehead, "this champagne is for everybody. I drink it because it steadies me. I can't drink whiskey. It's funny, but whiskey makes me want to kill somebody.

"So my father didn't come back. Smallpox broke out again that fall at the fort. My mother's father took it and died in a week. My mother was left alone. She was a thousand miles from any woman she felt she could

turn to. Don't be afraid of the champagne, gentlemen;
I tell you, it will steady you."

They watched the gambler pour and drink glass after
glass of the heady French wine—but seemingly without
effect on the iron restraint under which he held himself.

"My mother's condition," he resumed, "forced her to
go to my grandfather. She told her story. He asked for
her proofs—buzzards were picking them in the Crawling
Stone Wash.

"He told my mother his son had never married her!
He did, so help me God! The post surgeon was more
merciful. He defied the old man, took care of my little
mother at the hospital; and of all the damnable things
that could happen to a woman in that distress, my poor
mother gave birth to twins—a boy and a girl. I am that
boy.

"Even that didn't soften the old wretch's heart. He
was only broken over the death of his handsome son.
My mother had no place in his grief. Her very presence
at the fort seemed to irritate him. Before the snow was
off the ground he arranged to send her back to St. Joe
with her two babies. She was put in charge of two
drunken troopers to be taken down the river to a land-
ing where a steamboat, caught on the river the fall before, was going to St. Louis when the ice went out.

"The surgeon wrapped my mother and the babies up
in furs and made her as comfortable as possible—old
Roper came to the hospital then and offered her money
—she refused to touch it. A snowstorm set in after we
got started. By noon it was a blizzard. The troopers
lost their way and drove backward and forward all day.
By nightfall they had found the trail, but they were
drunk. When they struck timber along the breaks above
the river, wolves got their wind and followed them.
The horses got scared; the men whipped up and in a

few minutes the team was running away. The sleigh bounced along on the trail, struck a sharp turn, and my mother with the babies in her arms was thrown from the sleigh twenty feet down into a river break filled with snow—the wolves followed the horses.

"It was close to a village of Mandans. The Indians heard the noise and heard my mother's cries, dragged her out of the snow with her children, and got her into a tepee; they were kinder than the whites. They got my mother and her babies to the boat, and she reached the farm of her married sister in Missouri. But the hardships and exposure of the trip were too much for her. She lived, with what had come to her from her father, till we were twelve years old—never well, but devoted to her children.

"After that my sister and I went to live with our aunt. Her first husband had died. Her second husband was a hard taskmaster—he made us earn our keep. Three years of it was enough for me. It was too much —more than I ought to've tried. You can see for yourselves, gentlemen, there's not much underpinning to me. I couldn't stand ploughing from daylight to dark. I'm not lazy, I don't believe—but it wasn't in me to do heavy farm work, and I told my uncle so. He didn't care much; I was bleeding at the lungs by that time and not much good to anybody. I said good-by to my aunt, who was always like a mother to me, ran away and joined a party of emigrants headed for the mountains.

"A boy of fifteen gets a good many bumps on the trail. I paid for my experience, as all boys do. I fell in with Tracy. He was the first man I met in the high country who didn't try to get the best of me. I drifted here and there with him, but I always had in mind to hunt up Colonel Roper and tell him my mother's story after she left. In fact, my mother asked me to promise to do that much, and I had promised.

"I found him at the fort again—he had been sent back there. I called on him. I told him who I was. He flew into a rage and said my mother and her babies perished in the blizzard that set in the day they left the fort, and told me I was an impostor—that's what I got, gentlemen, when I was less than sixteen, from my own grandfather! Tracy made the trip up to the fort with me. I'd told Tracy that if my grandfather would take me I should quit him. He agreed that would be right.

"I'd thought the old wretch might have softened with the years; my mother told me he would; Tracy said he would—that it wasn't in human nature to act the way he was acting forever. He has a fine manner, you know —when I first went in he talked so nice I hoped he might ask me to stay. But when he heard my story—well, you know the rest.

"I told him I'd come back some day and make him eat his words. He ordered me off the reservation. Tracy and his deck of cards were waiting for me; I dropped my father's name and took my mother's—here I am.

"You know how I struck it a few years ago at Thief River. Dave Tracy was down and out. He thought if he could get a house started here, he could get on his feet. I backed him—why shouldn't I? When we took the trail, I slept under his blanket."

CHAPTER XIX

PARDALOE TURNS DIPLOMAT

GENERAL ROPER waited only till he was able to travel to go west with his location engineers. He said very little to Wentworth before he started; only that when he came back he would have a talk with Selwood.

Wentworth himself spent the week between Sleepy Cat and Thief River, disturbed only and surprised by Selwood's resignation as superintendent of the freighting line. It required all of Wentworth's and Carpy's powers of persuasion to induce him to hold on till an acceptable successor could be found—a difficulty in the circumstances, inasmuch as Wentworth had a pretty good idea of what would happen to his mules if a man less dreaded than Selwood were put at the head of the line in Sleepy Cat.

But, while Selwood was tractable, he was determined, and he stubbornly refused to "sign up"—at an increased salary and the promise that his duties should be only nominal—for another year. Neither Doctor Carpy, despite his blunt common sense, nor Wentworth, the long-headed master of frontier transportation, was capable of analyzing the mystery of the change that had come over Selwood. They wrongly surmised that his settled moodiness was due to the fresh outbreak of his grievance against his grandfather; had they been as close to Selwood as Bill Pardaloe was, and as good an observer, they would have known that less than a hundred pounds of Sleepy Cat femininity had wrecked his good nature, his optimism, and his peace of mind.

When they saw him finish, with libations of wine, the

recital of his family wrongs, they did not realize that he would likewise have been glad to drown all recollection of the last scene he ever expected to have with Christie Fyler. Moreover, Selwood, of a sort that habitually suppressed emotion, was the harder to know and understand; it was his business to mask his feelings. Bill Pardaloe, watching Selwood unobserved, knew better than to ask questions, but he himself had a soft spot in his heart for Christie, and though his duties no longer took him to the store, where Fyler's business was dwindling, Bill made it a point to drop around at times and see what he could see and hear what he could hear.

He always lounged into the store in the same manner —with the fingers of one long, ungainly hand resting on the haft of his bowie knife, stuck at his hip, and with his arms free for action. Invariably, too, with his head poked inquiringly forward—which set his long nose well ahead of his centre of gravity; with the corners of his mouth pulled down to suit his pessimistic mood, and with his small, piercing eyes wide open with suspicious gloom.

Nobody, by any chance, ever saw anything as cheerful as a cigar or a pipe in Bill's mouth—the only thing he could be accused of carrying regularly was a pack of cards so greasy that it was no longer possible in the light of a camp-fire to tell Bill's thumb-prints from the pips or the kings from the queens—and with the missing nine of diamonds replaced by a card photograph of General Grant. If dispute arose as to whether a face card was the knave of clubs or the queen of hearts, Bill Pardaloe decided this and like questions of identity, himself—on the ground that having carried the pack three years in the army, he ought to know it better than any expurgated stranger playing with him could possibly know it—and though his companions of the moment might never engage in play with him the second time, his decisions were more or less gracefully accepted. A chance companion to the cards, in another pocket, was an occasional flat bottle, to serve on the dusty road at points where desert water was reported to be impregnated with arsenic. But a pocket bottle was not a favorite equipment with Bill, who held that it was no more than an irritant; he preferred a jug somewhere about the wagon, and particularly where outsiders could not "locate" it.

Such a man would hardly be expected to make much of a hit with Christie Fyler. Yet Bill Pardaloe came to stand higher in her favor than any frontiersman in Sleepy Cat. Honesty underlay his crudeness, his great strength inspired respect, and Christie, with a woman's instinct budded on a girl's heart, liked him. When free to express herself, she naturally bubbled with humor, and Bill was fun; she liked to laugh at him, and he apparently did not object to being laughed at—by Christie; his gloom—like her seriousness—could be penetrated.

When Pardaloe could find Christie alone in the store he was happy. Fyler he detested as the man who had sold him an overcoat that fell to pieces in the first shower, and Big Haynes—like all mock-auction men— was a suspicious personage.

A fortnight had gone by since Christie dismissed Selwood, when Pardaloe, puzzled by the gambler's behavior and looking for some explanation, dropped in on Christie.

He stamped heavily up Fyler's steps one sunny morning. Christie was in the middle of the store with a feather duster in her hand when he arrested her attention. He did not know why her greeting was so very cordial that morning; but next to seeing the man she wanted to see and did not want to see, she was delighted

to welcome Bill—to see him was closest to seeing Selwood, anyway.

She laughed heartily at the condition of his boots.
"Bill," she exclaimed, "if you don't take some time off
and black those boots I won't speak to you again.
Honestly, Bill," she asked in pleading tones, "did you
ever black those boots?"

Pardaloe grinned; every time Christie said "Bill" he
melted like a roll of butter. "Christie, when I was in
the army I had t' black my boots every day. I swore
if I ever got out I'd never black a pair of boots again in
my life—'n', by cracky, I' kep' my word, too."

"But, Bill, wouldn't you break your word—just once
—for me?"

Pardaloe looked at his dust-covered footings, shifted
his cud, and countered craftily. "What difference would
it make to you?"

"Why"—Christie, nonplussed for an instant, looked
up innocently—"it would cheer me up so, Bill—I'm
blue!" And Christie laughed.

Pardaloe followed what looked like a trail. "What
you blue about?" he asked shrewdly.

"Oh—I don't know—can you tell whatever makes
you blue?"

Pardaloe swung up on the counter and sat down like
one at home. "I ain't blue," he retorted, bending his
beady eyes closely on the evasive Christie.

"I should be," she said demurely, "if I had to wear
boots like that." Her eyes covered the offenders re-
provingly.

"That's the pair of boots John Selwood give me the
day he booted the town. Them's opera boots. Happy
days them, in Sleepy Cat! Sleepy Cat ain't like that
any more. They just cold-blooded murdered a man
down street last night, again."

"*Bill!* What's going to become of this awful town?"

"Say, Christie," asked Pardaloe, taking a piece of plug tobacco from his pocket, "what's a-matter 'tween you and John Selwood?"

The shock to Christie was perfectly hidden in her astonishment. She opened her eyes as if inviting the most rigorous inspection. "Why, nothing! Why do you ask that? At least," she went on—and then a little hateful telltale color rose, "nothing that I know of— why, Bill?"

Pardaloe, having discharged his fowling piece, chewed his fresh morsel of tobacco into place, looking no longer at Christie but at the floor somewhat to one side of her, his mouth drawn down to a gloomy curve. "He don't come here no more," he observed at length.

Christie wavered. "Why, yes, I think he does, doesn't he?"

"When did you see him?"

"I can't remember just when—but he may have been here to see my father when I was out."

At this barefaced assertion Pardaloe's face took on an expression nothing less than painful. He tried to writhe —for he knew Selwood felt about as devoted to Fyler as he did—but he knew also that he was on delicate ground. He only chewed hard, looked hard at the floor, and repeated under the added gloom: "He don't come here no more."

Christie tossed her head. "Well, he's a very busy man, and, of course, has lots of friends besides us——"

Pardaloe groped steadily ahead. "Are you his friend?" he asked with nasal skepticism.

She professed astonishment. "Why, yes, I hope so. Bill"—Christie raised her voice—"what are you asking all these questions for?" Then a panic seized her. "What do you mean, Bill? Is Selwood hurt? Oh! Who was the man killed last night?"

For an instant the book of her woman's heart lay open before the big fellow—her look of sudden, deadly fear. Bill had a pretty good idea now.

He shook his head to her questions. "No, no—that hadn't a thing on earth to do with John Selwood—do you suppose I'd be a-settin' here if it had? Nothing like that at all, Christie. But what's wrong 'tween you and John?"

Pardaloe was treading on thin ice for a mule boss; and among the dangers he had not counted on was the reaction in a woman's feelings after she has betrayed her secret.

With a flush of anger Christie suddenly chilled. "I'm sure I've no idea what you're talking about, Bill. And it's very silly to keep on talking about it." So saying, Christie became very busy with her dry-goods and left Pardaloe sitting on the counter looking after her retreating heels and studying the floor with even more than his habitual concentration.

But he was not easily discouraged. Having thought seriously over the situation and braced himself slightly for a second attempt, Pardaloe returned to the store an hour later to straighten "the girl's"—for so he called Christie—troubles out.

"Christie," he insisted gravely, "it ain't no use our beatin' around the bush. There's trouble 'tween you and John—" She protested, denied, interrupted—it was all one. Pardaloe probed until poor Christie took refuge in a woman's last weapon—tears. This argument threatened to reduce Pardaloe to the same state, but it cleared the atmosphere, and Christie, touched by his honest interest, told him the story of the scene between Starbuck and Selwood and herself that eventful morning in the store. "It wouldn't have been so bad," trembled Christie, grieved and resentful, "if he had even tried to explain or excuse it——"

Pardaloe tried to effect a diversion by abusing Starbuck; it made no impression on Christie. She cared nothing about how bad Starbuck was, but a great deal about Selwood's reputation and calling. "He said himself," she murmured in final reproach of Selwood and his pleader, "he was just a common gambler."

This seemed to give Pardaloe a favorable opening. "Dash it," he thundered, not loud, but deep in his reverberations, "he *ain't* no *common* gambler. There's no man on the Overland Trail dast set up against him in a game of poker all night—if he *wants to play*. I tell y'—I know—I've tried it. Lately, I'll admit, he's fallin' off. I admit it—he don't seem to take no more interest in his game like he used to. But I want to tell *you*, John Selwood is strong as a bear in a game when he's all there —eye true and hand sure. And straight as an axe-helve everywhere and all the time. And why he can't talk up to you, Christie, is because, dash it, he's in love with you—that's why. I tell y'. I'm a married man, Christie, 'n' I understand such things."

She refused to hear another word, and Pardaloe went away not exactly knowing whether he had helped his favorite young man in Sleepy Cat or hurt him by extolling his technical skill.

Selwood slept later than usual that day. After his solitary meal in the dining-room, he went down to the barn, where Carpy found him later and took him to the Doctor's office in the hotel. There he sat for some time with Selwood in serious confab. "I'll agree, John," he said, countering a contemptuous remark of Selwood's, "there's been a good deal of loose Vigilante talk here, different times. But this time it isn't going to stop with talk. This town's got the worst reputation in the mountains."

"Whom are they going to clean it up with?" demanded Selwood contemptuously. "These old Indian traders—Roubidoux, Van Tambel, Otto Kickbusch—and the real estate boomers? I want to tell you it's a man's job to clean out Starbuck and Atkins's crowd."

"Well"—Carpy hesitated and summoned a twinkling smile—"they thought maybe you might take a small personal interest in the enterprise——"

"I shan't," declared Selwood without hesitation, "and you can tell 'em so."

"You certainly don't owe them river rats anything," declared Carpy with indignation.

"No," returned Selwood decisively. "But I'm getting to be a pretty fair hand at minding my own business."

"The drift now," continued Carpy, "is that if the town ain't cleaned up, the railroad will go clean around it and leave us out in the cold. The real estate men here say their business is ruined—it's got so bad folks is afraid to buy property."

Selwood was in a bad humor. "These bond crooks and town-lot boomers are the biggest bunch of thieves in Sleepy Cat," he declared, with unvarying contempt.

"I know it, John," persisted Carpy, patiently—and he could be very patient when he wanted to gain his end. "But boomers need live men to sell town lots to—a dead man is no good to a real estate agent. And it's getting so settlers are afraid to stay in Sleepy Cat overnight. Why, these river thugs go right into the emigrant camp and pull men out. Last night they killed a man, not ten rods from Dave Tracy's tent. Then there's the merchants—John Cole says if this keeps up they might as well shut up shop and ship their goods to Bear Dance or Medicine Bend."

"Well," exclaimed Selwood with an impatient expletive, "let 'em clean the town up. Clean it up—I've no objection."

"I can't say all's in my mind, John, without betray-

ing confidences. But things is set. This is Saturday
night, and on Saturday night, you know, every cattle-
thief and horse-thief from Calabasas comes to town for
a spree. To-night they'll all get in; but they won't
many get out. They're going to finish with every black-
leg and dive-keeper, bad man and gambler in this town
within the next twenty-four hours—that's exactly what's
coming."

Selwood bent a piercing look on his informant. "Does
that include me, Doc?"

"There's no objection to the way you run your place,
John—if yours was the only place or the other places
were like yours. And you'll have friends among the
Vigilantes, anyway. But when the thing starts there
won't be no fine lines drawn, John; you know that,"
continued the Doctor, trying to convey his warning in-
offensively, "and there may be mistakes when the torch
gets going. My advice is for you to pull out till this
thing blows over, and come back when you feel like it."

Selwood rose as to end the talk. Carpy had seen him
angry more than once, but never had he seen the mild-
mannered gambler enraged. Restraint was thrown to
the winds. He could no longer be talked to, no longer
be reasoned with. But in language so violent that he
would have been ashamed of it in cooler moments, he
expressed his opinion of all Vigilantes in general and
Sleepy Cat Vigilantes in particular. Carpy tried to interrupt, tried to listen, tried to calm him down—all was
useless.

"Dash it, John," he exclaimed at length, testy himself, "if I'm nothing else, I'm your doctor—hold on!"

"I expect to hold on," retorted Selwood rudely. "Tell
your Vigilantes they'll find me on the hill. And tell 'em
to come 'fixed,' for some of 'em will stay there with me."

It was his manner even more than his words that discouraged Carpy. There was not a hope of compromise in his determined resolve to resist to the end; and it seemed well-nigh hopeless to try to avert a tragedy. Carpy shrugged his shoulders. "You're your own boss, John," he said resignedly. "Do as you blamed please— I'm only trying to say what's right between friends."

"I *was* fixing to get out of this accursed town," interposed Selwood grimly. "It's no good to me—it never was any good to any white man. But if they want to drive me out—well, I'll go! But I'll take some of that bunch with me."

"Here's another thing I want you to think of, John," resumed Carpy, who was pertinacious. "What about Dave Tracy in all this? You'll have your fight—you'll damage some Vigilantes; maybe some of 'em your own friends; maybe get damaged yourself. Even supposing you make your getaway, what about Dave? He's helpless. How should you feel, John, if Dave was dragged out and strung up with that river bunch? Don't you owe it to Dave to get him out of the way before this thing begins?"

It was Carpy's last shot, and he had held it back till the brainstorm was somewhat abated. The suggestion came like a blow to Selwood. It struck home. Selwood had forgotten his wounded partner. His mind worked fast. He looked at Carpy—but not with less determination. "You're right," he said tersely. "I'll get Dave into the clear. But I'll be back on the hill by the time your friends get started."

He rose, very angry, to go; then he turned suddenly on the Doctor. "There's one thing I'll ask of you, Doc; while I'm getting Dave away, I want you to promise me to see that no harm comes to Christie Fyler——"

"John, I'll see to that if it's the last thing on earth I see to."

"I don't care much about her father—he's no protection to her; but he's her father, and no harm must come to him in this mix-up, either."

"You've got my word, John."

CHAPTER XX

MOVES AND COUNTERMOVES

THE Vigilante movement started in Sleepy Cat after the manner of a thunderstorm—with rumblings echoing faintly in the mountains and harmless-looking clouds gathering just out of sight, for a holiday. But the innocent clouds draw closer together and peeping over the range rise higher and higher till they frown with heads black as a hangman's cap above the Rat River Valley. Wicked flashes tear across the sky. Sharp crashes shake the gorges. Then, with all pretense cast away, they roll down together in a single deadly front, surcharged with lightning and seething with thunder. Only a moment and they were hanging above the peaks—now, with the roar of an avalanche, they twist the tree-tops. They loose a sudden flood on the helpless landscape, drenching hill and hollow. They strike with maddened bolts at man and tree and beast, their reverberations blend in a continuing roar, and their waters tossed by shrieking winds fall on the defenseless earth in blinding sheets and thundering cataracts.

Selwood was not a man to let his anger override his common sense for long. Most of all, the helpless condition of Tracy, like a relentless curb on a wilful horse, forced him to consider what must be done to save him from the mob fury. None knew better than Selwood what would be let loose when the fight started. He knew the men on both sides of the town and knew that once under way there would be no quarter for anybody—that behind the masks there would be more than one personal score to even up, regardless of right or justice; that there would be, in that mob, personal malice set on personal vengeance, and that Carpy's warning could not be disregarded.

Christie, on that fateful afternoon, moved about in her affairs quite unsuspecting any impending events. She had been in the habit for some time of visiting Tracy in the sick-tent and taking him such little delicacies as her ingenuity could supply. She realized how close he was to Selwood, and whoever was a trusted friend of Selwood's Christie, somehow, liked.

Pardaloe, feeling that help was needed in his efforts to straighten out the differences that kept Selwood and Christie apart, had taken Tracy into his confidence, and the old man was ready to do what he could to help.

On this Saturday afternoon he held Christie for a little chat, and as soon as he could introduced the delicate subject that Pardaloe had already broached to her.

"Bill Pardaloe," he went on, continuing his remarks, "said you was afraid of Selwood because you thought he was a gambler."

Christie's eyes fell—she would not comment on it; besides, Tracy himself was a gambler. "Mr. Pardaloe," she said impatiently, "says a great many things about matters that don't concern him—or anybody else, for that matter. How is your back to-day, Mr. Tracy?"

Tracy was not so easily thrown off. He said what he wanted to say. "I don't call Selwood a gambler—and I've been trying long enough to make him one. He ain't built for the business. The ice is too thin around his heart. Any old woman can come along to him with a tale of woe and he'll upset the whole durn town over it. He's fillin' in for me, at my place up on the hill," explained Tracy defensively, "that's about all."

"Why, with hands like them," he went on, in honest admiration at the thought, "that man has got more money in his finger-tips than's ever been panned out of Thief River. But he won't use 'em! Says he'll play square or he won't play at all! Nuthin' but a dum fool, in my opinion. I never seen such fingers on a poker table. Christie, did you ever see him tear a pack of cards in two, when he's mad? Didn't, eh? Well, he's got a grip like a grizzly in them paws. They ain't so awful big; but long and wiry."

Selwood, knowing nothing of the well-meant if misdirected activities of his two crude but stanch defenders, started for the horse barn, after Carpy's talk, and for Tracy's tent, reflecting that with Tracy himself he should have a delicate job on his hands; to induce the old man to move at all would be a triumph. He stopped at the warehouse first. John Lefever, whistling softly, sat in the shade of a freight wagon near the door, cleaning a revolver. The circumstance was merely coincident with Carpy's warning, but in Selwood's frame of mind it was a jar to his sensibilities. He told the wagon boss, briefly, what he had heard and what to do. "If there's going to be trouble here I don't want to get caught with a warehouse full of goods unprotected," he said to Lefever. "Get hold of every teamster we've got in town and hold every man here to protect company property. Work fast."

"I'll have 'em all rounded up in half an hour by the watch," returned Lefever. "What are you going to do, yourself, John?"

It was the second time Selwood had been asked the question. He did not know; but he flung some kind of an answer to the wagon boss, and crossed the street to the barn. McAlpin, in the front gangway, was washing a harness. Touching his hat—for his old-world manners still persisted in the Rocky Mountains—and wiping his hands on his trousers, the barn boss stood at attention.

Selwood's orders were brief. "Get up a team of saddle horses, Jim. Hitch 'em to the light democrat wagon —the one that's covered——"

"'The one that's covered,'" echoed McAlpin, his eyes glued on his boss.

"Muzzle Chloe carefully and put her under the seat. And give me the best team in the barn that's saddle broke——"

"Nance and Jim," interposed McAlpin, not losing a syllable between winks, "and they're crazy to go."

"Saddle my horse," added Selwood, "and put a couple of good saddles into the wagon, fill the bed pretty well with hay, and throw a couple of clean army blankets over it. Put in two canteens and enough food for four of us, two days." Pardaloe walked up from the stalls. "Get hold of Bob Scott, Bill," said Selwood to the mule boss. "I want to use him right away. He'll drive," explained Selwood to McAlpin. "And as soon as you find Scott," added Selwood to Pardaloe, "report to me at Tracy's tent. But don't talk before Dave—work quick, will you, Bill?"

Pardaloe hobbled briskly out after Scott, and Selwood spoke again to McAlpin. "I suppose you've heard this talk that's going around?" Selwood eyed the barn boss in sharply inquisitive fashion.

"Vigilantes?"

"They've been talking a good while," continued Selwood, purposely ignoring particulars, "but Dave must be taken where he'll be safe."

"He must, John."

"If things should get going we'll have our hands full looking after company property."

"You'll be going with Dave?"

"I'll be back sometime in the night," returned Selwood, evasively. "You've nothing to fear, McAlpin.

If things start, get the hostlers together—you've got guns and ammunition."

McAlpin, as Selwood walked away, flung one question after him. Just the question Selwood did not want to hear: "What'll you be doing, John?"

Selwood chopped him off. "Whatever's to be done !" he answered, snappishly.

He turned down the path to the tent quarter. Gamblers are fatalists, and, to the extent that temperament fits them to practise their philosophy, meet with coldness situations that give pause to other men.

McAlpin scratched his head as he studied the retreating footsteps of his taciturn boss; he had ventured one question. But he had forty questions that were burning the tip of his tongue, yet, without further courage to ask one of them, he saw Selwood depart—experience had taught him that no matter how many questions he put, he would get nothing pertinent in answer from John Selwood; that when Selwood was ready to answer such questions he would answer without being asked.

Who would lead the Vigilantes; how far they intended to go in their clean-up; when they meant to strike first and where; whether they could handle Starbuck and Atkins and their friends—for whose prowess McAlpin had a sneaking and canny respect; just where Selwood would come in in the fight; what measures he would take for his own safety; and lastly, what was to become of the big place on the hill that had cost so much money— these queries the Scotchman revolved rapidly in his mind, until Selwood, treading the path lightly and with the briskness of unreckoning manhood, turned the first corner and disappeared from view. But fate, greatest of all gamblers, quite understood how to upset a poise indifferent to the threats of men; just as Selwood turned the corner it presented to him, almost threw into his arms—rounding the corner from the other way and walking as briskly as he was—Christie Fyler.

She started visibly—as he did invisibly. Then in the suddenness of the encounter Selwood—never quick to adjust himself to meeting the woman whose mere glance could upset him—stiffly, almost ostentatiously, stepped aside, touched his hat, and hurried on a little faster. But after that, with his heart beating harder, he began to think and to surmise and to question himself and, of course, to regret. Their eyes, in this sudden and unexpected way, had met. It was only an instant, but the picture came back to him now of a sad expression in Christie's eyes—sad, at least, until she woke up and realized that she had run into Selwood, and then her eyes had quickly dropped; she had passed on.

It was his fault, he told himself. He had not even hesitated—he might have given her time to speak. Instead, he had stridden past even as she was looking at him. He cursed his stiffness and contemptible pride for not having given her even an opportunity at such a time —a time pregnant with threatening possibilities for them both as well as for Sleepy Cat. He longed for a chance to meet her over again; still, his vanity would not allow him to turn back. So—while Christie was reproaching herself for not making the quick advance she wanted to make and now felt it had been her place to make when she saw the only man's face in the world that meant anything to her—both, unhappy, passed on, little reckoning of when and where they should meet again.

Selwood quite knew that his mission to Tracy would call for tact. He sat down on a camp stool beside his friend, and after a few conventional passes opened the one subject of his visit with an abrupt question. "Dave, how much do you figure you've got in our Sleepy Cat place? Whatever it is," he continued, as Tracy dis-

claimed any equitable interest in the hall that Selwood
had paid for, "I'll trade you my interest in the Thief
River mine for your interest up at Sleepy Cat."

Tracy was taken aback. "What you tryin' to do?"
he asked presently. "Rob me or rob yourself?"

"I'm trying to rob you."

"Well, you're a long way from doing it. The mine's
worth half a dozen of our Sleepy Cat outfit."

"Then," said Selwood definitely, "the hall's mine
and the mine's yours. Is it a go?"

"Why, if you want it that way, yes—it is."

"All right. That's settled. Carpy," continued Selwood, "thinks this place is getting too noisy for you,
Dave. All these squatters coming in, and the clatter
they make. He says you'll do better out under the
pines a few miles up river, and I've got things arranged
to get you up there to-day. The weather's settled now,
and I've got time to move you—what do you say we
start to-day?"

Tracy scrutinized him. The old man's eyes were cavernous, but they were very much alive. Selwood well
knew he himself might be riding to an indifferent con-
sent or to a stubborn refusal. But he held on against
the cryptic silence, giving the wounded man the details
of his arrangements without revealing any of the anxiety
that underlay his methodical manner. When he had
done, Tracy shot an abrupt question at him. "You
didn't say anything about that this morning. What's
up?" he asked testily.

"Carpy didn't say anything about changing you till
an hour ago."

"I know where I'm comfortable, better than Carpy
does. I'll stay here."

Selwood, with patience, continued to dwell on the ad-
vantages of country life. But the old soldier resisted all

blandishments, and in the end his patience gave out first. "Look here, John," he exclaimed with a snap of disgust, "you're beating round the bush, like these crooked Sleepy Cat lawyers. I know what's going on, if I am flat on my back. The Vigilantes are ready to move."

Selwood met disgust with disgust. "Where did you get that story?"

"McAlpin."

"Hang McAlpin!" said Selwood fervently.

"You're trying to get me into the clear——"

"I hope that's no crime!" exclaimed Selwood, imbibing his wounded partner's impatience.

Tracy, raising himself half way on his elbow, eyed Selwood from his cot. "Where did you get the idea I was afraid of Vigilantes?"

Selwood shrugged his shoulders. "Where did you get the idea I thought you were?"

"Well, you're trying to ship me out of town—you and Carpy. Now, John, I'm not going—that's flat—not for all the Vigilantes in the Rocky Mountains."

As Tracy uttered his declaration, Bill Pardaloe, like a huge camel, stuck his head within the tent. The defiance seemed to stimulate him, for he worked his body inside the flap and standing half bent over to escape the ridge-pole, stood at attention, listening but holding his peace.

Selwood, paying no further attention to the intruder, vainly tried in low tones to persuade Tracy it would be sheer folly to remain where he was. He reminded Tracy of his helpless condition and of what his obstinacy might mean; he begged him to consider his—Selwood's—feelings, if there were none of his own to move him. The old gambler proved adamant to every consideration, and, not only that, he grew more and more set against all proposals. "John," he exclaimed, raging like a grizzly at bay, "are you running, too?"

"You know very well, Dave, there's a heap of difference between a well man's running and a wounded man's being carried out of the way of a fight."

"You going to stay?"

"There's no reason why I shouldn't."

"And fight?"

"Nobody will miss me if I do fight."

"If you stay, there's just one answer—you get killed," said Tracy. "Dash you, I know you better than you know yourself. Now, John, listen." The old man, gray, grizzled, unshaven, hollow-eyed, but stern, his iron-gray hair falling in a great mat over his wrinkled forehead, sat bolt upright on his cot. He tore open the breast of the coarse shirt he wore—his only upper garment—and pointed to an American flag, tattooed over his heart.

Selwood sat with the eyes of youth silently fixed on his country's emblem. Bill Pardaloe stepped closer in, craned his neck forward, pulled off his tattered hat to get still closer, and peered dumbly at the tattooed breast. It was a sight to see the grizzled mountaineer staring at the familiar symbol, pricked close as flesh and blood could bring it to the old soldier's heart; but his motionless silence paid the utmost tribute of mountain manhood to the flag, stamped on the heart of a man who had given the best in him to defend it. Bill Pardaloe, lifting his eyes from the flag to Tracy's eyes, drew his head slowly back, pulled himself up, looked about for a place to relieve his overcharged jaws, and, finding none, respectably restrained his impulse and chewed on in silence.

Tracy spoke to Selwood. "John, I don't say I've never done anything to disgrace it," he went on, "but I fought for that old flag nigh three year. I tramped down the Peninsula with McClellan, and double-quicked back again; I stood, best I could, against Pickett at Gettysburg, with George Meade; I went up against the Bloody Angle in the Wilderness with Grant. It don't mean a continental to a lot of folks nowadays, but it means something to me yet. Does anything you've ever seen me do, John, look to you as if I'd run from a blamed parcel of Vigilante crooks? I'll admit I'm no saint, I'm no preacher——"

"You're preaching right now, Dave."

"Then, damn it, let me preach—but the worst I've ever done was to invite a man to back his luck against mine. I've played crooked with crooks, I'll admit it, but no honest man can say I've ever stacked a deck against him—I took my chances, same as he took his.

"Now, a parcel of Vigilantes threaten to hang me—I know, same's if you'd told me. Well and good; there'll be lawyer sharks and land sharks and cattle sharks and mine sharks in that bunch—along, I'll admit it, with decent men and honest men. But that don't give them no right to hang me for a gambler. I left the best of my life in health and strength down on the Jim River for this old flag—that's why I can't put up a man's fight to-day—" He bared his right breast. There was a gap in it in which you could lay a hen's egg. "A Johnny Reb shell took that lung, John——" He tore open, with fierceness, the shirt sleeve of his left arm—"a minie ball splintered that arm, John—you know it's no good. It wasn't that fight with Frank Sanger that did for me. I was done for in the Wilderness and came out with no health to earn a living, and here I am—and not sorry for it. Well, they can hang me. But it'll be done after I'm dead. And then," he muttered with satisfaction, "the blamed skunks have got to hang the old flag with me. I tell you again, I don't say I've never done nothing to disgrace it. I don't say I'm proud of winding up as a gambler. But things is as they is. And if this is my last stand—why, it's all right."

He reached his hand out toward the tent pole. "Gi' me my gun, Bill." With Selwood sitting in silence, Pardaloe lifted from the nail on which it hung by the scabbard an old Colt's army revolver. Tracy took it almost affectionately. "Leave this with me," he said, falling back on his frowsy pillow. "Bring me a couple dozen ca'tridges—that'll be all I need."

Selwood smiled. "More'n you'll need, Dave," he said, quite undisturbed.

Selwood continued to smile; not mirthfully—seriously, rather. He just studied the mumbling old gladiator—half toothless, laid low after many a stout fight—stiffened in joint, frayed in nerve, caressing the old gun with a shaking hand, so enfeebled he could with difficulty hold up his head, and with only the gray eyes flashing the old fire as he hurled defiance at his enemies—it was not a cheerful picture! No home to die in; no woman to be tender with his pain or patient with his irascibility; no child's kiss to close the weary day—just a human derelict, cast by the storm and wave of civilization on its outermost shore—such was Dave Tracy.

"What you looking at me that way for, John?" demanded the old gambler peevishly.

"Nothing, Dave, nothing—just thinking. I'll be back again." He rose as he spoke. Pardaloe peered—as if in farewell—at Tracy and pushed his way outside. "See here," exclaimed Tracy, detaining Selwood. "You 'n' me's been partners, ain't we?"

"You picked me off the trail."

"You say you're stayin'. You talk about my getting killed — how d'y' suppose I'd feel if you got killed?"

Selwood laughed lightly. "It's what's comin' to both of us, I guess, Dave."

"Carry me up the hill to the hall, you and Pardaloe; I'll stay and you go."

Selwood shook his head with a smile—but not a yielding smile.

"Carry me up the hill, then, 'n' we'll both stay! We been partners in life—let's play it out together!"

Selwood stood half laughing, half smiling at the old soldier's plea, but shaking his head.

"Bull-headed as hell," muttered Tracy, discouraged. "Always was, always will be. I'd a blamed sight better be defending the hall than you. I'm no loss to anybody on earth——"

"Neither am I, Dave."

"What about the girl that brings me soup two and three times a week? What's she bringing it to me for? What did she bring me an apple for to-day? Because she thinks a lot of *me*—or *you?*"

Selwood winced. "Because she's kind-hearted," he said irritably. "Don't talk nonsense." But he was red in the face.

Tracy followed up sharply. "It's *you*, Selwood—not me—you. I don't have to be told what a girl's thinking when she'll set right there where you're settin' now, and listen as long as I'll talk about *you*."

Selwood shrugged his shoulders. "You're wasting your breath to talk about me." He flung out of the tent in no very pleasant frame of mind.

The valley, the river, and the flats were in shadow when Selwood stepped outside. The sun was sinking behind Sleepy Cat Mountain. He looked across the river. Well out on the Sinks dust rose lazily from a line of freight wagons heading south. Turning up street, Selwood's eyes fell on the hill, where the front windows of the big gambling-house burned in the glow of the sunset. Busy with his thoughts, he reached the barn, spoke to Scott, who stood in the doorway, directed him to bring Pardaloe with him as soon as it was dark, and, making sure that all ordered was in readiness, Selwood walked on up the hill.

CHAPTER XXI

THE RIVER BRIDGE

It was two hours yet to opening time. He unlocked the front door of the hall. The interior had never seemed ghostly before. He stood, surveying for a moment the array of dead tables and deserted wheels—thinking of the difference between the silent gloom of the empty dust and the boisterous crush of the middle night, with its glare and oaths and play.

Selwood, conscious of the echo of his own footfalls, crossed the room to his office, unlocked the door, entered, locked it behind him, sat down at his desk, unlocked it, and pulled open a drawer in which he kept his stock of ammunition. He drew from the breast harness, in which he carried it, his revolver and laying it on the desk, turned his attention to the drawer. Besides the boxes of cartridges and cleaning implements there were in it two cartridge belts and two Colt's revolvers. These latter were extras, one of them Tracy's and one his own. They were fitted with mother-of-pearl grips and finished more as show guns than the plainer everyday revolver of the same calibre that Selwood carried. There was still daylight enough for his purpose, and Selwood, taking first his own gun on the desk and in turn the two guns in the drawer, began the task of taking down, cleaning, and assembling the three.

It gave him plenty of time to think. Never in his life had he been in just such a position—faced just such a night. The frontier brawl is not advertised in advance. No stage is set for the death duel of sixty seconds in a crowded room. Apprehension, anticipation have only a minor place in the minds of men who know they must always and everywhere be ready for the instant appeal to mountain law.

This situation was strikingly different. Warning had come—his defiance had answered it—at least, for John Selwood. He had been told what to expect; he had said how he should meet it; there remained only the question of how far twelve cartridges loaded into two guns expressly for this occasion would carry him after the opening shot.

It was too much to hope that he should live to fire them all, and he fell to speculating on how many loaded cartridges would be found in the two guns when they picked him up. It enraged him to think of being cornered by Vigilantes; and escape now was so easy—and always there was Christie in the background of his thinking. But his word had been passed—whether foolishly or not, was beside the question. He had told the "real estate boomers" where they would find him.

Darkness was falling while he worked—the swift darkness of the high mountain valleys. In the street he heard a beating of hoofs and a chorus of whooping yells from horsemen heading down-town on a drunken spree. In the failing light he counted at one time through his window four men clattering along the street. Carpy's words came back to him: "It's Saturday night. All the Calabasas horse-thieves ride into town for a spree. They'll all get in. But they won't many get out."

He did not know the men—he only knew that in their company a skeleton horseman, astride a skeleton steed, galloped noiselessly ahead; that Death that night would slink, an invisible guest, in with these men as they lined up at the bar; unbidden, would sit that night with them at their tables and stake their evil lives against the caprice of frontier fate—as, indeed, he had already, for that night, staked John Selwood's.

He picked up, last of his job, the cartridge belt. It was too dark to see, but it was easy to feel with the fingers of one hand for the cartridges in the box, while in the other he held the belt and felt for the empty spaces to slip the brass slugs into place. Then he went patiently over the belt again, slipping it carefully through his fingers until he was sure every space had been filled. If he should never leave the hall, the supply would make little difference; but while a man may choose where his fight shall open, who can say where it will end? And with the thrift of Robinson Crusoe, he emptied a handful of cartridges into his trousers pocket, rose, buckled the belt about his waist, slipped the show gun into the holster and the plain gun into the breast harness. As he did this, he heard a loud knock at the outer door. It startled him; then he remembered that he had told Scott to bring Pardaloe to him as soon as it was dark.

He walked to the front door; the two men were there. While Pardaloe lighted up, Selwood, standing at the door, listened to Scott's report of the situation.

The street down below was unnaturally quiet. Not a store was lighted, not a man was in sight. Only toward the river were there lights and the ordinary noises of Saturday night carousing.

Bob Scott bared his tobacco-stained teeth as he smiled his report to Selwood. "They've put men on all the roads out of town except the upper river road. I guess the idea is to stop all the birds that try to fly the coop to-night. And they figured no one from Calabasas would be leaving town till pretty late, anyway." Pardaloe joined the two men. Selwood listened to all that was said and asked whether the team and horses were ready. Pardaloe had come straight from the barn. His eyes, set rather harder than usual with the prospects of the night, appeared closer, if possible, together, and glowed with a deeper light; while if suspicion could more completely characterize his manner, it seemed now heightened, in view of coming events. "They're hitched, John," he said darkly, "chewin' their bits in two and tearin' up the planks right now in the gangway."

"I suppose you know," said Selwood, addressing both men, "I'm going to take Dave Tracy out of town. He's my partner; I'll never see him hurt while I'm alive. He refused to go, as you know, Bill," he said to Pardaloe, "and he's bullheaded enough to put up a scuffle rather than be dragged out. He couldn't stand anything like that, so I had to be patient. He doesn't drink, and he's suspicious as an Indian—so I lost the best time to get him away, and this is why the team stood hitched up so long.

"No matter. Carpy put a sleepy dose in Tracy's coffee to-night. By this time he should be under; I hope he is. But he's got to go now, whether he drank the coffee or not. I won't see him strung up on a telegraph pole, if I have to kill him to get him out of town."

He turned to the Indian. "Bob, there used to be a trail the other side of the river, toward the old beaver dam—do you suppose we can get through it in the dark?"

"How you going to get across the bridge?" asked Pardaloe grimly.

"I'll attend to that. You say the river road isn't guarded, anyway." Selwood addressed the words to Scott.

"It wasn't when I rode up from the west bridge. The trail will shake Dave some, but we can get over it if we can get to it."

Big Haynes loomed up out of the darkness. "What's up, boys?" he asked as he walked in and saw the three men in confab.

"We don't know yet," said Selwood. "But I'll be away for two or three hours. There's talk of trying to clean the town up to-night. Skillman is in Medicine Bend, and I leave you in charge of the place here, Haynes. If you find yourself in danger, tell your dealers to close their games without any discussion and put out the lights. I expect to be back before anything much happens. But if you have to run, get a good start—you're fat."

Haynes, fingering a gun as big as a toy cannon, looked hurt. "Who'm I going to run from, John?" He glared at Scott and Pardaloe as if to challenge any comment they might incline to make.

"Well, Ed," said Selwood calmly, "I don't know as to that, much more than you do. But if they do chase you, throw away that gun or you'll never make the foothills—let alone the mountains."

Big Haynes ignored all raillery. "You're putting this place in my charge, John, till you get back?" he asked, to confirm his understanding.

"I am."

"What time'll you be back?"

"If I'm not back by eleven o'clock, don't look for me."

Haynes straightened up. "I'll hold this place against all comers till twelve o'clock," he said composedly. "Give me a couple of good men," he added, nodding significantly toward Pardaloe and Scott, "and I'll hold this place against all the Vigilantes in Sleepy Cat!"

"I need a couple of good men, myself," replied Selwood drily. "I might send up Bull Page!"

Pardaloe's respect for the boss had restrained his comment on the situation and on the resolute defy of Big Haynes; only his nervous demeanor indicated his feelings. The shifting of his feet, the acceleration of his jaws, the lantern-nosed stare into Haynes's face, the depth of his expression as he turned his eyes on Bob Scott—language could have conveyed little more of skeptical disdain than Pardaloe managed to express without it.

Adding only a few details to his injunctions, Selwood, returning to his room, picked up a shot-bag full of loose cartridges, and leaving the place that embraced all his earthly possessions walked rapidly down to the barn, followed by Pardaloe and Scott. The big doors, open night and day, were closed. In the office a lantern flame in a dingy globe burned low on the table. As the street door was opened by Selwood, McAlpin rose from the fringe of darkness.

"Things are fixed," the barn boss half whispered, as the three men entered the office. "Two men are watching the back door; they've got a couple ten-gauge guns and plenty of buckshot cartridges—loaded 'em myself—five drams and plenty of buckshot. 'N' I've got two men asleep here in the office—just in at dark from Medicine Bend—drivin' all day, so I fed 'em and told 'em to take the bunks till I needed their services—they've got shotguns. John Lefever has got six more men over at the warehouse, all heeled, and more a-comin'. If they get us, John, they'll know we're here!"

A minute later, men with lanterns were moving up and down the barn gangway. The waiting team, freshly fed and watered, was hitched to the light wagon. Beside the wagon was an extra saddle-horse for Pardaloe; Selwood had mounted up. "John," whispered the barn boss, clasping Selwood's knee as he stood beside his horse, "what's the place to find you, if I need you?"

Selwood hesitated. "We're trying for the south trail up the river, but I doubt we'll ever make it. We'll either be up at the beaver dam, or, more likely, at Calabasas. If you come after me, try Calabasas first."

At a signal from Scott, who took the reins, McAlpin

threw open the doors, and Scott, with Pardaloe at his side, carrying his redoubtable shotgun, and Selwood on horseback, clattered out of the barn.

Selwood, with a lantern, entered Tracy's tent. The old soldier had drunk his coffee. He lay heavily asleep. Pardaloe, waiting, peered inside. Selwood motioned to him. The wagon was backed close up to the door, and the big fellow, passing inside the tent, loomed a moment in giant shadow from the lantern, while Selwood gathered up Tracy's belongings. Then, at a nod, Pardaloe picked Tracy, bedclothes and all, up in his arms and, with Selwood holding back the fly, carried him out and lifted him into the wagon.

The cot was lashed inside the wagon; the tent was struck and stowed beside it. In less than ten minutes the little cavalcade was headed as quietly as the restive horses would let them for the bridge. The wagon turned down the rather steep approach, with brakes scraping to ease the descent—and to avoid standing the wounded man on his head—with the horses fighting the bits and Pardaloe, his shotgun between his knees, staring into the darkness. Selwood pushed ahead on his horse to try the passage.

He reached the bridge only to be halted by two men, who stepped out of the dark on either side, covering him with shotguns.

Selwood halted his horse. "What is it, boys?"

"Can't cross this bridge."

"Why not?"

"Nobody can cross the bridges to-night without a bridge pass."

"Well, we don't want to cross both bridges; one is plenty. And we've got passes—good on all bridges, trails, and boulevards—but they're not the kind of passes we like to use on decent men. We're crossing this bridge to-night, boys, but we're willing to play fair. Where did all the shotguns come from?"

Scott had pulled up the team just at Selwood's back. With entire good-nature, Selwood bandied phrases with the two guards—they were ignorant enough to be stubborn and wholly unconscious of their own danger. "Don't stick your guns into my ribs," suggested Selwood pleasantly. "I'll get down and we'll talk this over."

"No, you don't get down!" exclaimed the brighter of the two Vigilantes. "Stick to your horse."

"How many of you are there?" asked Selwood unruffled.

"Plenty to hold this bridge."

"There are just two of you—if there were any more they'd all be poking their guns under a peaceable man's nose. Listen! There are four of us. If you say fight, it's a fight, but you haven't a ghost of a chance. And you're doing nobody any harm in letting us take a sick man out of the fight up-town to-night. I'm going out over this bridge and coming back, myself, over this bridge inside two hours. I'll give you my word, I'm coming back."

He had talked only long enough to allow Pardaloe to crawl back over Tracy and out of the hind end of the wagon. Selwood told the guards, frankly, just who he was—they laughed at his claim to his identity; he offered to show them the sick man in the wagon—it was all in vain. He talked loud for a few minutes and irritated the guards; touched his horse enough with the spur to keep his feet shuffling, and Scott, trying to quiet his horses, kept them stamping and champing on the bridge planks. But all the while Selwood was making the noises, and all the while the guards stood their ground, his eyes were searching the circle of darkness to his right, where his eye, long practised, followed a hulking object

slinking slowly and noiselessly forward. So the eye of
the Indian at night follows the wolf sneaking about the
camp, when to the eye of the white man its stealth is
all invisible.

Creeping like a huge cat from behind the wagon on
to the bridge; pausing for loud words or the impatience
of the horses' feet; advancing, step by step, at the
champing of their bits and the straining at their harness,
Pardaloe crouched in readiness behind the nearer guard
waiting only for Selwood to act.

"It's foolishness, boys, to keep poking shotguns into
me," protested Selwood. "It would be better for you
and better for me if you'd stand back. And any man
that calls himself a friend of mine ought to be over *to
the left* by this time. If I'm shot *I fall to the right*. Man!"
he exclaimed, addressing the guard on his left hand,
"you're so close I can smell the powder in your cartridge. Well, if we can't cross, we can't. It looks to me
as if *you're ready*. And I'm ready. Go!"

With a lurch, sudden as thought, Selwood jerked
his horse to the right and throwing his lines, keeled from
the saddle to the bridge floor. As he did so, the toe of
his left boot caught the barrel of the shotgun on that
side with a blow that kicked the gun into the guard's
stomach. One barrel exploded; the charge went into
the air. In falling, Selwood, striking up with his hand
the barrel of the second shotgun, threw himself bodily
on the right-hand guard. The two men clinched to the
ground, and the gambler pulling, in the struggle, the
revolver from the breast harness, brought the butt down
twice on the fighting guard's head. Pardaloe, who had
placed himself, as directed, behind the left guard, butted
him violently from behind, above the knees, grabbed
both ankles, and as the guard's shotgun went off, threw
him with a grunt backward clear over his own head.

The man struck sprawling on the plank floor, and Pardaloe was on top of him before he knew what had happened. Selwood's horse reared and plunged at the discharge of the gun, but, fortunately, hit no one under foot. The struggle of the surprised guards was quickly over—neither had a chance against men practised in encounter.

Selwood was first to speak. "Throw me a piece of rope, Bob," he said, astride his man.

"Don't waste no rope on these birds," growled Pardaloe, "dump 'em into the river!" He was really picking up his yelling victim to follow his own advice when Selwood intervened. "Not by a blamed sight!" he exclaimed with a sharp expletive. "Dump nobody into the river. Hold that man till I tie him!"

"Don't waste a good piece of rope on a couple o' critters like this," pleaded Pardaloe in deep-voiced aggrievement, as Scott handed him rope; "keep it fur their betters."

"Hold the man—and tie him," said Selwood sternly, meantime trussing his own victim. "We may have visitors any minute—work fast."

Scott, and Pardaloe with much grumbling, carried the crestfallen guards, tied and roughly gagged, well into the bushes at the left of the roadway. "Sorry to gag you this way, boys," explained Selwood, leaving them, "but I'll be back by twelve o'clock and turn you loose, if you don't have better luck. Next time, stand back out of reach, as I advised you to. Don't expect to stick your shotguns into a man's ribs and not get kicked."

CHAPTER XXII

A RENDEZVOUS WITH DEATH

WITHOUT losing an unnecessary moment, the gambler, recovering his trembling horse, mounted up, crossed the bridge—the wagon close behind—and struck through the brush to the right and into the old trail.

They had hardly entered it before the serious difficulty of making their way up the river was evident. Halting the wagon before they had gone ten rods, Selwood pushed forward on the horse half a mile in an endeavor to find better going. The trail, heavily overgrown with brush, had become impassable by night, and the wagon track had been washed into countless gullies by the rains of years. He rode back trying to think out an escape from his dilemma. "We can never make it in the dark," he said in low tones to Pardaloe and Scott. "I could hardly find the wagon again. And the farther you go, the worse it gets.

"Dave has an old shack down at Calabasas. I hate to take him among the horse-thieves, but it's any port in a storm. There's a trail from Calabasas through the hills that comes out on the river just above the old beaver dam, and when I can get back to help, we'll get him to camp that way. The trick now will be to turn the wagon around. Unhitch the team and we'll do it by hand."

Selwood took the horses while Pardaloe and Scott, with many pulls, got the wagon to where the horses could handle it again, and the cavalcade struck across the Sinks on the Thief River road toward the famous water hole on the Spanish desert. An hour or so later, with good going, they had reached Calabasas—the haunt of men esteemed, of all men, meanest in the high country.

The holes in the canyons, the tumbledown shacks that sheltered these denizens of Calabasas were still as death when the wagon, guided by Selwood, by lantern, by Scott's instinct, and by main force, halted with as little noise as possible near what Selwood pronounced Tracy's cabin. The two lanterns had been hidden. Selwood got down from his horse and, calling to Scott for the dog, slipped Chloe's muzzle and held her on the leash. The mastiff whinnied and jumped at him, licking his hands as he caught her by the collar and led her toward the cabin door.

If the place were occupied, forcing an entrance would be a highly particular business. Selwood hoped that, with Saturday night and the constant probability that any squatter occupant was more likely to be sleeping there in the daytime than at night, the shack might be unoccupied.

Crawling on the ground and feeling his way to the door from the side, where he was partly protected by the sill log, Selwood got his hand on the lower part of the batten door. It hung, he remembered, on leathern strips, and it stood now in the night partly ajar, seemingly supported only by the upper thong. Chloe, his hand on her collar, pushed her nose—the best nose, the barn men thought, that was ever set in front of a pair of dog's ears—into the opening between the door and the jamb and strained at the leash, but she did not growl. Selwood allowed her to crawl inside, which she did with great gusto, held her a moment at the leash's length, and then released her. He could hear the dog scurrying about inside, but knew at once the cabin was empty. Gun in hand, he went to the wagon. Scott passed out a lantern, and Selwood, returning, carefully pulled open the door and entered.

The lantern light revealed a rough table, a rickety

chair, and a home-made stool. In the upper left-hand corner stood the double-decked bunk Tracy had built, and in which Selwood had slept the first night—and the only night—he had ever spent in Calabasas. There was coarse bedding in both decks. A rough rock fireplace stood at the lower end of the cabin. Beside the fireplace stood an empty box up-ended. Selwood knew well its use. Like a candle snuffer for a candle, it was there to set over and conceal instantly a fire on the hearth. The roof at the back of the shack rested on a shelf of rock.

In a few moments the three men, by the light of the lantern, had cleaned out the place. The bedding was dumped outside, together with a battered frying-pan and coffee-pot and some canned goods. Kerosene from a handy can was poured freely over the bunk, rubbish was pushed on the hearth and lighted. And with Chloe blinking at the flames, Tracy, still asleep on the cot, was lifted from the wagon backed up to the door into the shack and placed in the corner farthest from the bunk and near the open fire. When Pardaloe and Scott had brought in light supplies for breakfast, Selwood directed the two men to go to sleep in the wagon.

Re-entering the cabin, he sat down beside Tracy. A spasmodic flame on the rock hearth lighted the sleeping man's features. The face was haggard and the thin lips, lying feebly apart as the older man breathed heavily, were drawn and colorless.

Selwood turned his eyes about the squalid room. Partly lighted by the dingy lantern on the table, it was not inviting to the imagination—yet it looked as if it might be the last refuge of the human failure lying before him. Selwood had been long too busy with life to think of death; but in Tracy's appearance it had seemed more than once of late to stare at him; to-night the old face looked more like death than ever.

Impatient with his thoughts, he rose to his feet—yet there was something he could not shake off by rising. It was the thought that a death like this, of an old man, with more good in him than in the average man, was not pleasant; no decent surroundings, no comforts, forgotten or deserted by all the men he had ever befriended, except one—himself.

The thought of Christie kept flaring, like the fitful flame on the hearth, in his heart. She would have listened to him, he felt, had he been anything but what old Dave was, a common gambler. And what had he to expect but a death such as this if he ended a life like this? Only, at best, a quicker death, a violent death at the hands of some other outcast like himself.

He looked at his watch. To make his rendezvous by midnight he must be on the way home. Home! He had spoken the word in his mind. What right had a homeless man to such a word? Without a woman to make it, there was in his lexicon no such word as home —he had known one home. He woke Scott—Pardaloe was snoring unmercifully—asked the Indian to water his horse, and gave him such instructions as there were to give in case he should not be back by daylight—namely, to run Tracy up river until things had quieted down in Sleepy Cat; and if they heard the gambling-hall was burned to tell Tracy, Selwood had gone West.

He swung into the saddle with a light heart, for action is what the soldier, the adventurer, the gambler crave. There was no moon, and he met neither man nor beast on the desert trail.

Half way into town, emerging from the breaks that skirt the valley of the Rat, he caught a glimpse of a red glare on the northern horizon. He had no need to pause or to surmise what it might be; the Vigilantes were abroad.

Selwood presently halted; he struck a match and looked at his watch; it was only eleven o'clock—something had precipitated the fight—he might be too late to make defense. The faint crackle of gunfire reached his ears—told him more than he needed to know. He quickened his pace; if he were too late to fight for the hall, there was Company property to protect. But he had given his word to defend the hall, and wanted to meet the masked crowd where he had promised to meet them.

Urging his willing horse to his best, he pushed forward. The dull glare, rising and dying on the horizon, seemed a signal, beckoning him to violence and death. It spurred him to haste, and he bent forward in the saddle, with the keen night air burning his cheeks, and the eager horse, nosing the wind, leaping the long strides toward the river.

Reaching the river bottom, Selwood reconnoitred the bridge. Under the bluff it lay in the dark, with the flames of the town conflagration far above it. Hearted though he was to go forward, he dared not risk crossing it. If the guards had freed themselves, or been freed, they would be eager to shoot from ambush. He rode slowly down the river some three hundred yards. There was more light over the lower bluffs and the fire was plainly in the River Quarter. Selwood located an old ford and, guiding his horse cautiously into the rapids, allowed it to drink, crossed slowly, headed the horse up the rocky bank, rode up under the bluff, found a break he could get the horse into, and rode out on the river bench, in full sight of the town.

No more than a glance was needed to give the quick-witted gambler the situation. Vigilantes were pushing into the River Quarter below him, and burning as they went. But the gunfire, ceasing at times and breaking out sharply anew, told him they were meeting resistance.

He rode well outside the area of the flames and the fighting on the outskirts of the town. In the darkness he rode unmolested; indeed, encountered no one. Making a wide detour, he gained the upper part of the town, and came out unobserved on the Falling Wall trail, where he could command the lower end of Fort Street, which was on fire. Between him and the conflagration stood his gambling-hall, but this lay below the brow of the hill in front of him.

Down Fort Street, silent and completely deserted, he rode, wondering whether the smoke rising in the foreground included the ruins of his own building or others; and then, crossing the brow of the hill, he saw the gambling-hall just below him.

To his amazement, it stood apparently untouched. Lights were burning inside, and the grim outlines of the big building loomed before him in the glare of the general conflagration; to his straining eyes they seemed bigger than ever. He stopped and listened. Through the partly shaded windows of his place he could see no one moving, nor could he hear any sound. This was cause for suspicion, if not a symptom of danger.

With as little noise as possible, he rode into the grounds north of the hall, dismounted, secured his horse, and with his hand on the grip of his holster gun, walked to the door of his office, in the rear of the building. The office window near it was curtained and the room appeared dark. He slipped a key into the door lock and, standing to one side, pressed the latch and threw the door wide open.

Silence greeted the move. Selwood would have given much for a dog, but he had none, and, convincing himself that he might as well take a shot from the dark then as one in the light later, walked boldly into the room, struck a match, lighted the lamp, and closed the door behind him. The room was empty. Everything appeared as he had left it at dusk.

He threw open the door into the gambling-room. The lights were on—not a soul was in sight. But signs of disorder and evidences of hasty departure were everywhere. Glancing collectedly about, drawing rapid inferences from whatever he saw, Selwood looked at his watch. It lacked but a minute of twelve o'clock—perhaps the Vigilantes were coming back to face his threat and finish him and the hall together. As to Big Haynes and Haynes's defenders, he had never for a moment cherished any illusions; everything about the room indicated they had run like rabbits at the approach of danger.

He walked to the front doors. They stood wide open. He looked up and down the street; not a soul was anywhere in sight. Yet the hall, open, brilliantly lighted, stood silent and deserted; it was as if death had suddenly and completely wiped out its denizens—players, onlookers, dealers, everybody. The place stood directly in the path of destruction, the first to be attacked, the most solitary, the most conspicuous of the gambling-houses in Sleepy Cat—and these were all on the blacklist of the Vigilantes. He had returned to defend his place only to find that no one appeared to challenge its right to exist.

Puzzled at the situation, Selwood strode down the broad steps and started for the horse barn. To save time he crossed lots and approached the barn, seeing no one and, as far as he could tell, unobserved. He noticed that the barn lights were burning, particularly the stationary lanterns on both sides of the front door. At the moment he approached the front of the barn, in the shadow of its side a masked man, apparently a Vigilante, hurrying up street, encountered a man running out of the barn itself. The two almost collided. The man from the barn dealt the Vigilante a fearful blow across the head with a club.

The Vigilante, evidently a man of great strength, staggered, but grappled with his enemy, only to receive a second blow that would have felled any but the strongest. The handkerchief, symbol of the raiding party, slipped from his face to his neck, but, dazed as he was, he clinched with his assailant and struggled with him. Selwood, little as he liked the red handkerchief, liked a game fighter, and watched the struggle the dazed man was making against one evidently no better than a cowardly murderer. Though it might be one of his own men, Selwood liked less and less his manner of fighting, and saw, as the two men rolled, panting and cursing, toward him, that the man who used the club was fumbling for his knife.

It was too much to watch a murder Selwood, with an indignant oath, took a quick step forward. The Vigilante was under, and, as he was rolled on his back, the gambler recognized Abe Cole, the blacksmith; at the same instant he saw the knife raised above him. Selwood, with a vicious kick, sent the knife hurtling across the driveway, and, grabbing the upper man by the collar, brought the butt of his gun down on the man's head and turned his face to the light to see who it was. He had only time to ascertain that the coward was none of his own men, when McAlpin came running out of the barn. The hair of the barn boss was flying, his shirt was half torn from his body, and one side of his face was covered with blood. In one hand he carried a lantern, and in the other a hatchet—the front and picture of a wild man. Selwood, gripping the throat of the coward, looked up at McAlpin. "Who's this man, Jim?" demanded Selwood sharply. McAlpin, amazed at the sight of Selwood, was at no loss for words. "A firebug!" he cried, "Kill him! They're after horses. I caught him and he tried to murder me."

"Throw me a couple of halter straps or a piece of rope. You look to Cole," exclaimed Selwood. With a skull clearly club-proof, the fighting blacksmith was staggering to his feet. McAlpin, setting down the lantern and hooking the hatchet through his belt, steadied him. Cole recognized Selwood. "That was a close squeak, John," cried Cole. "He'd had a knife into me. I know the blamed thief. He's one of them river rats—kill him."

"Turn him over to your Vigilantes with my compliments," responded Selwood, rising from the man he had tied. "Why don't they come my way up the hill?" he asked of Cole, tauntingly.

"The orders is out not to burn you, John—that's why. Look after this bird a bit, Jim"—Cole pointed to the horse-thief and addressed McAlpin—"till I get help. We'll string him up."

McAlpin rubbed his hands in cheerful anticipation; Cole ran off, rubbing his head. Selwood spoke sharply to the barn boss: "What's become of Fyler?"

"The girl was over to see if they could get a team and a wagon, John. She was afraid they'd be after her father. I told her to come back for it—she didn't come. I drove it down to the store. The place was dark and locked up. They were gone—God knows where. I seen Bull Page. He's sober—scared to death for fear they'll hang him."

"Where are your hostlers?" demanded Selwood, upset.

"Out with them dashed Vigilantes—couldn't hold 'em back—not a man-Jack of 'em." Lefever's got his teamsters over in the warehouse and the bunkhouse."

The gambler hardly heard the answer. A panic had seized him. Too late he realized the danger to which Christie had been exposed—the danger to which he had left her.

He ordered McAlpin to put out the lights, close the barn, and shoot anybody who tried to get in. Down street he heard shouting; the Vigilantes were coming to get the horse-thief. McAlpin, with all speed, was closing the barn doors. Selwood, stooping, picked up the red handkerchief that had fallen from Cole's neck, and, thrusting it into his pocket, slipped around the corner of the barn and hurried up the hill.

A moment later he stood alone in the centre of the gambling-hall. His eyes, running over the room, fell on the shelf behind his desk. There stood the glass dome covering again the good-luck shoe he had brought from the Crawling Stone, and to which he still stubbornly clung. He set aside the dome and thrust the shoe into his coat pocket. Turning, he saw on the wall the print of the padre. He pried it loose, folded and put it into a breast pocket, and, going back to the middle of the room, drew down the big centre lamp.

It was a large, old-fashioned kerosene lamp, raised and lowered, in its shiny frame, on sticky brass chains and pulleys. The burner was large; lighted, it threw out the heat of a stove. Of all the lamps in the hall, the big centre lamp was Bull Page's pride, and its glass bowl held a quart of kerosene. Bull had tried more than once, when "absent-minded," to pour a gallon into it.

The lamp was hot. The blaze scorched Selwood's eyes as he looked into it. He lifted the bowl carefully out of the frame and balanced it. Once more he looked about him. Then, drawing back, he hurled the burning lamp with both hands far across the floor.

It crashed into a thousand pieces. There was a blinding explosion. A burst of flame leaped toward the ceiling. A hundred darting tongues licked at the gaudy velours hangings and ran like blazing powder up the silken shades; they careened wildly along the burning floor and wrapped their curling arms around overstuffed chairs and mahogany tables. Step by step, Selwood retreated before the destruction. At the door he paused—as if to make sure the hall was doomed. Then, running to his frightened horse, he sprang into the saddle.

Heading for the river, he spurred relentlessly. And not looking back, one man rode that night out of Sleepy Cat with a bad chapter in his life closed behind him.

CHAPTER XXIII

THE NIGHT AT CALABASAS

SELWOOD'S orders had been to leave Tracy in the shack in complete darkness, after the hearth fire died down, for the night. Scott, punctilious as a soldier and hardened to discomfort, had stood his watch outside. When, at the end of it, he called Pardaloe, asleep in the wagon, and the big guard, stiffened with the night chill of the desert, roused himself for his turn and pulled his shotgun out of the wagon, the nipping air settled on his neck and shoulders like moulded ice. After Scott had crawled into the warm place, a stern resolve to obey orders—orders that had been clearly repeated by Scott, who knew well his companion's weaknesses as well as his strength—gradually congealed within Pardaloe into the conviction that he could stand guard as well inside the cabin as outside. Where the silence was so intense that the sneeze of a gopher would alarm every living thing about a water hole, Pardaloe felt, perhaps rightly, that no human being could possibly sneak up on him unawares, and felt it would be no derogation of duty to stretch his orders a trifle.

Once inside, on the job, the embers dying on the hearth pleaded, together with Pardaloe's benumbed joints, for a new lease of life. Tracy was breathing regularly, and Pardaloe, cautiously scraping the fragments of fire together with the fireproof ends of his fingers, laid a few chips of wood across them and turned himself for a few minutes into a quiet but energetic bellows.

Sitting, giant-like, over the tiny blaze he coaxed thus from the darkness, the big fellow stared into it a few minutes, pulled his shotgun handily up beside him on the earthen floor, drew from a hip pocket his faithful pack of cards, dusted off a space below the fire with his hat, and began his solitaire.

When Tracy, half an hour later, woke from his heavy sleep and opened his eyes on the dim and mysterious scene before him, he might well have thought himself in a frontier nightmare. A smoky lantern burned vaguely on the hearth, and the uncertain light from the dying fire threw Pardaloe's huge bulk grotesquely up on the ceiling. Tracy, lifting himself slowly on his elbow, looked with blinking eyes and tried, as he stared, to collect his sluggish faculties. Instinctively he reached for his sole means of protection—it was gone; and Tracy, like a seasoned campaigner, lay noiselessly back to await developments.

It was not very long before he perceived that the fancied bandit, looming over the spurting flame while counting ill-gotten spoil, was only playing some sort of a game of cards. And when Pardaloe turned his head sidewise—as he did at intervals—Tracy thought that the bulky torso outlined on the wall and ceiling, the disreputable slant of the shapeless hat on the mule boss's head, and the lean and stubbly appearance of his lantern jaw, working in the silence of the night with the sombre irregularity of a hydraulic jack, betokened some one much like Bill Pardaloe.

Once convinced of this, Tracy was not slow in asking questions—which he made frequent and sharp. Pardaloe, beyond acknowledging his identity, was loath to talk. If he talked he would have to explain, and though not armed mentally at all points, the mule boss had a streak of cunning that served in default of a higher intelligence, and shrewdly reckoned that if there were explaining to be done, Selwood would prefer to do it himself.

In these circumstances, it was no time before Tracy and Pardaloe were at tart exchanges.

"Ain't no use your gettin' sassy, Dave, not a bit," urged Pardaloe at length. "Ain't goin' to git nowhere with your jawin' 'n' you won't find out no more from me than you would from a dead coyote. Wait till the boss comes, with your questions, 'n' be hanged to you."

"What boss, Bill?" asked Tracy, moderating his tone.

"John Selwood."

"Well, he may be your boss but he ain't mine, not by a jugful," sputtered Tracy. "Where is he?"

"Sleepy Cat, I reckon. No!" he exclaimed, contradicting himself suddenly, grabbing his shotgun and springing to his feet with all the celerity and something of the grace of a grizzly bear. "No!" he repeated, standing for an instant silent and alert; for as the radio picks the music of a human voice out of the silent air, Pardaloe's trained ear had drawn from the perfect silence of the desert night the echo of distant hoof-beats. "The boss ain't in Sleepy Cat. For if that ain't a hostyle visitor, it's himself a-comin' now!"

To scatter with a deft kick what was left of the fire, sweep up the grimy cards with the expertness of an old acquaintance, and to blow out the half-dead flame in the lantern, was all the work of a surprisingly few seconds, and Pardaloe in fewer added seconds was outside the tippy door, where he belonged, and on guard, as he belonged. It was Selwood, as he had surmised, and Scott's regular breathing in the wagon was checked only long enough to assure himself almost without waking that all was well in the coming of the horseman.

Pardaloe could answer all questions satisfactorily because there was nothing whatever to report. He argued mentally that as for Tracy being awake, Selwood could, and undoubtedly would, find that out for himself. He asked in turn for the latest news from Sleepy Cat; listened, wonderstruck, to the scraps of news from the fires and the fighting; shook himself at each startling sentence and complained he was missing it all.

Selwood had no sooner stuck his head inside the door of the shack than his impatient patient within called out: "Who's there?"

"Nobody but me, Dave," answered Selwood. But he spoke without much interest in the question or any enthusiasm on any subject.

"Where's my gun?" demanded the irascible gamester.

Selwood sat down beside Tracy and explained what had happened—told him what he had done in abducting him. Not without bitter remonstrance on Tracy's part, not without outbursts of protest at what the old gambler characterized as despicable conduct involving the loss of every dollar the two had in the world, at Sleepy Cat.

Selwood listened patiently. "Well," he suggested, good-naturedly, at length, "it's nothing new for a gambler to be broke—nor for a pair of gamblers, is it?"

Tracy was not to be placated, and he made no effort to conceal his disgust. "You're a queer kind of a gambler," he muttered. Then, gaining courage, as Selwood sat silent, to venture weightier abuse, he continued: "Fact is, you ain't no gambler at all——"

Selwood interrupted him with a somewhat disquieting assent. "So you've said before, Dave. I've come to the same conclusion, myself."

"—not accordin' to my notion," persisted Tracy, backing water just a little bit.

"Nor mine," interposed Selwood firmly.

But this was too much for Bill Pardaloe, who, on his knees, was preparing to work at the fire again. He whirled from the hearth. "Your old friend Roper thought he was a gambler," he snorted indignantly. "Roper cleaned *you* up without much trouble. But he ain't spent none of *Selwood's* money yet."

Tracy glared at the interloper. "Playin' poker don't make no gambler," he snapped. "If it did, every bible-backed mule driver in the Rocky Mountains would be running a game."

"Crawl into the wagon, Bill," said Selwood, "and get some sleep; we're pulling out for Thief River before a great while."

Pardaloe got up, and Selwood, pushing the ill-smelling lantern closer to the fireplace, picked up one of the half-burned mesquite roots, raked together Pardaloe's scattered embers, and after patient effort, interrupted to answer Tracy's occasional questions—and some patient feeding—he got a tiny blaze flickering. Having done this, he sat down on the blanket near the hearth, put out the lantern, and advised Tracy to go to sleep.

"What'll you be doin'?" asked the drowsy Tracy.

"I'll sit here for a while. Give me your cards, Bill."

Pardaloe was still wandering in and out of the shack. He had brought in an extra blanket for Selwood, who was coughing. As he reached into his capacious hip pocket for the cards, he framed an apology. "They're gummed up some, John."

"No matter," returned Selwood curtly.

"Been figurin' for a week now to buy a pack—never could get to it. This blamed freightin' keeps me too busy."

Selwood, familiar for at least a year with this favorite alibi, made no comment.

"Nine o' diamonds is shy, John," mumbled Pardaloe, still uneasy over the reception of his tried and true friends.

"Never mind," snapped Selwood.

"Lost it in Crawling Stone Canyon the night I had to pull for high ground in such a thundering hurry. This here photograph o' Gin'rel Grant——"

"Give me the cards."

Pardaloe handed the chilly gambler the greasy cards and withdrew. Tracy's talk gradually subsided; he was soon asleep. In the uneven play of light from the hearth, Selwood, the blanket spread before him, mechanically shuffled Pardaloe's cards. Whether he thought of the dozens of aristocratic packs he had but just sent up in smoke; whether he regretted his wilfulness; whether his slender fingers revolted instinctively at the smoke and grime of the mule driver's dog-eared pack, who could say? Not the firelight that peered, now furtively, now with a flare, into the set face above it; not the night wind that blew softly across the desert and puffed half-heartedly at the shack door as it creaked and swayed reproachfully on its crazy hinge; not the faint screams of far-off desert voices that rode the waves of the night air.

Selwood, absorbed and silent, held the pack in his left hand, impassively slipped the cards one by one to his right and faced them slowly on the blanket—pausing at intervals to mark their sequence and to read in it the answer to the question he kept asking.

Pardaloe's footstep was heard again. He came in with a handful of wood ripped from a window shutter and fed it, silently and skilfully, to Selwood's fire. When the blaze suited him, he turned on his hinges to read the story the cards were telling.

He kept silence till Selwood had finished. "Dead man in 'em to-night—eh, John?" he said in an undertone.

"A dead man," responded Selwood composedly, and added: "This last time there's something new, Bill."

"What's that?"

"A dead woman."

Pardaloe, cramping his grizzly neck at the surprising words, bent his beady eyes close down on the fate-bearing sequence. He stared for a moment. Then without words he drew back his head; the dead woman was there.

Tracy slept only a little while longer. Pardaloe had gone to the wagon, and Selwood felt presently that his partner was awake—and that very probably he lay watching him; but Selwood himself had no desire to break the silence. Tracy did not lie quiet long.

"What you doing there, John?" he asked at length—with something of a growl.

Selwood answered good-naturedly.

"It looks to me as if one of us, anyway, ought to be in Sleepy Cat a night like this," continued Tracy, with a suggestion of reproach. "Everything we've got up there in the world at stake."

"Everything *I've* got up there, Dave," amended Selwood. "You're a mine-owner now—I'm just plain gambler; remember that—will you?" He spoke the last two words with a touch of acid sharpness that did not often creep into his tone. Tracy recognized in it an invitation to quit. "I've been back up there to-night, since I brought you down," volunteered Selwood, to break the brusqueness of his earlier tone. "The Vigilantes are holding our part of the town, and they changed their minds, somehow, about burning us. Abe Cole told me we were safe. Of course, the other fellows might try it—but I just imagine they'll have most of the bunch on the telegraph poles by morning—if they've got enough poles. Dave"—Selwood asked the question in his accustomed kindly fashion—"you've played the cards a good while, haven't you?"

"Ever since I was big enough to set up 'n' play euchre

with my dad. Goin' nigh on forty year," grumbled the old man, appeased in turn by the friendlier tone of his protégé. The two men were talking in the almost total darkness of the cabin, for Selwood had neglected the fire.

"Do you believe in 'em, Dave?"

"Don't any man believe in 'em that ever handled 'em? Don't you believe in 'em?"

Selwood made no answer.

"I believe in the cards," continued Tracy meditatively, "all the time. I believe in dogs most o' the time; not many men I believe in ary time——"

"Do you believe in dead men, Dave?" asked Selwood.

"Don't talk foolishness," retorted Tracy. "And," he added with deeper pessimism, "I don't believe in no women none o' the time."

Pardaloe stuck his head in through the shack door just in time to hear Tracy's words. "Right for once, partner," he half bellowed. "Dead right—every word right."

Selwood showed impatience. "Wake Bob," he said to Pardaloe shortly. "Hitch up the horses. We'll be pulling out of here pretty quick."

"Which way you headin'?" asked Tracy as Pardaloe disappeared. His tone was irritating, and the question found Selwood irritable. The friction, suppressed for the most part between the two men, made itself felt again. "I don't know and don't care much," answered Selwood indifferently.

"Well, I'll tell you," remarked Tracy; "if you'll take me back to Sleepy Cat you'll oblige *me*. Oughtn't to've sneaked me out o' there. Then you bein' away from there, too; to talk it flat out, I don't like it. It bothers me."

Selwood tried to pass it off. He spoke with half a

laugh and in the manner of his partner. "Didn't think you'd take it *that* hard, Dave. I did what I thought was right——"

"Yes, but——"

"Sorry I bothered you. It won't happen again. I hope I shan't be bothering anybody very long."

Tracy threw a sharp question at him. "What d' you mean by that foolishness?"

"Is there any particular objection to my meaning exactly what I say?" The retort was too keen to pass unnoticed. Tracy was silent for a moment. When he spoke he made a gruff complaint. "Whenever you get a chance, you like to take me hard—don't you? Anything I say——"

Selwood suppressed a smile. "I wasn't thinking about you, Dave. Don't you know, a man can feel that his game's about played?"

Tracy snorted skeptically. "There you go again with your foolishness."

"Mine," continued Selwood, heedless of the interruption, partly as if to himself, "begins to look that way to me to-night."

"Shucks! you got a cough started again, that's all's the matter with you."

Selwood released a hard little laugh. "Coughs don't bother me. I've been acquainted with 'em too long. I asked you a while ago whether you believed in dead men. Last night I dreamed I saw Frank Sanger.

"I thought I was walking down River Street in Sleepy Cat. It seemed as if it was dusk—evening, or early morning—daybreak. I looked across the street. There was Frank Sanger walking on the other side, looking straight over at me. Looked the same as he did that night we—I—at Bartoe's. But his mustache was heavier. He had on a queer-looking hat.

"I tried to reach for my gun; I couldn't move a finger. All of a sudden, he started across the street toward me. His eyes were as big as teacups. And all the time I knew he was dead! I tried to cry out—I must have made some kind of a noise, for something woke me up. I grabbed my gun out from under my pillow. I was sure he was somewhere in the room. And there I lay in a cold sweat."

"Dead men don't walk the streets," growled Tracy. "Stir up that fire. What you sittin' there in the dark for? There's nothin' to a dream, man!"

Selwood made no move. "It's in the cards, too, Dave. I've tried 'em—three times. It always comes the same way—there's death in this deck for somebody. I guess it's full time for me to cash in, anyway. And remember, everything between you and me is fixed. You own the mine; I own the hall."

"Light the lantern, dash it," burst out Tracy, with a deepening growl. "Dreams don't mean anything! If there's anything wrong with the cards, it's because they're hanging men in Sleepy Cat."

Without a word Selwood rose, felt for a match, and, striking it, looked for the lantern. Tracy kept up a nervous running-fire of talk, punctuated at times by abrupt pauses, but persistent. Selwood, holding the lantern in his hand, slipped the globe down over the lighted wick; then he paused and, as he stood, listened. Doubtful at first of his sense of hearing, the faint, regular sounds of hoof beats soon fell unmistakably on his ears. He spoke to Tracy. "Hear anything?" he asked.

But too many "rebel" shells had exploded close to Tracy's ears to leave the drums as sensitive as those of the young frontiersman; he heard nothing. Selwood, extinguishing, by a short drop, the flame of the lantern, and bidding Tracy lie still, picked up the box and set it over the fire, stepped through the half-open door and stood for a moment just outside. He had not been mistaken; a horseman was nearing the cluster of evil huts known as Calabasas. In the wagon Pardaloe was snoring. To be prepared for whatever might come up—for the horseman was riding hard—Selwood called in a low tone to Scott, who slept like a cat, and bade him wake the big fellow.

Standing expectant in the full light of a late-rising moon, Selwood was joined by the silent Indian, who, waiting only to get his orders, stole forward under cover toward the main road.

He reached a point of vantage at the moment the horseman slackened his pace. The latter, after hard riding, appeared to be at a loss as he approached the shallow draw leading to the huts. Scott allowed him to advance and turn and rein about in his indecision only long enough to make him out. Pardaloe, in the interval, had joined Selwood and had moved with him from the door, which they left hanging awry on its one hinge, into the shadow. There they stood when, reining about, after speaking low to Scott, who had hailed him, the rider spurred again down the draw and halted before Tracy's shack. "For God's sake," he muttered, swinging from his saddle, "where is everybody?"

Selwood recognized the voice and the figure at the same instant, and, stepping out into the moonlight, spoke to McAlpin.

CHAPTER XXIV

THE CALL FROM CARPY

THE stout-hearted little barn boss staggered stiffly into the shack after Selwood, the two other men crowding in behind him. Pardaloe lighted the lantern, Scott lifted the box that Selwood had chucked, bottom up, over the smoking fire, and Selwood pointed to the stool.

McAlpin sat down. Neither friend nor enemy had ever accused the wiry Scotchman of lacking words to express himself. To-night he sat staring at Scott, who was mustering a blaze again from the discouraged embers, and the four men—even Tracy—waited impatiently for the newcomer to speak his mind; McAlpin seemed dazed. To Pardaloe's sputtering and to Tracy's jerky questions he paid no attention, except to bid the two shut up.

Neither Selwood nor Scott made any effort to hurry the foreman. It was enough for them to study his bloodshot eyes until he should be ready to explain what was responsible for his peculiar mental condition and his unexpected appearance at Calabasas. He sat on the box, fingering at and fussing with his left forearm. About him stood Pardaloe and Scott, who had risen from the hearth, while Selwood stood with his back to the fire, studying McAlpin by its light and the light of the lantern on the table, wondering whether McAlpin could be wounded, and how badly, or whether he was running a huge bluff.

"John," exclaimed the barn boss, darting his bloodshot glance at Selwood, "ha' y' got any ca'tridges?"

Selwood answered only after a pause and then impassively. "A few, Jim—why?"

McAlpin, holding his left forearm and hand pretty well up, spoke to Scott. "Bob," he said, "take your knife and slit that sleeve up a bit."

"Are you hit, Jim?" demanded Selwood, stepping forward as Scott drew his knive and slit the coat sleeve.

"I'm nicked in the arm, John, but it's naught; Carpy bound it for me. John, there's plenty doin' in Sleepy Cat."

"Have they hung anybody?" snapped Tracy fiercely.

"Hanged anybody?" echoed McAlpin, turning toward Tracy on the cot. "I want t' tell y', Dave, the biter's bit, th' night in Sleepy Cat. If anybody's hanged there the night, it'll be Vigilantes!"

Selwood alone made no exclamation. He stood quiet, with his eyes fixed on the wounded courier.

"What do you mean, Jim?" ventured Scott patiently.

"I mean," exclaimed McAlpin, "the gamblers are on top! They've turned the tables. They've rallied hell-bent, drove the Vigilantes to cover up-town—crowding 'em to the river close to the new railroad station—I mean John Cole is wounded, Abe Cole is wounded, Chris Kickbusch is dead, Doc Carpy is wounded, and Starbuck is boss of Sleepy Cat—that's part of it, and only part of it. How many ca'tridges y' got, John?"

"Meaning they need 'em?"

"Meaning, the minute Starbuck took hold of the fight he doubled the blamed Vigilantes up like a jack-knife—stole a march on the suckers behind their backs, got into John Cole's store, where was all their ammunition, stole it and burnt the store—that's another part of it."

"Are the barns gone?" asked Selwood harshly.

"Not yet. Lefever and the wagon boys are holdin' both the barns, but if the wind comes up, they won't save 'em. There ain't enough left of your big hall on the hill to roast a chestnut, John."

Tracy half sprang from the cot. He poured a torrent
of wrath on the Vigilantes and the gamblers, with inci-
dental shots at the fate that had kidnapped him away
from where he could stand in defense against any and
all comers, of his own.

While the old soldier exhausted his resources of protest and abuse in his fury, Selwood stood pat. Pardaloe,
Scott, and McAlpin kept a deathly silence in the face of
the outburst; for it was soon plain that Tracy's sarcasm
and wrath were aimed almost directly at Selwood. The
three subordinates in the scene knew too well that the
slightest word or comment on their part would be highly
improper; it was a moment for cool heads and cooler
tongues. Never had any one of the silent listeners seen
Dave Tracy so beside himself with anger as he raved at
the burning of the hall on the hill. In answer to his
wrathful questions, McAlpin could give no information
whatever; while he knew as much about the firing of the
hall as anybody in Sleepy Cat, that, it chanced, was
just nothing. More than one person in Sleepy Cat that
night, despite its tragedies, was asking himself who had
burned the place on the hill.

Selwood waited, without an interruption, for the fury
of the storm to abate. No thrust was keen enough, no
taunt biting enough, to penetrate his silence. Old David
stopped only when physically exhausted. "Now," he
panted, looking malevolently at Selwood, "I hope you're
satisfied. You've played your game, ain't you? Sent
everything we've got on the hill up in smoke. And I
can turn out, when I get up, with a pack of cards and
start all over again. I ain't but sixty years old! Why
don't you say something?" he demanded violently.

Selwood, turning toward his partner, rested his elbow
on the rock ledge above the fireplace, took from his lips
the cigar he had lighted, and spoke deliberately. "I'll

have a lot to say, I'm afraid, Dave—more than I want to say to a man half sick, but it's got to be said, whether I like it or you like it or not.

"I want you to remember, Dave, first of all—the hall is, or was, mine—all mine. I took over your interest yesterday afternoon in Sleepy Cat, and turned over to you my interest in the Thief River mine. It was a trade fair to you and fair to me; you said I was giving half a dozen times what I was getting—I wasn't; but I was giving you a square deal, and you said it was a square deal, and I know it was."

Tracy tried to interrupt; Selwood patiently but firmly protested. "I gave you your say, Dave. I waited for all your cards; I want a chance to face mine now—and," he added, with a touch that Tracy had rarely heard in his voice, "I'm going to have it."

"You've tried hard to make a good gambler out of me, Dave—and the only reason you couldn't do it is because it never was in me. When my own blood kicked me out, you took the place of my—father——"

"Shut up!"

"But, Dave, I wasn't cut to travel the lines you laid for me. You said it to-night—I knew it yesterday.

"So yesterday I closed my game, Dave. I'm done. Yesterday I traded you out of the place on the hill. I gave you a half interest in the best quartz vein along Thief River, and you'll never have to do another day's work in your life—Ben Wentworth, a man as square as you are, is your partner. You'll never know need while the pay ore lasts, and there's enough in sight to keep you twenty-five years. Besides, I'm able to work awhile myself yet. So I don't see why you should wear yourself out, raving about the place on the hill being burnt. I owned the place, Dave; it's gone up in smoke and it's my fault, for, Dave, I'm telling you now and telling the boys here, I smashed the big lamp on the floor to-night and fired the hall myself."

Selwood was perhaps better prepared for what followed than his companions, who listened stupefied. It was a moment before Tracy could frame words; then he launched at Selwood a further torrent of abuse. Selwood took it without a quiver.

"Perhaps I played you a low trick, as you say, Dave; perhaps I didn't. Anyway, *I meant to cut that string*, and that was my way of cutting it. I've done you no wrong—if anybody is loser, I am.

"You say you're done with me for good and all. That's pretty hard to take from you, Dave—it's hard because I owe you so much and you owe me just next to nothing. But whatever you say or whatever you feel, I can't ever honestly say I'm done with you; you're the only partner I ever had and you can't ever change my feelings toward you. You've said a few things to-night I wish you hadn't said—but most of what you've said was coming to me, and I wouldn't ask you to take a thing back."

Before Tracy could reply, Scott started to leave the room; Pardaloe would have pushed his huge bulk after him, but Selwood stepped between them and the door. McAlpin tried to shut Tracy off. Selwood silenced him. "There's nothing to be said here that you all ought not to hear," he insisted. "I want you to hear it."

"No!" burst out McAlpin, stepping hurriedly over to where Tracy lay, and talking angrily at him. "I won't hear a word of it—not another word," he shouted in profane excitement. "I'm here on life and death— away with your jarring and listen to me. If the place wasn't burnt by you, John, it'd been burnt a dozen times since. The gamblers is after you, John—after you and after this fool man Tracy. And he wants to go back to Sleepy Cat! They'll burn him with his bed under him.

They don't want no dead men in Sleepy Cat!" he
shouted at Tracy. "John!" McAlpin, wild with
anxious haste, whirled on Selwood. "Carpy told me to
ride the desert till I'd find you. 'Tell him,' he says,
'they're drivin' us—and they'll shoot or burn up every
man jack of us if we don't get help—and no more said.
If you find John,' says Carpy, 'he'll understand.'"

McAlpin stopped, out of breath. A stillness broken
by the wailing scream of distant coyotes followed his
words. Tracy, sullen, lay mute. Scott never by any
chance, at a critical juncture, intruded an unwelcome
word. Pardaloe, his head crooked forward under the curling brim of his broad hat—his eyes, keen and suspicious,
bent in the firelight on Selwood, as the eyes of a dog
are bent on a waiting master—only showed his emotion
by the rhythm of his jaw.

In the silence Selwood stood, his eyes on McAlpin,
pondering his words. Of all men in Sleepy Cat that
might have sent such a message to Selwood, Carpy was
the one whose call he could not ignore. Who had taken
care of him when he lay sick? When money could not
buy skilled nursing—when the ignorance of even well-
meaning friends might have been fatal to him? Who
but Carpy? Carpy, sitting with him more than once all
night in the dingy hotel, watching his weakness—guarding and nursing for days together his slender hold on
life—Carpy was calling him. With the tables turned
on the blundering Vigilantes, this never-failing friend—
always giving himself unstintingly, recklessly, to the
service of others, the man who never asked whether
one needing help was worthy or unworthy—who never
said pay, or asked for a fee—the man who was his own
worst enemy—needed help. Selwood to those about
him was grimly silent; but in his heart he said: "He
shall have it!"

And one more question was gnawing like remorse at

his heart. Where was Christie Fyler in all this deadly clash?

He shot a question at McAlpin. "Where is Fyler? Where is his daughter?"

"I don't know, John—nobody knows. Carpy's been tryin' all night to get track of 'em—if anybody knows where Christie is, it's Cliff Starbuck."

The name cut Selwood like a knife. "Starbuck!" he echoed, biting off the word, in rage. "Starbuck!" he repeated, as if to feed his wrath. "And Carpy gave me his word no harm should come to her."

McAlpin put up a hand. "Don't blame him—not for what he couldn't do, th' night. I'm hit myself"— McAlpin held up his forearm—"but nobody here seems to care a rap about that—where I got hit or how I got hit. But Carpy is a wounded man and his back's to the wall!"

Selwood seemed hardly to heed the interruption. "Starbuck!" he re-echoed, in lower but not less deadly tone. The fingers of the hand resting on his hip insensibly drew together. He seemed as he stood to shrink for a moment within himself. Then he started from his lethargy and, looking up, turned his eyes slowly from one to the other of his companions and back to McAlpin. "I can't pass up a call from Carpy," he said, speaking to all. "I wouldn't if I could; and I couldn't if I would. And it looks now," he added, "as if Starbuck and I have a score to settle. I hope not; but if it's got to be settled, the sooner the better."

CHAPTER XXV

BACK TO SLEEPY CAT

SELWOOD made his arrangements with decision. Taking what ammunition he could scrape together, he would ride, he said, to Sleepy Cat. McAlpin was to ride with him to reconnoitre the situation when they had reached town. Pardaloe, open-eared and chafing under his mask of quiet, listened intently but without approval. He coughed as if to signify that he was at least present, if not voting. Selwood was talking to Tracy; when he turned from the cot, Pardaloe was waiting for him.

"John," he said, taking Selwood aside and speaking in an undertone—biting at the same time with a jerk into his dry piece of tobacco—"where does all this leave me?"

"I was going to ask you to help get Dave down to Thief River till this blows over."

"John, if you was askin' me to head for Thief River same time 'z' you're headin' for Sleepy Cat, then don't ask me."

"What do you mean?"

"I mean," submitted the big fellow, "when you're headin' for Sleepy Cat, I'm headin' likewise. I ain't easy in my own mind, not a bit, since what the Scotchman says about a gurl I'm not namin'—no matter who she is. But she's worth a whole wagon-load of old buffalo bones like Dave's—not meaning no disrespect to nobody, whatsoever, at all."

"If that's the way you feel, Bill, what about me?" demanded Selwood, almost angrily. "I'm here to look out for Christie Fyler."

233

"That's just it, John," persisted Pardaloe, placatingly. "And to look out for Christie Fyler, now, single-handed, you know what you're up against—same as I know," snorted Pardaloe, "same as everybody here knows. That's why I say to hell with Thief River and Tracy; I'm trailin' you."

"But this is *my* fight, not yours."

"I'm makin' it mine, John."

"Stop talking, you old tub. If they can dig a grave up there big enough to hold you, I can edge into one corner of it. But, Bill"—Selwood raised one hand, simply—"who rides with me to-night ought not to care much about coming back!"

Pardaloe was chewing slowly, but with the steadiness of fate. "Nothin' particular, as I know of, John, callin' me anywheres back."

"Come along, Bill!"

A further parley was held; Tracy at last pleaded to be taken back to Sleepy Cat, and, as everybody else was for it, Selwood gave in. It was arranged that Pardaloe should ride with Selwood and Scott, and that McAlpin should follow in the wagon with Tracy, who was to be driven as far as the river and up to the barn, if it looked safe to make the attempt—otherwise he was to be secreted at some point in the willows until things looked better.

While Tracy's cot was hastily set back in the wagon and the horses were being got up, Selwood took the ammunition out from under the seat—a slender store, but, like a shower, a life-saver in a drought—and apportioned it into three parcels among Pardaloe, Scott, and himself. McAlpin sputtered a little at being held back with the wagon, but he could not be blamed for not having a keen appetite for the fast ride into Sleepy Cat.

It lacked but little of daybreak when Selwood reached

the river again. The three men had ridden separately, with a rendezvous below the bridge. Scott joined the gambler almost at once, and the two waited some moments for Pardaloe, who had harder work to make the time.

Fording the stream, the horsemen, once again together, secreted their horses in the undergrowth below the river bench, and climbed up the nearest gully to the flats that were being laid out for a railroad yard. Spreading out again, the three men circled this open space singly and without molestation, and came together on higher ground, where they could reconnoitre the town.

The fires that had lighted the sky earlier in the night had died down—chiefly for lack of material for the flames. An important part of Sleepy Cat lay in ruins, though the extent of the destruction was hidden in the darkness. One quarter of the straggling settlement had escaped the torch of the Vigilantes and the reprisals of the outlaws—this was the corner embracing the stage barns, Carpy's hotel, and the new railroad station.

Wind drifting down the canyon west of town carried fugitive clouds of smoke, strong with the acrid smell of burnt buildings, to where Selwood stood. It fanned into life little spurts of flame where nests of fire lingered amid fallen timbers.

From the hill where they had halted, Selwood and his companions, recovering their horses, made their way under such cover as they could, singly, to the stage barns.

Lefever met them. Selwood asked for the news. Lefever pointed to a pile of smoking ruins down the hill. "Some of them river rats have burned the bunk-house on us, John," said Lefever. "That's the way they keep their promises!"

"McAlpin told me nothing of that," exclaimed Selwood, looking angrily down the hill.

"Didn't know it was on fire when he started," returned Lefever. "But I'm telling you the teamsters are rarin' to go. They're only waiting for you."

"Just hold 'em till I get some bearings," was all Selwood replied.

Bull Page took the steaming horses back to their stalls, and Scott was sent out to scout. Lefever told Selwood and Pardaloe what more he could of the situation: Starbuck, who had been missing for a time at the outset, had taken the gamblers' fight in hand at a moment when the Vigilantes were driving all before them, turned the tables on the clean-up men, and now held the survivors of their disorganized force at bay in the unfinished railroad station. Starbuck, Lefever also said, would have burned the building over their heads but for the fact that he could not hold together enough sober men to rush the place. As it was, he had sent word by messenger that he would give them an hour to get out of the station and out of the town—coupled with the threat that if they didn't move they would be burned out by daylight. Starbuck's men, Lefever added, held the only building left in the River Quarter, where most of the burning had been—Bunty Bartoe's place down next the river; it had escaped the flames. In the upper town Carpy's hotel, which had been gutted, the gamblers had spared. He knew nothing about Christie.

Pardaloe had been despatched to the station with the ammunition. He came back with a long face, but a long face was nothing new for Pardaloe. Carpy, wounded, was there treating the wounded, who lay on the floor in the freight room. There was only a pretense of a guard kept about the building; within it, disgruntled Vigilantes nursed their grievances, railing chiefly at one another; and in one corner, with nobody to command, owing to the lack of ammunition, old General Roper, though hit, was maintaining headquarters, with neither head, as Pardaloe tartly put it, nor quarters. The only thing that prevented the refugees from running away was the fear of getting shot if they put their noses outside.

Selwood felt he must first of all see and learn what he could from Carpy. Directing his few companions to stick together and telling Lefever to throw out a stronger guard about the barn, Selwood started for the station.

By skirting the river bank and working from one to another of the breaks in the bench, he reached the rear door of the station without drawing any fire either from its defenders or its besiegers. He pushed open the door and entered the hall without being opposed or observed. Had anything more been needed to offend his instinct, inherited or developed, of self-preservation and defense, he saw it the moment he threw open the door into the waiting-rooms. These two rooms, half-finished and not yet separated by a partition, held the Vigilantes—particularly those wounded or those whose stomachs had lost taste for the deadly guerrilla warfare of the night. A glance into the lantern-lighted confusion of the place was enough to reveal to Selwood's unsympathetic scrutiny the complete demoralization of the Vigilante element. It was almost by accident that Abe Cole, the bandaged but still fighting blacksmith, saw Selwood and, running toward him, greeted him with a shout that drew attention to the long-hoped-for arrival of the taciturn gambler. As men, wounded and unwounded, crowded about him, he eyed the scar-faced, blurting blacksmith—his staring eyes bloodshot and his features disfigured—coldly, paying no attention whatever to his effusive welcome.

"You running this thing, Abe?" he asked.

"Running it?" echoed Abe hoarsely. "I *was* running it—nobody's running it. They wouldn't do a thing I

told 'em to do," declared Cole, with a plentiful sprink-
ling of profanity; "now they're cornered, jus' as I told
'em they'd be if they didn't obey orders, and there's
about as much fight in 'em now as there is in a bunch of
jack-rabbits!" He volleyed this, in disgust, for and at
whoever of his command wanted to take the compliment.

Selwood, ignoring impatient interpleaders that raised
their voices, some abusing the blacksmith and some one
another, looked about the two rooms. The figure that
instantly arrested his attention was that of Carpy, his
head swathed in a wild-looking bandage, moving about
among his wounded, who, filling one corner, lay on the
floor in various attitudes of prostration, anger, and
disgust.

Selwood, silencing those closest, spoke to Cole. "I
sent what cartridges I could rake up, Abe; it's all I know
of this side of Medicine Bend, outside what Starbuck's
got. So I'd advise you not to pass any of 'em out to the
jack-rabbits; put 'em in the hands of men that will use
'em."

"The teamsters, your men, are standing up," blurted
out Abe.

"What should you expect them to do?" asked Selwood, his gray eyes unsympathetic and unruffled.

"They stopped 'em from rushing us an hour ago,"
continued Cole. "But they ain't got six rounds apiece
left. Starbuck will come back."

Selwood's glance had wandered. "Hello, Doc," he
said as he saw Carpy elbowing his way toward him.

Carpy, wounded and infuriated, was grateful but
glum. Some stimulation brightened his one visible eye
and his dirt-stained, flushed face gave him rather the
appearance of a pirate than of a frontier doctor.

Selwood reached for the bloody hand stretched out.
He listened with patient attention to the wrought-up

surgeon, who tried to explain the wreck of their plans, though with an expression in his eyes that indicated his mind wandered.

Looking over the shoulders of those around him, Selwood saw the cowed spirit of the Vigilantes. One exception attracted his attention: one man appeared profoundly indifferent to the fortunes of the night. In a comfortable chair in the farthest corner of the second room, his long feet, incased in arctic overshoes, resting on the only table in sight, his bald head in a huge fur cap well pulled down, and his hands clasped in his lap, sat the queer pioneer trader of Sleepy Cat and of the mountain country—old man Van Tambel. Like another Casabianca, Van Tambel surveyed the scene before him. Everything he had in the world had but just gone up in the smoke of Fort Street, but the tragedy had apparently failed to shake his spirit. Composed and collected, he struck Selwood as an odd contrast to the welter of wrangling, confusion, and cowardice about him. The gambler silently laughed.

He turned his eyes on Cole. "Well," he said in response to many words from several mouths, "you've made a mess of it. They've got you cornered. Where are the bums that licked you hanging out? Does anybody know?"

He was assured that Bartoe's place was the only building that had escaped the flames in the River Quarter.

"That's where they are, then," was Selwood's comment.

"What are you going to do?" spluttered Cole.

Selwood paused. "I don't know what you're going to do," he said at length. "I know what I'm going to do. I'll take what men I've got with me at the barn and go after 'em."

"Wouldn't it be better to fight 'em here, John?" asked Cole.

"You're licked here," retorted Selwood. "If Starbuck stuck his head in the door most of these fellows would jump into the river. You've got no defense. I walked right in the back door just now. Go after 'em—that's your only chance. Get back to your wounded"—he took Carpy's arm—"looks to me, they're about all the fighting blood you've got left here."

As he spoke, he drew the surgeon apart. "You know the reason I'm in this mess, Doc," he said sternly and without wasting words. "Where is Christie Fyler?"

Carpy, controlling his excitement, caught Selwood's arm in his hand. "That's why I wanted you, quick as you could get here. So help me God, I don't know where the girl is, John. I only wish I did. This evening she and her father took supper at the hotel. I warned Christie privately to stay close—I couldn't trust Fyler with anything. Starbuck," said Carpy with a curse, "was prancing around her, and had the gall to try to stay to supper with 'em. I knowed Christie would stick close and would be all right, but I never figured on us getting drove like this. When I seen what was coming I run up to the hotel and told all hands to light out for the depot. Everybody was scared to death and tumbling over everybody else. I run to Christie's room myself and told her what was up, and to make for the depot——"

"Why didn't you bring her here yourself?" demanded Selwood.

"She wouldn't leave without her father," protested Carpy, defending himself, "and the dashed old mule wouldn't budge—I couldn't take her from him—she wouldn't go."

"So you left her there!!"

"What else could I do?"

"Knock him on the head and drag her here, yourself," said Selwood savagely. He made no effort to restrain himself, and his words fell like whip lashes. "You knew her danger," he thundered; "she didn't! So you left her there!" exclaimed the gambler, sardonic in his wrath. "A fine mess you've made of it!"

"John," protested Carpy, "I'll go over there this minute with you, myself——"

"And lock the barn after the horse is stolen! Stay where you are. What was the number of her room?"

"Twelve, at the top of the front stairs. John, I don't want you to go off mad this way. I did what I could— I tell you she wouldn't leave her father."

Selwood paused only to make a brief amend for his outbreak and to promise to return; he told Carpy he was going to look for Christie at the hotel—though in his heart he had no hope of finding her there.

On a table close at hand, where the doctor had set his instrument-case and dressings, stood a lighted pocket-lantern. Selwood, picking it up, closed the slide, put it out, and slipped it into his coat pocket.

"Hey!" exclaimed Carpy, "don't take that!"

"I may need it," said Selwood.

Walking toward the door with Selwood, Carpy pointed to one of the wounded men on the floor near where they were passing. He lay on his back, with his eyes closed, and his stertorous breathing was noticeable. "There's the old General," he said, "hit pretty bad, too; want to speak to him?"

"No," blurted out Selwood.

"He may die," observed Carpy critically.

Selwood was brutally resentful. "He won't need me to help him," was all he said. And flinging open the back door, he took one look out into the hall, slammed the door behind him, and slipped out into the night.

On the town side of the station he could hear sporadic firing answered at intervals by the fringe of guards defending the railroad building. He met no opposition on

the way to the hotel. It was far enough out of the line
of fighting to have been overlooked. Selwood wondered
why it had not been burned, but there it stood before
him in darkness. He scouted about the building for a
minute, and entered through a side door which he found
unlocked, opening into the dining-room. Without risking a light, he felt his way across to the hall, picking
up a wood-bottomed chair as he did so, and pausing at
intervals to listen for sound. He could hear nothing
anywhere, and walking up the front stairs without much
attempt to avoid the inevitable creaking of the treads,
he felt along the wall for the door of room number
twelve. Laying his hand after a moment on the knob,
he tried it. The door was unlocked. Without opening it, he knocked softly. There was no response. He
listened intently for sounds of breathing, but could hear
none. He then set the chair in front of the closed door,
lifted from his coat pocket the dark lantern, lighted it,
set it facing the door on the chair, pulled back the slide
of the bull's-eye, drew his revolver, and, standing to one
side, threw the door quickly open; if a shot were to come
from within, the lantern should draw it.

But no shot was hurled at him, no response of any
sort was made to the rude intrusion; the silence was almost ghostly. Selwood picked the lantern up from the
chair, threw its light rays from side to side of the room,
and, crossing the threshold with unabated caution,
looked about him.

The bed had not been disturbed. Selwood threw his
light on it; a Maltese cat, curled up asleep in the middle
of the counterpane, paid no attention to the intruder.
He lighted a lamp. One of Christie's familiar straw hats
lay on the bureau. Beside it he saw a pair of gloves
that he took up in his hand, felt of, and looked at. The
simple toilet articles of a frontier girl, the brush and

comb and lesser feminine accessories, together with a
black leather belt and a handkerchief, lay at hand.

Doctor Carpy's rooms had no closets, and Christie's
brown cloak hung from one of a row of pegs on the wall
—the knitted scarf that she wore about her neck, and
that Selwood liked so much, hung near it; the first time
he had met Christie in Sleepy Cat she had worn this
scarf, and he remembered how white her throat and
chin were, nestling in it, as she looked up in passing.

He caught the scarf in his hand, as if he would call
Christie back to it. He looked around the room, as if
she must appear from somewhere—but no Christie was
there.

Everything gave mute evidence that the defenseless
owner had been spirited away, or had fled without a
moment's warning. The indications were that a hasty
departure, a flight, perhaps, had been made, one in
which she had not had even time or been given a chance
to run to her room for her wrap.

To find himself standing thus surrounded by her most
intimate belongings—belongings so familiar, some of
them, to his observant eyes that in looking at them he
was stirred to a frenzy at the thought of danger coming
to her—was too much.

Without allowing himself to linger a moment where
sweetness seemed still to exhale from her former presence, Selwood, disregarding further precaution, hurried
down the hall to get a linen hamper that he knew stood
at the end. It was missing, and he hastened back to
the room, jerked the counterpane from under the frightened cat, and dumped into it, man-fashion, Christie's
belongings. He then emptied the bureau drawers, caught
up and tied the counterpane corners into a sling, and,
catching the bundle up on one arm, hastened down the
stairs and rejoined his men at the barn.

CHAPTER XXVI

COUNTER-ATTACK

HE got back without further incident, and deposited his queer-looking bundle with care inside a cupboard in the harness-room. Scott had returned and had covered the River Quarter, unmolested. His report confirmed all information that Bunty Bartoe's place had not been burned, and, Scott added, was now noisy with Starbuck's following, who, passing in and out, were celebrating their victory.

Pardaloe listened with snapping eyes. "How did you get through their guard?" he demanded.

Scott grinned. "Nothing much to hinder, Bill, till you get right down to Bunty's front door."

"Is Starbuck there?" asked Pardaloe.

It was a question Scott could not answer.

Selwood's mind worked as he listened. "I've got to know for sure where Starbuck is," he said, his eyes moving from face to face of those listening about him. "Where's Bull Page?" he asked after a moment's thought.

Bull was found rubbing down the horses.

"Get what men are in the office out, John," directed Selwood, "and call Bull Page in."

"Bull Page?" echoed Lefever, as if Selwood's mind were wandering.

"Yes, Bull Page," repeated Selwood testily. "Get him here quick."

Facing Selwood within a moment and alone with him in the office, the dilapidated but amiable Bull looked as surprised in being summoned at such a moment by the boss as the other men were.

Selwood spoke to him kindly and without haste, and

asked an odd question: "Bull, you haven't done the world very much good in your eventful lifetime, have you?"

Poor Bull, greatly taken aback, countered with a sickly smile. The words sounded to him like the dawn of a Day of Judgment. "Well—I—hope I ain't done nobody a whole lot o' harm—have I, John?" he asked in his quavering, throaty tones.

"Not to anybody except yourself, Bull, if the truth be told," replied Selwood evenly. "Not half as much harm as I've done, Bull, by a long shot. But to-night there's a chance for both of us to do something for somebody. You've seen that young girl whose father kept the mock-auction store down street, one of the stores that were burned to-night?"

Bull nodded. "I seen her, John."

"Somewhere in this row she's got lost. I'm afraid she's fallen into bad hands. You never can tell what will happen, you know, a night like this."

"Wouldn't want no wimmin folks of mine mixed up in it."

"Then listen," continued Selwood.

Bull, though appearing perplexed, listened very carefully to Selwood's further words.

"I've seen you many times drunk, Bull, trying to make me think you were sober."

Bull nodded as if confessing to the indictment.

"To-night I want you sober, trying to make everybody else think you're drunk."

Bull saw a flash of humor in the suggestion. "That," he returned, his chin pushed well down into his throat, "ain't goin' to be so awful hard, John, I don't think."

"There's one feature you may not like. But you're entitled, fair and square, to know it now. We may, one of us or both of us, get killed."

"Willing to go where you go, John," he replied simply.

Selwood showed his own surprise at the unassuming assent by a longer breath than usual. "John Barleycorn spoiled a man when he got you, Bull," he observed, regarding him gravely.

Bull's smile had long been in rags, but it shone brave through the tatters of his seamy face. He said nothing.

"When we do get into action," Selwood went on, "don't overplay your part. That's the trouble with these stage actors. They're sober men trying to look drunk, instead of drunken men trying to look sober."

Selwood believed that if any man at the barn could get into Bartoe's that night alive, it would be Bull Page. Bull, though janitor at Selwood's place, left his wages impartially at the various dives along the river front. He thus enjoyed a certain standing in the lower town as well as in the upper. He was not branded as a partisan, because no one thought him worth enlisting as one, and he moved without prejudice among the different factions of the town.

"I don't want to ask you to do anything I wouldn't do myself—if I *could*," said Selwood, explaining to Bull what he meant to attempt. "But you can get through doors barred against me and against any stranger; and with you to guarantee a stranger, I might make it. Anyway, Bull, if you're game we'll try; and they won't get us both without *some* kind of a hearing. No, don't take a gun; it wouldn't do much good and might do harm."

Pardaloe and McAlpin were called in. "If you'll hold your men together here a while," said Selwood to Lefever, "we'll know exactly what we are going to do. In, say, ten minutes, John, bring all of them that want to fight down to Bartoe's and maybe they can be accommodated. I'm taking Bull Page with me, and suppose you and Scott come along, Bill," he added to Pardaloe. "If we don't all of us get back, some of us might."

"What are you going to do?" asked Lefever.

"I'm going down to Bartoe's to look around."

Scott, with the quickest instinct of his listeners, looked at the gambler with a skeptical smile. "You're not going inside?"

"I am, if I can make it," returned Selwood. He began to unbutton his coat. "And I'll borrow your hat and coat and boots if you're willing, Bob," he added. As he spoke he took a cap of McAlpin's hanging on a nearby hook and stuffed it into his trousers pocket.

Scott began to take off his coat. Lefever sat partly on the table, with one leg swinging over the edge. He slipped uneasily from his perch and stood before Selwood.

"John," he asked, "what are you actually going to do?"

Selwood slipped his arms into the coat Scott held up. "I told you," he replied.

"You don't honestly mean you are going to try to go into Bunty's place to-night?"

"Why not?"

Lefever eyed him with indignation and contempt. "You're looking to quit, sure."

Selwood was already in Scott's rig. "Nothing is sure, John," he retorted amiably. "When my time comes, it comes."

"As McAlpin would say, you're talking like a blamed fool, John," rejoined Lefever.

Pardaloe grunted. "I'd say you're talking like one yourself, John Lefever, if I didn't owe you sixty dollars. That is," he mumbled, "if you think you can make Selwood change his mind by talking to him. If you're ready," he snapped at Selwood, looking around for his trusty shotgun, "let's go."

Selwood led the way out of the harness room through

the office and down the dark gangway to the back door of the barn. Lefever, still persisting in protest and caution, fastened the door behind the four men.

Separating as they left the barn, Pardaloe and Scott, and Selwood with Bull Page—a definite rendezvous named—worked their way down-town. Surprised at the lull in the fighting, they could only surmise that the Vigilantes were still at bay, with the gamblers still celebrating their victory.

The men stationed outside to guard Bartoe's place, the remaining resort on the river front, offered little impediment to a reasonably close approach. But Selwood, on one side, worked his way between the guards and the building, only to find that some one had sensibly drawn every window curtain and where there were shutters had closed every shutter. While Selwood and Scott scouted about the place, the front door could be seen to open at infrequent intervals for men to pass in and out; this much was all that a rapid inspection of the place disclosed.

Selwood joined Pardaloe where the latter awaited him on the river bank. "They've got it well hooked up, Bill," he said, looking toward the lone building where all was darkness save when a streak of light shot from the front door as it was opened. "I counted five men outside."

Pardaloe corrected him. "Count four now," he said with a certain grimness. "Rolled one of 'em down the river bank."

"You didn't kill him?"

"Choked him a little, that's all. These birds have got to have somebody to hang when we get through, 'n' it might as well be this buck as anybody else. No," he repeated indignantly, answering a second pointed question, "I didn't kill him. He's just gagged, and tied up tighter'n a bull's eye in fly time. If he wasn't fool enough to roll plum into the river when I started him he's all right. Now, speakin' of plans: I've got 'em laid out for this place, John."

"What are they?"

"Why, simple; I'll fire the back of the place and you pick 'em off when they run out the front. What?"

"Bill," said Selwood impatiently, "you missed one big bet when you didn't set out to keep Sleepy Cat supplied with fresh meat. First place, I don't know who's in there. If I did, I'm not a public executioner. I'm not a Vigilante. I'm just a plain gambler—not a butcher. And how," he continued, overriding Pardaloe's indignation, "do I know Starbuck isn't holding Christie Fyler or her father prisoner in there?"

Pardaloe drew a breath. "To tell the truth," he confessed, "I didn't think about her; the old man wouldn't make so much difference."

Selwood regarded the dim, forbidding outline of the tightly closed, ill-favored joint with half-closed, longing eyes. "I'd like," he said, much as if to himself, "to get one look inside that dive for just one minute."

"A look from you in there wouldn't last one minute," observed Pardaloe.

Selwood for a moment said nothing. "Well!" exclaimed Pardaloe impatiently.

"'Well,'" echoed Selwood, still reflecting, "before we do anything else, I'm going to take a look inside. I want to see just who's there—and what they're doing, Bill. We can talk a plan over afterward."

Pardaloe put some useless warning and much fervent scepticism into one ironical word, "Maybe!"

"Of course it's only 'maybe,'" admitted Selwood, not unamiably. "Got any whiskey with you, Bill?"

Pardaloe, after having so lately declared that no one could budge Selwood in his decisions, tried vainly to dissuade him from the undertaking. It was hopeless, he knew. But there was one thing Pardaloe could do—that was, obey orders.

A few minutes later, a man much under the influence of liquor, if one's nose could be trusted, for he strongly smelled of it, approached unsteadily the front door of the Bartoe place. In size, but in no other way, he resembled Selwood. Near the door two men, as he lurched toward them, stopped him roughly. They demanded his business, denied him entrance, and when he staggered toward the door itself, insisting he would have a drink, one of the guards, seizing him by the throat, threw him with brutal indifference backward into the street, where he fell prone and lay muttering to himself.

Presently he began to sing somewhat uncertainly a teamster's song. But the more he sang, the better, apparently, he liked the idea, for the longer he sang, the louder he sang, much to the annoyance of the truculent guard, who finally strode toward him with a curse to silence him—failing in his eagerness to note that the drunken man now lay much farther out in the street than he had been thrown. In the darkness he reached the object of his wrath, lying prone, and tried to kick it into silence. Beyond that point of the action, he had, afterward, for some time but the haziest recollection. His foot was caught in the air, he was snapped violently backward, and before he could utter even a warning cry, his head struck the ground like a stone. Two minutes afterward, still unconscious, he lay gagged and bound, stripped of his two guns and hat and coat, and rolled to one side into the ashes.

The guard at the door had fared in the brief interval

rather worse than better. Pardaloe timed his action to the thud he heard when the singing stopped; slinking up from behind like a mountain lion, he clapped one big hand over the second man's mouth, and with his other hand caught his victim's wrist in a vise; the next moment he had doubled him up in a bear hug and choked him into complete silence.

When the men were secured, Pardaloe dragged his prisoner, bound, around the corner of the building, arrayed himself, as far as he could get into them, in the accoutrements of his victim. Selwood, his face smeared with ashes, ran up. Not losing a moment, he whistled into the night for Bull Page, who, across the street, was awaiting his signal. "Now, Bull," he murmured, as the old man hastened to him, "for a look at the inside!"

CHAPTER XXVII

BARBANET IS PERSUADED

BULL caught hold of the iron latch-handle and pulled at the door. It resisted. Either bolted or barred on the inside, his efforts made no impression on it.

"Stand aside, Bull," said Selwood. He tried the latch, in turn, and, using more force when less failed, jerked at the door violently; still unsuccessful, he pounded on it with his fist.

A watchman within unbarred and opened the door a few cautious inches. Selwood, under the hat of the fallen guard, thrust forward his head. "It's Bull Page. Let him in! He's got a message for Starbuck."

The watchman took no chances. "Hold on," he exclaimed gruffly, and at once slammed the door shut and barred it. While Selwood waited his return—with perhaps more impatience than Bull, who must have felt that to oblige a friend he was taking a good chance of getting shot—the watchman took counsel. He opened the door again presently and with the same caution. "Come in, Bull."

Selwood in the interval had thrown away the guard's hat and put on the extra cap pulled from one of his numerous pockets; and when the watchman opened the door wide enough for Bull to enter, he attempted to walk in behind him. The vigilant guardian pushed him out again. "No, you don't——"

Bull raised his quavering voice. "Hit's all right— he's my partner——"

"Keep out!" exclaimed the watchman, shoving Selwood roughly back as he tried to edge through the half-open door.

"But he's got news Starbuck wants," persisted Bull, to whom the thought of entering the wolves' den alone was much more repugnant than that of making an appearance under the wing of a man who could at least shoot if shot at.

"No, you *don't,*" persisted the doorkeeper with a truculent aspect. "You come in, Bull Page—nobody else." With that, he jerked Bull in by the coat collar, and banged the door in Selwood's face.

The gambler took the rebuff impassively. He could have slipped his foot into the opening and scuffled an entrance, but this would only have defeated his purpose. It would, in the end, probably cost him his life and do Christie no good. Bull had his instructions: he was to tell Starbuck, Selwood wanted to see him at the barn—and was likely to get rough handling for his pains. Outside the evil joint, Selwood felt he held at least one portal and could afford to wait.

But he was beginning to count Bull's effort a failure and was trying to devise a new scheme when, after what seemed a long interval, the door was opened again. Selwood, as he saw Harry Barbanet coming out, followed by Bull Page, slunk into the shadow. Barbanet, sober, alert, suspicious, was the one man in the place that Selwood had most hoped not to encounter; at least, not until he had made more headway, for none, he felt, of the wolves within would so quickly penetrate his rude disguise. As the two men emerged, he retreated.

Bull looked vacantly around in the darkness as if to get his bearings. "He's here," declared Page in his trembling voice, trying as he spoke to penetrate the shadows. "I know that much; or was a minute ago—he'll help, if I c'n find him."

"You won't need any help," insisted the busy bartender, scornfully. "They're all locked up together right

inside here, back of the barber shop. Get old Fyler out
the back door, tell him you'll help 'em get away, him
first. He'll go out with you because he knows you—all
you've got to do is, throw him into the river. Starbuck
wants to get rid of him—you'll get paid."

"The old man's wiry," objected Bull, spinning out
the talk. "I want my partner outside the back door,
so the old man don't throw me in. Right wrongs no
man, Harry," persisted Bull, facing continued objection.
"I don't want to get throw'd in, myself—not for no
money. Of course, I'll try it alone if you say so, but if
my partner——"

An outburst from Barbanet cut short the talk; Bull
had said all he wanted to say, anyway. But, still maun-
dering on, he was unceremoniously pushed through the
partly open door back into the room. Selwood slipped
around the corner to where Pardaloe, close to a window,
was impatiently awaiting action. Selwood repeated
what he had heard, directed him to watch the back
door of the barber shop, take any necessary measures,
and to detain Fyler till Selwood could get back to him.

"Say the word," said Pardaloe, "and I'll fire the
whole dashed joint. I've got everything laid right here,
and good tinder to do it with."

"Don't set this place on fire till we get everybody out
of it," exclaimed Selwood. "Christie Fyler is more than
likely locked up in there with her father—hold your
horses, Bill."

"Yes, but it takes a few minutes to get a fire going,"
objected Pardaloe.

"I must see the inside of the place, first of all," continued Selwood. "I can't plan anything in the dark."

"Here's a sash loose," mumbled Pardaloe, balked of
his prey, "right here. Why don't you——"

Selwood, knowing the general layout of the inside of

the big room, jumped at the chance. "There's a curtain in front of it," continued Pardaloe.

"Out with the sash," said Selwood instantly. "Easy, Bill."

The window was a rather small, square, single-sash affair, set breast high. It needed no more than the prying off of a sash-stop, which Pardaloe managed with the blade of his bowie-knife, without making much noise. He lifted aside the sash. A curtain, tacked up inside, covered the window opening; and while Pardaloe noiselessly set down the sash, Selwood caught an edge of the curtain in his fingers and peered inside.

It looked like a fair chance. The corner was not dark, but it was not brightly lighted. A table stood close to the side of the window through which Selwood was looking. On one side of the table sat a man leaning forward, with his head buried in his arms, as if asleep. His hat lay on the table. Selwood watched him pretty closely for a moment—he was the nearest element of danger—but reached the conclusion he was stupid with drink. The curtain was short. Hung from hooks at the upper corners, it reached only to the window apron. Selwood could see men standing in small groups not ten feet away, but the entire room, probably for reasons of safety, was only meagrely lighted.

The gambler thought he could make it. He dropped the curtain from one hook. One end of the room stood pretty well revealed. No one apparently had noticed the partial fall of the curtain. He whispered brief instructions to Pardaloe.

"If you don't hear any shooting, Bill, you'll know I'm moving safe. If you hear *one* shot, just pay no attention. Have your shotgun up here on the sill; the instant you hear two shots, fire one barrel at that big lamp." Selwood pointed to the lamp hanging in the front end of the room. "Let the other barrel go into the middle of the crowd—that will give me a chance for the front door."

"John, I might hit y'," objected Pardaloe in a ferocious whisper.

"If I'm in that crowd, Bill, after *two* shots are fired, a few buckshot more or less won't hurt my feelings," said Selwood reassuringly. "Just let go quick at that lamp—that's the main thing. I'll make what noise I can with my gun to help you out."

Pardaloe, wrought up and listening with nervous intensity, was feeling in the darkness the hammers of the big gun. "Them hammer ketches is gettin' worn, John," he said warningly; "sometimes when I fire one barrel, the other goes off."

"Then get the lamp," returned Selwood indifferently; "give it both barrels at once. Now set down your gun and give me a lift—I must get in there with my back to the window and both hands free."

The mule boss took him under the armpits, that Selwood's hands might be free, lifted him, and the next moment Selwood, watching the nearest men closely, stood inside the room with his feet on the floor. Pardaloe quickly rehung the curtain.

It was the work of the next moment for Selwood to reel to and sink into the empty chair opposite the sleepy man and, peering from under his cap, to study the scene.

The interior of the place, of notorious repute even among case-hardened men, was not wholly unfamiliar to Selwood, nor had it changed much in the long interval since he had seen it. The fierce yellow glare of the big lamps was missing; a murky haze of smoke dimmed the atmosphere, and the heated air, with every door and window closed, was rank with the fumes of tobacco and the characteristic smell of liquor. The bar, in bartenders' parlance, was closed; but when drinks were demanded they were very carefully set out by one man only, the argus-eyed Harry Barbanet, evidently appointed to manage the motley ruffians—the refuse of Sleepy Cat and the aristocracy of Calabasas—who, filled with the success of their repulse of the Vigilantes, ranted, cursed, and boasted, or yelled and disputed, and drank when they could get drink, along the length and breadth of the bar. It was Barbanet's policy, as Selwood had no difficulty in discerning, to hand out enough drink to stimulate the fighting instinct, but not enough to befuddle it. It was the eyes of Harry—sober, plotting, vigilant Harry—that Selwood, rightly, feared more than all other eyes in the room. Neither Bunty nor Atkins was in sight, and Selwood's nervous glance searched the room vainly for a sight of the one man he had taken a desperate chance to see—Starbuck. Men came at intervals out of the back room, but each one closed the door most carefully behind him. It was there, Selwood soon found reason to believe, that the leaders were closeted.

To attempt the inner room meant, he knew, a showdown. Whatever eyes might be fooled in the front room, those in the back room would not be long in discovering his identity. But with a fatality either temperamental or due to his chance-taking career, Selwood made ready to penetrate the second room in a search for Starbuck. At the table where he sat, he felt now as much at home as if in his old gambling-room.

He pushed guardedly at the head of the man opposite him and found after a little fussing that he was fast asleep. The man wore about his neck a bandanna kerchief, and this, Selwood, keeping his eyes well on those about him, gradually disengaged with one hand —twisting it around to where he could loose the knot and draw it from the man's neck. His victim having taken this liberty good-naturedly, Selwood doffed McAlpin's queer-looking cap at a moment that no eyes were turned his way, and after another moment tried on the sleeping man's hat. It fitted well enough, and he did not take it off; but proceeding slowly, keeping a clear eye on the men nearest, and handling his right forearm as if wounded, Selwood slipped one arm and then the other out of the coat he wore, and laid the purloined neckerchief over the right forearm.

Drawing his revolver from the scabbard in which he had replaced it when sitting down, Selwood, with the grip of the gun in his right hand, wrapped the kerchief loosely over hand and gun together. When arranged to his liking, he drew his small hunting-knife, and gradually slit the bandage on the lower side from end to end, so that it lay hiding his revolver, but ready to jerk off with his free hand. Putting away the knife, he rose and, facing the room, reached with his left hand up behind him and jerked the window curtain from the remaining hook. Sitting down again, he made a rude sling of the curtain, hung it from his neck under his right wrist, and with his left hand slipped his coat back again over his shoulders. Sitting now quite at ease, he drew a leaf of cigarette paper from a waistcoat pocket, laid it on the table, fished a tiny bag of tobacco from a coat pocket, opened it between his teeth and his left hand, taking advantage of that proceeding to take an extra good look at the men in front of him, rolled his cigarette awkwardly on the table before him, pushed it between his lips, and rose to his feet. He drew his hat-brim evenly down, so it was neither high nor low, but exactly shaded his eyes where he stood, and with the cigarette hanging from his lip, moved toward a noisy group of men and asked the nearest one for a match.

Passing this inspection proved easy. One man asked him how he got hit; another, whether he was for burning the railroad station and everybody in it—which proposal Selwood heartily endorsed. Lighting the cigarette, and laying his left hand on his bandaged arm, he asked how soon they would be ready to begin action, and was told they were ready now. He moved from one to another of the talking groups—some of the men were examining revolvers, others stowing cartridges into various pockets, others adjusting ammunition belts—trading tobacco, boasting, and telling stories; but while Selwood recognized more than one of them either as Calabasas worthies or River Quarter "rats," none of them uncovered him.

His apprehension thus fairly well allayed, he made his way in easy measure toward the rear end of the room, where the crowd was thicker. He had approached within a dozen feet of the back-room door and was thinking of just how he should manœuvre an entrance, when it was suddenly opened, and out walked Harry Barbanet, followed by the redoubtable Bull Page, whose eyes showed mild stimulation.

The moment was delicate. It seemed to Selwood as if, of all men in the room, the bartender's sharp eye fixed instantly on him. To turn quickly away would only be, he well knew, to excite suspicion and even invite particular inspection; the utmost Selwood could do was to interrupt a conversation near at hand and ask whether the doctor had come.

Had Bull, the derelict, sold him out—disclosed Selwood's presence and told what he knew of his intentions? The gambler did not believe it. Men on the Rocky Mountain frontier staked their lives at times on what would seem very slender chances. But drunkard though Bull was, outcast among outcasts, Selwood would have risked his life that Bull, drunk or sober, would not betray him. The question that rankled in his mind was: Had Barbanet in that brief, piercing glance discovered him? Was it imagination that was already tricking him into thinking so? He could not be sure. But some instinct told him he had been detected and must measure accordingly. The next moment Barbanet, now following Page, passed Selwood without noticing him—and so close on his left that he brushed him with an impatient shoulder.

It needed only an instant for Selwood to reason that this was precisely the way he himself should have acted if positions were reversed; and he knew Barbanet's astuteness too well to believe he would act, in the circumstances, any differently.

Without hesitation, Selwood, taking advantage of Barbanet's broad shoulder, turned promptly to the left, and, falling into step, walked on directly behind the two—third and last man in a procession heading straight for the lower end of the bar. For with his instinct, right or wrong, Selwood would not have kept his place and exposed his back to a shot, until he could put at least a partial screen of men between himself and his enemy.

It seemed strange to find himself heading so briskly in such company and at such a businesslike gait for a corner of the room that he had so good reason to remember. The old archway had been boarded up, and a batten door had been set roughly into it to lead into the barber shop; it was for this door that Barbanet was heading.

Nothing could have suited Selwood better. But just before reaching the door, Barbanet caught Page's arm, told him to stop, and attemped to turn in behind the bar. At this juncture Selwood in turn caught Barbanet's arm and stopped him.

"Don't bother, Harry; you won't need that gun. Face about—keep straight ahead."

Barbanet felt the quick and unpleasant sensation of a revolver muzzle held to the small of his back. A hand with fingers like steel slipped down his forearm and over his left wrist. Without trying to turn his body, he looked back over his shoulder, surprised, but making no pretense of not knowing who spoke.

"First time I've seen you to-night, John," he remarked, quite undisturbed by his situation.

"No," retorted Selwood in like tones, "this is the second time, Harry."

"I noticed you had a long arm on when I passed you," responded Barbanet, less amiably.

"Not for my friends, Harry—there's a good many strangers in town to-night. Open that barber-shop door, Harry—do it quick."

"There's two men behind it with shotguns."

"They're friendly—you're walking right in there ahead of me. Go on! The way we stand now, there's not a man in this room that could tell whose gun went off if you got hurt, Harry. Open that door."

No frontier crook in his senses would choose certain death before a fighting chance. Barbanet knew perfectly well the alternative. Selwood might not himself escape, but his fate would no longer interest Harry. With ill grace, but without imprudent delay, Barbanet advanced to the door, his left wrist gripped in Selwood's left hand.

"Key's in my left-hand pants pocket. Let loose my wrist."

"What's a right-hand man doing with a key in his left-hand pocket?" asked Selwood. "Page," he added, pulling Barbanet's arm back, "take the key out of Barbanet's right pants pocket and unlock that door, quick."

"Page," interjected Barbanet, jerking the words out viciously, "you'd better keep out of this."

Bull Page grinned brokenly. Perhaps the remembrance of old abuse at Barbanet's hands—the times he had come thirsty and broke, and gone from Barbanet's bar thirsty and broke, decided him. At all events, after a rapid search, Bull found the key in Barbanet's right-hand trousers pocket, unlocked the door, pushed it open, and Barbanet, followed by Selwood and Bull, passed through into the barber-shop.

CHAPTER XXVIII

SELWOOD FINDS CHRISTIE

THE barber-shop was dark. "What are you looking for," asked Barbanet, lazily sarcastic; "soap or towels?"

"Two men with shotguns," retorted Selwood, while Page fished a match from his pocket and lighted a lamp. "It may be they're in the back room; push ahead; open that door in front of you."

"Another man's got the key to that door," asserted Barbanet, surly now. "You'll have to talk to Starbuck about that."

Selwood, without raising his tone, tried out a double-edged bluff—one that would work either way. "Bull!" he said. "Go back to Starbuck. Tell him Barbanet wants the key to the barber-shop back room. He may give you an evasive answer. If he does, tell him Barbanet is in trouble in the barber-shop and says to give you the key or come a-running if he wants to save what's in the back room.

"If he follows you back, Bull," continued Selwood carelessly, "come as far as the door with him. Keep out of the shop here till the smoke settles."

Bull nodded. "I understand."

"If you know what's good for your hide, Bull," interposed Barbanet, "don't take any talk like that to Cliff Starbuck. Don't play traitor to Starbuck. He'll kill you—or I will."

"Why, Harry," said Bull Page, asserting what manhood Barbanet's whiskey had left him—and though his deep, throaty voice shook, there was no hesitation, no fear in his utterance—"what do you think you're talking about? Do you think I'm afraid of you—or your kind?

What have you ever done for me but fill me with poison when I come to town with money from the mines, you snake!" exclaimed Bull, gathering force with his invective. "Where did I go for a grub stake when I was hungry? To John Selwood!"

"Oh, shut up, Bull," blurted out Selwood.

"No!" exclaimed Page, rolling up resentment till it amounted to defiance of all comers. "I'm blamed if I'll shut up! This skunk's goin' to hear for once what's coming to him and his slut breed."

"Shut up, Bull," snapped Selwood impatiently. "Dash it, do as you're told."

"Why, Harry," exclaimed Bull, paying no attention to the protest, "I'd take that man's message through hell and back. I'd walk in on Starbuck with it if I knew he'd fill me with lead the next minute.

"But he won't. You fellows are done."

"Bull!" cried Selwood. "Get out! And get back here quick with that key or with Starbuck."

"I'm flyin' right now, John. Do you know what this rat asked me to do a few minutes ago? To knock old man Fyler on the head and throw him in the river— that's all."

With this parting shot, Bull was opening the door through which they had come in. Barbanet saw the jig was up. "Hold on," he said, bitterly sulky, "call off your rabbit. That key will unlock either door."

Bull lost no time in starting for the inner door. "Stop a minute, Bull," interposed Selwood; "take those aprons on that chair to tie this fellow up with before you open the door. Got 'em? Now put out lights and unlock."

Page threw the back door open. Light streamed into the barber-shop from a lamp set on an up-ended barrel in the apparently empty room. Silence greeted the opening. Selwood pushed his sullen prisoner forward across the threshold. A suppressed cry acknowledged the sight of him. "Harry Barbanet!" exclaimed an unsteady voice. "What do you mean by keeping us locked here all this time? You promised we should be free in a few minutes. When are we to get out?"

Margaret Hyde stood to the left of the doorway; and clinging with clasped hands to Margaret's arm, hatless and shrinking under a cape, her eyes filled with fear, Selwood saw Christie Fyler.

Christie's startled glance fell on him. He was looking fixedly at her. To their meeting eyes the exchange was an electric shock. There was only an added mystery to Christie in his unexpected appearance. Of all men, she would have wished to identify Selwood last, despite what had passed between them, with these detestable surroundings in which she was held prisoner. To see him suddenly in this forbidding place in company with the ruthless tool of the man she had now so much reason to fear, was like rudely stripping her of what faith she had left in men. It was hardly a moment before the situation cleared, but for Christie it was a painful moment.

Barbanet halted before Margaret's question. He nodded coolly back over his shoulder. "I ain't bossing this procession." He spoke with a contemptuous spite. "This man with the gun is running things—for a few minutes—talk to him."

Fyler emerged from the gloom of a corner, with a look of expectancy. His thin hair was pretty much on end, or would have been seen to better advantage if it had been, and his large eyes shone wildly in the lamp-light. But as little as Selwood liked him, he realized that he had at least stuck to his daughter and had just now escaped death by a mere scratch because of doing it.

Barbanet's words directed all eyes on Selwood. He spoke to Margaret Hyde. "If you are kept here against your wills, you're free to go now—or will be in a minute. This is a good place to get away from. It will be burned before daylight."

"They brought us here because they said the hotel would be burned," declared Margaret Hyde, in agitation.

"They dragged us here," exclaimed Christie. "They threatened to kill us."

"What can we do?" asked Margaret Hyde, appealing to Selwood so quietly that it seemed as if she were anxious not to dwell on what had gone before.

"Who is 'they'?" asked Selwood.

Margaret hesitated. "All of these men," interposed Christie, tremulous and eager. She pointed to Barbanet. "This man, and most of all—Starbuck. It was he who had us brought to this vile place," repeated Christie, with gathering anger and courage. "We don't know yet why we should be locked up in this way. Who are all these men we hear in the next room? That man"—she pointed her finger, with flashing eyes, at Barbanet—"and another tried to drag me here, alone. Margaret wouldn't let them—they almost tried to kill my father!"

Selwood stood the sullen bartender facing the wall, with his hands up. "I'll have a job for you in a minute, Barbanet," said Selwood in an undertone. "You may want to save your own skin with it. When these people get out of here, you can take word in to Starbuck he's cornered. Lefever's men have surrounded this place, and they're out to get him and his crew for burning their bunk-house. Starbuck can either fight, or come out and talk. If he fights, there won't be any talk—not so far as I know. If he doesn't come out he'll be burnt out. If he fights, he—and the rest of you—will get the rope."

He turned away without waiting for an answer. Bull

Page had unbarred and knocked the rim lock off the flimsy back door, and opened it. Pardaloe, waiting impatiently in the dark, and itching to train the big shotgun on somebody, loomed up in the doorway.

"They're here," he said to Selwood significantly. He looked enviously at Selwood's victim, standing with his face to the wall—he offered so tempting a cushion for a handful of buckshot—but was appeased when Selwood seriously put on him the responsibility of taking the three refugees through the burnt district to the barn.

Christie, listening eagerly to all the words passed, edged up so she could ask Selwood a question apart. "You are not coming?"

He hesitated as she spoke, and looked at her almost curiously. The old fever in his blood rose at the sight of her. But pride ruled his will, and Christie, looking questioningly up at him as if she, too, longed to say and to hear more, saw nothing of what was hidden behind the unbending expression. "Not yet," was all he said when he answered. "But you oughtn't to lose a minute—follow Pardaloe and keep close to him."

Pardaloe himself seemed in haste. "Don't lose no time, Christie," he urged; "come along!"

She could not be hurried. "Then surely," she faltered to Selwood, "I shall see you again to-night—to—to say *something*—to thank you for——"

Selwood held on to his words as if they were diamonds. "Glad to do it," he murmured, stubbornly laconic.

His gaze was so steady that her eyes fell. However, she would not give up—and when she looked at him again her eyes were glistening a little. "I know I hurt you terribly," she began. He offered nothing to help her out. "I did not want to," she persisted, resolved to soften him. "Can't you—come with us now?"

It was his turn to squirm. He did not risk his eyes

directly on hers—only repeated, almost mechanically, "Not yet."

She dropped into a low, quite matter-of-fact tone—Christie knew how to close in on a man. "Then let Father and Margaret Hyde go," she urged. "Let me stay here till you are ready."

He replied with quick decision: "That wouldn't do."

"Are you going to—to fight?" She could hardly breathe the hateful word between her reluctant lips.

"I may have to." Without looking at her, he raised his hand toward the open door. "Follow Pardaloe."

She made her last appeal—save, perhaps, that deepest appeal that until now had lain unspoken in her eyes. But Christie could say things, too. As she stepped toward the door her eyes flashed back at him. "If I didn't fear endangering your life—I'd stay anyway!"

The suddenness, the surprise, the intimate defiance, brought the care-free old laugh for a moment to Selwood's lips—the laugh of the summer auction days, the laugh that Christie remembered and had missed so long. But without giving him time for a word she stepped out into the night. It was not till then that he imagined he heard in the darkness something like a suppressed sob.

CHAPTER XXIX

SHOW-DOWN

SELWOOD knew that for every moment lingered with Christie he had been gambling with a relentless enemy —time. He knew that when dangers multiply no moment can be called your own—that at such a time fate holds many cards—you but one.

With Christie on the way to safety and Lefever's men at his call, he started Barbanet back to Starbuck.

But Barbanet had only disappeared when Selwood heard a woman's scream. Christie had but just crossed the other threshold—it was her voice.

He sprang out of the open back door and ran around to the front. In the street, lighted by the gray gleam of daybreak, he saw a little group of struggling figures. To his left, out of the wide-open doors of Bartoe's place, Starbuck's men were crowding. What Selwood feared had happened: a door guard, freeing himself, had given the alarm. As they ran out they were met with the gun-fire of Lefever's men, and in what seemed no more than a second the two parties were at grips with clubs and guns.

Before Selwood could dash across the sidewalk, the group in the street was surrounded by a crowd of yelling men. In the thick of it Selwood made out Pardaloe, whirling about like a bear and furiously shaking off a man who clung to his back; a second man, gun in hand, jumped around the two, evidently trying to shoot the mule boss without hitting his assailant; Christie, screaming, her father and Bull Page urging her away, stood by, wringing her hands. And at that moment an active man, dashing out of Bartoe's and brandishing a revolver, ran between Christie and her protectors and caught her up with his free arm.

Had the confusion been less, had the uncertain light been less certain, Selwood would have been at no loss to recognize this man; the commonest instinct in the nature of men would have declared Starbuck to him in the man assailing Christie. He did not realize that smoke was now rising about Bartoe's place, that Pardaloe had made good his threat to burn it, and that the men running out of the door were crying "Fire!" He had eyes for no one but Starbuck and heard nothing but Christie's angry, rebellious cries as she struggled to free herself. And he ran toward her with an answering cry.

Starbuck saw him leap into the street; and, still holding the frantic girl, he brought down his gun like a flash on Selwood.

It was a reckless, a useless shot. With Christie fighting him with her puny fists, the bullet flew wide. Not deigning to reply, not even drawing his own gun, but maddened to fury, Selwood dashed forward; before Starbuck could pull up and cover the second time, the gambler was on him. Bull Page had caught Christie by the wrist and was dragging her away. She screamed at Bull and resisted him. She tried to get back to where she knew a deadly moment had come between the man she hated and the man she loved; but she could not.

Pardaloe, like a beleaguered giant, had shaken off his enemies, recovered his shotgun, and above the sputtering crack of revolvers, its roar sounded on Christie's ears. Then, clubbing the gun and shouting imprecations at his enemies, the mule boss swept an open space between them and two men who, locked in a death struggle, rolled in the middle of the street.

Despite a terrific blow across the head from the flat

of Selwood's revolver, Starbuck's weight and bulk had borne the gambler to the ground; and Starbuck, to avoid a fatal dexterity with the same revolver, had clinched with him.

Neither of the infuriated men—seasoned to death grips—wasted another instant in trying to shoot. But Starbuck had a further resource lacking to his enemy. Selwood knew precisely what it was—the deadliest of weapons in a clinch. He knew as grips, like lightning, shifted, eyes strained in fury, blows rained remorselessly, and the gage of life and death slipped from hand to hand, precisely what Starbuck was trying to do—he knew almost precisely where the heavier man carried the coveted weapon, and now not one man but two were exhausting every resource of strength and stratagem to reach the haft of Starbuck's bowie-knife at his hip.

It was an unequal struggle. Starbuck's weight and strength almost continually overbore the gambler's agility. Each advantage for the mastery hard-gained by Selwood was soon lost to the heavier defense of Starbuck. With Pardaloe's piercing eyes taking note of every turn, he could see but one hope for the lighter man, a hope that vanished when Selwood seemed weakening. If Starbuck's wind should outlast the other—Selwood, Pardaloe told himself, could not win.

So deep had become this conviction that more than once Pardaloe would have interfered, would have knocked Starbuck on the head or rammed him with his gun-stock—would have taken for himself the badge of disgrace from the wrought-up teamsters, watching—had he not known that Selwood, living or dead, would never forgive a stigma put on him by the aid of a friend. With hungry eyes and ears, the powerful mule boss watched the doubtful issue and listened to the sharp, broken breaths of the struggling men. But again and again

Starbuck would roll his enemy under, only to have Selwood squirm free and slip himself out.

The contest fast narrowed to one point—the possession of the knife. Pardaloe saw and he understood; his fingers itched and his muscles twitched in his fever to pass his own knife into Selwood's hand; and almost as if timed to the last moment of the encounter, Starbuck, once more freeing his right hand, restrained till then by Selwood's left, slipped it from the leash of muscles, and whipped out his knife.

But in gaining this deadly advantage he had laid himself open to an unlooked-for danger. As a boxer, defeated in every tactic of defense, sees himself going and turns to the attack, Selwood's right hand, releasing Starbuck's left, shot out and clutched Starbuck's windpipe. The sinewy fingers that could tear a pack of cards in two like a sheet of paper, closed relentlessly on Starbuck's throat, and, squirming from under him, Selwood threw himself across his enemy and overlay the arm slashing at him with the knife. Pardaloe, wild with anxiety, knew the end was in sight. But could Starbuck inflict a fatal injury before he should succumb to the grip that had cut off his breath?

Throwing himself frantically about as he felt consciousness going, striking blindly at Selwood from the forearm, Starbuck tried to land a fatal thrust. But Selwood, as Starbuck, plunging and rearing, slammed him from side to side to shake loose the deadly grip, took the slashing as best he could, clinging all the while like a panther to the throat of his foe.

Above the din about him, Pardaloe shouted and yelled. Hope had returned. He saw how the fight went. And, stamping his clumsy feet in a frenzy, he watched Selwood's left elbow gradually straighten and saw his left hand slide slowly, unevenly, but certainly up to Starbuck's right wrist. Again the two men meshed. Pardaloe could see their straining muscles shiver in a climax of struggle. Then, Selwood had wrested the haft of the knife from his strangled foe, let go his throat, and raised his arm to strike.

Not till then did Pardaloe jump in. He caught the uplifted arm. The gambler, covered with blood, looked angrily up. "Not yet, John," cried the big fellow, low and ferociously. "Hang him!"

Panting as if dazed, Selwood looked again to see who spoke. The voice that entered his ear sent no message to his brain. He shook away the matted hair that fell before his eyes. Pardaloe, gripping his arm, looked intently at him and repeated his words. Whether Selwood understood or not, he knew Pardaloe. He looked down on his gasping enemy, and, stretching out his left hand, laid the ugly knife in Pardaloe's hand.

With a cracked laugh, he staggered to his feet, groping about with his hands for support.

Pardaloe steadied him. "Cut much, John?" he asked, bending anxiously over him.

"Why—no." Trying to pull himself together, Selwood panted the words. "I guess—not."

"You're chipped a little," commented Pardaloe, taking hold of his blood-soaked left arm and peering with melancholy sympathy into the strained eyes.

With the fingers of his left hand, Selwood felt uncertainly around his heart. "One jab," he said, breathing hard, "I thought went through me. His grip must have slipped," he added, as his fingers ran vacantly over his chest, trying to find a particular spot, "or something —turned the knife. What's here, Bill?" he asked, feeling blindly at the slit breast-pocket of his woollen shirt.

Pardaloe set down his lantern, and, using both hands on the slashed pocket, succeeded in fishing out the remains of a pack of cards. He stooped to examine the cards by the light of the lantern; the point of Starbuck's knife had gone half way through them. "My cards, by gum!" exclaimed Pardaloe, as his face fell. "Plum' cut to pieces, too. That deck ain't worth shucks to nobody now—look at 'em!" He held the pack up for inspection and looked indignantly down at Starbuck, whose wrists and ankles were already bound by Lefever and Scott. "No matter, old boy," he growled; "we'll fix you in a minute so you won't cut up no more cards for nobody."

Such of Starbuck's following as could escape the clutches of Lefever's angry men were scattering in the thickets along the river, where most of them had horses hidden, and by fording or swimming the stream could spur out on the Sinks for Calabasas.

Smoke was billowing from the doors and windows of Bartoe's place. Flames were lighting for the last time the interior of the empty barroom and licking its evil trappings. Selwood, steadied by Pardaloe, looked blankly at the scene before him and backed away.

The teamsters were dragging off their prisoners. In the crowd that closed in on the scene there rose up sudden bosses, and a confusion of orders as to how Starbuck should be disposed of. In the midst of the shouting, jostling throng, Selwood stood once more clear-headed. When a cry arose to run Starbuck to a telegraph pole, he intervened. "Hands off," he said. "This man is my prisoner. Take him to the barn, Pardaloe, with the others—and hold him till I get there."

CHAPTER XXX

THE PADRE

Torn by anxiety and racked with fears, Christie hovered as long as she could on the edge of things. But poor Bull Page, with more sense of the fitness of things than should be expected, refused her entreaties that she be allowed to see Selwood. "Safest place fur wimmen folks to-night's inside," he insisted. "John is O K, that I know," he declared; and with that assurance she had to content herself. "You two," he suggested to Christie and Margaret, when with Fyler they reached the hotel, "get into the kitchen and get some coffee going for the bunk-house boys. If they hadn't got out when they did, there wouldn't be any hotel now. Them fellows sent word to Carpy that if he didn't come down to Bartoe's to look after their wounded men, they'd burn the hotel on him; he told 'em—well, to burn and be hanged."

Selwood walked to the hotel. Scott trailed him close, and, running ahead, lighted a lamp in the office. When he walked with the lamp into the dark hall, he found Selwood sitting on the first tread of the bare stairs, twisting the tourniquet on his left arm, and storing strength to get up to his room. When he got on his feet again he waved Scott aside, climbed the stairs, and got to his room alone.

He had hardly thrown himself on his bed when Carpy's boisterous tread could be heard on the stairs, and the next minute Selwood was in the hands of the rough, cheerful surgeon—most cheerful now, for the night skies had cleared, and cleared his way.

While Carpy, with Scott helping him, was dressing the wounds, Pardaloe came in to see how Selwood came on and give him the news. Atkins had been killed in the street fight. Barbanet, sullen, and Bartoe, struggling and screaming, had been cruelly dragged from the barn to the fate of their kind. "Abe Cole," said Pardaloe in reciting the incident, "wanted me to go 'long and sit on the court. 'No,' I says, 'I won't sit on no court for nobody.' 'Why not?' says he. 'Why not?' says I. 'Why, dash it, before they get through they might take it into their heads to hang me!'" McAlpin, Pardaloe continued, had prevented "the boys" from taking out Big Haynes.

"The boys aren't afraid of McAlpin, are they?" asked Selwood, watching Carpy's bandaging.

"No," thundered Pardaloe mildly. "But he's got Haynes hid and they can't find him."

"I don't think it right to hang him either," said Carpy. "He's nothing like as bad as the others. Haynes claims Atkins and Bartoe threatened to kill him if he didn't turn in with them."

Scott proved a good assistant. But when Carpy had finished and Pardaloe was still talking, the Indian regarded Selwood with a peculiar smile. There were many lights and shades in Bob Scott's very homely smile, many varieties of meaning—and those who knew him well could read them pretty well. Selwood, taking keen note again of what was going on around him, perceived that the smile Scott now wore meant news; but the wounded man was too used up to ask for it. He only looked his own inquiry into his retainer's eyes and waited for him to speak.

The half-breed, treading about the room even in boots almost as lightly and silently as his moccasined kind, gathering up the odds and ends of Carpy's work, did not lose his smile of import, nor did Selwood's expression lose its demand for information.

"What is it, Bob?" he asked at length.

Scott, lifting his eyes, answered with a broader smile and another question: "Got any money?"

No inquiry could have surprised Selwood more. "Not a whole lot," he confessed with abating interest. "How much do you want?"

"Two thousand dollars."

Selwood took it for a joke. "Well, I'm broke just at present; but if it's coming to you, you'll get it. What do you want with two thousand dollars?"

"I've got a man down below the barn you been wanting to see."

"Do I owe him anything?"

Scott shook his head. "I guess not."

"Who's the man I want to see?" asked Selwood, with only moderate interest.

"The old padre."

Carpy was stowing his instruments away in his bag. He looked up with an exclamation of astonishment. Selwood regarded Scott searchingly. "You mean the old padre I wanted to see?" Scott nodded.

Selwood, who had taken a chair, rose to his feet, and with one hand picked up his coat to throw over his shoulders. Scott helped him. "Where in thunder did the old padre turn up?" asked Carpy.

"McAlpin passed him on the Calabasas trail about an hour ago, when he was bringing in Dave. He had a couple of Gunlocks with him." Scott so designated the Indians from Gunlock Reservation. "McAlpin told me he met a black-robe and that he was on his way up here and going to camp along the river. So I rode down there and talked with his guides. They told me they had a very old black-robe along. So I talked to him.

They're heading for the Blackfeet country. 'I saw the big fire in the sky,' he told me, 'and I said to my men the new town is burning; many people are in distress. We will go there before we start up the river!'

"I held my lantern into his face," continued Scott. "He is a gray-headed—an old man. But," added the half-breed, with the certainty of men of his kind, "he is the same man whose picture you had in your room up at the hall. And I told him there was a white man here wanted to see him. And to go to the horse barn if it wasn't burned. But he said he would camp down by the river. He's there."

If there was a surprise for Carpy in the recital there was a greater one awaiting him in Selwood's reception of it. For a moment Selwood did not speak. When he did, Carpy stood open-eyed. "Well—" said Selwood deliberately. "If you've got the man, the money is coming to you—when I can dig it up. But don't hold him on my account—I don't care about seeing him."

Carpy was well nigh speechless with amazement. "What!" he exclaimed, recovering his breath. "'Don't care about seeing him?' Man!" he cried. "Don't want to see the man—if it is the man—that's got your whole story? Have you lost your senses?"

Selwood, standing unmoved, parried the attack with stubborn indifference. He felt that Christie had cast him off—what did a name, good or bad, mean to him now? But he would say not one word, and Doctor Carpy, unable to stir him with eloquent reproach, in the end lost his own temper. "Here, after all these years," he protested, "that blamed old martinet Roper has been running over you, and you get a chance to nail him, by Jing, you won't take the trouble to do it!

"All right. I'll do it myself," the Doctor exclaimed. "I won't let that old buck run over *me* any longer.

Bob," continued the incensed surgeon, pointing his finger at Scott, "hold on to your black-robe and his redskins. If we can't find anything else for breakfast, bring 'em up here for a cup o' coffee, anyway." And with Selwood staring at the wall, and the half-breed grinning perplexed, Carpy flung out of the room.

CHAPTER XXXI

MARGARET'S STORY

In the gloom of the hall, Carpy, still exasperated by Selwood's obstinacy and talking resentfully to himself, almost ran into Christie, a pathetic figure, he thought, waiting for a chance to speak to somebody. As he stopped with an apology, she seemed encouraged, for she stepped close to him. "Doctor!" she exclaimed, in a frightened whisper, "*is* Mr. Selwood terribly hurt?"

"Well," said the surgeon, half smiling, "John's cut some—yes. Did McAlpin bring your things back?"

"He did. Did you take them away?" she asked.

"Selwood took them. There was no one left to guard the hotel, so he carried them down to the barn."

"Doctor," asked Christie plaintively, "will he get well?"

Carpy laughed as he looked into her appealing eyes—one of those reassuring laughs that would bring life and hope to a dying man. "Christie," he murmured, "there's more the matter with that fellow than just Starbuck's slashing. I think," continued the Doctor, eyeing her with a significant expression, "that if *you'd* talk you could tell—better than anybody else—what's a-matter with him." Christie tried to brave it through with innocent astonishment. Her attempt did not deceive the Doctor; he retorted in raillery. "Listen to the little bird!" he purred, smiling. "Christie, you're a fine girl, good enough for the best, or I wouldn't talk to you so plain. But you're in love with John Selwood and he's in love with you. There, there! I didn't mean to make you cry, child."

She looked up. "What can I do, Doctor?" she

pleaded. "I thought the world of him—why shouldn't I confess it to you? You wouldn't betray me. I do yet. Now he has saved my life—and more than my life. But how do you think I felt when I was told by that vile man—and by him—that he was a gambler?"

The Doctor looked perplexed. "I knowed it, Christie. I knowed that was what made the trouble 'tween you," he said. "I couldn't blame you so much, neither," he added regretfully, "even if I'm nothing but a poor drunken doctor myself."

"You shan't say that!" she exclaimed indignantly. "You're nothing of the kind! You're the kindest, best doctor in the whole world!"

He shook his head. "Tell the truth, girl, and shame the devil. If I wasn't I wouldn't be wasting out my life in this hell-hole. But I want to say only this: I wisht somehow it could be fixed up. I may not be able to speak it in words, but I know what goes into the making of a man, my girl; and whatever it is, it's in John Selwood. And if he ever quits the business he's in, you'll see a man all through him."

A flood of words broke through Christie's pent-up feeling. "Oh, I believe every word of it, Doctor. You've no need to tell *me* that. He's just the finest man in the world, if he'd only—" A timid suggestion occurred to her. "You, Doctor, if *you'd* ask him to give up that business—you have more influence with him than any one else——"

Carpy cut her off. "Christie," he said, emphasizing every deliberate word with a shake of the head, "you've got more influence over him in your one little finger than I have all over me.

"But, Christie, I've noticed this: it ain't so good when somebody coaxes a man to quit anything—even if he does quit it—as when he quits a thing himself, out of just his own free will. Now if John Selwood ever quits the game of his own accord—bet on him!

"Well," he said in parting, "things is working, anyway; they're working right now, maybe, to clear things up, that I can't tell you about just yet—only this: count on me to stay with you, will you?" The look she gave him as she went back to her room made him ten years younger. He strode toward the stairs, only to encounter Margaret Hyde hurrying to meet him.

"Why, yes, the boy's chipped up a little," grumbled Carpy in answer to Margaret's manifest anxiety—for he was thinking of his own perplexities—"nothing to hurt much," he added. "And, Meg, don't give nobody no more of our sheets to tear up for bandages," continued the landlord-surgeon emphatically. "Tell 'em to use buffalo robes. This hotel will be out of business at this rate, before daylight. You look queer: what's a-matter with you? Ain't shot anywheres, are you?"

The drawn face and the sunken, anxious eyes of his housekeeper made his question almost an involuntary one. She answered to reassure him, but she could not hide her distress. "I'm not wounded, Doctor. But might I, I wonder," she managed to say in her low, restrained voice—a voice that, no matter how often it broke, never wholly lost a note of once gentle breeding— "might I," she added, repeating her plea, "speak to John Selwood right away—just for a *few* minutes?"

Doctor Carpy lifted his eyebrows with a grating laugh, and as if things were getting *too* complicated. "So *that's* what you're hanging around for? Why didn't you say so? Well, now, I'll tell you; if you're worrying about John, don't do it——"

Margaret flushed. "But, Doctor——"

"That boy ain't hurted none to speak of. Shucks!" Doctor Carpy faintly grinned. "I never thought——"

She caught her breath. "It's *not* about him," she exclaimed, in distress, "far from it! But I *must* speak with him."

"'Fraid it's too late to ketch him now," objected the Doctor, still mystified by her strange interest. "The boys are waiting to set up another telegraph pole party. And they're waiting for John to come down to the station before they begin. See him when he comes back, Meg."

Carpy knew nothing of what those words—and particularly the last words—meant to Margaret Hyde. But he could not help seeing the suffering in her face strangely intensified. "You're sick, Meg," he exclaimed, not unsympathetically, "that's what's the matter, girl. Go to bed till breakfast time—don't believe there's a thing in the house to cook, anyway."

Her lips could scarcely frame words. "I *must* see John Selwood," she repeated, with a supreme effort at self-control. "I must see him now. Who is in there with him?"

"Bill Pardaloe and Bob Scott."

"Doctor," she exclaimed, stepping closer in her almost frantic appeal, "help me! Ask them to step out a moment—I tell you, I *must* talk to him alone—*now*."

It was impossible not to acknowledge her extremity. Carpy reopened Selwood's door. He spoke to Pardaloe and Scott. "Look here, boys," he said, beckoning with his head, "both of you. Step out here a minute. Meg wants to talk to John, private."

Selwood, cleaned up and brushed up as decently as he could be with his bandaged arm and hands, stood before the table preparing to go to the barn. He was buckling on his cartridge belt; his coat was thrown over his shoulder. Hearing Margaret's footsteps, he looked around. One glance revealed the agony in her face. He laid unlighted on the table a cigarette that Scott had rolled for him, and spoke. "What is it, Margaret?" He pointed to a chair. "You're not hurt?"

Looking at him like one dumb with emotion, she sat down. When she spoke, she had already forgotten the question he had just asked. "Mr. Selwood——"

He interrupted her. He had taken his revolver up from the table and was slowly slipping cartridges back into the cylinder. "Since when," he demanded with good-natured unconcern, "did I stop being just plain 'John'?"

"Never, to me—never," she said brokenly. "But to-night I come to beg my life at your hands—hoping, praying you won't deny me. Let me tell you what I mean—tell you my story. I was married ten years ago, when I was eighteen. Oh, yes," she said, to cut off his surprise, "I know how old I look—trouble has done that. For three years I had the best husband in the world—kind, considerate, devoted. His friends persuaded him to go into politics. They elected him city treasurer of the little town where we lived in Michigan. That was his undoing; it meant being out nights, being a good fellow, drinking, spending, wasting.

"It lasted two years. And during that time I fell sick. I was very sick, a long time, and he did everything he could in the world to care for me—to relieve me. I cost him so much, oh, so much for doctors—more than I wanted him to spend; but he would try everything that gave us the least hope. He said I should have the best care, and he gave it liberally, extravagantly, to me. Then—one night he came home. He had been drinking." She stopped an instant. "It was the first time in my life, John, I had seen him in drink," she went on. "He told me that night his accounts were short—that the next day his books would be examined; that he must face the penitentiary—or run away."

In her agony she sat, now twisting and clasping her fingers, now her hands; now looking at the floor, now looking at Selwood imploringly—her words wrung from her reluctant lips. "When he told me that," she faltered on, "I was frightened. I was so weak that night! And I was wicked. I told him to go, John—to go at once. But to write me. And that when he found some safe place far away in the West, I would join him."

Selwood only looked at her—not unfeelingly, but as one who could say nothing because he knew of nothing to say. Margaret moistened her parched lips. "He never wrote me," she said, in a low, hard voice; "if he did, I never got the letter. I made up my mind he must have been hurt, or killed, and that I would find out, or find him, myself. And after weary, weary months of search I did find my husband—here—in Sleepy Cat."

Her eyes had dropped from her listener's eyes. Her head hung. Her voice fell still lower. "He was not hurt, not dead. But worse for me—his feeling—for me —was dead. He cared nothing for me—nothing——"

"But you," interposed Selwood coldly, "you cared for him. It's an old story. Well, what then?"

"I stayed here while he was here; then I went to Thief River to be near him—not chasing him, not bothering him—hoping sometime to repay him for his old goodness to me. But he had chosen bad company, and through drink was going from bad to worse. I can't excuse him for the evil. But I *know* there is good in my husband. I've come to you to plead for his life."

"To *me?*" echoed Selwood, mildly astonished. "Why to me? What's his name?"

It took all her courage to speak. "He doesn't use his real name here," she said in strained, broken tones.

"You wouldn't know it if I mentioned it. He is known here—as Cliff Starbuck."

"Starbuck!!"

She heard the name blurted out in hateful amazement. With dry, despairing eyes she watched the passionless features before her harden into the cold refusal that she saw was coming.

Leaning against the table, with his back to it, the gambler shifted from one foot to the other. His eyes, that he might avoid her eyes, fixed on the floor; he flattened his left hand at his side on the table, and his right hand rested on the grip of the revolver he had slung in the scabbard at his hip.

"I'll tell you, Margaret," he said at last—speaking with apparent unconcern but with deadly point—"I'm sorry you're mixed up with that fellow. But I couldn't do a thing for you, if I wanted to—and I can't honestly say I'm looking to do anything for that man. They're going to hang him—and it's almost too good for him— that, if you want it, is my honest opinion. But you might go and talk to the two Cole boys, John and Abe, if Abe's alive yet; and to the teamsters. If they're willing to let him go"—he shifted again on his feet—"I won't say anything."

"But, John," she pleaded in heartbreaking tones, "if you won't say anything, I'm lost. None of those men would have any mercy for me; or for him but to hang him. They have no hearts, no feeling—you know, I might as well go out and beg the stones in the streets for mercy."

Selwood stood motionless. "He pulled a knife on me in that clinch to-night," he muttered.

Her plea was so swift. "He was drinking to-night——"

"He dragged Christie Fyler out of this hotel down to

that—" Words could convey no more of hateful, bitter anger than his words carried.

"He was drinking, John—drinking! And the others were going to burn the hotel—I was here, I know—and *I* went with her to protect her, John. *I went with her!* I'd have given up my life rather than she should come to harm. I thought of her. I thought of you——"

"My advice to you would be to let him hang."

"John——"

"I don't want to hurt your feelings by saying how I feel toward that man——"

She sprang up from her chair, and clasping one of her bony hands in the other, at the waist of her worn dress, stood, dry-eyed, before him. "John, listen! Have you never done things you wish you hadn't done?"

He snorted. "I hope they don't class me with that——"

"You know what whiskey will do to a man——"

"For God's sake, don't blame *his* meanness on whiskey—whiskey's got enough to answer for!"

"I don't, I don't. I blame it on myself. When I should have told him that terrible night to do right, I told him to do wrong. Pity me! Have a little mercy for *me*, John. Think of the old padre whose picture you kept here on the wall so long—who has spent his life forgiving men, helping them. Oh, I'll pray that you find that padre, John. If he were here, he would ask you for the sake of Christ and His Mother to pity me to-night, to let Cliff go. Think of Christie, John. You love her, she loves you. Would you spare him if *she* asked you? I've told her all this. She's in my room now down the hall. She'll beg for his life of you this moment if you'll let her—she told me she would. *She* has forgiven him. Oh, God!" Her words poured out in a torrent—low, tearless. She sank before him on her knees. "I'll do anything for you you could ask of a woman, John. I'll pray for you every day and night of my life. Have pity on me! Spare him to me for one more—just *one* more chance!"

She had caught his bandaged hand in her thin, knotted fingers and covered it with her forehead. He stood irresolute, wanting to pull it away and ashamed to—uneasily listening and thinking. A long time he stood.

Then, suddenly, his face darkened. He jerked himself angrily up.

"What do you want me to do?" He threw the words at her with a rude savageness that would have frightened another. But Margaret knew what his words meant. She scrambled to her feet and caught his hand again in her hands, and broke into a flood of tears. "Oh, I don't know. I don't know," she sobbed; then she lifted her streaming face with the tender confidence of a child. "*You* will know, John."

"Sit down," he snapped. She shrank away. From her chair she only looked her hope and her gratitude and watched anxiously the play of his features. Selwood, with a vacant expression, took up from the table Scott's cigarette, put it between his lips, and slowly felt for a match. He felt first in one pocket of his waistcoat vainly; then he felt in another; he felt for a match in a right coat-pocket, and again he felt for one in a left coat-pocket. It seemed to poor Margaret as if he never would find that fatal match; for even while he searched and decided, her husband, she knew, might be hanged. In her fearful anxiety she was about to run out and find a match for him, when finally, and with his eyes still fixed on the floor, he felt once more in the first pocket he had tried and drew out the match he had missed. He held it a moment, paused, rolling it between his finger and thumb; then, in com-

plete exasperation, he snapped the unlighted cigarette
back on the table, put the match in his pocket, and
turned his bloodshot eyes on Margaret.

"I'm doing something I don't approve of," he said
sulkily. "Nobody else will approve of it, that's a cinch.
This buck has tried his blamedest to kill me—and done
worse'n that. Nobody outside a lunatic asylum would
turn a hand to help him. If I wasn't a blamed fool,
I wouldn't."

Margaret, with only the tears that had been shed
brimming in her eyes, sat looking at him. Her subdued
fingers worked unseen together. "I'm doing what I do
for *you*," he said harshly. "Not for that——"

She bowed her head. "Ask Bob Scott," he went on,
"to bring McAlpin in here—McAlpin is waiting for me
down-stairs. But if you want to save your man, don't
let Pardaloe come in. When Scott and McAlpin come
in here, stay outside the door till I send for you."

"Boys," he said to McAlpin and Scott the moment
the door of his room closed behind them, "Meg, out
there, is the wife of this hound Starbuck. You didn't
know it; I didn't—nobody around here knew it. I can't
tell you everything she told me to-night—if I stopped
to, they'd have Starbuck hanged before I got down
there. And I can't tell you why I've promised her his
life—but I've been just blamed fool enough to do it—
that's all. And"—he spoke low and with stubborn in-
toning—"when I make a promise, I don't allow any man
to interfere. To begin with, Starbuck is my own personal prisoner. I want to get him away without hurt-
ing some people's feelings—you can understand that.
Will you help?"

"Well," he continued, as he listened to their protests
of loyalty coupled with an ungrudging assent, "I thought
maybe you would. Now call in Meg."

Scott opened the door, and Margaret Hyde, looking questioningly from one to the other, as if to read her fate in their eyes, stepped inside, and the door was closed behind her. Selwood spoke again. "Starbuck and Big Haynes," he said to her, "are tied up and locked in the harness-room at the barn. Lefever's men are guarding them. I'll go down with you all and take care of Lefever. He'll call off his men and leave me to look after my prisoner. Bob, you cut Starbuck loose. McAlpin, you have horses saddled at the back door of the barn, and Bob will ride with Meg and—him to the east end of town. Nobody," he spoke now to Margaret Hyde, "will bother you beyond that. Keep out of the way of travel and of our men, but get East as fast as you can. If you can get to Medicine Bend, you'll be all right—nobody there to bother. But between here and there you'll have to look out. Any of our boys or the Vigilantes will shoot him on sight. Leave the horses at Medicine Bend in our barn— Well, I guess that's all.

"Not quite, either," he added, still thinking. "Barbanet's gun is at the barn; Starbuck can take that. Pick up some grub at the barn for 'em, Jim, and a couple of canteens. Give 'em some matches and a flint and a pair of blankets." He started forward on his feet. "We'll head for the barn. Hang it!" he exclaimed, suddenly recollecting himself, "there's Bill Pardaloe yet. I'll never square it with him if I talked an hour. He'll never give in—where is he?"

Scott grinned. "Hanging over the bar, when I come up."

"Who's behind it?"

"Bull Page——"

"Tell him to hold Bill there for ten minutes, anyway —to lock him in if he has to. There's no time to lose."

CHAPTER XXXII

REPRIEVE

UNDER one pretext or another, Lefever, amenable to Selwood's plea for Meg Hyde, who, for Lefever, had never refused to take care of a sick teamster, got rid of the harness-room guards. It was more trouble for Lefever to dispose of the remainder of his fighting men, but on the strength of burning rumors in the invention of which the wagon boss easily excelled, the men were sent on various but pressing wild goose chases and Selwood's way was cleared.

He left Margaret in the office and took McAlpin well down the dark gangway, near one of the big oat-bins.

"Where have you got Haynes?" asked Selwood.

McAlpin shuffled about and scraped his feet. "John," he said apologetically, but speaking fast to skate over very thin ice, "it's this way. Haynes wasn't the worst of them devils—now, was he?"

The barn boss looked hopefully for a sign of assent from his listener, but Selwood was silent and emotionless. It made it a little harder to go on, but McAlpin pushed ahead. "The teamsters was for stringing up everybody they ketched after this last fight down at Bartoe's. But I just stood 'em off on Haynes. He told me how come the bunk-house burned. Starbuck and Bartoe sent him to tell you that they wouldn't touch Company property if you stayed neutral. But he couldn't find you and gave the word to Lefever, and Lefever said the teamsters would stay out of it. But some of the teamsters had grievances agin the gamblers, and went out with the Vigilantes, so Starbuck said that released 'em and they fired the bunk-house."

McAlpin talked fast. "But I didn't think it right

291

to take Haynes out, not till you come," continued the Scotchman artfully. "But now you're here—and of course you'll do as you please," he added, tinging his submission with an appeal, "only, I——"

"Where is Haynes?"

"Right here in this bin," explained McAlpin, pointing to the bin at their hand; "he's under the oats—tied up and all safe till you decide whether you'll let them dashed Vigilantes hang him—but he wasn't the worst of them devils, John, not by no manner o' means, at all."

"Get him out," directed Selwood, still non-committal.

McAlpin, handing his lantern to Selwood, sprang into the bin and began to paw down into the oats. In one corner he had left an airhole, cunningly contrived with empty sacks, and after digging at this corner so deep that Selwood felt confident his friendly offices had resulted in smothering the auctioneer, McAlpin uncovered Haynes, cut the ropes from his arms, and, digging out his feet, cut the rope from his ankles. He then waited for Haynes to get up. But Haynes seemed to take no particular interest in getting up. After some prodding and some assistance, however, from his self-appointed keeper, the big fellow pulled himself together and staggered to his feet.

Selwood held up the lantern. Falstaff, victim of the Merry Wives, presented no more desperate appearance than the old-time confidence man and mock-auctioneer.

He blew the oats from his mustache, blinked, and spoke huskily. "If it's time to move, boys, I guess I'm ready. I'll ask you to remember I've got a weak heart —don't hang me high. You'll get just as good results if I'm six inches off the ground as if I was six feet."

"Don't make a blamed fool o' yoursel'," sputtered McAlpin. "Here's John Selwood. Mind yoursel'; don't fall into the gangway."

"Ed—"! began Selwood.

Haynes interrupted him. "Don't say anything, John. I can't help the way things have gone. But I'll say this: I don't know no more'n a child unborn who fired the hall. Bull Page told me the Vigilantes were coming up the hill after me, so I had to light out."

"Well, whatever's coming to you, Ed, there's nothing coming to-night. You know this country 'tween here and Medicine Bend?"

"Backwards and forwards, John."

"Meg Hyde has begged Starbuck from me. It's not coming to him, but I've been fool enough to give in. If they can get to Medicine Bend they'll be safe. If one of the teamsters catches sight of Starbuck he'll shoot him. They've got to get to the Bend, by keeping off the big trail and sneaking through the canyons and behind the rocks. It's your chance, Ed. I've got nothing like hanging against you—not anything like it. McAlpin will have the horses at the back door, and you can do your best to make it with Starbuck and Meg Hyde. Hustle."

Leaving McAlpin to explain, Selwood walked rapidly back to the dingy, smelly office. Margaret Hyde was feverishly waiting. He directed her to go into the harness-room and apprise her husband, making only the request that Starbuck under no circumstances speak to him. After Margaret had gone in and come out again, he told her to go to the gangway door and wait, took the lantern from her hand, went into the room himself, and, bending over Starbuck, cut the ropes that bound him, steadied him on his cramped feet, unlocked the gangway door, threw it open, and pointed to Meg outside.

Starbuck, blear-eyed and blood-crusted, his hair dishevelled and his trousers and shirt awry, was a desperate sight. He gazed at Selwood standing with the lantern in one hand and Barbanet's gun in the other. Selwood silently handed him the gun.

Starbuck had been forbidden to speak. His lips were sealed. He tucked the gun into his trousers waistband, and took a step toward the door that meant freedom. Before the threshold he stopped, turned to Selwood, and spoke.

"John," he said in a tone that surprised his listener, "I've been a ——." He applied to himself the scurrilous epithet so commonly and freely used among frontier men. But Selwood heard it from the lips of one who meant now to condemn fittingly only his own shame, not his mother. "I've been one—I know it," he hurried on. "But if I can ever make it up to—Meg—and you——"

Selwood waved him on. "Never mind me," he said evenly. "Your chance lies ahead of you." He pointed to the door. "Take it."

CHAPTER XXXIII

FACE TO FACE

The sun rose Sunday morning on a ruinous scene in Sleepy Cat. With a good part of the town burned, most of the people in hiding, and with few provisions saved from the burned stores, Sleepy Cat lay stunned by its misfortunes. An effort to break away from the rule of the disreputable element and purge the town had reacted almost to the complete destruction of the town itself, and the tent colony of transients and emigrants had fled with stories wilder than the facts.

From the cross-bar of the first telegraph pole planted in Sleepy Cat with grandiloquent words, hung two sinister reminders of the work of the reinforced Vigilantes. But sensational was the upheaval when it became known that Starbuck, organizer and brains of the crooks, had, together with Big Haynes, made his escape.

No explanations were forthcoming from the stage barn. It had happened—that was all. The man captured by Selwood was his own prisoner, it was said, and he was the person to feel most aggrieved.

McAlpin had, from the first, claimed Big Haynes as his own take. And as McAlpin had never up to that time been known to brave a bad man, much less to capture one, it was believed by some that he had succumbed to the excitement of a night of terrors and fought and won a real fight. Others held that as between McAlpin and Big Haynes it must have been chiefly a contest as to which should surrender to the other first. But Big Haynes had gone.

Bill Pardaloe, when told that Starbuck was missing, stamped and snorted; but under the skilful ministrations of Bull Page was diverted from his noisy intention of heading a death chase after the fugitives, and was persuaded instead to go to bed.

The breakfast served that morning in Doctor Carpy's Sleepy Cat hotel was unusual. At sunrise a barrel of salt pork was luckily found in, and rolled from, a dark corner of the stage warehouse, and, together with a barrel of flour and a sack of green coffee, was commandeered for public need. The hotel was accorded these provisions and a barrel of army biscuits.

Not until he had assembled this provender could the busy surgeon-landlord get away to interview the padre, who, he was then told by Scott, had gone up to the railroad station to visit the wounded.

Carpy opened the waiting-room door to look for his man and paused.

At the far end of the room, sitting on an up-ended keg, his back supported against the wall, Carpy saw one of his much-bandaged Vigilantes. Bending over him with a cup of water while the wounded man drank was a man of advanced years, whose dark soutane easily identified him as one of that small but widely scattered band of men known to the Indians of every tribe of the West, from the Staked Plain to Hudson Bay, as black-robes.

When the padre lifted the cup from the bandaged lips he straightened up, and Carpy perceived how tall he was and spare. The priest and the surgeon saw each other at the same moment. Carpy noted the straight iron-gray hair, brushed back from the wide forehead; the strong, almost stern, features, bronzed to the color of the red men to whom he ministered; and the lean hand holding the tin cup.

"Padre," said the surgeon, coming up with blunt raillery, "I'm glad to see you making yourself useful.

If you want a job nursing, I'll hire you right now; I'm doctoring this outfit."

When the black-robe smiled, his features lost their stern repose. "It would not be new work," he replied in a heavy foreign accent, "but I'm sorry to see such warfare, such bloodshed—and what about?"

"Padre, some of this Sleepy Cat blood needed to be shed—in fact, a good deal of it," observed the Doctor evasively. "I'll tell you all about it. First, though, I want to ask you a few questions, Padre, about something that happened in this country a long, long time ago—going on thirty year. I want to see whether you can throw any light on it; then I'm on my way. But I've told Bob Scott, that half-breed you came in with, to bring you up to my hotel with your Indians for something to eat this morning. How long have you travelled this country, Padre?"

Carpy was not a hard man to read. Single-minded, bluntly outspoken, his honesty of intent was written on his open countenance, and the experienced reader of men before him perceived it all. The composed black-robe parried his question, all in good part, with another: "How old are you, Doctor?"

Carpy laughed and shook his head. "Doggon'd near forty, Padre—if I must say it."

"Then I crossed these mountains, first, a good time before you were born."

"Why, you must remember old Fort Pierce."

"I was here years before Fort Pierce was built."

"Well and good. Do you remember an old fellow there named Colonel Roper; he commanded there a long time—of course," added Carpy apologetically, "he wasn't as old then as he is now."

"I did not know him."

"Ever know his son, Lieutenant Roper?"

"I never knew any of the officers at the fort."

"Were you ever there?"

"No."

The good-hearted surgeon began to grow uncomfortably warm in his difficulties. "Well, then, you never married anybody at the fort?"

"Never."

"Was there any other black-robe through this country thirty years ago, Padre?" he continued, with oozing hope.

The padre answered after careful thought. "No," said he.

"Doggone it!" exclaimed Carpy, knitting his brows, but reduced in the clerical presence to his one effeminate epithet; "I can't see how it is—and Bob Scott swears you are the man!"

"What do you mean, my Doctor?"

"Did you ever marry *any*body out here?"

"Many of the Indians, of course, my Doctor; sometimes a white man—a trader or a trapper, and an Indian woman—very rarely a white couple, very rarely—usually on the steamboat. Once, camping on the river below Fort Pierce, I married a young army officer to a young white woman. But that poor man was killed soon afterward——"

"In the Roper Massacre at Crawling Stone Wash! My God!" exclaimed Carpy, the perspiration starting from his forehead. "That's the very story!" He seized the padre incontinently by the arm. "Come!"

The padre looked at him astonished, and pointed to the room. "But your patients?"

"All attended to—most of 'em junk, anyway——"

"'Junk'!" echoed the padre, shocked. "Men with human souls, junk! Doctor!"

Carpy hastily shook his head. "They ain't men—

just coyotes, most of 'em—they ain't hurt anything much. Right over there in the corner," continued the Doctor, pointing but forgetting his decorum in his excitement, "is that same dashed old Colonel Roper himself—I'll tell you all about it—come right along with me, Padre, and save a *man's* life; then fill up with breakfast and come back here, fast as you want to."

Before the two men reached the hotel the padre, urged to a brisk pace by his companion, had all of the story the Doctor had. Selwood had brought Tracy up from the barn to the hotel, made him comfortable in a room, and was walking down the stairs when Carpy opened the front door of the hall and ushered his companion in.

Unable to repress a start at the unexpected appearance of the venerable missioner, whose spotted, shabby soutane pictured well the accidents of mountain travel, Selwood paused. But apart from the rough exterior, it was the piercing eyes, the gray hair, the bronzed features, the expression of a grave face that he had studied since he was a boy, and that now walked out of a tragic past into actual life before him—it was this that shook the gambler to the depths; he knew before a word was spoken that this man was the man of the picture.

"He's got it!" cried Carpy to Selwood, loudly, and before any one else could speak a word. "He's the man! He married them." Carpy, in his excitement, caught the padre's arm with one hand to urge him forward, and shot the other like a semaphore out at Selwood. "He's got it, John," cried the Doctor. "This is the man! He married them. He knows everything. Padre"—Carpy turned to his companion and pointed to his friend— "that's their boy standing right there!"

Selwood had need of all his restraint. He stood, motionless, on the lowest tread of the stairs. The missioner scanned the serious features before him with composed and penetrating eyes. "Is this, then," he said, for Selwood made no attempt to break the silence, "is this," repeated the black-robe slowly, "the child of my marriage of that young lieutenant so long ago?"

The gambler made no answer. Instead, he sat down on the stair and buried his face in his bandaged hands.

CHAPTER XXXIV

CARPY STARTS THINGS

SELWOOD spent long hours that morning with the black-robe. He urged him to come up to the hotel and remain over night. But the old campaigner would not leave his Indians, and professed himself unwilling to risk sleeping in a room lest he take cold; he preferred to camp with his escort, who had pitched his tent down by the river—and could not be dissuaded. But he wrote out for Selwood such details as he could remember of the eventful night of the marriage of his father and mother, and gave it to him.

Since he would not remain up-town as Selwood's guest, Selwood declared that he himself would spend the night with the padre down at the river; and, having escorted him to his simple camp, Selwood, still much bandaged, returned to the hotel to forage for a blanket and filch what could be found in the way of delicacies and supplies for the Indians.

While getting together, with Bob Scott's aid, what he could of sugar, flour, meat, and tobacco, Carpy came in on the marauders of his store-room. He dragged Selwood out into his office, planted him in a chair, and sat down facing him, eager to hear all of the padre's story. When the younger man had recounted it in full, Doctor Carpy told a story himself.

"John," he chuckled with much enjoyment, "I've been kind of mean."

"What have you been doing?"

"I've been riding the old General—told him the padre's

here and proved all you claimed up to the hilt. Then I says: 'What have you got to say to that?'"

"What did he say?"

"What the blazes *could* he say?"

"But the old man's changed, John. He's broke—old age a-comin'. Then somebody planted a bullet close to his ribs last night, and that annoyed him consid'able. He was hit in the back—they had the Vigilantes plumb surrounded one time. So when I poked him with the probe I says, 'Which way was you running, General?'

"Well, if the old man had got mad, I'd had some fun out of it. But he never said a single word, and that made me kind of ashamed—so I apologized and told him he mustn't mind an old army surgeon. Then I told him about you going down to Bartoe's alone, and leaving directions for Lefever to bring the teamsters into action, soon as you got Christie out. And how you cleaned up Starbuck and cleaned out the place and burnt it. Well, that pleased him. I was poking him with the probe pretty hard, but he just kept asking questions about you and didn't wince. 'Dash it, Doctor,' he says finally, 'blood will tell; it *will* tell! The boy's got it in him.' Taking the credit all to himself!" laughed Carpy. "Could you beat that?

"Now, John," continued the Doctor, "I had him brought up here to the hotel. He's asleep now. After a while go up and see him. He wants to see you——"

Selwood shook his head. "I don't want to see *him*."

Carpy raised his chin. "Don't be a mule; that's some of your old *grand*father coming out in you—not your mother. Some while later go up like a man and see the General—to tell you the truth, he ain't a long time for down here, even if he gets well of this wound—which I think he will."

Then, in Carpy fashion, he sprang a further surprise. "How you feeling this morning, John?"

Selwood almost stared at him. This was a question the Doctor never asked of anybody under any circumstances; Doctor Carpy's patients were told, not asked, how they felt. But Selwood was ready for him. "I'll ask a question, myself, Doctor. Did you come out here in a wagon train?"

"I did."

"The first job I got west of the Missouri River," continued Selwood, "was driving a team of mules."

"Same as I, John—same as me."

"I was a youngster—and you know I wasn't a husky one. By the time I'd driven those mules a week, if the owner had knocked me on the head I'd have thanked him for it. Everybody in the outfit was dead afraid the Indians would get us; after the first week I was dead afraid they wouldn't. I had sneezed and coughed and snorted in that alkali dust till my nose and eyes and throat were plum burnt up. Then one evening, after the hottest, scorchingest day I'd ever felt in my life, on the Platte bottoms——"

Carpy nodded hard. "Hotter'n blazes on those bottoms, wa'n't it——"

"—somebody up ahead yelled! I was just about able to raise my head and look over the mules' ears. There, ahead of us—far, far away—I saw snow, the snow on top of the Rocky Mountains.

"You're asking me, are you, how I feel to-night? If it wasn't just for one thing, I'd say I felt better than I've ever felt since that evening I saw that snow on top of the Rocky Mountains."

"What's the one thing?"

Selwood shrank in a little. "You couldn't mend it."

"John, you're a blamed fool."

"If I were saying it, I'd put it stronger."

"I know what's a-matter with you. And, maybe, I *can't* cure you—not I, myself. But there's a little huzzy up-stairs with her head as full of you as your head is full of her. That girl can do a thing *I* can't do. And there she is a-sitting alone all this long morning, crying her eyes out—now what do you think's wrong with her? That's all I'm asking. Go up-stairs, man, knock on her door, and if you can't tell her anything else, tell her some of the good news you heard to-day. I gave her a hint. But she'd like to hear a few things straight from you——"

"Did she say that?"

"That and a whole lot more," averred Carpy, making his prevarication violent, since he felt he had gone too far to retreat. "Go on up-stairs and have a face-to-face talk with brown-eyes."

Perspiration dewed Selwood's forehead. He gazed at his bandages. "I'm not in very good shape to talk to anybody, the way I look now." But, encouraging him in roughly honeyed fashion, Carpy got him to the foot of the stairs. Selwood demanded and was accorded some shifting and smoothing up of bandages before he would move farther and, being then assured he looked fine, nerved himself for the ascent.

He never did remember just how he got up the familiar flight that morning. But, once above, he had wit enough to turn toward his own room to consult the looking-glass about his hair.

What was his surprise to find the door of his room open and, looking inside, to see Christie smoothing up the counterpane on his bed. He stood perfectly still, watching her. In a moment she had finished and, turning as she straightened up, she saw him in the doorway. She gave a startled little cry, and her face was a picture of crimson confusion. "Oh!" she exclaimed, trying to speak and to laugh at once, "You can come right in! I'm all through. Margaret has gone, you know, and Doctor asked me if *I* wouldn't tidy up his room and yours just for this morning—I—so I made the beds—and I—oh, Mr. Selwood, were you *very* much hurt in that dreadful fight?"

Selwood protested he had received no serious injury, but seemed unable to add much to his disclaimer. "And all this morning," continued Christie, hardly giving him time to speak, anyway, "I've been trying to get a chance to thank you over and over again for all you did for me and for Father last night—I don't know *what* would have become of us—where should I be now, if it hadn't been for *you!* You can come right in," she repeated, growing a bit hazy herself; "I think things are in *some kind of order*," she faltered, not only out of breath but out of thoughts, for she had stood his silent eyes, and something she saw in them, about as long as she could stand them and keep her senses. "And," she said, dropping her own eyes before him, "I'm just going."

"Don't be in a hurry," he suggested, standing exactly in the doorway through which she was trying to make her escape.

"Oh!" she exclaimed for the fourth or fifth time—and her eyes bulked large with fear and apprehension. "I must go to the Doctor's room now—his bed isn't made yet!"

If Christie's burning cheeks and distressed manner were to be believed, this fact pictured a terrible situation. But it did not impress Selwood. As Christie showed fright, he showed composure.

"If Doc Carpy ever saw his bed made, he wouldn't know where to get into it," he retorted unfeelingly. "He sleeps in a buffalo robe. Christie," he added, "I'd like a little talk with you. Do you remember the morning I met you and your father on the Crawling Stone Trail?"

Christie spoke up promptly. "Indeed, I do."

"Do you remember whether you lost a shoe that morning?"

She looked at him blankly. "How in the world did *you* know anything about that?"

"I think," continued Selwood, "I've got a nice new shoe that belongs to you—did you happen to keep the mate to it?"

"Why, it's in my trunk, down at the tent—if the trunk hasn't been stolen. What about it?"

"I picked up a girl's shoe that morning on the trail. I thought it was about the prettiest shoe I'd ever seen. There was a horseshoe lying there on one side of the trail and this girl's shoe on the other. I'd had nothing but horseshoe luck all my life out here, and it had been rotten luck. So I thought I'd take a chance on that girl's shoe—and I picked it up."

Christie laughed. "What an idea! And what did you do with it?"

"I've got it. And what I want to find out from you right now and right here is, what kind of luck it's brought me. Sit down a minute, will you?"

Christie, somewhat flustered, did sit down.

"I said to myself," continued Selwood, "it must be a nice girl that owned that shoe. And if I could find her —and ever get some things in my own life straightened out—I'd ask her whether she'd marry me——"

He seemed to be running out of words and ideas, and Christie came to his aid. "Well, of course, I *hope*"—her eyes fell—"it's my shoe, John. It's going to be a terrible temptation to—to claim it. Couldn't we make believe it's mine, John, *anyway?*"

"Do you really want it to be yours?"

Christie looked up very simply. "How could I want it to be any one else's, John?"

Five minutes later Doctor Carpy's loud whistle echoed up the hallway. Christie Fyler, in Selwood's arms, started like a frightened fawn. She tried to break away, and could not. "John!" she whispered frantically. "Some one's coming! Let me go!" With tear-brimmed eyes she looked pleadingly up. He would not release her. "He's down-stairs," murmured Selwood reassuringly. "There's nobody at all up here."

"You'll start your arms bleeding again, John," she whispered in alarm. "I can't get a breath!"

"Christie!" Selwood looked down at her face, her head cushioned in the hollow of his arm. "I've got to tell you this, too—I'm dead broke."

She laughed—who as well as lovers can face the world broke? "I guess everybody is broke in Sleepy Cat, John. Then, besides risking your precious life for me, you've had a terrible misfortune—they burned your hall, didn't they, John? And you lost everything?"

He looked down at her. "Christie," he said seriously, "I suppose you'll be willing to prove property by letting me try that shoe on you to see if it fits?"

"Oh, it isn't necessary to bother you—I can try it on, myself."

"If you'll let me try it on you, I'll tell you a secret."

"Go ahead, then."

"I burned the hall, myself. Yes," he continued, as she looked at him amazed. "Why? Well—I was done with it—and everything in it. All that's behind me, Christie."

There was just an instant of breathlessness. Then she tipped up on her toes just as high as she possibly could, and flung her arms as far as she possibly could around his neck, and smothered the rest of his words.

In the hallway below Carpy was whistling. They heard his heavy tread on the stairs. Selwood was for closing the door and preserving the situation. But he had found a new boss now—and one who knew what was proper and what was not. The door of his room remained open.

But nothing short of an operation would have released Christie from Selwood's arms. The Doctor was called by Selwood to the open door only to be brazenly invited to look in.

CHAPTER XXXV

THE DEATH IN THE CARDS

AFTER supper James McAlpin, with some ceremony, drove Selwood's team—the rangy American bays—up to the hotel. Owing to McAlpin's personal manipulation, the coats of the horses glistened in the after-glow and the tan road-wagon shone like a mirror. A canker of dull days in the barn had put the team on edge—they champed at McAlpin's bits.

Christie came out on Selwood's arm, bandages and all. It was their first ride together, and Christie was to be driver. Selwood went through the etiquette of seating Christie carefully in the wagon, with various of his loafer friends peeking around the corners and out of the office windows, and with McAlpin officiously running in to spread the dust-robe across her knees, tuck it in, and running back to the heads while Selwood got in.

They drove out on the divide for a few more minutes to themselves, and then down and around by the river to the camp of the padre. They found him before a little camp-fire. An Indian held the horses and the padre pointed them to a seat on a ledge.

"You married my father and mother, Padre," said Selwood, when he had told his own and Christie's story. "We want you to marry us."

While they talked, Selwood fed the little fire with the driftwood the Indians had gathered. The padre told of that other marriage—of the night, the storm, the flooded river, and the pine-torches of the Indians.

After leaving the camp, Christie and Selwood, loath to part, drove again out on the divide. The stars of the night shone wonderfully. The Lady in her Chair was slowly

rising in the northeast, and the Big Bear, Arcturus looking on, was retreating in the northwest. The Northern
Cross stretched its broad arms across the meridian, and
the Eagles, almost overhead, looked down on these two
mountain lovers—lost in the immensity of the desert
spaces—as they had looked down so many autumn
nights on so many millions of lovers gone before. Low
in the west the heart of the Scorpion burned in a red
flame, and in the east the Sea Monster peered up into
the sky. To the south of this, a single mass of cloud
puffed out like a great explosion above the horizon and
from it darted incessant tongues of lightning.

It brought to Selwood's mind a memory. "You remember when and where I first saw you, Christie: it was
down in the Crawling Stone Wash the morning your
father's freight wagon got stalled. When I was driving
away, I looked over to your wagon, and saw your face
between the end curtains."

They drove back to the hotel very late, hoping everybody had gone to bed, but in this they were doomed to
disappointment. In the brightly lighted office a brave
company of frontier adventurers, closely tuned to Selwood's movements, were tirelessly sitting in a suffocat-
ing atmosphere around a seriously overheated stove.
McAlpin was there, waiting to take the team back to
the barn; Lefever was there as hero of the secondary
attack on Bartoe's; Scott, so quietly that no one heard
him, had sneaked in out of the evening chill; Pardaloe,
after trying all day to "locate" and "lick" the man
responsible for Starbuck's escape, had come in to go to
bed and had forgotten what he came in for. Tracy, in
one corner, lay on his cot because he could get no one
to carry him out into the hall. Fyler was there because
he had no friends and was trying to make some. Bull
Page was present to prevent bootlegging from the bar-

room; and Doctor Carpy was there, after his calls, to dispense general good-feeling, of which he had that night an ample supply—and to keep his guests from burning the lining out of his office stove.

Christie was allowed to go up-stairs unmolested; indeed, she was ignored with chivalrous ceremony. Selwood, on the other hand, was dragged into the office and held a victim till he could negotiate peace with his retainers, and effected his escape, in the end, only by inviting them all to a wedding at sunrise down at the river in the camp of the padre.

In the dawn of a glorious morning they were married —perhaps on such a spot as that to which Selwood's father had brought his bride-to-be, in the storm, so many years before. Selwood, taking on family responsibilities, was asked by Carpy whether he would elect to use his father's name, Roper, or retain his mother's name, Selwood. He found no difficulty in deciding. As Selwood he had been known, well or ill, from the beginning of his frontier days, and as Selwood, baptized John, he wished to be known to their end. His unfortunate father's family name had been to him too long and too much a source of humiliation and unhappiness.

After the wedding breakfast, attended by all the guests, with the padre as a special guest of honor, Christie persuaded her new husband to go up with her to General Roper's room. The old man, weakened by wounds and softened by years, broke and asked his grandson to forgive what had past.

It was one of those moments for banishing resentments and forgetting the cruelties of pride and obstinacy. Christie wiped the tears from the old man's eyes, and he repaid her by throwing a bomb into her unsuspecting camp when he sincerely congratulated them both and named as the only favor he would ask

that the first boy be named John Roper Selwood and
sent to West Point.

For a day or two, no trip and no escape from work
was possible for Selwood. He was up to his neck in
work at the barns and the warehouse, straightening out
the tangle into which the conflagration and the rioting
at Sleepy Cat had thrown the stage and wagon sched-
ules. During the day scattered lots of supplies began to
filter in from Medicine Bend, and by nightfall the hotel
cook was able to promise Doctor Carpy a respectable
wedding supper as his compliment to the bride and
groom, and to a company from which no loyal friend
was excluded.

At nine o'clock in the evening behind the closely curtained windows of the dining-room, wedding guests
made merry. Christie, flushed with happiness, had
stolen from the table for a moment to run up to the
General's room with a piece of wedding cake, when one
of the two waitresses, coming up behind Selwood's chair,
whispered in his ear.

The bridegroom's face clouded. "Who is it?" he demanded in an impatient undertone. "Is it one of my
men?"

"I don't know, Mr. Selwood. I don't think so. I
never saw him before."

"Tell him," directed Selwood, vexed, "to come around
in the morning; I've worked about fourteen hours to-
day."

The waitress appeared perplexed. "I told him you
wouldn't want to be interrupted," she said in an earnest
whisper. "But it seemed like he was in terrible trouble.
He told me to ask you for God's sake to come out to
see him for just a minute."

Selwood muttered a protest. "Where is he?" he
asked in an aside.

"At the kitchen door."

The girl thought that Selwood's keen eyes would have burned her up during the instant before he spoke again. "Tell him," he continued in a low voice, "to go around to the front door and sit down on the porch with his face to the street—understand? To go around to the front door and sit down on the porch with his face to the street," he repeated, "and his back to the door."

The waitress passed out into the kitchen. When she returned she whispered again. "He's gone to the front door, Mr. Selwood."

The talk had all been going on around the table, but Pardaloe's snaky eyes had not lost sight of the low-spoken colloquy. "What's a-matter, John?" he demanded suspiciously.

"Some stranger outside wants to see me," answered Selwood, rising. "I'll be right back."

Pardaloe was on his feet before Selwood had taken a step from the table. He put up his bear-paw of a hand. "Hold on, John!" he said definitely, pushing back his chair. "You don't go out alone to see no stranger to-night, 'specially not in your recent shape—hold your horses."

The table rose as one man. There was a momentary upset, and some conflict of claims as to who should accompany Selwood. Without passing on these words, Selwood nodded to Pardaloe, and the discussion ceased. The mule boss followed him in long strides toward the dining-room door. Hardly missing step, and with one swoop of his long arm, the big fellow snatched up his blunderbuss, which stood in a handy corner, and, stooping to get through the door, passed out behind Selwood.

Bob Scott, at the table, sat close to the door leading into the dining-room from the kitchen. The other two men had not got out of the room when Scott, with his

habitual smile of apology—the smile that drew about
his mouth and drew his lips back in such homely lines
that, but for its kindliness, it would be taken for a grin
—rose in perfect silence and with incredible celerity
slipped out into the kitchen and was out of the back
door and half way around to the front of the hotel in
the dark by the time Pardaloe had carefully drawn every
shade in the hotel office and beckoned to Selwood to
come in from the hall. He, himself, then slipped across
the hall into Carpy's private office, and, throwing up
the sash of the window that commanded the porch,
trained his shotgun on the outer gloom.

Selwood, his revolver in his left hand, threw open the
hall door without exposing himself. The hanging lamp
at the foot of the stairs threw a light out through the
opening. Seated on the porch, his face to the street,
sat a large, loosely built man with his head hidden in a
dark pull-down cap. "Who are you and what do you
want?" asked Selwood, inspecting his caller from behind the hall door and through the crack of the opening.

"You know me, John," answered the man, hoarse and
short in utterance. "But I ain't very popular in these
parts just now."

"What's your name?"

"I'd like to give that to you private, John. I'm keeping some under cover."

Something in the cadence of the words told Selwood
that he knew the man. A question that followed was
only a precaution, for he felt sure from the cracked and
husky tones that the man was Big Haynes.

"Whoever you are, you're well covered where you
sit," remarked Selwood, with apparent indifference.

"I know it."

"Put up your hands. Stand up and turn around here,"
came the next order from the hall.

The man did as he was told. A disappointment

awaited Selwood's confidence in his usually keen ear. The pinched, haggard, and unshaven features now turned toward him could not be those of the bluff, portly auctioneer; a hasty glance told him this could not be Big Haynes. The cheeks were bruised and swollen, the eyes sunken in hollow sockets, and the man's clothing was in tatters.

"Who are you and what do you want?" repeated Selwood, astonished, impatient, and suspicious. "Speak up before you get blown off the porch."

The man answered with a question. "Who's covering me from Doc Carpy's office?"

"Bill Pardaloe." Selwood fairly snapped the words.

"Who's this man at the other corner of the house?"

Before Selwood could speak, a voice came from the darkness, and a second man came forward. "Bob Scott is at the corner of the house," said the voice. "It's Big Haynes, John," continued the Indian, low voiced; "he's alone."

Selwood stepped from behind the door out on the porch. He could hardly credit his senses. It was two days since he had seen Haynes; but those two days had aged the man ten years. Selwood had but just seen this man and seen him with the rope almost around his neck. Facing that situation the old man had not winced, not shown the white feather. Torn now, bedraggled, completely whipped, he stood before Selwood like a ghost of his former self.

"Put down your hands before they fall down," directed Selwood, half in pity, half in disgust. "What in God's name has happened—did our men catch you? Have you had a fight?"

"Not the kind you mean, John. Give me a drink, for God's sake, and le' me sit down and tell the story. I ain't had a bite to eat since last night."

They led him into the office, helped him into the

washroom, and Scott went to the kitchen for strong coffee. Big Haynes drank four cupfuls before he could quit; then, sitting in front of Selwood, who stood with his back against the writing table, and with Pardaloe and the Indian listening, he spoke.

"We got away from here yesterday morning O K— after you turned back, Bob—Starbuck, Meg, and me, and we made time on the Medicine Bend trail till daylight. When sun-up come, we struck off into the rough country south and worked east, best we could, till noon; then we stopped for to eat and rest up. The going was pretty bad, especially on Meg. Her horse picked up a stone and went lame early in the morning, and that held us back. Then we figured out nobody would molest her, alone on the trail, nor the teamsters wouldn't bother her none about the horse, for they all knowed Meg—so we rode her over to the trail, and Starbuck and me made up to meet her at Crawling Stone Creek that night—so we parted." Haynes shook his head. "There was a game woman, John, if ever there was one——"

"'There *was* a game woman, John,'" echoed Selwood, suspicious and angry. "What do you mean?" He started. "Is Meg dead?" he thundered at Haynes. "Did Starbuck kill her?" he asked in a rage.

Haynes put up his hand. In all the wreck of his sorry plight, whatever it might be, there was something, for the first time, that commanded respect. "Let me alone, John—you'll hear it all soon enough.

"She was there ahead of us at dark, waiting—down by the quicksand crossing. Meg said there was a good many teams along the road. We planned to take the trail when the moon came up and ride all night, but we was plum tuckered, all three of us. So Starbuck said we would go up the canyon a ways and camp for

the night and rest up Meg's horse all the next day—
that was to-day—and ride all the next night—that was
to-night.

"When we thought we was up far enough for to be
pretty well hid, we staked the horses up above, where
there was a little grass, and built a fire down on a ledge
and had supper. I never knowed, no more than a baby,
that Starbuck and Meg was former man and wife—
never drempt it. After supper they told me their story.
Meg said she told you——"

"What story?" demanded Pardaloe peevishly.

"Never mind now, Bill," said Selwood, adding sharply
to Haynes: "Go on."

"Starbuck said he'd got another chance from a man
he never expected to get a chance from——"

"What man?" roared Pardaloe, starting up.

Selwood whirled on him, throwing up his hand at the
same time to shut off Haynes. "Dash it," he cried, "let
the man tell his story, Bill! Ask questions afterward.
No matter what Starbuck said."

"Hold on!" exclaimed Pardaloe, pointing an accusing
finger at Selwood. "Do you know the name of the
man?"

"Yes," retorted Selwood severely, "and I'll give you
his name in good time."

Pardaloe drew in a long, hissing, satisfied breath.
"I'll kill that cuss," he muttered to Scott, "if it's the
last thing I do on earth!"

"Well, there they were," continued Haynes. "Starbuck said she'd saved his life and they were going to
head for the Panhandle and start over again. We didn't
talk long. All Meg said was she wanted me to know
she was Starbuck's real wife and she didn't like to be
called just Meg, but Margaret Starbuck.

"Anyway, the two of 'em went to sleep close to the

fire—I moved off a way. I was so blamed done out I just couldn't sleep—so there I was lying on my back on the rock, thinking where'd I land next, when I began to hear a funny kind of noise. And it kept getting louder 'n' louder, 'n' funnier and funnier—up the canyon. I lifted up to look, and there, away up the canyon, I seen a big white streak stretched clear across it, right from wall to wall, and roaring. I set up and called down to Starbuck, and pointed. 'What's that white thing?' I says.

"He jumped like he was shot. 'WATER!' he yells. 'Margaret!' he yells. 'Cloudburst! Quick! for your life! Grab your saddle, Haynes! Get to the horses! Up! Up!'

"He grabbed their two saddles. I grabbed my saddle, and we made, hard as we could, up the canyon wall. You know about what kind of time we'd make on loose rock in the dark—there was a little moon over the wall —not much. I'd got maybe ten feet above 'em when I heard Meg scream—she'd fell down. The water was crashing and roaring down on us like all hell was let loose. She yelled to Starbuck to save himself. He dropped the saddles and picked up Meg and started climbing with her—and the water struck us.

"I was maybe twenty feet higher than Starbuck and Meg. If I'd been forty feet it wouldn't have helped; that water was a hundred feet deep. It picked me up like a match, and picked them up, and picked the horses up—I never knew a thing till I come to, on a shelf away down the canyon. I was pounded clean to pieces. How I ever lived I don't know—but there I was.

"It was dark; the moon was gone. I yelled out their names, both of 'em, loud as I could—didn't get no answer. So I shivered and shook and stomped around till daylight. Then I walked on down the creek bottom toward the main trail. The water was down. I looked careful for signs and kept calling Starbuck and Meg— but didn't have no hope much of ever seeing 'em again till I spied something, down at the mouth of the canyon, and pretty well out in the creek on a gravel bar. First I thought it was a big piece of driftwood; then I thought it was one of the horses. I seen, when I got closter, it wasn't. It was Starbuck and Meg.

"I waded a ways out into the creek and got pretty near the sand bar to see if either of 'em was alive. Meg's skirt must 'a' caught in a snag on the bar, and that held 'em there when the water went down. There they were, lying on the up side of the bar, with their arms tight round each other—and their heads part under water— Starbuck's head was clean under water."

Hayes wiped his forehead with the back of his grimy hand. "I waded back ashore and kept on down the Wash till I got to the main crossing, and set down there to wait for help. Inside an hour a couple o' your wagons come along, headin' west. I told the boys the story jus' 'z' 'twas. They'd heard about the trouble at Sleepy Cat but didn't know nothin' about it. They agreed to help me. We unloaded most of the hay on one wagon and drove the wagon up the creek, close as we could to where they lay. We waded out and one of the boys took aholt of their feet, and the other one and I took their shoulders together, so we got 'em out to the wagon the way they lay, 'n' got 'em into the wagon. I asked the boy to take 'em to Medicine Bend—offered him what money I had, 'cause I knew I could get coffins at Medicine Bend, and I hated to see Meg put under like a dum' animal. He wouldn't hear nothin' to turnin' back—said this was closter and he was due here in the mornin' for a return trip, anyway. So, John—well— here we are."

Hollow-eyed, he said no more. Selwood, after a moment's silence, spoke to Scott. "I guess everybody's out of the kitchen," he said. "Get hold of Bull and tell him to cook some supper for Haynes and hunt up a bed for him." He turned back to Haynes. "Where are they?"

"John, we laid 'em down at the barn in the harness room—there wa'n't no other place, 'n' I jus' plum didn't know what to do with 'em till I seen you. If you don't think it's right——"

He hesitated. Selwood finished the sentence. "It's all right," he said, rising. As he started toward the dining-room, Pardaloe laid a heavy hand on his shoulder. And he looked down at him with serious eyes. "John," he said solemnly, "remember what the cards said Saturday night at Calabasas? We couldn't figure out just how it was coming, could we? But the old deck didn't lie; death was in it that night, sure enough, wasn't it?"

Selwood stepped into the hall, to find Christie, wide-eyed, at the open door. She caught his hands. "When I came down-stairs they told me you had been called from the table. I was frightened and I ran out to see where you were," she whispered. "I heard that terrible story! John, what shall we do?"

They called Carpy, and while Pardaloe told the story to the merrymakers, Selwood and Christie told the Doctor.

"Caught up the canyon in one of them blamed cloud-bursts," mused the Doctor. "Them twisters form right out of the blue up there in the Crawling Stone Mountains. They'll circus around like a balloon till they hit a peak; then they burst—and God help who's camping below. In thirty minutes they'll tear the whole side out of a mountain. Well—it's done!"

But the Doctor vowed with hardened oaths that Meg Hyde should have the best there was to be had in Sleepy Cat; and the three started for the barn—for Christie would not be denied. "Let me go, John," she pleaded. "I'm a woman, she's a woman—let me go."

They lay on a blanket rudely spread on the harness-room floor, still locked in each other's arms. Carpy held a lantern to their faces; Selwood and Christie stood at their side.

"There's a considerable bruise on his forehead," said Carpy, speaking after his brief examination. "When the water struck him, I guess it knocked him flat on the rocks. That water coming down the Crawling Stone hits a man just like a sledge-hammer would hit him. It slams him down like a ton of brick on the rock 'n' then tosses him up like a cork and away he goes!

"Starbuck knew all that, too; but with Meg in his arms, he maybe tried to break her fall and in that way hit the rocks wrong himself." The Doctor walked slowly around the bodies. "Cliff was a powerful man," he went on. "If any one could have landed in the clear out o' one of them hell twisters, he could. But two of 'em—and one a woman—that's different. Well—load 'em into a wagon, John. We'll take 'em up to the hotel."

"To the hotel, Doc?" echoed McAlpin, who with the rest had followed from the hotel and crowded into the room.

"Where else?" roared Carpy. "Up to the hotel 'n' into my office."

Christie knelt at Margaret's side. The men stood by. Her tears moistened the dark, sand-strewn hair, as she tried to gather it up and knot it a little at Margaret Hyde's neck.

When she rose from her knees, she buried her cheek on Selwood's breast. "At least, John," were her half-whispered words, "she died where she would have asked to die—in his arms."

CHAPTER XXXVI

HEARTS IN THE WEST

"What's Selwood going to do?" asked Wentworth. He was sitting with Carpy in the sunshine on the hotel porch, having come up to see where the losses of the Vigilante outbreak, and its reprisals, had left him. A week had passed since the Crawling Stone tragedy, and Sleepy Cat, though badly scarred, had already profited, rather than lost, by the efforts to exterminate its crooks and murderers.

The tent camp, deserted awhile by frightened emigrants, was filling up again. The traders were rebuilding —the coming of the railroad was close at hand, the real estate offices were once more open, and the unquenchable optimism inspired by the only pure air in the world again prevailed.

Doctor Carpy took Wentworth's question seriously. "It's not so much, Ben, a question of what *he's* going to do," he replied. "There's two figuring in that camp now; the question is what are *they* going to do?

"Selwood," continued the Doctor, "talked about going back East. 'Jing!' I says to him. 'If you're goin' back East I'll hand you a letter to a friend of mine there; he'll give you a job counting grass.' 'Counting grass?' he says. 'Sure,' I says. 'He's superintendent of an insane asylum. That's what they do with men that leave Sleepy Cat for to go back East.'"

Carpy hardly paused to continue. "Christie was a good deal upset about this roughness that's been goin' on here—men gettin' killed and that kind. 'Well, Christie,' I says, 'it's partly the fault of the climate. You've got to remember it's mighty hard for a man to

323

die here—I mean, to die the old, bed-fashion, natural death. This is a wonderful climate; it's given you, my girl, a fine husband. He came out here half dead, and if he hadn't come, he'd 'a' been dead long ago. And look at him now! Why, Christie,' I says, 'if they didn't kill off somebody by main force once in a while out here, or bring in some more doctors to reduce the population, people would get so thick, they'd be laying out the mountain-tops for town lots.'

"Well, of course, she didn't like that kind of foolery much; but it's so—you know it, Wentworth.

"Then," the Doctor went on, "Selwood talked about California. 'California!' I says. 'California? Sand! Fleas! Greasers!' Well, he thought he was goin' out there, anyway, to get hold of a little freighting business of his own, and 'live down' some things he claimed he wanted to forget. I says to him: 'You'll live 'em down faster right here, John. The population of this town changes every three weeks. In three weeks nobody here will ever know you run a place here and things will be 'lived down' a week before you'd get to California if you travelled night and day.' But I'm kind of afraid the cuss is going, anyway. Don't seem to be no business here he likes. I offered to sell the hotel to him."

"Well," remarked Wentworth, "if a freighting business of his own is all he's looking for, he needn't go to California for it. I came up here to offer him a third interest in our line. When the railroad gets here, we'll have to run wagons west to Bear Dance for another year. Then the business is growing all the time at Thief River—that line across the Sinks will be running ten years yet. If he'll live here and spend part of his time at Thief River, he can run this west end of the line to suit himself."

"Do you mean that?"

"I mean it."

"Well, by gum, I'm thinking that'll settle it," averred Carpy. "We've got something now to work on."

"How's old Dave?" asked Wentworth.

"Goin' to get well. It's what I'm telling you—you can't hardly kill 'em out here. He and old Roper are in bed yet; their rooms are next to each other up-stairs, and they get out of bed every day now for a little game of poker—first in one room, then in the other. You can't kill 'em and you can't stop 'em, neither—they're too old dogs. Dave has sent old man Fyler down to Thief River to run the mine for him. He give Fyler a share in it. I fixed that up," explained the innocent-looking doctor. "You see, Christie didn't want to go clear out to California and leave her father here! So that put her agin California. Now let's hunt up John, and drive that partnership nail into him while the iron's hot!"

It was not, perhaps, most of all, the bribe of an already established and congenial business that held Selwood on the crest of the Rocky Mountain Divide. Every morning he walked down to the barn after he had announced he was going to California, it made him sick to look into the faces of his men. Gone were the snap and the dash of their normal manner; gone the smiles, the "joshing," and the jokes. And, what was as painfully significant, gone were the care-free fits of anger and "cussing" and complaints and of argument hotly threatening blows that he, Selwood, had always been called on to settle.

McAlpin's tail-feathers plainly drooped; Lefever's snug trousers waistband grew a world too wide for his shrunken sides, and new notches had to be cut to tighten his cartridge-belt; Pardaloe moped in and out of the stable like an ailing mule, peevish, stooped, and hollow-eyed; Bob Scott, in desperation, had had his hair cut, and no self-respecting Chippewa squaw would longer have acknowledged him a brother in blood.

And with all of this, the work went on quite as capably as before; it was the spirit that had fled—not the faithfulness.

How much of this desperation was weighing on Selwood's heart as he listened, sober-faced, to Wentworth's calm proposals? How much did the claims of such a man-for-man friendship as men never know, and never can know, outside the wild life of a mountain frontier, pull at his heart while he was debating what to do in a crisis of his checkered life?

But one morning there were heard at the barn more noise, more shouting, more profanity, more laughter, and more arguments—more fights were in the offing and more symptoms of crude, heartfelt rejoicing were manifest than had been known there since before the days of the Sleepy Cat riots. For that morning Selwood and Christie had come down to their hotel breakfast just as Carpy and Wentworth were leaving the dining-room. And there was that in their manner that Carpy read the moment he looked into their faces. He was not a bit surprised, even if Wentworth by any chance was, when Selwood—holding Christie in his arm—said to them both: "Well—I guess we're going to stay!"

THE END